WATCH
HER
DISAPPEAR

BOOKS BY LISA REGAN

WATCH HER DISAPPEAR

LISA REGAN

bookouture

Published by Bookouture in 2022

An imprint of Storyfire Ltd.
Carmelite House
50 Victoria Embankment
London EC4Y 0DZ

www.bookouture.com

ISBN: 978-1-80314-320-0
eBook ISBN: 978-1-80314-319-4

*For my mother, Donna House, for nurturing my dreams
and for picking me up whenever I fell down*

PROLOGUE

WESTERN PENNSYLVANIA, 1994

The men were visible through a tear in the heavy blind. There were at least a dozen of them, maybe more. Some wore police uniforms. Others wore suits. Some arrived dressed all in black with stiff, bulky vests wrapped around their torsos and helmets protecting their heads. Some of them crouched next to their vehicles while others stood around, eyes searching the surroundings. All of them carried guns: handguns and larger, longer, sleek guns. The men in the tactical gear approached the house first, picking through the weedy, trash-strewn front lawn. Their boots pounded out a staccato beat. When their feet reached the wooden porch, the entire house shook. There was shouting and then the sounds of a large object ramming against the front door. Wood splintered and then they were inside. Running, shouting, smashing in doors.

"Clear!"

"Clear!"

"Jesus, what is that smell?"

"Someone check the back."

"This place is a mess. We need more guys in here."

No one noticed the man in jeans and a plain black T-shirt

with a pistol in his hand. He was the first one through the bedroom door. A cough erupted from his throat. He gagged and covered his mouth with his free hand. Edging around the room, he found the window and tore the shade down. Light exploded across the ugly tableau. The pistol clattered to the floor. Falling to his knees, the man crawled across the dirty hardwood floor and gathered the small girl in his arms.

It was his keening that drew the attention of the other men, finally. Great, eerie, high-pitched wails filled the air. For a few seconds, the entire house went silent. Even with all the activity outside, the exterior fell preternaturally quiet. Then the battering boots returned. Men's shadows filled the doorway.

"Jesus! Oh Jesus."

"What the hell?"

"What is he doing here? What the hell is he doing here?"

"Oh God."

"Someone get him out of here. He's contaminating the scene."

In the hall, someone retched.

"How did he get in here?"

"Oh shit. Oh no."

From the crush of bodies just outside the room came the sound of someone crying. "How could someone do something like that?"

A radio squawked. Movement from the corner of the room caught the eye of one of the men. He let out a gasp. Then he yelled, "Help! We need help in here!"

ONE

Lindsay Jones was going to kill someone. She didn't care that it was prom night. What she cared about was that some skank on the junior varsity cheerleading squad had just posted an Instagram live story gushing about how Lindsay's boyfriend, Brody Ford, had promised to meet up with her at a hotel after prom. Except that one of the girl's followers on Insta had told Lindsay's best friend about the whole thing.

Now Lindsay stood in the girls' restroom just outside of Denton East High School's auditorium waiting for her best friend, who had promised to get a copy of the video. She checked her make-up in the mirror, leaning over the sink and using one of her long nails to scoop out a glob of mascara that was lodged in the corner of her eye. She patted down her long blonde hair, which her mother had spent over a hundred dollars to have blown out that day, and studied her dress. It was all slits and deep cuts in an elegant black that accentuated both her bony parts and her curves. Why Brody wasn't satisfied with this, Lindsay would never understand.

She had noticed him flirting with other girls from time to time: in the halls at school before homeroom and sometimes at football games, but he'd sworn to her that he hadn't done anything with any other girls. They were going to graduate from high school in less than two months. Then they were supposed to spend the summer traveling together before they went to separate colleges.

Lindsay wasn't about to let some thirsty junior ruin her senior year.

The door to the bathroom banged open, letting in a blast of music and flickering colored lights. The auditorium was crammed with people dancing in the semi-darkness. Wearing a short, strapless blue dress covered in sequins, Lindsay's best friend, Deborah Hart, strode over and handed Lindsay a phone. A sheen of sweat covered her round face and her chest heaved. "That's Mary Jo Chachakis's phone. She screen-recorded the Insta live video. We should be able to watch it."

Lindsay beckoned Deborah closer and the two watched the video twice. It was exactly as bad as Lindsay expected. Tears stung the backs of her eyes, but she refused to let them fall. Deborah stared at her with a sympathy so saccharine it made Lindsay's stomach turn. Lindsay thrust the screen into Deborah's face. "Where is she?"

Deborah blinked and stared at Lindsay.

Lindsay rolled her eyes. Sighing, she said, "What?"

"Don't you think that Brody is the one you should be confronting? I mean, like, you can go off on this junior, but that's not going to stop him from trying to get with other girls."

Lindsay hated admitting that Deborah was right. That was not the dynamic of their friendship. Lindsay was the alpha and Deborah followed. But Deborah had a point. "Fine," Lindsay sighed. "First we find Brody, then we find this girl."

It took fifteen minutes of weaving through packed bodies on the dance floor and shouted conversations with a dozen people to find out that Brody had gone outside to smoke. As Lindsay left the auditorium and stomped down the hallway toward the front of the building, Deborah hurried to catch up. Her heels clacked against the tile. "Where are you going?" she called.

"To the alcove," Lindsay said over her shoulder.

"How do you know he's out there?"

Lindsay stopped walking and turned on Deborah. "Where else would he go to smoke? God!"

A few minutes later, after convincing the faculty stationed at the front entrance that they needed something from Lindsay's car, they rounded the back of the building. They walked through a grassy area on the east side of the school and through the parking lot used by the custodial staff. Four dumpsters lined the wall to their left. Lindsay stalked past them with Deborah in tow. The alcove was a small outdoor space between two parts of the building that jutted outward. It was a windowless recess that wasn't quite large enough for a full parking lot. Long before Lindsay was even born, the school had attempted to make it into some kind of outdoor theater with fifteen curved steps that cascaded down toward a basement entrance to the school. At the bottom, next to the basement door, was a small, curved concrete stage. What they hadn't counted on was that rain, snow, autumn leaves, and trash would gather there far too consistently for it ever to be kept completely clean, much less used.

Not many kids went down into the theater. It was dirty and creepy, and mostly unlit. They usually sat along the wall that separated the theater from the rest of the alcove to engage in activities the school didn't allow. Only one dim light hung over the entire area. Lindsay's skin prickled as she and Deborah stepped into the shadows. She felt some of her resolve weaken. She'd been out here plenty of times with Brody during school hours while he smoked. She usually had her vape pen. On occasion, she and Deborah had smoked pot out here. But they'd never been in the alcove at night.

Deborah's fingers wrapped around Lindsay's upper arm, pulling her back. "I don't think he's out here."

Lindsay's eyes searched the darkness ahead. A small orange circle flared in the distance. Lindsay shook Deborah's hand away and tromped toward it. "He's here," she said. "I can see his cigarette."

As they drew closer, Lindsay's eyes adjusted. Along the wall sat Brody, cigarette in hand, just as she'd told Deborah. Beside him was his best friend, Mark Severns. Lindsay recognized the profile of his spiky hair even before she heard him laugh and say, "Busted."

The orange circle flared again, illuminating Brody's face. "I'm coming back in, babe," he told her. "I just needed a smoke."

"Where is she, Brody?" Lindsay demanded.

A light sparked beside Brody. Mark had turned on his phone's flashlight app. No, Lindsay realized, not the app. He was recording them.

Deborah said, "Turn it off."

Mark laughed. "No way. Your girl is about to go off, and I'm going to get every second of it."

Lindsay swallowed and faced Brody, launching into the tirade she'd been preparing in her head since they left the bathroom, not even caring if Mark got it all on camera. Let him record it, she thought. Maybe it was better for every girl at school and on social media to know what a slimeball he was for trying to cheat on her.

She hadn't even gotten halfway through her rant when Deborah lunged for Mark's phone. He held onto it, but the tussle knocked him off balance. As he fell backward over the wall, one of his hands grabbed at Brody's jacket.

"Bruh—" Brody started to say before he, too, tumbled off the wall and into the blackness of the theater below.

"Oh my God," Lindsay shrieked. She ran along the wall

until she found the opening to the theater steps. "Deborah, come on! They could be seriously hurt! Oh my God."

She fumbled inside her purse for her own phone. Her fingers trembled as she pressed the power button to bring the screen to life. Somewhere behind her, Deborah said, "I can't see anything!"

Lindsay found the flashlight app and tapped it. She used the beam to pan the area, searching for the boys. But instead, the shaft of light caught something else. Not some*thing*, she realized as she carefully made her way down two of the steps toward the stage. Some*one*. A girl. Sprawled across the stage on her side, one pale cheek resting on her folded arms.

"Lindsay?" Deborah called.

"Damn, man," Brody said from nearby. "That hurt like hell. Mark, you okay?"

"I'm fine. I just—"

He fell silent as Lindsay took two more steps down toward the stage, her flashlight illuminating the girl more sharply. Her brown hair had been carefully styled into a chunky braid updo with a thin, sparkling headband across the front of her head. Her make-up was perfect. It looked as though she had simply laid down and fallen asleep. Lindsay left the flashlight beam on her face for a long moment. Pressed between her cheek and wrist were the wilted red roses of a corsage. Lindsay felt Brody limp over to her side. "You know her?"

Lindsay shook her head.

Deborah's voice came from behind them, closer this time. "Who is that?"

Then Mark, drawing up on Lindsay's other side. "I don't recognize her."

"What do we do?" asked Deborah.

Lindsay took one more step, scanning the rest of the girl's body with the light. A strapless dress clung to her frame. Lindsay recognized the color: champagne. She'd wanted to get a dress that color, but her mom told her she'd look washed out. This girl, with her pale skin and dark hair, wore it perfectly. The bodice was beaded and embroidered with a floral pattern and the skirt was tulle with an unexpected splash of red along the base.

Lindsay realized that the red wasn't part of the fabric about a second before Deborah started screaming.

TWO

Detective Josie Quinn and her investigative team stood around waiting for all hell to break loose. So far, the night had been unusually quiet, which always set Josie's nerves on edge. No one on the Denton police force looked forward to prom night in the city. Nestled among some of Central Pennsylvania's most breathtaking mountains, the city of Denton spanned twenty-five square miles with a population edging over thirty thousand —higher when the university was in session—and enough crime to keep their small police department busy. It was also home to several different high schools, and all of them held their proms on the same night in May. Josie still couldn't figure out why the school board had thought a city-wide prom night was a good idea. It was absolute chaos, and no matter how many officers they called in, there never seemed to be enough to handle all the car accidents, fights, underage drinking incidents, and other misdemeanors that the youth of Denton were hell-bent on committing.

Yet, here stood all the detectives, in the police headquarters second-floor great room. They'd already burned through four pots of coffee. While Josie sat at her desk, everyone else gathered around the corkboard above the desk of their press liaison, Amber. Josie's husband, Lieutenant Noah Fraley, pointed at something on the corkboard and said, "I like this option."

Detectives Gretchen Palmer and Finn Mettner nodded. Finn tapped his finger against a different item and said, "I think you get more for your money with this package, though."

Amber pushed her long auburn hair behind her left shoulder and picked her tablet up from her desk. "I have three more I can print out."

Gretchen said, "I've never been to any of these places. Any one of them looks like it would be amazing."

"You've never been?" Amber said. "Never?"

Gretchen smiled, the lines at the edges of her brown eyes crinkling. In her mid-forties, she was the oldest and most experienced of the team. Before joining Denton PD as a detective, she had worked on Philadelphia's homicide unit. "Never," she confirmed. "Too much work. Work, work, work."

Amber rolled her eyes. Josie didn't miss the playful way she poked Finn with her elbow. "You all work too much," she said. "Way too much." Quickly she added, "But I do appreciate it."

Finn slung an arm around Amber's shoulder. He was the youngest and least experienced detective. He'd been brought up through Denton's own ranks by their Chief, Bob Chitwood. When Amber came on as their press liaison almost two years ago, the two of them had quickly fallen in love. "We know you do," he told her.

Behind her, the Chief's door creaked open. He'd been in his office most of the night. Arms folded across his chest, he sauntered over and stood beside Josie, staring at everyone else's backs. Chief Chitwood rarely made an appearance in the great room unless it was for an update or to ream one or all of them out. He was a lot like sandpaper. No matter what kind of contact you had with him—good, bad, or indifferent—it was going to be uncomfortable. Although, to be fair, in the previous six months he'd made some awkward efforts to be less abrasive toward everyone.

Josie waited for him to start yelling. That was his default setting. Instead, in a normal speaking voice, he said, "What the hell is this?"

Josie sighed. "They're planning my honeymoon."

The four of them turned and looked at Josie and the Chief. Noah, who was typically not fazed by the Chief, gave her a disarming half-smile. "We will plan it for you if you don't chime in. Have you given it any thought?"

She shook her head. "We've been married for over a year. We've been on vacation since then."

Amber frowned. "But you guys never went on your honeymoon."

The Chief took a few steps toward the corkboard. Gretchen and Noah made room for him.

Josie didn't speak. She couldn't remember whose idea it had been for her and Noah to actually take a real honeymoon finally, nor could she recall how they'd all ended up perusing brochures for island getaways that Amber had pinned to her corkboard.

Noah said, "You love the beach."

Josie gave him a tight smile. He was right. She did love the beach. She'd love to be there right now. She just didn't want to have to do any of the planning or decision-making. Or think about why they'd never made it to their honeymoon in the first place. Just over a year ago, on their wedding day, a body had been found at the venue. It had thrust them all into a double murder case with more twists and turns than a Hershey Park roller coaster and had eventually led to the murder of Josie's grandmother, Lisette Matson.

As an infant, Josie had been kidnapped from her biological family and passed off as another woman's child. That woman had told her then-boyfriend, Eli Matson, that Josie was his daughter. Eli and his mother, Lisette, had no reason to believe otherwise and they had loved Josie fiercely. The woman Josie had believed was her mother had been abusive, lending new meaning to the word evil, always devising some new form of torture for young Josie. After Eli died, Lisette spent years and every cent she had gaining custody of Josie. She finally got it when Josie was fourteen years old. Lisette had been the foundation on which Josie built a new life, free from the terrors her abductor had put her through. Lisette had been everything to Josie—her rock, her anchor, her rudder, and her guiding light. Since her murder, Josie had been floundering, trying to find her footing in her new world where every surface was coated with grief and every joy, even the small ones, was tinged with sadness.

As if he knew she was thinking about Lisette, Noah added, "You know damn well Lisette would be mad if you didn't go."

He was right about that, too.

The Chief pointed to a pamphlet that showed a candlelit dinner on a deserted beach, surrounded by palm trees. "This place is nice. At least it was when I went there, which was about a hundred years ago..."

He drifted off, oblivious to all the eyes on him. Chief Chitwood never spoke about his personal life. They didn't even know if he was married or had children.

Noah cleared his throat. "Honeymoon?"

There was a long, silent moment as the Chief continued staring at the photo. Then he chuckled under his breath. "No, no. Not me. I was young and stupid and thought I was in love. It was before Kel—it was a mistake. I was trying to impress a woman. Took her there. Spent a ton of money. Had a great time. Didn't last."

Turning back to face Josie, he blinked, as if coming out of a stupor of some sort. "You should do it, Quinn. You've certainly earned the time off."

Josie could count on one hand the number of times the Chief had given any of them compliments. Dumbstruck, she caught Noah's eye. He gave a barely perceptible shrug. On the Chief's other side, Amber held back a smile. Gretchen and Finn simply watched the Chief with raised brows.

Josie sighed and stood up. "Fine," she said. "Let's see what you've got."

Before she could take a step, the phone on her desk jangled. They all stared at it as if it were some alien object that had just landed there. "You've got to be kidding me," Noah said.

Josie snatched up the receiver. "Quinn."

She listened, making mental notes as dispatch filled her in. Then she hung up. "We've got a body."

Gretchen sighed. "So it begins."

THREE

In all the years she had been on the Denton police force, Josie had never encountered a dead body on prom night. Well, at least not related to prom celebrations. Now, she and Noah stood in the dark pit of Denton East High School's notorious alcove, their flashlight beams focused on a young girl lying in a pool of blood. Josie didn't need to check her pulse to know she was already dead. Her form was preternaturally still, and her skin had taken on a waxy appearance. Beneath her lower body, blood congealed in black pools.

As if reading her mind, Noah said, "The principal said that he checked her pulse—touched her throat—but there was nothing."

"I think she's been gone awhile," said Josie.

"We need lights down here," said Noah. His voice was low and held a note of sadness.

Josie shone the light on the girl's face once more. It looked as though she'd simply laid down for a nap. Nothing about her hair or make-up was disturbed. There were no defensive wounds that Josie could see—at least not from the way that the girl was positioned. As Josie studied her more closely, she felt a flicker of recognition, but it was fleeting. "Do you recognize her?" she asked Noah.

"No, you?"

Josie stared at the girl's face a bit longer. Her mind worked back through where she might have seen the girl before. Coffee shop? Grocery store? One of her recent cases? The girl who delivered their pizza last week? Nothing came to mind. With a sigh, she said, "No. I guess not. Okay, listen, we need to call the Evidence Response Team."

Noah turned and looked back toward the top of the steps. The responding officers had cordoned off the theater area so that no one could enter, but that hadn't stopped a group of people from gathering near the separating wall. The crowd of onlookers seemed to grow with each minute. There were a handful of teenagers, the principal, two teachers, one school police officer, and two Denton patrol officers. The Denton officers had flashlights. Everyone else's faces were illuminated by the glow of their phones. Gretchen had her notebook out, scribbling as she spoke with one of the students. Mettner took his notes on his phone as he interviewed a teacher.

"You think this is a homicide?"

Josie said, "I think it's suspicious. That's a lot of blood. Plus, what's she doing out here?"

Noah continued to study the crowd above them. "You never used the alcove when you went here?"

Josie said, "I knew about it. Even the kids who didn't come out here knew about it. But when I went here, it was used for smoking or doing drugs. Not... this. I could understand if she had taken some sort of illicit substance, come out here, and passed out, but that doesn't explain all the blood."

"Nothing good ever happens in this place," he muttered. "I find it hard to believe she was out here alone." He turned back, shining his flashlight on the girl's lower body once more.

"There's no trail. No droplets. No spatter. Whatever happened to her, happened right here in this spot."

"You're right."

His flashlight beam drifted over to the single door that opened into the theater area. It was to the right of the stage, painted a slate gray. Trash, leaves, and dirt gathered along the bottom of it. A cobweb sparkled on its handle.

Josie said, "The door doesn't look like it's been opened in a long time."

"The principal said it's padlocked from the other side. Too many kids were sneaking out here during class."

"How long has it been padlocked?"

"For the last four months," Noah said.

"Has he checked the padlock?"

"Not him but his vice principal. He ran inside to check it right after they found her to make sure no one could get out that way. The lock is still intact."

"Meaning this girl came from up there, not down here."

Josie turned now and stared at the people above them. "We need everyone's phones. Especially the ones from the kids who found her. I don't want this poor girl's face—or any part of this horrible scene—shared with every person in this school, or worse, on social media. We should try to get all the photos and videos taken inside the building as well, see if we can catch her on camera in photos or the background of photos. We also need to check with the prom photographer and get any pictures he took of her and her date, assuming she came with one. We definitely need to find that date—as soon as possible. Someone knows who she is. Find her friends. I didn't see a phone or a purse near her. If they're not still inside, then maybe they're under her dress or somewhere not immediately visible but we need to locate those things. We need to talk to every student and teacher here, Noah. Also, we'll need Dr. Feist to come out to the scene."

As they trudged back up the steps, Josie continued, "We're also going to need someone to deal with the parents. Word will get out as soon as we tell everyone they can't leave until they've talked with us. Parents will be over here in no time, rightly panicked."

Noah said, "I'll put Gretchen on that. You call the ERT and Dr. Feist while I have the uniformed guys expand the scene perimeter and make sure no one but our people go in. I'll get the phones from the kids who found her and see if the principal can lend us a room where we can question everyone."

Josie took out her phone as they reached the top of the steps. "I'm also going to call in some patrol units. There are a lot of kids here. We're going to need bodies to keep everything under control."

While Noah herded everyone away from the steps, Josie made the necessary phone calls. By the time she finished, all but a few uniformed officers had disappeared. As she recalled, the front entrance was the only way to get into the building from outside and it was a five-minute walk from the alcove. She started off in that direction, looking up at the two brick walls to her left and right that closed in the area. There hadn't been cameras when Josie went to Denton East, and there weren't any now.

She took one last glance behind her before she turned the corner, thinking about the girl all the way down in the dark recess of the alcove, alone. Were her friends looking for her? Had anyone noticed that she was missing? Were they looking at some kind of bullying incident, or a domestic issue with a boyfriend? Josie felt a small ache in her chest as she thought about the parents who had sent the girl off to prom that evening. They'd probably exclaimed over her dress, her make-up, and hair. They'd probably taken a hundred pictures of her. They'd probably made her pose for awkward photos with grandparents, siblings, and neighbors both inside their home and out. It had been a perfect May day, the sun shining, the temperatures in the high sixties. Driving to work that afternoon, Josie had seen a handful of prom-goers out on their front lawns with their families taking endless photos.

Now Josie was going to have to break the news to this girl's loved ones that their worst nightmare was real.

FOUR

The next few hours went by in a blur. There was so much to be done and over four hundred kids to question—the prom was a combined event for juniors and seniors. Josie knew they'd be at the school until daybreak. The teens who had found the body were interviewed, their parents were called, and they were released with strict instructions not to talk with anyone about the body they'd discovered at least until the girl was identified and her family notified. Josie didn't want her parents to hear about her death from the town rumor mill or social media. Only one of the teens, Brody Ford, had taken a photo of the body and from a thorough search of his phone, it did not appear he had had time to send it to anyone or post it anywhere. Josie took his phone into evidence, which went over about as well as the prom being abruptly canceled.

Gretchen began herding arriving parents into a couple of classrooms near the front entrance while Josie, Noah, and Mettner dealt with the crowd of kids and staff members in the auditorium. Noah interviewed adults in one classroom across from the auditorium while Mettner began interviewing students in a separate room. Since they still had no idea who the girl was or how she had died, and none of the students were being questioned in connection with any crime or as suspects in any crime, they were able to speak to them without their parents present, although the students had that option if they preferred. The principal and vice principal, as well as several uniformed officers, stood sentry around the cavernous space, ensuring that no one left without speaking to the police.

The celebratory mood that had been in full swing when Josie and her team arrived was gone. There was no more music or colorful strobe lights. No more dancing or laughter. Now the students sat at the tables on the periphery of the auditorium looking exhausted. They sat slumped in chairs. Many of the boys had taken off their jackets and strewn them across the backs of their chairs. Several of the girls had kicked off their heels. The glitz and youthful energy that had seemed to radiate from each one of them when Josie first walked into the auditorium—before the principal stopped all the festivities—were completely gone. Now they were by turns somber and skittish. Some played on their phones while others stared at all the police officers. Others chatted quietly, but Josie could tell by the hushed whispers that they were all just trying to figure out what the hell was going on. Once a student had left with Noah to be questioned, they were released to their parents. Josie tried to see it through the eyes of the teenagers—their peers were leaving with a detective and not coming back. Of course, judging by the number of chirps and dings issuing from all their phones, word was getting back to them.

Josie stood in the corner of the auditorium where the official prom photographer had set up. He had uploaded all his photos onto a laptop and Josie was clicking through them. She sat at a folding table that had been set up next to the backdrop and carefully went through each photo a third time. The photographer stood over her shoulder, his teeth working a hangnail on his right index finger. Josie put him at about thirty years old, tall and thin with a neatly trimmed goatee and shaggy brown hair. He was dressed in brown slacks, a white dress shirt and a black tie, but they seemed to hang on him, as if they belonged to someone larger than him.

"You're sure this is all the pictures?" she asked him for the second time.

"I'm absolutely sure," he replied. "I told you. That's everything. Those are all the photos I took tonight."

There wasn't a single photo of the dead girl. Josie gave a frustrated sigh and closed the laptop. "Were these prepaid?"

"Yes. All the packages are prepaid before prom."

She stood up from the table. "Do you do a lot of these?"

He shrugged, nibbled on his finger again. "They pay well, so yeah."

"Do you get a lot of students that decline the photos?"

"It's tough to say," he told her. "I'm not privy to how many students attend versus how many purchase photo packages."

When Josie had gone to her junior and senior proms, they'd had to buy tickets. She handed a business card to the photographer. "You're free to go."

He let out a long breath, relief loosening his posture. With a weak smile, he breathed, "Thank you."

Josie left him packing his things and strode across the auditorium to where the principal stood, texting furiously on his phone. "Mr. Broadbent," she said.

He looked up from his phone and managed a pained smile. "Detective Quinn."

"Did the school sell tickets to the prom?"

"Yes. I can tell you how many—"

"Do you have the names of the students who purchased them?"

"Oh. Well, yes. Listen, I'm really sorry that I didn't recognize her—that poor girl. You must understand how many students we've got in the whole school—"

Josie cut him off. "I do understand, and there is a possibility that she's not a student here at all. Someone could have brought her as their date. Or she could be from another Denton high school entirely and somehow, she ended up here. It is prom night in the entire city. I'll have my team check with other schools once we're done here if it becomes necessary. Right now I want to figure out if she was a student here. We'll have a much better idea once my team has interviewed everyone. Until then, I'm going to need a copy of the list of students who bought tickets to the prom. Also, I need a copy of your current yearbook."

He nodded. "Sure, sure. Of course."

"What about security cameras?" asked Josie. "Where are those located?"

When Josie was a Denton East student, they hadn't had security cameras but today, high school was a very different monster.

"We don't have any in here, I'm afraid," Broadbent told her. "They're in all the halls and the main office. None in the parking lots. Other than prom and homecoming and a few theater productions during the year, most of the activity here takes place during the day—while classes are in session. Our school police regularly patrol the parking lots. We've never had any issues."

The lack of cameras might seem ridiculous to most people, living in an age where cameras of every kind were ubiquitous and violence in American schools was endemic, but Denton was a city plopped into the middle of Central Pennsylvania. Much of it was rural. That's not to say the schools there weren't without problems, but as educational institutions went, Denton East reported very little crime. Even nuisance incidents were low there. Josie could understand why the administration had not chosen to spend money on expensive security cameras for the parking lots when their more urgent needs were for educational materials. Other schools like Bartz High in South Denton had so much crime, they spent the majority of their budget on security measures.

"What about the exterior of the building?" Josie asked.

He hung his head. "We have cameras out front so we can see who is coming and going during the day. During school hours, all entrances are locked except the front. If any exterior doors are opened while classes are in session, an alarm goes off in the main office. The front doors are locked as well. All visitors have to use the intercom to announce themselves and their business. Since we try to ensure that anyone entering the building is coming through the front, the only cameras are there."

"None in the back?" Josie asked. "At all?"

Sheepishly, he shook his head. "Detective Quinn, we're very lucky here at Denton East that our students are not generally disruptive. Once we closed off the exterior door to the alcove so that we didn't have to send someone down there every time one of the kids tripped the alarm to vape between classes, things became even less troublesome, so no, we do not have exterior cameras at the back of the building."

She pointed to the auditorium entrance which stood open, double doors revealing a large swath of blue-tiled hallway. Across from the doors hung a student-made banner that read: *GO DENTON EAST BLUE JAYS*. Someone had hand-printed the words "Football Team" below that and someone else had crossed it out and written "Soccer."

"Is this where the kids came into the auditorium tonight?"

He nodded. "Yes, right here. They gave their tickets to a faculty member at the front entrance and then I met them all here, gave them table assignments, and directed them toward the photographer. They were supposed to find their table and then get their photos taken immediately."

Josie put a hand on her hip. "You're telling me you looked at the face of every person who came in here tonight, but you don't recognize the girl in the alcove?"

A blush crept up from the collar of his light blue shirt to his balding scalp. "Detective Quinn, I told you, we have hundreds and hundreds of kids at Denton East. I'm afraid I don't know each one of them by sight."

"But do you remember seeing the girl come in? Do you remember handing her or her date a table assignment?"

He shook his head. "I'm afraid not. Again, we have hundreds—"

She cut him off. "I know. Hundreds of students just at the prom."

"And some of these attendees are not students here. Some of our students brought dates from other schools."

"I'm aware," said Josie. "Do you have security footage from this hallway?"

"Oh, well, yes, I'm sure we do. If you'll follow me, I can take you to the school police office and they'll help you. I did call in the entire school police staff."

Josie's phone chirped a few times, indicating she had text messages. As she followed the principal out of the auditorium and down the hallway toward the main office, she took out her phone. It was the group thread that she and her team used to keep each other apprised of their progress.

Gretchen had written: *In the interest of quelling some hysteria out here, I instructed all parents to text or call their children if they have not already made contact. So far, all the kids whose parents have come are accounted for.*

Mettner responded: *I've told all the kids to immediately contact their parents if they haven't already for that reason. I asked one of the school police to go around and instruct all the kids still in the auditorium to do so as well.*

Noah: *I'm almost done with faculty and staff. No one knows who this girl could be.*

Josie tapped in a message about the prom photographer being a dead end, and a quick recap of her conversation with the principal, including that they'd likely have to check with other city schools once their investigation at Denton East wrapped up.

Mettner typed: *So far I'm getting the same as Fraley—no one has any idea who the girl could be. No one remembers seeing anyone meeting her description. No missing dates or friends yet. Still have a lot to talk with.*

Noah replied: *I'm finishing up with the adults. Will join you to interview the rest of the kids.*

"Right here, Detective," the principal said as they pushed through a set of double doors and turned left down another hallway. Ahead was the main office but just before that was a heavy door with a glass inset marked "School Police." The lights were on inside and two officers in plain clothes hunched over computers.

The principal made introductions and the two men began queuing up the night's footage for Josie. "Principal Broadbent," she said. "I'm going to need that yearbook."

"Yes, I'll get it."

"Actually, if you could, I'll need yearbooks going back two years just in case this is someone who already graduated."

Broadbent left and Josie sat in front of one of the computers. Her phone chirped again. Officer Hummel this time, the head of their Evidence Response Team.

Dr. Feist is here. We're still finishing up. It will be some time before we can let her near the body. Come out when you have a chance.

Will do, Josie typed back. Then she turned her attention to the prom night footage.

FIVE

The footage wasn't as illuminating as Josie had hoped. The cameras were set high above the hall, angled downward so that they didn't catch the teens' faces head-on. Most of them arrived at the auditorium in groups, making it more difficult to isolate particular people. There were two girls mixed in with other groups that Josie thought might be their Jane Doe, but it was too difficult to tell without another careful look at the girl herself. Josie made notes of the timestamps and turned her attention to the footage from the front entrance and other hallways. She found footage of Brody Ford and Mark Severns leaving through the front at 7:47 p.m., followed about fifteen minutes later by Lindsay Jones and Deborah Hart. No other teens exited the building before or after.

She rewound the footage to its earliest point, watching as eager teens arrived for the prom. Again, she found the same two girls embedded within a group of teenagers as well as a third girl whose dress looked similar to the one Jane Doe wore. The clarity of the videos wasn't good enough for Josie to make a firm determination. Also, she'd only seen the girl in the alcove for a few moments, in the dark, using a flashlight. Not exactly reliable. Josie noted the timestamps on the other videos and asked one of the officers to make her copies of everything. Later, if it turned out the girl had been murdered, they'd need to account for the movements and whereabouts of each and every faculty and staff member during the evening.

Principal Broadbent had brought a stack of yearbooks to the police office and set them on the narrow table positioned just inside the door. Josie stood and stretched her arms over her head. It was late and her eyes felt dry. She decided to remain standing as she leafed through each yearbook. As she had with the video footage, she found a handful of junior and senior girls who resembled Jane Doe but Josie would still need a better, more careful look at the girl to be certain. She folded the corners of the pages on which she'd found candidates and tucked the yearbooks beneath her arm.

Thanking the school police officers and Broadbent, she made her way to the rooms in which Noah and Mettner were interviewing teenagers. She poked her head into the room where Noah sat with a young man. "Lieutenant? A word?"

Out in the hallway, Josie handed Noah the books. "Any luck?"

He shook his head. "It's looking more and more like she didn't attend the school but came with someone who does. We haven't found her date yet. You get anything on the footage?"

"Nothing definitive. I asked for copies so we can review later, together, after these interviews are over if necessary. These are the yearbooks. I folded down the pages with students who bear a resemblance to Jane Doe. Can you and Mettner cross-check them against your lists of interviewees?"

Noah nodded. "Will do. Where are you headed now?"

"The alcove. Hummel should be getting close to finishing by now, and Dr. Feist is waiting to get onto the scene."

"Great. Also, I had the patrol officers work their way

through the tables inside, looking for any unattended purses or phones. Nothing."

Josie sighed.

"You think her date did this?" Noah asked, his mind working through all the same possibilities as hers.

"Well, that's the most obvious thing, isn't it? Domestic violence among teens is a real problem. We just had that case at Bartz High where the boyfriend tried to strangle his girlfriend, remember?"

Noah grimaced. "How could I forget? They were only sixteen. All right, let's say she doesn't go to this school but her boyfriend does. He brings her to the prom. They have some kind of altercation. Maybe they were arguing—although no one so far has reported seeing anything like that—and they went out to the alcove. Things got heated. He killed her."

"Without getting any blood anywhere?" Josie remarked.

"I don't know. We really need to know the mechanism of injury. Hopefully Dr. Feist can lend some insight when you get out there. If we assume stabbing, then maybe he got blood on himself when he did it but then left before she actually bled out —which would explain why there are no footprints."

"But Noah, they would have had to leave the prom and come out here, and no one left early. I checked the footage. The only way in or out was the front entrance. If the killer left through another door, it would have tripped an alarm in the office. None were tripped tonight. The only kids who left through the front door early were the kids who found her."

"None of them had blood spatters on them," he said. "They all had the same story, and it was consistent. Not only that, but if one of them had done it then the other three of them had to have known. They'd all be lying. How long was it between the time that Brody Ford and Mark Severns left the building and the time that Lindsay Jones and Deborah Hart followed them?"

"Only about fifteen minutes. I don't think that would have

been enough time for the boys to have killed her and gotten rid of the murder weapon and their bloody clothes," Josie said.

"Right," Noah agreed. "Unless they never went inside and came right to the alcove after parking their car. Boyfriend murders her and then goes home without ever entering the building."

"If that's the case," Josie said, "we'll be able to narrow down his identity when we check the tickets purchased against attendees. Right now, I need to get out to the alcove."

She didn't need a flashlight to find her way to the alcove. Hummel had set up so many lights, you could probably see the nook from outer space. The parking lot had been cordoned off. One uniformed officer stood in front of the yellow crime scene tape, guarding the scene. He let her through to the staging area where the ERT had left equipment and an ambulance waited to transport the body. A few feet from the ambulance stood a man dressed in jeans and a button-down shirt. Josie had met him before. As she recalled, he was a college professor. At his feet lay a drone. With him was Officer Jenny Chan, a member of the ERT. Josie walked over.

"Drone footage?" she asked.

Chan nodded. "With a scene this bloody, outdoors, we had to start with overall pictures before we moved close up. The drone footage helps us ensure the integrity of the initial photos. Makes sure we don't miss anything and that everything is documented fully before we start tracking blood everywhere, although Hummel has already started doing that. You might remember Dr. Chris McAllister. He teaches at Denton U, but we bring him on as a consultant when we need drone footage."

Josie managed a smile for him as she shook his hand and introduced herself. "Right," she said. "Drones aren't in the budget."

Chan pointed over Josie's shoulder. "The doc is just waiting to get in."

Josie turned. Starting at the steps to the theater was a second area that was taped off, this one guarded by an officer with a clipboard. No one could get in or out of the crime scene below without signing in with him. Dr. Feist stood a few feet away, sipping coffee from a stainless-steel travel mug that read: *A Medical Examiner Loves You For What's On The Inside.* She was already dressed in a Tyvek suit, complete with booties. Her silver-blonde hair was tucked beneath a skull cap. She gave Josie a grim smile as she approached. "They're almost ready for me."

"Did Hummel tell you what we've got?"

Dr. Feist nodded and set her coffee mug on the ground beside a leather tote bag. "I'll need to determine where the bleeding started. I'll take a few of my own photos and then you guys can transport her."

From the corner of her eye, Josie saw Hummel emerge from the theater. He waved at them and jogged over. "We haven't found a weapon of any kind or any personal belongings, but we didn't move the body. It's possible there could be something beneath her. Other than the blood around her body, we only found two other drops on the steps leading up here which we marked and photographed." He looked at Dr. Feist. "We're ready for you, doc."

Dr. Feist lifted a camera and some gloves from her bag. To Josie, she said, "Suit up. You can come with me."

SIX

In the stark glare of the halogen lights that the ERT had set up at various places in the theater, the scene was much more disturbing. Twigs, leaves, dirt, and trash littered the stage. In the center of it, the girl lay as if she were part of two very different pictures: her upper body was clean and, in her elaborate bodice, make-up and carefully styled hair, she looked quite lovely, while her lower body was bathed in blood that now curdled darkly against the slate-colored concrete. The sight made Josie's stomach churn. She could see where Hummel's booties had stepped in the pools of blood so that he could take up-close photographs as well as all the places he had tracked the blood thereafter. The closer Josie got, the sharper the coppery smell became.

Dr. Feist circled the body, snapping photos with her own camera before kneeling in the blood that had pooled in front of the girl. "Hold this," she told Josie.

Josie took her camera, bringing the strap over her head, careful not to disturb the skull cap she had donned along with the rest of her crime scene garb. She watched as Dr. Feist used gloved hands to gently peel the girl's dress from her legs. Like her dress and the two-inch heels she wore, her legs were drenched in blood.

"I don't know if you want to watch this," Dr. Feist muttered. "But I need to pull her legs apart and make sure we're only dealing with one body."

Josie's stomach roiled again. She'd been so focused on securing the scene and getting everyone present catalogued and interviewed that it hadn't even occurred to her that this might not be a homicide.

Dr. Feist went to work, still talking in a low voice. "Remember the fourteen-year-old from last year?"

Josie echoed Noah's earlier words. "How could I forget? She gave birth in a Stop-N-Go bathroom and bled out."

"Looked like a murder, didn't it?"

Josie recalled the scene, pushing down the nausea that accompanied it. In her line of work, she saw the worst of the worst. Horrific things that stained her psyche so deeply, it would take God himself to repair the damage. For some who had done the job as long as she had, her nausea, disgust, and sadness were considered a sign of weakness. But for Josie, it meant her humanity was still intact. The feelings didn't stop her from doing her job—if anything, they made her more motivated to work to make her community safer—but she tried to make a habit of noting them and moving forward. "Sure did," she croaked. "Don't you think, though, that if this girl was in labor or miscarrying, she'd look more... disheveled?"

Dr. Feist popped her head up and glanced at the girl's face. "Sleeping beauty," she muttered. "I suppose you're right, but you never know. Remember how we talked about individual health factors the last time you had a murder victim on my table?"

"I do," Josie said. "You're saying some women can give birth without breaking a sweat?"

Dr. Feist laughed. "That I'd like to see. No, I'm saying that all people are different. Maybe she had a higher pain tolerance than most girls, or the pain made her pass out before she bled out, or she could have been under the influence of something that made her sleepy..." She trailed off. Josie waited for her to pick up her train of thought again but instead the doctor made a *hmmph* sound, her hands searching along the girl's left inner thigh.

"This is not that at all," said Dr. Feist, her tone growing more urgent.

"What do you mean?" asked Josie.

Dr. Feist changed positions, moving her face closer to the girl's leg, her fingers probing something that Josie could not yet see. "She didn't give birth or miscarry. She's got a wound."

"Stab wound?" Josie asked.

"You know I can't say for sure until I get her on my table but yes, it looks to me like someone stabbed her deeply enough to hit her femoral artery, but like I said—"

"I know, I know," said Josie. "You can't say for certain until after your exam. I'm not asking for official findings here, just your impressions."

"All I am seeing at this point is what appears to be a single stab wound, likely to her femoral artery."

"If you're right, and it's an arterial wound," Josie said, "that wouldn't have left her with much time to get help."

Dr. Feist held out a hand for the camera and Josie pulled it over her head and passed it to her. As the doctor took up-close photos of the wound, she said, "If she bled out from her femoral artery, she would have lost consciousness in about thirty seconds. Without intervention, she would have died in less than five minutes."

"Arterial bleeding spurts," Josie said.

Dr. Feist continued taking photos. "Yes, but the way she was positioned, her right leg would have redirected a lot of the blood back toward the ground. I imagine the person who stabbed her got some blood spatter on them, but they pulled her dress back down which obviously contained the bleeding somewhat, causing it to pool underneath her rather than shoot upward and outward."

"Covered her up," Josie echoed softly, more to herself than the doctor. To contain the spurting blood, she wondered, or because he felt some sort of remorse for what he had done? Or both? In spite of the gruesomeness of the scene, Jane Doe had been left in a more dignified manner than most dead bodies Josie saw on the job. Oftentimes, the way a killer left a body said a lot about their state of mind and how they felt about the victim. Given the location of the body, the killer had clearly staged the scene in a very specific way. Josie gave her head a small shake, forcing herself to focus on the present. "The two drops of blood Hummel found on the steps—those are likely from blood that got onto the killer and then dripped as he left the scene."

Dr. Feist handed the camera back to Josie. "Yes."

"Do you see any weapon?" Josie asked.

"Help me roll her over."

Josie put the camera around her neck again and then flipped it around to her back so it wouldn't hang over the girl's body. Gingerly, she knelt in the blood beside Dr. Feist. Josie placed one hand under the girl's hip and another under her shoulder while Dr. Feist maneuvered her lower body. Even through her gloves, Josie could feel the deep cold that settled into a dead body. It was a cold unlike anything else she had ever touched. From the stiffness of the girl's frame, Josie knew she was entering rigor mortis. Together, they rolled her onto her right side, but all they found was more blood.

"Whoever did this to her took the weapon with them," said Josie.

"Looks that way," Dr. Feist agreed. "I'm finished here. Let's have her transported. I want to get her on my table as soon as possible."

SEVEN

The sun was coming up when Josie and the team wrapped things up at Denton East High School. At some point during the night, Noah and Gretchen had been dispatched to other areas of the city to check with other high schools to ensure that the girl hadn't gone missing from one of the other proms going on that night. Denton East students and their parents had gone onto social media to lament the terrible ending to the prom, and in the middle of the night, someone from the local television station, WYEP, had found out. A news van waited in the parking lot, its occupants jumping out to shout questions at Josie and the uniformed officers still on scene as they left the building. She said "no comment" like a broken record. The other officers remained impassive.

By eight a.m. Josie, Noah, Gretchen, and Mettner were all back at their desks in the great room. As they began writing reports, Amber sailed in with a bunch of coffees from their favorite café, Komorrah's Koffee, which was just down the street from the stationhouse. She distributed them, her sunny smile growing dimmer by the moment.

"It was a bad one, huh?" she asked Mettner softly.

He squeezed her hand briefly. "Pretty bad, yeah."

Amber set the rest of her things down at her desk. In her hand was one more paper coffee cup. She looked around the room, her eyes finally landing on the Chief's closed door. "Where's the Chief?"

"He went to get breakfast," Noah answered. "He was out all night. Spent some time at the high school checking in with us and then went around scene-hopping after that. We had some more calls, but nothing as serious as what we found at Denton East."

Gretchen directed her gaze to the cup in Amber's hand. "Did you get him a coffee?"

Amber, too, looked at the cup. "Well, yeah."

Josie asked, "He told you how he likes his coffee?"

"I asked," Amber said.

"And he told you?" Mettner laughed. "Did hell freeze over, or is the Chief becoming... friendly?"

"I wouldn't go that far," said Noah.

Gretchen sipped her own cup and asked, "So what is it? Black? He seems like he'd take his coffee black."

"Well, it's a Red Eye," said Amber. "Black coffee with two shots of espresso plus two pumps of vanilla, topped with half-fat foam."

They all stared at her.

"We don't know him at all," said Mettner.

Amber shook her head, set the coffee meant for the Chief on her desk and snatched up her tablet, powering it up. All business, she stood before their desks and said, "Talk to me about the Denton East case. I'm sure I've already got messages from reporters on my line."

Josie rubbed her face with both hands. "Guaranteed. WYEP was there when we left. A dead body at a prom is not going to stay under wraps for long."

"Do you have an ID?" Amber asked.

"That's just it," said Noah. "No one knows who she is, or if they do, they're not admitting to it."

Mettner added, "We interviewed over four hundred kids. No one was unaccounted for."

Noah said, "Everyone came with someone, but no one reported anyone missing."

"No parents showed up looking for their daughter," Gretchen added. "Mett and I checked with the faculty of all the other high schools. There were no reports of any missing teens. They checked their list of attendees against tickets sold and no one was unaccounted for. Everyone who was expected to be at their proms was there and everyone who was expected to bring a date brought one. We woke up prom photographers and had a look at their photos. Didn't find the girl in any prom pictures. Still, we asked all the principals to send over yearbooks."

"She wasn't a student at any local high school?" Amber said.

"Looks that way," Josie said. "Noah, did you get anywhere with the Denton East yearbooks I gave you?"

"All the girls you flagged were accounted for. One of them did not go to the prom but we got her number from one of the other students, called, and verified that she's just fine."

"The footage?" Josie asked.

Mettner said, "We still have to go over that in more detail, but I don't think we'll find anything."

Josie looked back at Amber. "Either someone is lying, or she never made it inside. What about the list of people who bought tickets? Noah? Mett? Did you cross-reference it with the kids you interviewed?"

"Yeah," Mettner answered. "All the kids who bought tickets were interviewed. Alive and well. All reported that their dates were accounted for."

"Anyone buy tickets and not show?" Josie asked.

Mettner shook his head. "No."

"You two checked phones for videos and photos to see if

you could find our Jane Doe either in regular photos or in the backgrounds?"

Noah said, "We found nothing. Josie, I don't think she ever made it inside."

Gretchen said, "Maybe someone invited two dates."

Noah said, "And what? They found out about one another?"

Gretchen shrugged. "Don't know. I'm just saying maybe there was some kind of cheating situation that blew up."

"Still, someone would have seen or heard something," Mettner said. "Teenagers love drama. There's no way something like that would have been secret. The whole reason the kids who found her in the alcove were out there in the first place was because a girlfriend thought her boyfriend was cheating on her. It was all over social media, apparently."

"Then we need to be looking at these kids' social media," said Gretchen.

Noah grimaced. "We're talking over four hundred kids. Not sure that is feasible. Plus, that stuff would be set to private, I'm sure, and we'd need either consent or a warrant to get into their accounts."

"Which means we need to narrow down the list of teens whose social media we should look at," Josie said. "Although now that they all know a body was found, anyone who was posting about anything would probably delete it. We might be able to retrieve deleted information with a warrant and help from a computer forensics expert, but for that we'd need to home in on a particular kid or group of kids, and we're just not there yet."

"Someone—or several someones—have to be lying," Mettner said.

"We're not ruling that out at all," Noah said.

Josie took another sip of her coffee, the feel of it sliding down her throat like a balm to her nerves. She couldn't get the image of the girl's bloody dress out of her head. But there was something else, something even more alarming to her. "No parents showed up last night either at the school or here to report their daughter missing."

Gretchen said, "Don't they all go to hotels after the prom? Or elsewhere? That was a tradition in Philly. These kids were out all night and usually most of the next day."

"Cell phones," Noah said. "If I'm a parent, I'd at least expect her to check in by phone. A text or something."

"Maybe she has crappy parents," Mettner remarked.

"Or she's from a foster home," Gretchen added. "One where no one is looking for her just yet."

"I feel like we're missing something," said Josie.

Amber sighed. "Maybe you'll know more after Dr. Feist's autopsy. For now, I'm going to need to field press calls. What are you comfortable releasing?"

Josie took another long sip of her coffee. "The body of a female who appears to be a teenager was found on school grounds last evening during the prom. Give her description: Caucasian, brown hair—call Dr. Feist's office and see if they can give you an eye color—about five foot two inches tall, maybe one hundred twenty pounds. You can say that no one at the prom remembers seeing her, nor does it appear that she was there with anyone. Autopsy is pending. Anyone with information call us. We can release more after Dr. Feist does her exam if we still haven't identified her."

Amber tapped away at her tablet, her lips pursed. "Do you want to describe the dress?"

"Yes," said Josie. She nudged her computer mouse, and her screen came to life. Clicking several times, she located the file that had been started for their Jane Doe. Hummel had already uploaded the crime scene photos and drone footage. Josie selected a thumbnail that captured only Jane Doe's upper body and her slumbering face. Enlarging it, she said, "It's almost like a tan-gold color."

Amber circled the desks and looked over Josie's shoulder. "That color is called champagne, I think."

She punched at her tablet again.

Noah said, "If we can't get anywhere with an ID, we can try locating places where the dress was sold."

"Good idea," said Josie. "Dr. Feist usually has Hummel come over and take the personal items into evidence. I'm sure he'll upload those photos and information within the next few hours."

Josie was aware that Amber's fingers had stopped moving across the screen of her tablet. She looked up to see Amber staring at the photo of Jane Doe. Josie glanced back to double-check that she hadn't accidentally chosen a more gruesome photograph. But it was only of Jane Doe's body from the waist up. No blood was visible. Still, seeing a photo of a dead body could be jarring no matter what the circumstances.

As if sensing the change in Amber's mood, Mettner said, "You okay?"

Amber blinked and looked up. "She looks familiar."

"What?" said Josie and Mettner at once.

Amber pointed an index finger toward the photo. "You don't think she looks familiar?"

Mettner, Gretchen, and Noah all got up and walked around, gathering behind Josie and Amber to study the picture. Josie focused on the girl's face. Had she missed something? Had they all missed something? They'd been working at a breakneck pace since the night before, more consumed with securing the scene and interviewing prom attendees than anything else. Something scratched at the back of Josie's mind.

Noah said, "I don't think so."

Neither Gretchen nor Mettner recognized her.

Josie looked back to see Mettner rest a hand on Amber's shoulder. "Sorry."

She shook her head briskly and offered them all a tight smile. "No, I'm sorry. I don't know why I said that."

Josie said, "Because she looks familiar to you. I thought she looked familiar the first time I saw her as well, but I have no idea where I might have come into contact with her. Don't discount it. You may have seen her somewhere. Think about it for a while, see if anything comes to you. In the meantime, we'll finish the mountain of paperwork we've got and then we'll take shifts going home to sleep."

Josie's desk phone rang.

Gretchen said, "Who needs sleep?"

"Quinn," Josie said, after snatching up the receiver. She listened for a few seconds and said, "Thanks, Doc. We'll be right over."

EIGHT

She woke to a blinding light. It seared her pupils, causing a stabbing pain that shot all the way to the back of her head. Squeezing her eyes shut, she threw an arm over her face. Something cold touched her bare shoulder and she yelped in surprise, flailing to get away from it. But she couldn't. It took her several seconds to realize the pain she felt was from fingers digging into her flesh. Then came another hand, pinning her shoulders down.

"Stop!" she cried out.

Opening her eyes again, she caught only a blurry glimpse of the room she was in—mattress, rumpled white sheets, wood paneling, an indistinct figure looming over her. Then pressure on one of her shoulders was gone and light invaded her field of vision, blotting everything out.

A disembodied voice said, "Stop moving."

But she didn't want to stop moving. Panic built in her chest, filling up her heart, her lungs, pressing on her diaphragm so hard that she couldn't get air. Her head felt heavy. In fact, her entire body felt sluggish, like the day after she snuck almost an entire bottle of her mom's vodka—filling the near-empty bottle with water so her mom wouldn't notice right away. Everything felt foggy except where the terror had opened a seam in her chest, piercing like a hot knife.

"Where am I?" she said.

The fingers squeezed her shoulder so hard that the pain sent a wave of nausea crashing through her stomach. She willed her body to remain still, but she wasn't sure if she succeeded. Between the haze inside her head and the blinding light whenever she opened her eyes, nothing seemed real, not even her own body. Had she died? Was this hell? Was she finally going to pay for all the stupid shit she had pulled just like her mother said? "One day, you'll be sorry," her mom always yelled.

Why didn't I listen?

"You're exactly where you should be," said the voice in a tone that felt like a serpent sliding along her skin.

"In hell?" she squeaked.

The fingers digging into her flesh let go, relieving some of the pain. A moment went by, or maybe it was an hour. It was too hard to tell. Everything was upside down and disconnected and her brain wasn't working right. Then came a noise that her mind couldn't process at first because it seemed so out of place. Laughter. But not the good, infectious kind. The creepy, bone-chilling kind. Abruptly, it stopped. Then the voice said, "You'll see."

She rolled onto her side and vomited.

NINE

Denton's morgue was located in the basement of Denton Memorial Hospital, which sat high atop a hill overlooking the city. Their footsteps echoed through the long hallway leading from the elevator to the suite of rooms that the morgue occupied. No matter how often the hospital housekeeping cleaned the hall, it always looked grimy, its walls filmed over with decades of dirt and its tiled floors yellowing. As they approached Dr. Feist's exam room, they were hit with the unique and wholly unpleasant odors of death and decay combined with a strong chemical smell.

Inside the room, a body lay beneath a sheet on top of one of the large stainless-steel exam tables. Given the size, Josie was certain it was their Jane Doe. Although Dr. Feist's laptop was open on one of the countertops that ran along the wall at the back of the room, she was absent. Noah sent her a quick text while they waited. A few minutes later, she sailed into the room from her adjoining office. She wore blue scrubs and her shoulder-length hair hung loose. Josie noticed smudges beneath her eyes. Lifting a paper coffee cup to her lips, she drained whatever was left in it and threw it away.

"Sorry," she said. "I needed that."

"We understand," said Josie.

Dr. Feist walked to the back of the room and tapped the mousepad on her laptop, bringing the screen to life. "Hummel took this girl's fingerprints and ran them through AFIS, but he said he didn't get any hits. Not surprising, given her age. You guys have any luck identifying her?"

"No," said Noah. "I don't suppose you found any personal items when you removed her clothing?"

Dr. Feist shook her head. "Nothing. Hummel came and took all of her clothing into evidence. She didn't have a purse."

"Identifying marks?" asked Josie.

She held up an index finger, her eyes brightening. "I might have something for you there. Let's start at the beginning." She strode over to the table and carefully pulled the sheet down to the girl's neck, exposing her head. Jane Doe still looked peaceful although her skin had taken on even more of a pallor. Dr. Feist had cleaned the make-up from her face and removed all her hair ties, pins, and headband, leaving her brown hair loose around her head. She looked different without the heavy make-up, but still naggingly familiar to Josie. Again, she went back through the last several weeks of her life, trying to figure out if she had somehow run into this girl. Had she passed her on the street while walking Trout? Had Josie seen her at the ice cream parlor the day she stopped on her way home from work for a banana sundae? Had she jogged past her in the city park? She couldn't bring any encounter into sharp enough focus to remember where she had seen this girl's face before.

Dr. Feist began, "I would estimate that Jane Doe is an adolescent girl between the ages of sixteen and eighteen. You may recall from other cases that we look at the growth plates when we're trying to determine the age of a John or Jane Doe—especially if we believe the victim is a teenager. Obviously, this girl appears to be a teenager. The growth plates confirm that.

"With growth plates, we look at the long bones in the body, like the femur. Long bones have three different parts: the shaft, which is called the diaphysis, the wide flared part at the end of the bone, which is called the metaphysis, and the end cap or epiphysis. The end cap is the growth plate. In children and adolescents, there will be a gap between the growth plate and the knobby end of the bone—between the epiphysis and the metaphysis. As we grow into adulthood, the growth plates fuse to the metaphysis. The growth plate at the proximal end of the femur fuses to the metaphysis between fifteen and nineteen. Jane Doe's are fused."

"So she could be as young as fifteen?" asked Noah.

"Actually, I believe she is sixteen, based on the fact that her distal radius is also fused. That happens at age sixteen. However, typically, fusion of the growth plates of the clavicle at either the medial or lateral aspect doesn't occur until age nineteen, and Jane Doe does not show fusion of the growth plates of her clavicles, so she hasn't yet reached age nineteen."

"That narrows it down considerably," Josie said. "Thank you. What else can you tell us?"

"She is well-nourished, five foot three inches tall, one hundred twenty-five pounds. I did not find any fresh bruises, lacerations or abrasions on her body other than the femoral wound, which I will get to in a moment. She shows no signs of sexual assault, although her hymen was not intact. That could mean that she was sexually active at some point, but I cannot say for certain. The only thing I can tell you with any degree of certainty is that I found nothing to suggest she had had sexual intercourse in the seventy-two hours prior to her death. First—"

Dr. Feist moved to the top of the table and pointed to a section of the girl's hair. "Her hair's been cut. It looks like just one lock. Maybe two inches across and, assuming it was the same length as the rest of her hair, four inches long."

Josie and Noah crowded closer to get a better look. The

doctor had carefully combed Jane Doe's hair out so that it fanned around her skull like a halo. The missing section of hair was clearly visible now that her hair was loose.

"That's strange," said Noah.

"Yes," said Dr. Feist. "It is."

Josie said, "Maybe whoever killed her took it as a souvenir."

"This job never gets less creepy, that's for sure," Noah muttered.

Dr. Feist moved down the right side of the girl's body and peeled the sheet back to reveal a pale forearm. She turned Jane Doe's palm downward and pointed to the meaty part of her forearm just below the crook of her elbow. Josie and Noah rounded the table. Josie noted the five faded pink horizontal lines scarring her skin, like stripes. Noah leaned in for a closer look. "You think she was a cutter?"

"Hard to say," said Dr. Feist. "But those are most definitely scars of some type, and they look intentional. That does not appear accidental to me."

"Each line is identical," said Josie. "How long are they?"

"Just about two inches across," Dr. Feist said.

"How old are these?" asked Noah.

Dr. Feist gave him a rueful smile. "I can't date a scar, Lieutenant. Individual health factors, remember?"

"Yeah, yeah," he muttered. "Everyone's different. Well, what are these scars consistent with? Timewise?"

"All I can tell you is that these scars are consistent with injuries sustained less than six months ago," Dr. Feist explained. "And that is just an estimate. They could be older or younger than that by weeks or possibly even a month or two. The six-month thing is just a general rule. Every person heals differently. A lot depends on the location of the wound and nature of the injury. These are pretty clean, linear cuts which typically heal more quickly. However, if they'd been inflicted more than six months ago, I'd expect them to be more silvery or pale than red. I know that's not helpful."

"What about distinguishing marks?" Josie asked. "Do you have something besides this? Anything we can take to the public?"

"I'm afraid not," said Dr. Feist. "Also, if you're interested, given her stomach contents, it appears that she ate only a couple of hours before her death. I've sent the samples to the lab for analysis, but it looks as though she had lobster, pasta, and cheesecake."

Noah turned to Josie. "What were they serving at the prom?"

"Not lobster," she responded. "But it's possible she had dinner elsewhere before arriving at the prom. When Ray and I went to our senior prom, we had dinner at the fanciest place in Denton beforehand. We never even touched our grilled chicken and roasted potatoes."

Noah said, "Well, maybe we need to start talking to local restaurants who serve lobster and see if anyone remembers her coming in. There could be footage."

"That's potentially a lot of restaurants," Josie noted. "But we haven't got much else to go on, so let's get on it. I'll text Gretchen and ask her to make a list of restaurants that serve lobster and have her call around to each one to find out if they had any prom-goers last night."

Dr. Feist waited for Josie to put her phone away before she continued. "There's something else. I normally wouldn't bring this up at this point—not until toxicology was in—because I am not one hundred percent certain, but I just..."

She trailed off. Her eyes went to the girl's toes which, Josie noticed for the first time, were painted a pale rose color.

"What is it, Doc?" asked Noah.

Dr. Feist looked back up, her eyes going back and forth between the two of them. Josie knew how exacting and how careful the doctor always had to be when giving her findings and preparing her report. In the case of a murder, she would one day have to testify in a court of law as to the contents of her report. A good defense lawyer would take her to task for any small thing that she could not opine with absolute certainty. Then her credibility would be shot. Not only could she not afford to be wrong, she could not even afford to be vague, or to present her own private thoughts or theories about a case. There was only the physical evidence and what she could say with medical certainty.

Josie said, "It's just the three of us here. Tell us. It won't be written down anywhere unless toxicology confirms your suspicions."

Wringing her hands, Dr. Feist took another moment to consider it. Then she said, "This is a disturbing case."

"It is," Noah agreed.

"I see a lot of disturbing cases," she pointed out.

"We know," Josie said.

She hesitated another moment. Noah glanced at Josie and then back at the doctor. "Tell us what you think you found in the stomach contents."

"Benadryl," Dr. Feist blurted.

There were a few seconds of silence. Then Josie said, "You mean the allergy medication? Over-the-counter Benadryl?"

Dr. Feist nodded. "Again, I can't tell you for certain. I only observed some small chunks of what looked like partially dissolved pills in her stomach, and they were pink, like Benadryl. But lots of drugs have pink coatings."

"Then why do you think it was Benadryl?" asked Noah.

She shrugged. "Benadryl would sedate her but not necessarily kill her. I mean, it could kill her, but it would take massive amounts. It would make her more..."

"Pliable," Josie said.

"Yes. Plus, it's easy to get."

Noah said, "She was stabbed. Why would someone need to give her Benadryl?"

"So they could stab her," Josie said. "Without her putting up much of a fight. Without her knowing it, even. She could have been asleep when the stabbing happened. That would explain why it didn't look like she struggled at all."

"It's just a theory," said Dr. Feist. "Like I said, toxicology would have to confirm."

"That takes weeks," Noah said. "Sometimes months."

"Yes," Dr. Feist agreed.

"Do you think that she died from a Benadryl overdose?" Josie asked. "And the stabbing was secondary?"

"No," said Dr. Feist. "This girl bled out. I'll show you the wound."

She lifted the sheet higher, exposing Jane Doe's upper legs. Toward the inside of her left thigh, almost in the crease of her groin, Josie saw the wound, now cleaned up and gaping beneath the harsh lights of the morgue. Dr. Feist traced a wedge shape around the wound, starting at the crease where Jane Doe's leg met her groin, then toward her outer thigh a couple of inches, and then downward and up again, back toward to where she started. "This is the femoral triangle which, as you can see, is located on the superomedial aspect of the lateral thigh. There is one on each side." Dr. Feist moved her hand to the girl's other thigh—the one without the stab wound—and pressed a finger into the femoral triangle there. "You can see there is a depression here in the thigh muscles. For the sake of simplicity, all you need to know is that this is where a lot of important stuff passes from the pelvis into the thigh. You've got muscles, ligaments, veins, lymph nodes, nerves—"

"And the femoral artery," Noah interjected.

"Right," said Dr. Feist. "In fact, this is where you palpate the femoral pulse. You can try it on yourself later, but it's quite easy to find. As you probably know, the femoral artery is the main supplier of blood to your lower body. It's pretty important. Like Josie and I discussed at the scene, a severed femoral artery can cause you to become unconscious in as little as thirty seconds and without intervention, you'll die within five minutes. In fact, the cause of death here is exsanguination secondary to a stab wound. You should also know that these types of stab wounds—in this location, to the femoral artery— are not common. I have only ever seen them happen when people are drunk and get into fights. Things get sloppy and someone inadvertently gets stabbed in this area. I've also seen some freak accidents with penetrating wounds involving glass and other items. But what you're looking at here, it's unusual."

Josie took another look at the wound, steeling herself against the hideousness of it. She thought about the way that Jane Doe had been positioned. Staged, even. Everything about this case so far was unusual, including the singular appearance of the wound. "There was only one stab wound?" Josie said.

"Yes," Dr. Feist replied. "A very clean stab at that. Straight to the artery."

Noah said, "Whoever did this knew exactly where to stab. Either he's done it before or he has some kind of surgical or medical background—or both."

"He must have," Josie agreed. "Otherwise, we'd see evidence of previous attempts."

"Right," Dr. Feist noted. "As we discussed earlier, if she was sedated, stabbing her in this location would have been easier. If you look at the angle and the precise cut of this wound, it seems very likely that the victim was not moving at all. I didn't even find evidence within the wound that they'd moved the knife blade around to try to find the artery. They knew precisely where to stab and how deeply and by all appearances, Jane Doe did not put up a fight. I didn't find any defensive wounds."

Noah said, "Not even any bruising?"

"Nothing to indicate that she was conscious enough to put

up a fight at the time the stabbing occurred. My best estimate as to the size of the knife is that the blade was approximately one half to five eighths of an inch wide and two to three inches long. Sharp point, single-edged, smooth, not serrated. The killer was extremely precise."

Josie asked, "Is this stab wound precise by virtue of the fact that Jane Doe was passed out, or do you think that the killer has some prior medical experience?"

Dr. Feist frowned. "I can't say for certain. This is very clean, but I'm not sure it rises to the level of surgical precision. Also, as I said, it's not difficult to find the femoral pulse here. You would need enough knowledge about anatomy to understand what the femoral artery does and where to locate it, but once you find the pulse, you don't need a very deep cut to reach the artery—at least not here in the femoral triangle."

Noah rubbed a hand over his chin. "But you said yourself, this kind of stab wound where the manner of death is homicide is unusual."

Dr. Feist began pulling the sheet back down toward Jane Doe's feet. "The homicides by stabbing I typically see are very often fatalities that occur as a result of some kind of heated dispute. Domestic violence situations, bar fights, scenarios in which things escalate and then someone grabs a knife and attacks."

Josie said, "In other words, you don't have people looking for an arterial pulse before they stab."

Dr. Feist gave a cross between a wry smile and a grimace. "Exactly. I can't say for certain that's what happened here, and I can't put that in my report and testify to it because I can't tell you what was in the mind of the person who did this to Jane Doe, but I don't see the kinds of indicators of intense rage I'm used to seeing with stabbing deaths."

"It's not messy," Noah mumbled. "Whoever did this is... it almost feels..." He drifted off, and Josie could tell by the way his mouth dimpled in the corner that he didn't want to say what he was thinking.

"What?" she prompted.

Noah gestured toward Jane Doe. "It almost seems merciful. In a sick, twisted way. Think about it. He sedated her so she wouldn't know what was happening to her, he put her in a sleeping pose, and then even after he stabbed her—"

"He covered her up," Josie finished for him. "Pulled her dress down to give her some twisted semblance of dignity—at least in his mind. Yes, I get what you're saying. If he'd wanted to humiliate her in death, he could have left her positioned differently or even left her in a more public place. If he'd wanted to make her suffer, he also could have done that. The way he killed her ensured that she passed quickly. There's a good chance she had no idea what was happening at all."

Noah said, "She gets dressed up for the prom, has a fancy dinner that is likely laced with something—toxicology pending—and then she starts to feel woozy. Tired. Maybe she passes out or she falls asleep and the next thing she knows—"

"Is nothing," said Josie. "Because she's dead."

TEN

They drove back to the stationhouse, Noah at the wheel. Josie stared out the passenger's side window, watching the streets of her city flash by in a blur of color. Spring had arrived in full force with its lush greenery and vibrant blooming flowers. It seemed as though wherever it was possible, life sprang forth. From garden beds, front lawns, outdoor planters, even the cracks of the sidewalks. Yet, Jane Doe was in a drawer in the morgue, cold, lifeless, and utterly alone in death as it seemed she had been in life.

Josie searched her tired brain once more, trying to figure out where she had seen Jane Doe before. Amber recognized her as well. Where would both of them have seen the girl?

They got out of the car, dodging the reporters' questions about what they'd dubbed the "Prom Queen Death" until they got inside the building. Trudging up the steps to the great room, they found Gretchen at her desk, an empty carton of takeout in front of her and a phone pressed to her ear. They sat down and waited for her to finish her call.

"So far I've got nothing in terms of restaurants," she told them. Putting on her reading glasses, she flipped a page in her notebook, which sat beside her desk phone. "But I've still got a few more places to call. By the way, Mett went home to get some sleep but first, he finished going through the footage from the school hallways and he was able to identify all the teenage girls you flagged. They're all accounted for."

Noah said, "You mean there is no evidence that Jane Doe ever made it inside the school building."

"Correct," said Gretchen. "Also, we got yearbooks from several of the other high schools in the city. I checked them. Didn't see our Jane Doe. Listen, I think we need to go after the dress. There aren't that many places that sell prom dresses around here. We might have better luck trying to track down where she bought the dress."

Josie booted up her computer and started pulling up the photos of the dress that Hummel had taken and uploaded, looking for a picture showing the least amount of blood. She found two that would work. She couldn't use photos of the entire dress, but a close-up of the bodice and the top of the skirt would do. She also brought up a photo of the clothing tag from inside the dress, noting the brand and size. "Let me make a list of stores, and we'll start on that now," she said. "You go home and rest, and when Mett comes back in, Noah and I will go home and sleep."

Gretchen didn't argue.

Four hours later, Josie and Noah had each had a quick lunch and several more coffees. They'd also been to every bridal shop, department store, and boutique in the city that sold dresses fit for prom and returned back to the station-house with no leads. Three of the shops carried the brand of the dress and two salespeople from two different shops thought they remembered having the dress in stock, but a cursory review of their records didn't turn anything up. The managers from all three stores promised to do a deep dive into their receipts and store footage, but that would take time, which meant that Jane Doe would spend another night unknown.

By the time Mettner returned to the stationhouse around dinner time to relieve them, Josie and Noah were falling asleep at their desks. Still, once they got home, they took their Boston Terrier, Trout, for a walk. Their friend Misty had stopped over several times to feed him and let him out while they worked the prom murder case, but Josie knew he'd never be able to quell his excitement at having them back enough to sleep right away. Once he was properly worn out, the three of them collapsed into bed.

The next morning, there were still no calls or tips about their Jane Doe. No wailing, worried parents. Even the reporters had begged off, leaving in search of a new story—one with more leads, Josie thought. By noon, the four detectives were seated at their desks again, this time staring at one another. Amber watched from her own desk, her tablet hugged to her chest. They'd gone over the theories again and again as to what had led to the girl's death, but none of them accounted for why no one was looking for her and no one recognized her description.

"What do we do?" asked Mettner. "We've got nothing."

"Maybe she's missing from some other jurisdiction," Gretchen suggested.

"Missing," said Noah. "How many missing persons show up at proms?"

"She's right," Josie said. "She could be a runaway for all we know, or taken by a noncustodial parent. It's worth a shot. We should check the PA CIC alerts."

The Pennsylvania Crime Information Center sent daily emails to law enforcement throughout the state pertaining to everything from suspicious vehicles to missing persons.

Josie logged into her email and began searching her messages. As she worked backward though the last week, she recognized some of the faces. She checked the PA CIC messages daily. Communication between departments went a long way to solving and preventing crimes.

Josie was vaguely aware of a presence hovering over her shoulder. Then she heard Amber say, "You're right. It was from one of the alerts. That's why she looked familiar to me."

Josie stopped scrolling through the emails and looked at Amber. "You don't usually look at the alerts."

"Right," said Amber. "I don't because I'm only here to handle the press—"

In the back of Josie's mind, something clicked into place. "But she was so young."

Noah, Gretchen, and Mettner all stared at them.

"Yes," Amber said. "I said something to you about it."

"Now I remember," said Josie, still frantically searching through the old alerts. "It was months ago."

"How many months?" asked Gretchen.

Amber said, "It was right after the new year. January. I had just returned to work. I saw the alert. She reminded me of... of me and my sister when we were that young. I was upset about it."

Josie nodded. "We talked about it."

Mettner walked over and touched Amber's shoulder. "You never told me about it."

Just before Christmas the year before, Amber had been abducted and nearly killed after several long-held family secrets fell into the wrong hands. It had been a tough road back to normalcy for her. They were all doing their best to help whenever and however they could.

Amber said, "It was stupid. I don't know why it even bothered me at all."

Noah said, "We all have triggers, Amber. After something traumatic happens. We just don't know what they're going to be until they happen."

Josie understood that better than anyone. She was still

balancing her childhood trauma with the traumatic loss of her grandmother in adulthood. Some days she was fine, but others, just a word or an image sent her spiraling into depression and made it hard for her to breathe, let alone get through the day.

"Do you remember her name?" Josie asked.

"It started with a G. I remember that."

Josie went back to January and tried to refine her search. Finally, she found the alert. "I've got it!"

She hit print and the ancient inkjet printer in the corner of the room whirred to life, slowly spitting out a page. Gretchen, Noah, and Mettner joined Amber behind Josie's chair, crowding in to get a look at the computer screen. From it, stared a smiling fifteen-year-old girl with long, straight brown hair and blue eyes. It looked like a school picture taken outdoors. Behind her, a rolling green field undulated into the distance. She stood next to a wooden fence, her body turned forty-five degrees toward the fence but her head canted toward the camera. Both her hands rested on top of one of the fence posts. She wore a bright red sweater and a pair of jeans with knee-high black boots. As always, looking at her in life, even in this artificially posed photo, Josie was astounded by the spark that death took from its victims. When Josie had seen her in the alcove and again on the autopsy table, she'd seemed familiar, but Josie would never have connected her with this smiling girl.

"Gemma Farmer," read Noah. "Fifteen years old. From Keller Hollow. Went missing on January second of this year. Last seen at home."

"Keller Hollow is an hour away," said Mettner. "It's barely a town."

"Seriously," said Gretchen. "When we worked the Bone Artist case, the boss and I were out there. It's literally a bunch of houses along a very long road. They don't even have their own police department."

Josie studied the alert, taking in the details. "Right. I think their population is around three or four hundred. The sheriff handles most stuff for them but in this case, the state police were brought in. Looks like Detective Heather Loughlin was assigned."

"Last seen at her home?" Mettner said. "Meaning what? She disappeared from home? Was abducted? Parents left her there and came home and she was gone?"

Josie frowned. "It doesn't say. Let's just call Heather. We'll put her on speakerphone and find out all the stuff that's not in this report."

They had all worked with Heather Loughlin at one time or another in the last several years. She was a thorough, no-nonsense investigator whom Josie respected. Plus, she always picked up when Josie called, which she did now, barking "Loughlin" into the phone.

Josie took a few minutes to explain why they had called, including that they believed that their Jane Doe was actually Gemma Farmer. When she finished, the line was silent. Josie counted off three beats before prompting, "Heather?"

Behind them, the door to the stairwell opened and closed. Glancing over her shoulder, Josie saw the Chief walking toward them. He raised a bushy brow at the group of them. Noah sidled over and, in a hushed tone, began bringing him up to speed. Josie heard only snatches of the update. Autopsy. Femoral wound. Missing lock of hair. Missing Persons. Gemma Farmer.

"Heather?" Josie said again, although she was still watching the Chief's face. His usually flushed, acne-pitted cheeks grew paler with each word that Noah said.

Finally, Heather said, "Gemma Farmer went missing from her bed four months ago, Quinn. What would she be doing at a prom in Denton?"

Josie reached for her mouse and pulled up the Jane Doe file. "I'm going to send you a photograph. You tell me."

Once the email was sent, they all waited, the room now silent. The Chief muscled his way through the others to Josie's right shoulder. They heard clicking on Heather's end and then a long exhale of air. "Oh no," she said. "No, no, no."

"It's her, isn't it?" Mettner said.

A heavy sigh filtered through the line. "Yeah, it's her all right. I'm going to have to contact the parents to make an ID. It's Sunday morning. Will your ME be available to meet us at the morgue?"

"She will if we ask her," said Josie.

Noah took out his cell phone. "I'll call her now."

Heather said, "Can you meet me at the morgue in about an hour?"

"Of course," said Josie. "Do you need to go to Keller Hollow?"

"No," said Heather. "I just need to get from where I am to the morgue. Her parents live in Denton now."

ELEVEN

Once they hung up, everyone dispersed, heading back to their own desks. Only the Chief remained by Josie's side. She glanced up at him, expecting to hear him bark orders, but his eyes had taken on a glassy, faraway look, as if he were watching a film only he could view. Josie followed his gaze across the room but he stared at a blank wall.

"Chief?" Josie asked softly. "Is there something I can help you with?"

Silently, he shook his head.

Josie waited for him to say something or retreat to his own office, but he stayed next to her, lost in thought until Noah stood, walked over, and said, "Dr. Feist is already there. She said it's no problem to meet there. She'll wait for us. I'll go over to the morgue with you."

"Sure," said Josie.

"I'm coming," said the Chief.

Neither of them argued. Josie wondered if he'd insist on driving with them, but he followed them in his own vehicle.

"Any idea what's going on with the Chief?" Noah asked as

he drove them back to the hospital, occasionally looking in the rearview mirror to make sure the Chief was still tailing them.

"None," Josie said. "But I'm sure he'll tell us when he's ready."

At the hospital, the Chief was a silent companion, riding down to the basement on the elevator with them, and trailing them down the hall to Dr. Feist's suite of rooms. Before they got there, Josie could hear a woman wailing. The sound went through her, shredding her insides. The sound of grief. Her soul yawned toward it like a tuning fork. Still, she kept her chin up, eyes forward, steely and resolute. This was part of the job. The worst part, but it was what she had signed up for. What they had all signed up for. Watching loved ones bear the impossible and then trying to give them the cold comfort of justice.

Inside the exam room, Dr. Feist, Detective Heather Loughlin, and a man and a woman stood around one of the exam tables. Gemma Farmer's parents. Gemma's body was there, covered up to her neck in a white sheet. Her mother threw her upper body over the girl, weeping uncontrollably while Heather and Dr. Feist looked on. Mr. Farmer kept one hand on his wife's upper back, his head slowly shaking from side to side.

"Nooo," Mrs. Farmer keened. "Not my baby. Not my baby."

Josie, Noah, and the Chief stopped just inside the doors and waited, watching from a respectful distance. It took several minutes for Mrs. Farmer to calm down. Her husband pulled her away from Gemma and into his arms, patting her back. His eyes stayed on his daughter as Dr. Feist covered her face. She walked to the door that led to her office and gave two curt knocks. A moment later, her assistant, Ramon, appeared and transferred the body out of the room.

Heather gestured toward Josie, Noah, and the Chief. "Wes and Diana Farmer, these are my colleagues from the Denton Police Department." She rattled off their names. "As I told you,

Gemma was found here in their jurisdiction, so they will be handling the murder investigation."

"We're very sorry for your loss," Josie offered.

Up close, she could see Gemma's resemblance to her parents: her mother's pointy chin and round cheeks. Her father's thin lips and eyes. Her mother's hair was dyed almost as black as Josie's own hair and her father's hair was almost a rust color. Gemma's brown hair likely came from Diana Farmer. Whereas Gemma had been thin and lithe, her parents wore the weight of middle age around their waists. Both were short. Gemma had probably just outgrown her mother in height.

Diana sniffed, leaning her head into Wes's chest. "Who would do this to our baby?"

"We'll do our best to find out, Mrs. Farmer," said Noah.

"On her birthday!" Diana added. "Who would do this to her on her sixteenth birthday?"

For the first time, the Chief spoke. "When was her birthday?"

Wes squeezed his wife's shoulder. "Friday. It was Friday night. The same night you say you found her at the prom."

The case got stranger by the second. The Chief shot Josie a look but she couldn't divine what was behind it. Heather stood between them and the Farmers in her brown suit, hands folded at her waist, blonde hair tied back neatly in a ponytail. "Mr. and Mrs. Farmer, I've got to speak with Detectives Quinn, Fraley, and their Chief about Gemma's case. They'll probably need to talk with you very soon."

On cue, Josie pulled out a business card and handed it to Mr. Farmer. He took it and stared at it, mystified.

"I want to talk now," said Diana, lifting her head. "I want to know who did this. How did my baby end up at a prom, of all things? Where has she been all this time?"

"That's what we need to find out," said Josie. "Heather was going to bring us up to speed."

Wes Farmer looked at Heather, his gaze intense. "Then do it. I don't want another minute wasted. Someone killed my kid! You need to find him."

Josie sensed the tension in Heather's posture, but she maintained her professionalism. Turning to Josie, Noah, and the Chief, she said, "On January second, Mrs. Farmer got up at six a.m. to see her husband off to work and make sure that Gemma ate something before school. Mr. Farmer left the house at six thirty. Gemma had not come to the kitchen for breakfast yet, so Mrs. Farmer checked her room and it was empty."

Diana said, "All her things were there. Her bed was messed up like she had slept on it, but she was gone."

Noah asked, "She left her phone behind?"

"Yes," said Diana. "Her phone and the little backpack she takes with her everywhere."

"What about her clothes?" asked Josie.

"She changed," said Wes. "That's what we think. 'Cause her pajamas were on the floor next to her bed."

"And her sneakers were gone," said Diana.

Josie said, "It appeared as if she'd woken up, gotten changed, and left?"

"Someone took her!" Wes exclaimed. "She wouldn't just leave like that! Not without telling us something."

"Not without her phone," Diana added. "She was glued to that thing every second."

Wes released his wife, putting a couple of inches of space between them. Almost under his breath, he said, "I told you to limit her screen time."

Diana's posture stiffened instantly. "Limit her screen time? She's a fifteen-year-old girl. If you wanted her screen time limited, you should have parented her—"

She broke off, her eyes going wide as the reality hit her once more—Gemma was dead. It was clearly an argument they'd had on a regular basis, and Diana was so used to it that without thought she'd launched into her position on the matter. Josie watched her knees tremble. Luckily, her husband took mercy on her at the last moment and caught her before she collapsed. Dr. Feist pulled a metal rolling chair from the corner of the room and waited while Wes settled Diana onto it. She covered her face with both hands, sobbing anew.

Heather's mouth tightened into a straight line. "Mr. and Mrs. Farmer," she said. "Why don't we get you home, and if these detectives need anything further from you, they can call or stop by."

TWELVE

THREE MONTHS EARLIER – CENTRAL PENNSYLVANIA

The next time she woke, her head didn't feel any clearer, but she wasn't trapped in darkness any longer. Pain pulsed through her head when she tried to sit up, so she laid back down, curling on her side, bleary eyes taking in the details of the small room. Sunlight snuck around the edges of heavy miniblinds affixed to a window directly across from her. The walls were wood-paneled, dark and dated. Brown water stains leeched through the white paint of the ceiling like a series of Rorschachs. Green shag carpeting. A gold doorknob gleamed from a pressed-board wooden door that led... where? She didn't know. The effort of looking around the strange, unfamiliar room was exhausting. Closing her eyes, she tried to piece together what was happening—what had happened to her.

Had she imagined the voice?

No. That wasn't right. The voice had helped her get cleaned up after she puked everywhere, given her something to drink, something else for the pain in her head. Taking a sniff, she detected only the faint florid scent of laundry detergent mixed with some kind of disinfectant. Opening her eyes again, she looked down at herself to see a pair of pajama pants and a

T-shirt that she didn't recognize. What the hell was going on? Had someone kidnapped her, or had her mother finally sent her to rehab like she threatened all those times?

Her mom. She thought about the last time she'd seen her mom. Fighting, arguing, screaming. The usual. She'd stormed out. Not for the first time, but for the last time.

"For the last time," she mumbled to herself. Her body shot upright so quickly that dizziness hit her like a slap, sending her backward onto the bed.

She'd had somewhere to go. Finally. Somewhere safe. Somewhere fun, where parents never yelled or judged or tried to ruin your life. Somewhere without so many rules. That's why she'd left her phone behind, so they couldn't track her. That's why she'd gotten into the car. That's why she hadn't paid attention to where the car was driving, why she accepted the bottle of peach schnapps, sticky-sweet, sliding down her throat like juice. Then pills in her hand because why not? A new life was about to start, and she was feeling good.

Then nothing.

This was not the new life she was promised. This time, she steeled herself against the pain and sat upright, sucking in several deep breaths until she felt strong enough to stand. It was much easier than she'd anticipated. She lurched toward the window and threw the miniblinds open. Trees as far as the eye could see.

She swore.

Turning to try the door next, she had a full view of her side of the room—the mattress on which she'd slept—and at the foot of it, in a heap on the floor, was another girl, naked, bruised, and chained.

There was no stopping the scream that ripped from her chest.

THIRTEEN

Once the Farmers left, the detectives stepped out into the hall to discuss the case, leaving Dr. Feist and her assistant to the rest of their work. The Chief was silent as ever, but Josie felt a strange tension radiate from him, filling the space all around them. Heather glanced at him twice, as if waiting to see if he had any questions or anything to offer, but he merely stared at her, eyes burning with intensity, arms folded over his chest, waiting.

Noah said, "Why don't you give us the rundown of the case?"

Heather looked down the hall toward the elevators that the Farmers had disappeared into. Sighing, she said, "To be perfectly honest, I thought she was a runaway. There was no evidence that she was abducted or taken against her will."

"Any grooming activity?" Josie asked. "Someone older online trying to connect with her before she went missing?"

Heather shook her head. "I thought of the trafficking thing, too. Obviously. Pretty fifteen-year-old girl? That was one of the first things we looked at, but no, no evidence of it."

"Boyfriend or girlfriend?" asked Noah.

"Neither. We talked to all her friends. They all checked out. There were no major red flags leading up to her disappearance. Her friends said her parents fought all the time—in case you didn't pick up on that—and it wore on her but that was nothing new, apparently."

"They moved to Denton since she went missing," said Josie. "Was that planned?"

"Unfortunately, yes. That was one of the things that they fought often about. The dad needed to take a job here as a manager of a Spur Mobile store. He said they weren't making ends meet in his last position. The management job was more money. Gemma didn't want to leave her friends. Diana was trying to convince him to at least let her and Gemma stay in Keller Hollow until the school year ended so Gemma could finish tenth grade, but financially, it wasn't feasible. They needed to sell the house right away. I even wondered if she took off because of the move, but when we couldn't find her right away and she didn't come back, I started to wonder. It damn near killed Diana to sell that house thinking that if Gemma came home, she'd go there and they would be gone. They left word with the neighbors that if Gemma showed up, they should call immediately, but that never happened."

"She didn't pack anything when she left?" asked Josie.

"Not that the parents can tell. The only thing out of the ordinary was that her mom had taken her to the mall a few times in the months before she disappeared. That big one in the middle of nowhere?"

"Yeah, I know it," Josie said.

The Oak Ridge Mall sat just off the interstate, about a half hour from Denton. It was surrounded by mountains but centrally located so that all the small towns scattered to the east of Denton could easily access it.

"Gemma and her mom typically split up when they got to the mall and when her mom went to meet her in the food court, she was talking with another teenager that the mom didn't recognize. Mom said she thought she knew all Gemma's friends but had never seen this girl before."

"Did Gemma introduce them?" Noah asked.

Heather shook her head. "No. The mom said as soon as she started toward them, the other girl took off. Every time. For a bit, she worried that the other girl might be selling Gemma drugs or something like that, but she never found any drugs in Gemma's room and Gemma never appeared to be under the influence of anything."

"How many times did Diana see them together?" asked Josie.

"She said maybe three or four times over the course of a few months. She described the girl as about five foot four, blonde hair, thin. We asked all of Gemma's friends and her ex-boyfriend about the girl, but no one recognized the description. We canvassed the mall and didn't find anyone working there. Nothing on the cameras."

"That could be nothing," Noah said. "The phone was clean? Nothing on social media?"

"We scoured Snapchat, Instagram, TikTok, and Twitter. On the phone we found nothing. When we subpoenaed records, we also found nothing. Everyone in her life checked out."

Josie said, "Everyone checked out, but she disappeared. What you're telling us is that she got up sometime in the middle of the night, got dressed, left all her stuff behind, and walked out of her house."

"That's how it looked, yes."

Josie said, "Keller Hollow isn't exactly an urban hotspot. Where could she have gone?"

Heather nodded along with Josie's words. "You're right. Unless she was headed to a neighbor's house, we're talking about a large rural area for miles."

Noah said, "So either she was at a neighbor's house in Keller Hollow this entire time or someone picked her up. But I assume when you say everyone checked out, you mean neighbors, too."

"We went door to door," said Heather. "That's not to say that if someone was hiding her, we would have known, but I'm inclined to think someone picked her up. What I can't figure out is if it was planned or spontaneous. If it had been planned, we should have seen something on her phone or social media platforms. But if it was spontaneous, what are the odds of her getting snatched from Keller Hollow in the middle of the night by a stranger?"

"She left her phone," Josie said. "She obviously knew or suspected she could be tracked by her phone. Why else would she leave it behind?"

"So you think it was planned," Heather said.

"I think teenagers are smarter, savvier, and sneakier than anyone gives them credit for," said Josie.

"What about self-harm?" asked Noah. "She has those slashes on her arm. Did anyone mention them when she went missing?"

"No. They never came up. When we asked about scars or birthmarks, her parents said there was nothing. Listen, this kid didn't want to move, and I don't think her relationship with her parents—particularly her dad—is that great, but by all accounts she was not severely depressed or in any kind of distress. She hated that her parents fought, she didn't want to move away from all her friends in the middle of the year. That was the extent of her issues. Neither her parents nor her friends mentioned self-harm."

"That doesn't mean she wasn't doing it," Josie pointed out. "Did she know any kids here in Denton, by any chance? Anyone who goes to Denton East High?"

"No. She didn't know anyone here. That was a big issue for

her when her parents told her they were moving. Her friends said she was devastated at having to start over completely without knowing even one student and in the middle of a school year," Heather explained. "And before you ask, there was no talk of her going to the prom—certainly not here. It was only January when she went missing."

Noah asked, "Did you check out the parents?"

"First thing," said Heather. "They're each other's alibis, though."

"Because everyone was home during the night," Josie filled in. "Mom and Dad sleep in the same room?"

"Miraculously, yes," said Heather. "Or so they claim."

Noah said, "So you really can't rule them out altogether. They could be covering for one another or the dad could even have done something to her while the mom was asleep."

Heather nodded. "You're right. I haven't cleared them completely, but we didn't find anything strange around the house. No blood evidence or freshly dug graves in the backyard."

The Chief's voice made them all jump. "It wasn't the parents."

They all turned to stare at him. Heather's eyes narrowed. "I don't think it was either but like I said, them giving one another an alibi isn't airtight. Not in my book. Not when there were only three of them in that house that night and one was a minor who is no longer with us."

Josie took a step closer to the Chief to catch his gaze, but his eyes were locked on Heather. "Do you have a theory, Chief?"

Ignoring her, the Chief said, "Fraley, you'll go with Detective Loughlin and gather copies of all the case files she's got. Bring them back to the station. Write up your reports. Get all your paperwork in order. You, Palmer, and Mettner should be working every lead until we get back."

Noah looked from the Chief to Josie and back, one eyebrow raised. "Get back?"

Without an explanation, the Chief turned away from them and started striding toward the elevators, leaving all three of them gaping at his back. He shouted over his shoulder, "Quinn! Let's go!"

FOURTEEN

The Chief didn't speak in the elevator or on the way out to his car. He opened the passenger's side door for Josie and gestured for her to get in, which she did. She had never been inside his Lincoln Continental before. It smelled like tobacco, which was strange because she'd never seen him smoke or even smelled smoke on him. In the center console a Komorrah's Koffee cup sat in the cupholder. Josie wondered if it was regular coffee or his drink of choice—a Red Eye. A glance at the back revealed several items thrown haphazardly across the seats. A light Denton PD jacket, a couple of binders marked with the Denton PD logo, half-empty water bottles, an umbrella, and several crumpled, empty plastic bags. She felt her cell phone buzz against her hip and checked it quickly. It was Noah. *Let me know what the hell's going on as soon as you know.*

She tapped back: *Will do.*

The Chief folded himself into the driver's seat and slammed the door. He fired up the engine and pulled out of the parking lot, heading down the long hill from the hospital into Denton. Josie watched his profile. When she could stand it no longer, she said, "Are we going to talk about what's happening here?"

He said nothing.

"Fine. Will you at least tell me where we're going?"

"I need to show you something," he said tersely.

"Right now?"

Instead of answering, he said, "Gemma Farmer. You're the lead. Tell me what you think."

As usual, Josie felt like Chitwood was giving her some kind of test that she was destined to fail. Rather than blurt out her thoughts, she took a few moments to think it over. Then she said, "Missing for just over four months but with no marks indicating torture or even that she was bound. No evidence that someone took her, but she had to be somewhere for four months. She met someone. That's the only possibility. The question is how and where, if she didn't use her phone to arrange it, especially living in a tiny rural area like Keller Hollow."

"The murder, Quinn. I'm talking about the murder."

Josie let another few beats of silence pass between them, her mind picking through the details of the crime. "A single femoral wound, a missing lock of hair. Returned to a public place on her sixteenth birthday. This isn't his first time. That's what I think. He is experienced. Gemma Farmer was found at a prom, but I don't think her killer is another student or even a teenager. Given the fact that there was virtually no evidence left behind, the staging, the planning involved, I think the killer skews older. I don't know if this is a serial killer, but Gemma Farmer's murder has a level of sophistication I've only seen once or twice before—with serial killers. They re-enact their fantasies over and over again, refining things until they get... better. Better at killing. Better at creating whatever scenario they're obsessing over. What are you telling me? This is a serial killer? You could have told me that at the hospital. What's going on?"

Chitwood turned off onto a road that led to Southwest Denton. It was rural and Josie knew that in a few miles they'd be driving past a number of farms sprawled out over fields where Alcott County met Lenore County. "I don't know if this is a serial. What I know is that we have a problem."

"We?" Josie asked. "Are you going to tell me what's going on, or are we just going to drive around all day while you say cryptic things?"

He shot her a dark glance and at once, she regretted her tone. He didn't scold her, however. Instead, he said, "We're going to my house. There's something I need to show you."

Josie felt a small uptick in her anxiety although she couldn't say why. She didn't think the Chief was a threat, no matter how strangely he acted. Still, she didn't know where he lived. None of them did. He'd been with the department for almost five years and none of them knew anything about him. He had always been a closed book.

They traveled a few more miles in silence. The mountains gave way to rolling fields. Farmhouses dotted the sides of the road. Chitwood slowed at a black mailbox and turned down a long dirt driveway. Josie held onto the door handle as they bounced toward a small, two-story house with white siding and red shutters. Beside it was a detached two-car garage, a hulking concrete square with utilitarian white bay doors. Chitwood parked between the buildings and got out. Josie followed, headed toward the porch of the farmhouse.

"Not there," he called to her. "The garage."

Josie glanced at the house. It was difficult to contain her curiosity now that she was so close to Chitwood's abode, but she walked over to the garage instead. A ring of keys appeared in the Chief's hands. He picked through them until he found the key he was looking for and then used it to open the padlock at the base of one of the doors. Putting the padlock into his pocket, the Chief heaved the door upward unleashing a series of creaks and groans. From inside, dust swirled in the sunlight. In the center of the garage bay was a riding tractor and all around it were metal shelves with cardboard letter boxes on them. It looked like the evidence locker at Denton PD. Josie knew the Chief had been on the job for decades. She wondered how many copies of old case files he'd kept during that time. Typically, detectives weren't authorized to keep any official case documents or make copies of them, although some departments allowed them to keep their own notes and make copies of items that were not considered sensitive.

Along the back wall was a scarred wooden table with a saw and several woodworking tools scattered across it. Above the table was a two-by-four with hooks affixed to it. From each hook hung a different tool. In the center, between a hammer and a wrench, was a photograph, yellowed with age.

"Come in," Chitwood said.

He walked along the left side of the tractor, eyes searching the boxes. Josie couldn't see any labels. She moved to the right side of the tractor, drawn toward the work table and the photo. As she drew closer, she saw that it was a photo of a teenage girl with long blonde hair and a wide toothy smile. She wore a Catholic school uniform, a green plaid pinafore over a yellow blouse. Thick saddle shoes and ankle socks completed the outfit. She stood in front of a large stone building, a long set of steps behind her. Her arms were spread out before her, as if she were in the middle of throwing them out at her sides. Josie leaned in and studied her face. The photo didn't have the crispness of modern pictures. Her features were blurred but not so much that Josie couldn't see the resemblance between her and the Chief.

Chitwood began pulling boxes from the shelves and bringing them over to the table. Josie pointed to the photo. "Is this your daughter?"

He didn't look at her, instead taking a lid from one of the

boxes and riffling through its contents. "That's Kelsey," he said. "My sister."

Josie felt her heart sink. If this was the most recent photo of his sister he was keeping on display, Kelsey was likely no longer with them.

"She's dead," he told her, answering the unspoken question. "In fact, that's why I brought you here. I need you to look at Kelsey's case files."

He started pulling manila files from the box and spreading them over the table. Josie glanced at a date listed on one of the folders: 1997.

She stared at him, waiting for him to stop, to notice her, to say something that sounded reasonable. When he didn't, she said, "Chief, I don't think we should—"

He stopped taking the files out and put his hands on his hips, looking down at her. For the first time that day, Josie felt like he really saw her. "Quinn, this is important."

"I can see that," she said. "But maybe this is something we should take back to the station. Have the team go over it when we've got time. Gemma Farmer's murder is our priority right now. This is—where did you get these, anyway?"

"Never mind where I got this stuff. Quinn, I need you to go over these files. I need to know what you see."

Spreading pages out before her, Josie saw report after report. Many of the documents were written on plain copy paper in the Chief's own scrawl. The rest were official reports. Josie knew that whatever the Chief was getting at was important, but she really didn't want to give Gemma Farmer's murderer any more time than necessary to potentially strike again. "I am happy to look at anything you want me to review, Chief, but it might be faster if you just tell me about the case."

He flicked a long finger off one of the reports in front of them. "I need to know what you see, Quinn. I may never get a chance like this again. Listen, I know I give you a hard time and that's because you're a royal pain in my ass. I don't even know how Noah stays married to you because when you get your teeth into a case, it's all you see."

Josie held up a hand. "You can leave my marriage out of this."

He waved a hand dismissively. "Quinn, listen good, because I'm not going to say this again, and I'm sure as shit not going to say it in front of anyone else. You're the best investigator I've ever seen. I want you to review my sister's murder case."

Murder. Just like Josie, just like Noah and Gretchen and countless others Josie had met during the course of her career, the Chief had lost someone important to him to violence. It was a pain she wouldn't wish on anyone, a lifelong cross to bear. Time dulled the jagged edges of the wound but never healed it completely. Life always picked at the scab. The scar never disappeared, it just changed shape. "Chief," said Josie softly. "I'm so sorry."

He shook his head. "The time for sorry is past. Long past. I just need your help with the case."

"I can help you," she replied. "But Chief, this case is twenty-five years old. And right now I've got to prioritize Gemma Farmer."

He shook his head. "But they're connected. I think there's a good chance that my sister's killer also killed Gemma Farmer."

FIFTEEN

"Start at the beginning," Josie said.

Chitwood turned away from her and started pulling more boxes from the shelves, setting the ones that didn't fit onto the table on the floor instead. He pulled off their lids and searched through them. "Kelsey was fifteen when she went missing," he said. "Almost sixteen."

Josie made some calculations. "She was fifteen twenty-five years ago?"

"She was missing for four months and seventeen days."

Again, she worked through some math. "Wait. You had to have been in your forties. You had a teenage sister when you were in your early forties?"

Chitwood stopped, hunched over a box, and looked up at her. "We didn't have the same mother, obviously."

"Your dad remarried?"

Chitwood barked a laugh. He stopped what he was doing and straightened his back. Irritation flickered across his face. "Let's get this out of the way, okay? My dad is a bastard. A rotten, disgusting, piece of crap who doesn't deserve to walk

God's green earth. But he's still here. He's always been here. Like a malignant cancer. You can't stop him."

Josie quirked a brow. "He sounds pretty awful. What are we talking about here? Is he a serial killer?"

"Worse. He was a cop."

Josie said, "Where was he on the job?"

Chitwood knelt on the ground, hands back in the box, searching again. "He started on patrol and moved to detective in the Brighton Springs Police Department. Fifty years he was on the job."

Josie recognized the name of the city. It was the name listed on the official reports in front of her. Brighton Springs was in Western Pennsylvania, north of Pittsburgh. Not as large as that city but large enough to warrant a sizable police department. "Is that where you were before you came here?"

Chitwood shook his head. "Never worked there. Wouldn't work in the same department that would keep him employed."

"He was corrupt?"

"As corrupt as the day is long," Chitwood agreed. "He wasn't exactly a great father either. He cheated on my mom from day one, stepping out on her until she started drinking just to numb her humiliation. Back then, divorce wasn't a great option. She was practically a kid when they got married. I still can't figure out how he did it. She wasn't even eighteen yet when they tied the knot. Basically, she felt stuck. Married to this shithead who controlled everything, including the money. It wasn't like she had job skills or anything. She used to tell me, 'Bobby, your dad set a trap for me, and I walked right into it.' Drank herself to death before I even turned twenty-one."

He talked about it with the detachment of someone recapping the plot of a soap opera.

"I'm sorry," said Josie.

He didn't acknowledge her words. "I think my dad was relieved when she died. He didn't have to listen to her crying anymore. When I was twenty-five, he showed up on my doorstep with this baby. Said it was his kid."

"Kelsey?"

He nodded and closed the box he was looking through, standing up and searching the shelves for a different one. "He was sleeping with an informant. Drug addict. Got her pregnant. She had no interest in raising a kid. My dad didn't either. I still can't figure out why he even brought her home."

"He brought her to your home," Josie said. "Right?"

"Yeah. He said, 'Bobby, I need some help with this kid.' He didn't know the first thing about babies."

"You did?" Josie asked, again wondering if Chitwood had a whole family somewhere that none of them knew about.

He laughed. "Of course not. I was a twenty-five-year-old patrol officer! All I cared about was women and trying to catch a case more exciting than a traffic stop."

"I don't understand," Josie said.

Chitwood threw another box onto the floor and sighed. "He left her with me because he knew I'd take care of her. He knew how much I hated him. How I never wanted to be like him. My mom wasn't perfect, but she wasn't a monster. He knew I tried always to be more like her than him."

"You raised your sister."

Chitwood stopped and fished inside his jacket pocket for a tissue. He wiped at his nose. Josie had never seen him show this much emotion, but tears glistened in his eyes. "I changed all her diapers. I made her bottles. I took her to the doctor. I sang stupid songs with her and taught her numbers and letters. The first word she ever said was 'Bah.'"

"For Bobby," Josie said, feeling her throat constrict.

He nodded, now dabbing the tissue at the corners of his eyes. "Cost me a lot, too. Remember that woman I told you about? The one I spent the weekend with on an exotic island? I thought I had something with her, but she didn't want to raise

Kelsey. She wanted us to start our own family, not raise another man's kid. She thought I was pathetic for not standing up to my dad, making him take responsibility for Kelsey."

Josie stepped closer to him, watching his face as he visited the past. "But it wasn't about responsibility," she murmured. "You loved her."

"Like my own," he croaked. "Like my own."

"You said she went missing when she was fifteen," Josie said. "What happened?"

"The same damn thing that happened to Gemma Farmer," he said. "That's what happened."

SIXTEEN

Chitwood moved the tractor out into the driveway and then Josie helped him spread reports and crime scene photos across the garage bay floor. Kelsey Chitwood's case had produced a lot of paperwork, most of it generated in the nearly five months between her disappearance and her death and consisting of what turned out to be false leads. From the number of hand-written documents, it was clear that Chitwood had conducted his own private investigation during the time she was missing. He tried to arrange things in chronological order. Josie started by reading the initial missing persons report.

"Kelsey disappeared from a Catholic school? A boarding school?" she asked.

"Yeah," he said. "When she turned fourteen, she was a little rebellious. Kept getting in trouble with the law. I managed to keep her out of juvenile hall because she was getting into trouble in the same jurisdiction where I worked—Lochfield. It was about an hour east of Brighton Springs. I had things handled, I thought. Unfortunately, because I didn't have legal custody of her, when things got a little more serious, Dad had to get involved. His solution to her acting out was to take her out of the public high school she was in—where all her friends were—and send her away to a Catholic boarding school. I hated the idea and so did she. Worse, she was closer to him than me because the school was in Brighton Springs."

"Your dad wouldn't let you assume guardianship?" Josie asked. "After fifteen years of raising her?"

Chitwood shook his head.

"You didn't sue him for custody?"

"Of course I did," he responded. "He had the judge in his pocket. After hearings and piles and piles of evidence that I raised Kelsey, the judge ruled I wasn't fit to have custody of her. My dad got to keep her, which was his intention all along."

"That's terrible," Josie murmured.

Chitwood shrugged. "Like I said, he was a bastard. Still is. He's in his nineties now. He lives alone over a bar, not too far from where Kelsey was found. I just keep waiting for the call from his landlord that he's dead, but as horrible as he is, he'll probably outlive me."

He passed her a document written in his own handwriting, and Josie realized it was a collection of notes from his independent investigation. She read over the details. "She disappeared from her dorm room at school?"

"Went to bed in the evening and the next morning when she didn't show up for breakfast, the nuns checked her room, and she was gone. Pajamas were there but one of her uniforms and a pair of her shoes were missing. They didn't have cameras, but there was no sign of a struggle or forced entry or anything like that."

"She was marked a runaway, wasn't she?" Josie asked.

"That was the theory, yeah. Especially since she hadn't wanted to go to that school in the first place." His voice wavered. "She wanted to stay with me."

Josie turned back to the Brighton Springs report. Her gaze

landed on the name of the investigating officer. "Wait," she said. "Harlan Chitwood. Your dad was the lead investigator in her case?"

Chitwood said, "Like I said, I'd never work for a department that would employ him."

Josie read over the official report again and then she dropped to her knees, searching for the first series of follow-up reports. "Well," she muttered. "We don't have room to talk. You let me work my own sister's case."

"Yeah, I guess that's true," he said. Kneeling beside her, anticipating what she was searching for, he began handing her reports. "He had a partner back then. Young guy. Travis..." He drifted off as he paged through another document. Finding the name, he read, "Benning. Travis Benning. My dad got him as a rookie detective. Tried to teach him the Harlan Chitwood way, but Benning wasn't having it. He worked the case, too."

Josie was reading through the paperwork as fast as she could. "Where are the interviews with friends? Classmates? They only talked with the nuns."

"There are a lot of gaps in their investigation," Chitwood said. "I interviewed and interrogated anyone who ever came into contact with her. Turned up almost nothing. It was like she vanished into thin air. A couple of her school friends said they saw her talking to an older woman—a lady with long white hair —a few times in the month before she went missing. Kelsey used the public library a lot. The school had one, but using the public library got her off campus for a while. She took the bus from her dorm to the library. Her friends saw her talking to the woman at the bus stop near the dorm."

"Did anyone get a description of her?"

"Short, thin, Caucasian, white hair," Chitwood said with a slight roll of his eyes. "Like half the elderly population in that damn city."

"No one got close enough to work with a sketch artist?"

"No."

"Did she talk—"

"Quinn," the Chief said, his voice almost a shout. "I thought of all these things. No, Kelsey didn't talk to any of her friends about her. Yes, they asked her who she was but she said she was 'just some girl' she saw at the bus station. I searched nearby businesses for cameras. I talked with the bus driver on that route, the passengers. So did my dad and his partner. Those reports aren't in there, but it doesn't matter. The woman was a ghost. A nobody. I don't even know if she was connected to Kelsey's disappearance. Maybe she was just some lady Kelsey talked to at the bus stop. My sister vanished into thin air."

"Except she didn't," said Josie. "Where are the rest of the reports from the Brighton Springs Police Department?"

"I got everything I could," he told her. "I'd rather not say how. It's incomplete. Either they tampered with the records or they didn't do their jobs. But here, this is the important stuff. Not how she went missing. How she was found."

He handed her a sheaf of photos, and Josie steeled herself before paging through them. The first photo showed Kelsey from behind, kneeling in what looked like a church pew. Only her head and shoulders were visible, long blonde hair cascading down her back. Around her were heavy wooden pews, empty, and ahead of her was the nave leading to the apse. Its dome was painted sky blue. Angels knelt, peering down at the church in what looked like a cross between dismay and hope. Josie flipped through the next several photos, disconcerted by the feeling of getting closer to Kelsey with each one in real time. From the side, she could see that Kelsey's arms were hooked over the top of the pew in front of her, holding her up. For some reason, Josie had expected her to be positioned in prayer, hands folded before her. Instead, she was semi-slumped, with the edge of her chin resting on the top of the pew in front of her. Her eyes were closed, her face pale and peaceful. If she hadn't been positioned so oddly, she might look as though she had fallen asleep during Mass.

From over her shoulder, Chitwood said, "Keep going."

Josie wondered how many times he had looked at these over the years. Their edges were soft and worn. The next series of photos showed her lower body. She wore her school uniform. "When you found her, she was—"

"It was her sixteenth birthday," Chitwood said. "Keep going."

Josie felt a wave of dread wash over her. She flipped through more photos. Kelsey had been positioned with her knees resting on the kneeler. Beneath her, a pool of blood spread outward in every direction. Chitwood was at Josie's shoulder now. When he spoke, she felt his breath tickle her hair. "Cause of death was exsanguination from two stab wounds to her femoral artery. Toxicology showed Benadryl poisoning."

Josie felt her breath catch. She tried to speak, to ask a question, but shock paralyzed her vocal cords. Chitwood took the photos from her hands, riffled through them, and then thrust one in front of her face. It was Kelsey on an autopsy table from the neck up, looking very similar to Gemma Farmer with her hair fanned out around her. Josie noticed the missing lock of hair immediately.

Every internal alarm bell she had clanged inside her mind. Swallowing, she tried to speak again. "How—how many? How many girls?"

Chitwood pulled the photo back toward his body, cradling the pile of them against his chest. "Two," he said. "Kelsey and Gemma Farmer. I've searched for years for other crimes that match up to Kelsey's. I've checked VICAP, NCIC and the PA CIC. I've never found any others except for Gemma Farmer. I'm assuming that Gemma and Kelsey's murders are connected.

The similarities are so striking, I feel like someone clubbed me in the head. The disappearance, the body found on their sixteenth birthday, the femoral wound, the missing lock of hair. I know Dr. Feist won't officially say Gemma Farmer had near-toxic levels of Benadryl in her system without proof from toxicology, but I'd bet a vital organ that's what the labs are going to show. This has to be the same guy. It's too close."

"One happened to your sister and the other happened in your jurisdiction," Josie said. "Do you think it's someone you know? Someone you knew back then?"

Chitwood sighed and looked around the garage, which was now a mess of papers, files, folders, reports, crime scene photos, and half-open boxes. "I don't know, Quinn. I've spent the last twenty-five years trying to find this guy. Not so much recently because I exhausted every lead. Believe me, I've given this more thought than you could ever possibly imagine. This has been my life. This and nothing else. Quinn, if I'm right, and this guy is back—if he's done it again—I might have a chance at catching him this time. So I need you to look through every page in here, compare it to the Gemma Farmer case, and tell me what you see."

Josie walked over to the table and studied the photo of Kelsey once more. She had been tall and thin like the Chief, and although Josie had only seen him smile once or twice, they definitely shared the same grin. "This is an inactive case from someone else's jurisdiction," she said.

"I know."

"These files—everything you've got here from Brighton Springs—you shouldn't even have it."

"I know."

"That said, these files are incomplete. We need to see what you couldn't get from them."

"I agree."

"You understand that if the person who killed your sister also killed Gemma Farmer twenty-five years later, I can't use anything I find in these files, right? Your files. None of it would ever be admissible in any court of law."

"But you see it, right?" said Chitwood, a desperation to his tone that made Josie wince. He didn't seem to notice.

"Of course I see it. Anyone with two brain cells could see the connection, but if you want it to count, we have to go through official channels. Contact this police department. Ask for copies of the files. Maybe we should consider the FBI."

She thought about the sophistication of the crimes—the staging, the taking of a souvenir, the efficiency with which the killer dispatched his victims. "This guy has been operating for a long time. Maybe he's not committing crimes that exactly match Kelsey and Gemma's murders, but there is no way he's been silent and inactive all this time."

"Unless he was in prison," said Chitwood. "That's just it. What if he was in prison for something else? Twenty-five years. What if he just got out and he's starting again. Quinn, we can't let this guy take another child from her—"

He broke off. Josie could see the war in his eyes as he fought for composure. He had been about to say "parents," she was sure of it. Kelsey had been his sister by birth, but he had raised her. In his heart, she had been his child. Josie felt a pang in her chest. An emotional ache spread from her heart through the rest of her body. Her grandmother, Lisette, had known fairly early on that Josie wasn't her biological granddaughter and yet, she had loved Josie as her own child in every way. The bond between them had been immense. Living a life without that bond was a struggle that Josie endured every minute of every day. Josie tried to imagine Chitwood's loss, equally as huge and all-encompassing, and how it echoed through his life to this day.

"I'll help you," she told him. "You know that. I'll do everything I can to find Gemma Farmer's killer and if we can connect him to Kelsey's murder, even better. But Chief, I'm only as good as my team. If you want to know what I see, then let me bring all of this back to the stationhouse. Let us all go over it together."

SEVENTEEN

Back at the stationhouse, Josie and the Chief enlisted Noah, Mettner, and Gretchen to bring the boxes from his car into the first-floor conference room, stacking them on the table and along one of the walls. Josie stood beside the Chief at the head of the conference room table. In awkward, stilted sentences, he brought them up to speed and then hastily retreated, leaving them all gawking at Josie, waiting for an explanation. The Chief was about as good at discussing things that were emotionally important to him as Josie.

Mettner crossed his arms, leaned a hip against the back of one of the chairs, and said, "He wants us to work a cold case from a different jurisdiction in the middle of the Gemma Farmer case? We can't work this case, even if we wanted to—it's not our case."

Gretchen tucked her notebook between two stacks of boxes on the table and turned toward him. Sighing, she said, "That's not what he said, Mett. Did you listen to any of it?"

"You know what I mean," Mettner said. "This isn't even in our jurisdiction."

Noah began taking the lids off the boxes. "If Chitwood is

right and there is some kind of serial killer operating in Pennsylvania, then we need all the information we can get. It won't hurt to familiarize ourselves with Kelsey Chitwood's case."

"Which we'll have time to do when, exactly?" Mettner asked irritably.

Gretchen's voice dripped with sarcasm. "Yeah, 'cause we're so busy and stretched thin chasing down all the leads on the Gemma Farmer case."

"What we really need to do," Josie interrupted, "is try to track down any cases that might have come between Kelsey Chitwood and Gemma Farmer."

"The Chief said he hadn't found any," Noah said. "You think we're going to find something he hasn't in the last twenty-five years?"

Josie, too, uncapped a box and began pulling out file folders. "I think we have more information now than he did before. We have two murders with multiple similarities. That means we may have more parameters within which to search than the Chief has had in the past."

Mettner plopped into a seat at the table. "Fine, then. Where do we start?"

Josie pushed a box toward him. "We figure out all the things that are similar and then we search VICAP, the NCIC, and the PA CIC for those characteristics going back twenty-five years. Someone has to call the Brighton Springs department and formally request these files. We're not even supposed to have these." She thought about all that was missing from the Brighton Springs folders: interviews with Kelsey's friends and classmates; evidence logs; and a host of other reports. If Harlan Chitwood had been a corrupt police officer, was it possible he had tampered with the police files on his own daughter's kidnapping and murder? What reason would he have to do that? Or had someone else interfered? If Harlan's superiors at Brighton Springs had known he was dishonest and even criminal and still let him operate for fifty years, Josie wasn't sure anyone there could be trusted. "Actually, I think we should go there once we've familiarized ourselves with the Chief's notes," she added. "We can drop in on the police department there. We can interview the Chief's dad, while we're in Brighton Springs. I'll look up his address, and we'll pay him a visit."

Noah said, "That's a good place to start. Someone needs to take a closer look at the Chief's life. Right now, he's the main connection."

"True," said Gretchen.

"To Mettner's point," Josie said. "We do still need to focus on Gemma Farmer. She takes priority. Now that we have a positive ID, someone needs to take a photo of her—one that her parents provided to the state police when she went missing—and go to all the restaurants we've already called as well as the dress shops, and see if anyone remembers physically seeing her in the last weeks or months. Tomorrow, someone should also go out to all the high schools and see if we can show the students her photo as well. Before we were only working off a description of her and her dress. Maybe a photo will jog people's memories."

"I'll do it," said Mettner, walking to the door.

"I'd also like to look at cases of missing girls who are under sixteen in Pennsylvania," Josie said.

Noah frowned. "That could be a lot of people."

Gretchen stared at a report she had pulled from one of the boxes. "True, but we can probably narrow the list to girls aged fifteen, missing for a year or less. Gemma Farmer was missing for four months. Kelsey Chitwood was missing for almost the same amount of time. If we round up to a year, that would be a good place to start."

"I know it may still be a long list," Josie said. "I understand that, but what's the alternative?"

"Maybe if we can find commonalities between Kelsey Chitwood and Gemma Farmer, other than how they were killed, we'll know better what to look for in terms of missing girls," said Noah.

It took days to get through the files that the Chief had compiled on his sister over twenty-five years. The amount of work he had done was staggering and yet, Josie knew she would have done exactly the same thing. The team rotated, two of them working on familiarizing themselves with Kelsey's case as well as looking for similar cases and missing girls under the age of sixteen, while the other two worked the Gemma Farmer case, showing her photo all over town in the hopes someone would recognize and remember her. The list of missing fifteen-year-old girls in the state was shockingly long, although many of them were marked as custodial kidnappings—meaning a parent absconded with them—and almost all of the rest were considered runaways. It would take time to track down the detectives assigned to each runaway in different jurisdictions to get a better idea as to whether or not they were similar enough to Gemma and Kelsey's cases that they bore further scrutiny.

The team also took turns tracking down people in Chief Chitwood's past, namely criminals he had caught and arrested across multiple police departments in his decades-long tenure as a law enforcement officer, focusing first on people who had recently been released from prison after twenty or so years of incarceration. After several days, they hadn't even compiled a complete list, let alone checked out everyone on it. Josie feared it would take weeks or even months to track down everyone associated with him. She decided to assign the task to their desk sergeant, Dan Lamay, who was only too happy to do the online research and make all the calls required while the rest of the team were out on the street working the Gemma Farmer case.

Once Josie was thoroughly acquainted with Kelsey's case,

she made numerous calls to the Brighton Springs Police Department and even sent a few emails, but to no avail. As she hung up her desk phone for the fifth time that week, she looked across the desks to Noah. "I'm going to Brighton Springs first thing tomorrow morning. Their department isn't returning my phone messages or emails. If I show up in person, which was my intention all along, it will make it harder for them to ignore me. Plus I want to talk with Harlan Chitwood face to face."

Noah looked up from his computer screen. "Better let the Chief know."

From behind her, the Chief spoke, startling them both. "I'll go with you, Quinn. Everyone else can stay here and work the Gemma Farmer case."

Josie spun her chair around to face him. "Chief, I can talk to him myself. You don't have to—I mean, if you don't want to see him."

"We go together," he insisted. "Tomorrow morning. Pack a bag in case we need to spend the night."

EIGHTEEN

THREE MONTHS EARLIER – CENTRAL PENNSYLVANIA

She tried to force a breath out of her lungs, but nothing came. The edges of her vision blurred. Stumbling back to the mattress, she tripped on the shag carpet and fell half on, half off the mattress. Blinking, she willed the room to stop spinning. This wasn't from a hangover. This was anxiety. A panic attack. She'd been having them since she started high school. Her parents thought she was full of it at first. Like she was making it up, being overly dramatic. Her dad was convinced she was faking them to get out of doing hard things because there didn't seem to be any rhyme or reason as to when they happened. "Stop being such a prima donna," he spat at her. He said it so many times, he just started calling her "Prima" for short. Even when her mom told him to stop, he still did it. She had always hated it, but now she'd do anything to hear her dad call her Prima again. If she ever got out of here, she would tell him he could call her Prima for the rest of her life. She didn't care. She just wanted to go home.

She tried to do a breathing exercise. When that didn't work, she crawled all the way up onto the mattress and flopped onto

her stomach, burying her face in the pillow. It smelled vaguely
of smoke. Like a campfire.

The campfire.

The clink of chains stole her attention. Raising her head,
Prima looked over her shoulder, toward the foot of the bed. Like
some kind of zombie, the naked girl climbed to her knees,
swaying and groaning. Eventually, slowly, she turned her head,
peering at Prima with dark, glistening eyes.

"Hello?" Prima said stupidly.

The girl licked her cracked lips and arched her back.
Bruises mottled the skin over her ribs and her upper arms. A
green-yellow blotch the size of a hand curved around her hip.
Prima gathered the blanket in her arms and inched toward the
bottom of the mattress. "Here," she said, holding the ends of the
blanket and spreading it out so she could lay it over the girl's
shoulders.

But the girl shrugged it off and quickly moved as far as the
chains would allow, pressing into the wall. "No," she rasped.
"Don't do that."

"But you're naked and you... you must be cold."

Those dark eyes glared eerily from beneath a shank of her
dull brown hair. "You can't. You're not allowed. If you try to
help me, we'll both suffer."

NINETEEN

Josie could think of about a million other things she'd rather do than spend three to four hours in a car with Chief Chitwood, much less take an extended trip with him, but no one knew more about Kelsey's case than he did, and he was intimately familiar with Brighton Springs whereas Josie had never been there. Plus, there was no guarantee that Harlan Chitwood would agree to talk with her, but there was a very good chance he would agree to talk with his son, even if they were estranged. The next morning, Josie left Noah and Trout snoring in bed and picked up coffee on the way to the stationhouse.

The Chief waited in the parking lot, leaning against the side of his car, a small black suitcase at his feet. She parked beside his car but before she could get out, he tossed his luggage into the back of her vehicle, and got into the front seat next to her. "Let's go," he said.

She set her GPS coordinates for the Brighton Springs Police Department and pulled out of the parking lot. Once on the interstate, she tapped the lid of the unopened paper coffee cup in the center console. "That one's for you," she said.

He made a noise in his throat and shook his head.

"It's a Red Eye," Josie said. "The way you like it."

She kept her eyes on the road but felt his eyes boring into her. From her periphery, she saw him pick up the cup and take a sip. Then he grunted.

"Was that a thank you?" asked Josie, smiling.

Instead of answering, he reached toward the screen in the center of the dashboard, punching buttons for the radio stations. "You got music? I don't want to spend the whole drive like this."

"Like what?" Josie asked as he cycled through stations with dizzying speed. She caught only snatches of songs—a chime here, a note there, sometimes a word.

"Awkward silence," he answered.

This time Josie laughed. "Who said it has to be awkward?"

He settled on a station that played eighties music. "I'm not a big talker."

Josie thought about him living alone for the past twenty-six years—in the time since Kelsey went missing—with no family, no spouse, no companionship except his work. She understood his drive, perhaps better than anyone, but she wondered what it must be like to live a life void of people. "Do you have any pets?" she asked, wondering if he at least had his own version of Trout. Or perhaps he was a cat person like Gretchen.

He glowered at her. "Quinn, we're not doing the talking thing, you got that?"

She nodded and focused on the road while he turned up the radio.

Luckily for them, the weather was beautiful—sunny and warm in the high sixties—and the traffic was light. The lush green mountains of Western Pennsylvania rose up all around them, making Josie feel like a speck on the breathtaking landscape. They passed through the small city of Lochfield first. Its streets were laid out irregularly, like the city planners hadn't really planned at all, instead tacking on more homes and businesses without any regard to traffic patterns or ease of travel. As they wended through the streets, the Chief pointed out a playground. It sat behind a sagging chain-link fence, its jungle gym and playhouse a faded blue. Small dents marred the shiny slide. "That's where I used to take Kelsey," said the Chief. "I lived not far from here when she was little. Every afternoon we'd walk over together. She played for hours."

Josie slowed as they passed. By the time she glanced back at the Chief, he had turned his gaze back to the windshield. Only a small tremor in his jaw betrayed his emotions. "That must have been fun," Josie said.

Chitwood turned his face toward the passenger's side window. "It wore her out, that's for sure. Take the next left or you'll never get out of here. This street just loops around and around."

Josie followed his instructions and soon they were leaving Lochfield behind, mountains around them melting into rolling hills. An hour later, they drove into Brighton Springs. It was larger and more sprawling than Lochfield. Its streets were much like Denton's, laid out in a grid fashion, easy to follow. As Josie drew nearer to the Brighton Springs Police Department, she noticed from the corner of her eye that the Chief was clenching and unclenching his fists.

"Is this where you grew up?" she asked.

"Yeah. I left after high school and never came back. Except after Kelsey disappeared. Then I was here every hour that I wasn't working in Lochfield, trying to track her down." He pointed ahead of them to the left where a large stone church rose up toward the sky. "That's Saint Agnes."

Josie slowed as they passed the massive church. A waist-high stone wall separated the church property from the sidewalk. From what Josie could see, a neatly kept garden area lay between the wall and the large stone steps leading to the main doors.

"Were the dormitories near here?" asked Josie.

"Behind the church," he said. "This whole block used to be the campus. Over the years the enrollment dropped so much they had to close the school. Then the church sold off most of the property. I'm pretty sure only the church remains. Everything else was knocked down, replaced by townhouses."

"Did someone from the church give you the rosary bracelet?" Josie asked.

When her grandmother was in the hospital, dying, the Chief had given Josie a bracelet made of rosary beads. It was beautiful. The beads were green like polished stones and the medal attached showed a woman in flowing robes beneath the words: *Our Lady, Untier of Knots.* Josie wasn't particularly religious, and she had told the Chief so, but he had insisted that she take the beads. Josie remembered the conversation with pristine clarity.

"Someday, I'll tell you the story of how I got that thing," said the Chief. "All you need to know right now is that even if you never prayed a day in your life, when someone you love is dying, you learn to pray pretty damn fast. Someone who believed very deeply in the power of prayer gave that to me, and at the time, it was a great comfort. Maybe it won't mean shit to you. I don't know. Regardless, if this is Lisette's time, nothing's gonna keep her here, but you? You're gonna need all the help you can get. You hang onto that until you're ready to give it back to me, and Quinn, I do want that back."

"How will I know when I'm ready to give it back?" Josie asked.

Chitwood started walking away. Over his shoulder, he said, "Oh, you'll know."

"The story behind those beads," Josie added when the

Chief didn't answer. "It's Kelsey's disappearance and murder, isn't it?"

"Sister Theresa," he muttered. "She gave them to me when Kelsey disappeared. For four months and seventeen days I prayed that Kelsey would be found. I just wanted answers."

"The not knowing is the worst," Josie agreed. In her line of work, she had seen how not knowing what had happened to a lost loved one consumed people, how it could stunt or ruin a life —or both.

The Chief sighed, his eyes still on the houses flashing past them. "God answered those prayers. She was found in that church."

"But she was dead," Josie said. A long moment lurched past. The up-tempo beats of an eighties song filled the silence. Josie had never used the beads to pray. She wasn't Catholic. She didn't know the first thing about saying a rosary. Plus, she had found out at an early age that prayers would not keep bad things from happening or evil people from committing the worst savagery.

Mouth suddenly dry, Josie swallowed. "Why did you keep the beads? If you prayed that much and Kelsey still turned up dead? Why would you—"

Chitwood turned to her and gave her a pained smile. "The same reason you still have the beads, Quinn. You do still have them, don't you?"

"Of course," said Josie.

They were in her pants pocket at that moment. When her grandmother first died, Josie carried them with her everywhere, not praying, just touching them, holding them, feeling their weight. Eventually they ended up in her nightstand and she took them out when she couldn't sleep and squeezed them in her palm, a talisman against her grief and unease. But her grief was unpredictable, like a crocodile languishing in shallow water

—it appeared calm and still but in the blink of an eye it could charge at you, knock you down, and with a snap of its jaws, plunge you into a hell you had little chance of battling back from. You just had to let it have its fill and once it was done, hope you could get back up. So she'd started carrying the bracelet with her again, the sound of the beads clinking in her pocket and the feel of them against her fingers grounding her in the moments when the crocodile rushed at her.

"Comfort," Josie choked out. "You kept them for comfort."

"Yes," said the Chief. "Sister Theresa gave those to me, and she had the strongest, most unwavering faith of any person I've ever seen. It seemed like that made them more powerful, in my mind. God knows, my own faith wasn't strong enough. The only thing I have faith in now is that people will always do terrible things because this world is a terrible place. We're born knowing we're going to die. The only things we're guaranteed in this life are death and suffering. That's it."

"I thought faith was about believing in what you can't see," Josie pointed out.

He gave a dry laugh. "You have faith?"

Josie shrugged. "I don't know. You're right—we can count on suffering and death. Those are absolutes." She thought of her grandmother in that moment, visualizing Lisette's mischievous smile, the glint of her blue eyes, the bounce of her soft gray curls. The image filled Josie with warmth. She missed her grandmother so badly that it took her breath away, and yet, she wouldn't give up the years they had spent together for anything in the world. She added, "We're not guaranteed love or joy, but they exist. Sometimes I think..."

She drifted off. After a beat of silence, the Chief said, "You think what?"

"I think maybe that's why we're here: because we're supposed to be looking for joy, for or love, or both. Or maybe we're here to create them—or something. The way things are, it's a miracle if you find them at all, in any form or fashion."

"For me, finding Kelsey's killer and putting him away would be a miracle. Look over there. I think that's it." He pointed to a large, flat-roofed building that sprawled along the side of the road ahead. It was one story, its brick face a faded salmon color, and as they pulled into the parking lot, Josie could see the ghostly letters from a sign that had once hung from its front: *Brighton Park Elementary.* Now, above that, a new sign announced: *Brighton Springs Police Department.*

"This is new," said the Chief. "They used to be downtown."

They stepped out of the vehicle and Josie stretched her stiff limbs. Inside the main entrance of the building, the lobby was tiled in white with blandly painted white walls. A large circular desk took up the middle of the room. Behind it was a set of steel doors with windows that revealed a long, wide hallway on the other side. A small black device affixed to the wall beside the doors told Josie that they were locked, and you likely needed some kind of badge to swipe in order to get through them. Vinyl-cushioned benches lined the walls, all of them empty. A man wearing a blue Brighton Springs police uniform sat behind the desk, a phone receiver pressed to his ear. He looked up as Josie and the Chief walked in and then went back to his conversation, focusing on the desktop in front of him. Josie walked right up to the desk and waited while Chitwood paced the lobby.

Josie listened to the officer discuss his current child support arrangement for ten minutes before he finally hung up. Still, he didn't acknowledge her presence until she thrust her credentials into his face and said, "Maybe you can help us. We need to speak to whoever is currently handling the Kelsey Chitwood case."

Slowly, he studied her ID and then looked up at her. Josie sensed the Chief behind her and wondered how much longer it would be until he blew up at this desk officer. The Chief wasn't known for his patience.

"Chitwood?" he said. "As in, old Harlan Chitwood? Related to him?"

"Kelsey Chitwood was his daughter," Josie said. "She was murdered at Saint Agnes's Church twenty-five years ago. The case is still open—or at least, it should be—and I need to speak to the detective handling it."

Pushing himself away from the desk, he said, "Uh, sure. Hang on a minute."

He disappeared through the double doors after swiping a badge hanging from a lanyard around his neck. Through the windows, Josie watched him shuffle down the hall and disappear into one of the doors on the left.

They waited. After twenty minutes, Josie walked behind the desk and pounded on one of the doors. Another officer poked his head out of a door down the hall but didn't come to see why she was knocking. She counted off another fifteen minutes while the Chief paced the room, saying nothing. His reticence shocked her. Finally, after yet another fifteen minutes, the desk officer returned. There was no apology for keeping them waiting so long. He simply told them, "That is with our cold case unit."

"You couldn't figure that out from the fact that the case is twenty-five years old?" Josie snapped.

Ignoring her, he said, "That unit is in the annex."

"Where's the annex?" asked Josie.

"Go outside, around the back of the building, in the rear parking lot. You'll see it."

Josie didn't thank him. Outside, they got back into her car and drove around to the rear of the building. All she saw was a line of shiny Brighton Springs police cruisers and at the very back of the property, a trailer sitting on top of concrete blocks. A small sign next to its door read: *Annex.*

"You've got to be kidding me," she muttered as she parked.

"I see things here haven't improved at all since my father retired," the Chief said as they got out of the car and approached the trailer.

"Should we knock?" asked Josie.

"And wait another hour?" The Chief said irritably. "Screw that."

He muscled past her, up the single step, and swung the door open. Josie followed him inside. The trailer was filled with filing cabinets and stacks and stacks of letter boxes. The only other things crammed inside were a mini refrigerator with a coffeemaker on top of it and a black metal desk to the left of the door. A woman sat behind said desk, tapping away at a computer keyboard. She wasn't in uniform, instead wearing a pink sweater. A lanyard hung around her neck, but Josie couldn't see her badge. Her silky brown hair was tied back in a neat ponytail at the nape of her neck. Her skin had the soft, supple look of a teenager. Swiveling her head toward them, she said, "Can I help you?"

"Is this the cold case unit?" Josie asked.

She gave them a wry smile. "Sure."

The Chief said, "You don't sound certain."

She laughed and stood up, moving around the desk so that she could shake both their hands. "I wouldn't call it a unit, that's why. It's just me. My name is Detective Meredith Dorton."

"Detective?" the Chief blurted out.

Slowly, Meredith frowned, folded her arms across her chest, and stared up at him. An awkward silence ensued. Meredith waited comfortably. Finally, the Chief said, "How long have you been at Brighton Springs?"

She smiled. "Well, that's the most diplomatic way anyone's ever asked me how old I am."

Josie took out her credentials and showed them to Meredith. "Josie Quinn. This is my Chief."

"I recognize you," Meredith said, studying Josie's ID. "I've seen you on television."

Josie gave a tight smile. She'd not only been on her local television station to discuss cases she worked on, but she'd cracked some cases so scandalous that they'd garnered national attention. In addition, her own complicated and sordid family history had been the subject of two episodes of *Dateline*.

"What are you doing all the way out here?"

"We're here about a cold case," Josie said. "The murder of Kelsey Chitwood."

Meredith's eyes widened. "Any relation to the notorious Harlan Chitwood?"

The Chief said, "If we say yes, are you going to disappear, not come back for an hour, and then send us somewhere else?"

"That depends," said Meredith.

"On what?" asked Josie.

"On whether or not you two have an interest in protecting him and the shoddy work he did in this department for fifty years."

The Chief grinned. "So that's why they stuck you back here in this trailer with all these old files. That's a big hornet's nest you're referring to. You must have poked it pretty damn hard."

With a sigh, Meredith moved back to the other side of her desk, fishing inside one of its drawers until she came up with a stack of foam cups, a few coffee stirrers, and a handful of sugar packets. "I've been on the force here for about ten years. I'm older than I look. I was promoted to detective about three years ago. After about a year, I caught an armed robbery. Two guys— one old-timer and one young guy. I got the young guy to flip on the other. In fact, he told me about this murder his mentor did thirty years back. I didn't pay much attention to it until after the case was wrapped up. Then I started looking into it. Someone was already in prison for that murder. Guess who put him there?"

"Sounds like Harlan's work to me," said the Chief.

"Long story short, Harlan bribed a witness, got an innocent man put away for life, and left the actual killer out on the street. I did what I could to get the innocent man exonerated and released. Then I started looking at some of Harlan's other cases."

"Which made you persona non grata in this department," said the Chief.

Josie said, "I thought you said Harlan was over ninety years old. How does he still hold so much sway here?"

Meredith walked over to the coffeemaker and punched some buttons until it spluttered to life. "He was on the force for fifty years."

The Chief glanced over at Josie. "That's fifty years of cases, Quinn."

Josie pieced it together in her mind. "If you start looking too hard, find too much corruption, then all his cases are tainted. Every case he ever worked on. The DA would be looking at decades of overturned convictions."

The Chief said, "He was corrupt, no doubt, but I'm sure he got it right every now and then."

"He did," Meredith said, returning to her desk. "But your colleague is right about the DA not wanting to be on the hook for all those tainted convictions. Then there's the exposure to the police department."

"And lawsuits," Josie said. "Detective Dorton, I'm not an attorney but I'm pretty sure they have whistle-blower laws in place to protect people like you."

Meredith grinned. "There are. I've already looked into it. I can't let this stand. How many other innocent people did he put in prison? I can't let them rot. Just as soon as I have definitive proof of every time Harlan Chitwood broke the law, I'm going to burn this whole place down—figuratively, of course."

The Chief regarded her with an appreciative smile—an

expression Josie didn't remember ever seeing on his face. "I look forward to that day."

"I didn't get your name," said Meredith.

"Bob," the Chief said. "Bob Chitwood. I'm Harlan Chitwood's son."

TWENTY

To her credit, Meredith handled the revelation with poise. Her poker face was impressive, and Josie got the feeling that every single person she came into contact with vastly underestimated her. She studied the Chief for a long moment and then she said, "I'm sorry to hear that."

Josie couldn't stop the laugh from escaping her mouth. Immediately, she clamped a hand over her lips, but it was too late. Both Meredith and the Chief stared at her. The Chief said, "I'm sorry, too." He turned back to Meredith. "But I'm glad to hear you're not letting him or this department get away with anything. Kelsey Chitwood was my little sister. Like Quinn here said, we're here about her murder case."

While Meredith poured black coffee into foam cups and offered it to them, Josie gave her a quick rundown of Gemma Farmer's peculiar case and the similarities between it and Kelsey's cold case. "What we really need is to have a look at your files," she concluded.

Meredith nodded along as Josie spoke. Occasionally, she jotted details down on a small notebook next to her computer.

"You find any other cases like these two in VICAP, NCIC, or the Pennsylvania CIC?"

"No," answered the Chief.

Meredith put her pen down and gulped the rest of her coffee. "Okay, so you just need Kelsey's files."

"Yes," said Josie.

"I think I know where they are."

"They're not computerized?" asked Josie.

Meredith laughed. "Please. This department computerize cold case files? That's one of the things I'm supposed to be doing. You know, after I blew the whistle on that old murder case, they created this department just for me. I've been working through these cases one by one. I scan the documents, reports, and photos into the computer system and then I review it, see if there is anything that I can do now to move it along or solve it, but there's a reason these are cold cases."

"And these files keep you from poking around in the files of Harlan Chitwood's solved cases," Josie said.

"Exactly."

"My dad was the lead detective on Kelsey's case," said the Chief. "Would you have access to the files?"

Meredith pursed her lips momentarily. "If it's a cold case, yes. I haven't gotten to that one yet. I'd remember it. But I do have a system of sorts. Give me a few minutes."

She disappeared behind a wall of letter boxes. They heard her opening file cabinet drawers and sliding them closed again and then moving boxes around. A few minutes later, she reappeared, sweat beading at her hairline. In her hands was a yellowed letter box with the name *Chitwood, Kelsey File No. 97-324/97-419* written in black Sharpie on its side. Meredith hefted it onto her desk and took off the lid. Dust floated from inside the box like a cloud. Waving it off, she began pulling out folders and paging through them. Her earnest expression turned to one of frustration. "Wait a minute," she mumbled.

"What's wrong?" asked Josie.

"This is not Kelsey's file. These folders. They're from a completely different case."

"Meaning what?" said the Chief. "Where are Kelsey's case files?"

Meredith looked over her shoulder at the countless boxes and file cabinets. "I don't know," she said.

Josie glanced at the Chief. A flush started in his cheeks, the precursor to an outburst of rage. She put a hand on his forearm, feeling his arm muscles tense beneath her touch.

Meredith threw the files onto her desk. "I really do hate this place. This isn't the first time this has happened. I had another set of boxes filled with the wrong case files. Like they'd been completely switched out."

"You think someone did this on purpose?" asked Josie. When she felt the tension in the Chief's arm lessen, she retracted her hand.

Meredith sighed, shoulders slumping as she emptied the last of the files from the box. "I can't prove it, but the last time this happened? It was like a shell game. It wasn't a case of a few folders being misfiled or one case file being put in the wrong box. The entire case file was mixed up, and there were two other cases involved. Case one was in the case three boxes; case three was in the case two boxes and case two was in the case one boxes."

The Chief said, "That sounds purposeful. When's the last time anyone handled the files?"

"Ages ago," said Meredith. "Decades, probably. All the cases in question are now considered cold."

Josie asked, "How did you find the other files?"

"Weeks and weeks of searching," said Meredith.

"We don't have weeks," said the Chief.

She smiled. "It's not going to take me weeks this time. If I'm right and someone switched the files, I know their system." Glancing behind her, she said, "Can you give me today?"

"Of course," the Chief said. "We were going to stay overnight. We could check back in tomorrow."

Josie took out a business card and grabbed a pen from Meredith's desk, scrawling her cell phone number on the back. "Call us if you find Kelsey's file or if you need any help."

In return, Meredith gave them her personal cell phone number, instructing them to contact her there rather than trying to reach her via the department.

Outside, Josie and the Chief got back into her SUV, but Josie made no move to leave the parking lot. Instead, she eyed the trailer, thinking about Meredith's suspicion that some of the cold case files had been purposely switched around. No filing system was foolproof. In the Denton PD, there were sometimes folders or reports that were misfiled. But it was unusual for an entire case file to be put in the wrong place. "Why would someone switch out the files?" she said aloud.

Chitwood sighed. "To make it harder for them to be found."

"Why not just destroy them?" Josie asked.

"Maybe they weren't able to. Some of those old cases take up boxes and boxes. At the old building, you couldn't access any case files without someone seeing you. The bullpen and evidence locker were right outside of the file room. There really wasn't a way to get in and out without someone seeing you. No one would be able to carry a bunch of letter boxes out of the building without arousing suspicion."

Josie thought about all the documents that Chitwood had had in his garage. He knew this because someone had helped him get copies of many of the documents in Kelsey's case file. Those documents and photos had likely been snuck out of the old police department building a little bit at a time.

"Okay," she said. "Why doesn't someone want the files to be found? They're cold cases. Unsolved cases." She took out her cell phone and fired off a text to Meredith. "I'm asking Meredith to make a list of the other cases that were switched around to see if there is any connection among them. In the meantime, we've got a day here. If we can't look at the case files, the next best thing is to talk to the lead detective."

The Chief grimaced. "I suppose there's no avoiding it."

TWENTY-ONE

Tappy's Lounge was one of the most depressing places Josie had ever seen. It was three stories of crumbling red brick with a rickety, rusted fire escape clinging to one side of it. The windows on the first floor, occupied by the bar, had been boarded up long ago. Dark red paint chipped away from the wood where it had grown soft with moisture. A sad neon sign hung over the door, only half its lights blinking. The building was squeezed onto a lot between the ramp to the interstate and an abattoir. The parking lot was broken asphalt and held only four spots. Luckily, when they arrived, one of them was open. Next to the bar door cigarette butts overflowed from a standing ashtray. There was no knob on the door, just a hand-sized spot where the brown paint had rubbed away from patrons pushing the door open.

The Chief pushed against it, stepping inside. Josie followed. In spite of the fact that it was nearly seventy degrees outside, a blast of hot air enveloped them as they crossed the threshold. The smells of old, stale beer, piss, and cigarettes rushed at them. It was so dark that they paused for a moment to let their eyes adjust. The only lights came from two televisions and three neon signs advertising different beers. Everything about Tappy's felt too close, overly cramped. The bar took up so much of the room that there was only a few shoulders' width of space between the barstools and the single pool table in the place.

Behind the bar, a bartender rinsed glasses while watching a baseball game on one of the televisions affixed to the wall. Pittsburgh Pirates versus the Philadelphia Phillies. A battle of Pennsylvania's two major league teams. The sound was turned down low, the words of the announcers indistinct. There was only one patron, sitting at the end of the bar, eyes fixed on the half-finished beer before him. Neither man turned when they entered. Josie and Chitwood walked up to the bar and waited. Just like at the Brighton Springs Police Department, no one was interested in helping them. Josie waited for the sixth inning to end and then she banged on the bar. "We're looking for Harlan Chitwood."

The bartender looked over his shoulder. "Second floor. Go around the back. Up the steps. First door you see. Down the hall. Door with the gouge in it."

The fresh air was a relief. Josie and the Chief circled the building. Behind a dumpster that somehow didn't smell as badly as the inside of Tappy's, they found a set of wooden steps leading to a deck, its surface black with age, grime, and dirt. A single camping chair sat in one corner next to a two-liter generic cola bottle. Debris swam in murky brown water that reached up to its narrow neck. On the other side of the deck was a solid door painted dark green. A small laminated sign at eye level read: *No bar patrons past this point.* The faded gold doorknob felt loose in Josie's hand as she twisted it and pushed the door open.

A hallway stretched out before them. From the ceiling hung a single naked bulb, casting a drab, dull glow that did little to illuminate the space.

The Chief leaned down and whispered into Josie's ear, "I always hoped he would end up in a shithole like this."

The doors in the hall were unmarked. No sounds came from beyond any of them. When they found the door with the gouge in it—a chunk of wood missing from the area beside the lock—Josie knocked.

No noise came from inside. Josie knocked again. "Harlan Chitwood?"

They waited a few minutes and then Josie knocked and called out for him again. This time, she heard footfalls from inside. A moment later, the door swung open.

Harlan Chitwood was taller and broader than his son, even in his nineties. He looked both powerful and frail at the same time, his posture cocky and self-assured, but his age evident in the saggy, lined skin of his face, the handful of gray hairs that gathered on his scalp, and the orthopedic shoes on his feet. His flannel shirt and jeans were threadbare.

"Mr. Chitwood?" Josie said.

Before he could answer, the Chief stepped in front of Josie. "Dad."

Harlan blinked twice and said, "Who are you?"

"Bobby," said the Chief.

Harlan stared at him for a long moment. Long enough for Josie to register the low hum of a television inside. From the sound of it, he was watching the same game as the bartender.

The Chief said, "I know you know who I am, Dad."

Harlan opened his mouth to speak but instead started coughing. His entire body seized, muscles stiffening, as the wet rattle tried to work its way out of his chest and up through his throat. From the cuff of one of his sleeves, he pulled a folded tissue and pressed it to his mouth. When he finally settled, he said, "I know who the hell you are, Bobby. Come inside."

He turned his back and the Chief and Josie filed in after him. Josie was surprised to find that he lived in a studio apartment. The scents of bacon grease and Bengay were overwhelming in the small space. In one corner, the fridge, oven, and kitchen sink had been crammed together. An unwashed frying pan languished on the stove, grease congealing into a thick white paste along its bottom.

A droopy, stained recliner sat next to a full-sized bed. Beside the recliner, a tray table held a pair of glasses, a remote control, and a can of beer. On the other side of the bed Josie noted a tall wooden dresser with a television on top of it. Beside that were three picture frames, each one holding a newspaper clipping from the *Brighton Springs Herald* with a headline about Detective Harlan Chitwood.

Detective Cracks "Unsolvable" Murder Case of Brighton Springs Socialite

Brighton Springs' Finest Stops Series of Armed Robberies

"I'm so Grateful." Mother of Missing Girl Found Safe Thanks to Local Detective

No photos of his children or his wife or even of friends or colleagues. Josie turned her attention back to the men who now stood at the foot of the bed, facing one another.

Harlan said, "What the hell are you doing here? Someone tell you I'm dying or something?"

"No," said the Chief. "I'm here about Kelsey."

One of Harlan's bushy brows kinked upward. "Who?"

Josie could see the Chief's face flushing. One of his fists clenched at his side. He showed remarkable restraint, though, when he simply answered, "Your daughter."

"You cracking up, Bobby?" said Harlan. "Kelsey's dead." For the first time, he looked over at Josie. A slow, lascivious smile spread across his face. Although she was wearing jeans, a

Denton PD polo shirt and a light jacket, Josie felt naked beneath his gaze. "Who's this little minx, Bobby? Your girl-friend?" His gaze flickered from Josie's breasts down to her feet, and back again. "You have good taste, son. I liked 'em young, too. Back when I could get 'em."

The Chief snapped his fingers in Harlan's face. "Hey," he said. "Stop being a pig for five seconds and look at me. This is my colleague, Detective Josie Quinn."

"Detective," Harlan scoffed. Another cough erupted from his diaphragm. On a wheeze, he added, "More and more broads on the job now, huh? Bet it makes it easier to get—"

"Shut up," the Chief said. "You keep disrespecting Detec-tive Quinn and we're going to have a repeat of that night down-stairs in 1999. I don't give a damn if you're ninety years old or if you've got COPD. I also don't give a damn if I get dragged out of this shithole in handcuffs. It will be my absolute pleasure to recreate that evening. Is that what you want?"

Chastened, Harlan snuck one last glance at Josie, this time meeting her eyes, and then he looked back at his son, bravado gone. Shuffling over to his recliner, he sat down and waved a hand in the air. "Fine, fine. Whaddya want, Bobby?"

"I want to talk about Kelsey's case. We went to the police department. Her file has been 'misplaced.' You know anything about that?"

"How would I know about something like that? I been retired a long time now. Stuck in this place. You're wasting your time anyway. Wasn't ever going to find who killed that girl."

The Chief opened his mouth to speak, but Josie cut him off. "Why not?"

Harlan looked over at her, mouth agape, as if he was surprised she was able to speak. "What kind of question is that, sweetheart?"

Josie took a step closer to him, hands on her hips. "Well, tiger," she responded. "Looks to me from those newspaper arti-

cles over there that you were quite the legend in the Brighton
Springs Police Department. In fact, we just came from there,
and you're an icon."

He smiled but then uncertainty crept across his face as she
continued. "How is it that the great Harlan Chitwood"—here,
she pointed to the frames on his dresser—"who was able to crack
'unsolvable' cases like the one of the Brighton Springs socialite,
couldn't solve the murder of a sixteen-year-old Catholic school-
girl? His own daughter, no less."

She could feel the Chief staring at her. Harlan looked at his
lap where his hands fidgeted, trying to tuck the folded tissue
back into the cuff of his sleeve. "We didn't have anything," he
mumbled. "No leads, no clues. We never even had any suspects.
You can't get blood from a stone. Is that what you want to hear?"

"You stopped looking," said Josie.

Harlan's gaze lifted. For a fleeting moment, she saw the
resemblance between him and the Chief in his flinty eyes. "You
never had one, did you?" he muttered.

"One what?"

"A whodunit. A head-scratcher."

"Every investigator has them," Josie said. "But this was your
own kid. You stopped looking. Why?"

Harlan said nothing, instead, reaching for his beer and
taking a long swig.

Josie glanced at the Chief, whose face was approaching the
color of beets. Josie wondered if he had ever posed this question
to his father—or if he had but it hadn't been answered. Had that
been part of whatever happened between them at Tappy's in
1999?

The Chief said, "Answer her, you son of a bitch."

Harlan gave a slow shake of his head and set his beer can
back on the tray table. "You don't want to hear this, Bobby. You
never did."

"Oh, what? How Kelsey was a 'troubled teen' and how she

got herself into whatever it was that happened to her? How she walked away from her life? You're right. I don't want to hear it because it's horseshit. Kelsey would not have left. She was fifteen years old."

"She didn't want to go to that school, Bobby. For the love of all that's holy, the two of you fought me tooth and nail on that damn school. You know it. You also know she was in trouble. You're the one who got the charges in Lochfield dropped. Underage drinking. Drug possession. Shoplifting."

"That was kids' stuff. She was acting out because she had no mother and a garbage father. It was a mistake sending her to that school. You could have given me guardianship and let me handle it but you didn't. You had to be in control. You had to punish me. For what?" Spittle flew from the Chief's mouth as his voice rose to a shout. He started to pace the room. "I still don't know. To this day, I don't know why you did it. You put her in that school, and it got her kidnapped and killed."

Harlan's fists clenched atop his thighs. He raised his voice. "It's my fault? You think it's my fault? Open your eyes, Bobby. That kid left the dorm on her own. She got out of bed, got dressed, and walked out. We didn't find her because she didn't want to be found. She got herself into something and it got her killed. That's the harsh truth, Bobby. All these years later and you still can't accept it. She ran away, Bobby. She ran the hell away."

The Chief leaned down, his index finger inches from Harlan's nose. "She didn't run away. Someone lured her and kidnapped her."

"Oh, how the hell would you know that, anyway?" Harlan said, pushing the Chief's finger away.

Josie watched a tremor work its way through the Chief's body. When he spoke, his voice was low and calm. His words ripped a hole right through her heart. "Because if she had run away, she would have run home to me."

Before Harlan could respond, he turned on his heel and stormed out of the apartment, slamming the door behind him, but not before Josie saw him wiping tears from his eyes with the heels of his hands. Josie did her best to keep her own composure, putting the emotions that threatened to overtake her in a box inside her heart for another time. Later, she would replay the scene in her head, feel again the rage and grief radiating from the Chief so strongly that they were like palpable sound waves. Later, she would sit with the pain of knowing that the Chief had lived with such guilt and regret for so many years, unable to get out from under it. For now, she focused her attention on Harlan.

"Just what do you think Kelsey got herself into?"

His head jerked, as if he was startled to find that she was still in the room. "What?"

"You said that Kelsey got herself into something. Like what?"

He picked up his beer again, drained it, and crumpled the can in his palm. "How the hell should I know?"

"You were an experienced investigator. You didn't have any ideas?"

He sighed. "I thought human trafficking. A boyfriend. Maybe he groomed her, told her how pretty she was, how smart. How he couldn't live without her. Made her feel like she was special and like he was finally going to give her all the love she never got anywhere else. All the stuff dumb teenage girls believe when they've got low self-esteem."

It couldn't have been easy growing up with the knowledge that your father was a cold, misogynistic, corrupt police officer who had fathered you with an informant who chose not to keep you, but Josie was certain that the Chief had given Kelsey a stable and loving home for fifteen years. The Chief was right. Underage drinking, shoplifting, and even experimenting with drugs were not uncommon in the teen population. Those things weren't necessarily indicators that a teen was, as Harlan had vaguely put it, "troubled," or that there were issues with their self-esteem. There were a whole host of reasons that teenagers experimented with drugs and alcohol or shoplifted and many of them had nothing to do with having low self-esteem. Besides, Josie doubted that Harlan had ever had enough of a conversation with his own daughter to make that determination.

"Why do you think that Kelsey had low self-esteem?" Josie asked.

"Listen," Harlan said. "This didn't make it into the autopsy report, okay, but Kelsey was a cutter."

"What? What do you mean?"

"She had scars on her arm, okay? The medical examiner thought they were self-inflicted. He said she must be a cutter. I told him I didn't think he could say that based on a couple of marks, but he said they were 'consistent with' self-harm and that even though there weren't a lot, it didn't matter. He told me most of the time, cutters don't leave scars. He was insisting on it, you know? He was gonna put that in his report. But I said that he couldn't say that unless he was one hundred percent sure, 'cause if the thing went to court, a defense attorney would have a field day with that—*oh, she was a cutter, she must have been real messed up.* She already had the charges for drugs and shoplifting."

"You thought if you found her killer, a defense attorney would attack Kelsey's character," Josie said.

"I've seen it a lot," he said. "They put the jury's focus on how messed up the victim was, like they deserved whatever they had coming to them. Normally, I didn't give two shits. Most of the victims whose cases I worked were messed-up, shitty people and getting killed was probably a favor to them and society."

Josie tried to keep the disgust from her face. "But for some reason, it mattered when it came to Kelsey?"

"Well, yeah. She was a Chitwood."

Josie didn't point out the flaws in his logic—that he seemed to care nothing for either of his children; that he hadn't had a meaningful relationship with either of them; and that he didn't much seem to care that his teenage daughter had been abducted and murdered but that somehow, the assassination of her character in a potential murder trial was an issue for him.

He continued, "My partner, Benning, he agreed. We convinced the ME to keep the self-harm thing out of the report."

Josie thought back to the autopsy report that the Chief had had in his files. There was no mention of self-harm and if she was recalling correctly, the only mention of scars was one on her knee which was quite old. "You said you didn't want him opining that the scars were a result of self-harm, not that you didn't want them in the report."

"Right, yeah."

"But they weren't in the report at all," Josie said.

He shrugged. "Yeah."

"The Chie—Bobby doesn't know about them?"

"Nah, and I wasn't going to tell him, as hot-headed as he gets about that kid. He never wanted to hear anything I had to say anyway."

"How many scars are we talking about?" Josie asked. "Where were they exactly?"

Harlan held out his arm and with his other hand, pointed to the meaty part of his forearm just below the bend in his elbow. "Right here. Two slashes. About an inch, maybe two inches long."

TWENTY-TWO

Josie found the Chief outside the bar entrance to the building, pacing. When he saw her, he started walking to the vehicle. They didn't speak as Josie drove around Brighton Springs looking for a hotel. He didn't look at her even at the hotel. Once they checked in, they went to their separate rooms. Josie stretched out on the bed and ordered room service. She closed her eyes and did a breathing exercise her therapist had taught her while she waited for the food to arrive. She still wasn't sold on the whole breathing-as-a-solution-to-sadness-and-anxiety thing, but she kept doing the stupid exercises anyway. The events of the day replayed on a loop in her mind. Each time she relived the moment, the look on the Chief's face before he stalked out of Harlan's apartment felt like a stab directly to her heart. She barely tasted the hotel food, but she scarfed it down anyway, wishing more than anything that she was home with her husband and her dog.

But when she called Noah, he was still at the stationhouse. She briefed him on her day and asked him to send her any photos he could find from Kelsey Chitwood's crime scene that might show the slashes on her arm. She also requested the crime scene photos from the Gemma Farmer case for comparison.

Sitting cross-legged on the hotel bed, her cell phone tucked between her cheek and shoulder, she opened her laptop.

"It's late," said Noah. "You must be exhausted. Did you eat anything?"

"I ordered room service," she told him, waiting for her computer to boot up. "You guys get anywhere with the Gemma Farmer case?"

"Nowhere at all," he said with a sigh. "Morale is low on this one."

Josie pulled up what she had come to think of as the "Sleeping Beauty" photos of Gemma on the alcove stage, her head resting on one arm, eyes closed. The faint trace of the pink scars on her forearm were just visible. With so many other strange characteristics to the crime, the scars had become an afterthought, not even discussed. But according to Harlan Chitwood, Kelsey had had scars in exactly the same place. It couldn't be a coincidence.

"Keep working at it," she said. "Something has to break."

Even as the words were out of her mouth, she was haunted by Harlan's question as to whether or not she'd ever had a whodunit or a head-scratcher. In other words, a case she couldn't solve. There had been plenty of less serious cases she hadn't been able to solve, and a few murders that she was quite certain were drug- or gang-related where the evidence was too scant to build a case, but she hoped that the Gemma Farmer homicide wouldn't end up in a cold case unit in Denton in twenty-five years. She'd sure as hell do everything she could to avoid that.

"Are you looking at these too?" she asked Noah.

"Gemma or Kelsey?"

"Gemma," said Josie. "I'm going to look at the ones you sent of Kelsey now."

She switched over to Kelsey's crime scene photos, clicking through each one and studying them closely, paying particular attention to the girl's forearms—what she could see of them. When she spotted what Harlan had been talking about, her heart did a double tap. She enlarged the photo on her screen, wishing the crime scene photos from twenty-five years ago were as crisp as today's pictures.

"They're the same," she said.

She heard noise in the background from Noah's end of the line. "I'm putting you on speaker," he told her. "Gretchen and Mett are both here. Which photo are you looking at?"

She mumbled the number attached to the photograph and waited until he said: "Got it."

"Right arm," she told him. "Draped over the top of the pew in front of her. She's got slashes on her forearm. Just like Gemma Farmer. They appear to be about the same approximate length and width from what I can see. Also kind of pink. Damn near identical to Gemma Farmer's wounds."

Gretchen's voice came through the line. "Zoom in," she told Noah.

Josie clicked back to Gemma Farmer's photos. "Pull up the Farmer photos again. Gemma has five of them."

"We weren't sure what they meant," Mettner muttered. "Or if they meant anything."

"Josie," said Noah. "Have you talked with the Chief about this?"

"Not yet," she said. "I wanted to be sure first." She didn't add that he had already had a pretty tough day.

Mettner said, "What do they mean? If we assume the killer gave them to these girls, what do they signify?"

"It's impossible for us to know what's in this guy's sick, twisted head," said Noah.

"He could be marking the number of his victims," said Gretchen.

Josie had been thinking the same thing, but hearing it out loud sent a chill straight down her back. She brought photos from each scene up on her screen side by side. "Which would mean Kelsey was victim number two and Gemma Farmer is victim number five."

Gretchen said, "Which means there are more out there. We just haven't found them yet."

"We have to keep looking," Josie said. "Maybe we're missing something."

Her phone beeped, indicating she had another call. Pulling it away from her face, she looked at the incoming number. It was local to Brighton Springs. "Guys? I think that might be Meredith from the cold case unit here. I've got to go."

She ended the call with her colleagues and swiped answer for the incoming call. "Detective Dorton?"

"Hello?" said a female voice that sounded older and reedy. "Is this—is this Josie Quinn?"

"Yes," Josie replied. "Can I help you?"

"Um, I hope so. My name is Sister Theresa. I'm a nun at Saint Agnes's Church in Brighton Springs."

"I know who you are," said Josie. "How did you get this number?"

There was a hesitation. Sister Theresa lowered her voice. "It's the only number he would give me."

"Who?"

"Bobby. Bobby Chitwood. He's over here at the church and I'm afraid he's quite a mess."

Although Sister Theresa couldn't see her, Josie shook her head. "I'll be right there."

TWENTY-THREE

A circle of yellow light illuminated the landing outside the double doors to Saint Agnes. Sister Theresa had left the doors unlocked, as promised, and Josie slipped inside the dimly lit antechamber. Directly ahead were two more large wooden doors which had been left ajar. Beyond them, the main area of the church was better lit. Two rows of wooden pews were bisected by a wide marble-tiled aisle that led to the altar. To one side of the altar, several candles burned, the flicker of their flames dancing off the stained glass above them. On the other side, a statue of the Virgin Mary stood atop a table, her hands extended outward, palms up, as if inviting parishioners to kneel before her in prayer. Along the walls were confessional booths.

Josie looked around, searching for Sister Theresa or the Chief. "Hello?"

"Over here," said the female voice from the phone.

Josie looked to her left where a small woman with short gray hair popped up from between two church pews closest to the back of the nave. "I'm Sister Theresa," said the woman, beckoning Josie toward her. She wore a simple gray sweater, a pair of khaki pants, and clunky black shoes that favored function over fashion. The only indication of her faith was a simple gold cross around her neck. As Josie walked toward the nun, she felt dread building in her stomach, her room service dinner churning in her gut.

"Thank you for coming," Sister Theresa said softly.

Her blue eyes gleamed with concern and, Josie thought, pity. She stepped out of the way and Josie's heart sank. Between the pews, flat on his back, was Chief Chitwood. There wasn't much room between the two pews. The space was normally taken up by a kneeler but that had been stowed upright. One of its legs was jammed into the Chief's rib cage. An open bottle of Jameson whiskey stood on the seat of the last pew. The smell turned Josie's stomach.

"How did he get in here?" Josie asked, stepping between his ankles, trying to get closer to him.

"He called me," said Sister Theresa. "We've always kept in touch, although I haven't seen him in probably six or seven years. He said he was in town and that he had a possible lead in Kelsey's case. Then he asked if I could let him into the church so that we could pray together."

With her foot, Josie nudged the Chief's leg. He didn't move. "Did you two pray together often?"

"Not often but sometimes. Over the years."

"Chief," Josie said loudly and firmly. "It's Josie Quinn."

She nudged his foot again and this time his head rolled back and forth. He opened his eyes and blinked rapidly. "Quinn!" he said. "You're here."

"Did he show up like this?" asked Josie.

"I think so, yes," said Sister Theresa. "I was late, although I had left the doors unlocked for him. When I got here, he was in quite a state."

"Chief," Josie said again. "Can you sit up?"

"Quinn!" he hollered as if she wasn't standing over him. One of his arms flailed in the air, knocking over the whiskey bottle. Josie lunged forward to right it but still, it splashed over both of them. "It was right here, Quinn," the Chief mumbled. "She was right here."

Josie backed out of the aisle and went around to the other side of the pews, entering from the side of the confessional booths rather than the main aisle.

"Quinn!" the Chief shouted. "Where'd you go? I need to show you something! This is where she was, right here! Quinn?"

Josie approached his head, squatting down and hooking both hands under his armpits. "I'm right here," she said. "I'm going to lift you up, try to get you seated in this pew. You think you can help me?"

A sour cloud of whiskey hit her face as he said, "This is the pew! This is it!"

Josie lifted using her knees, dragging him upright. "I need you to stand up," she told him firmly.

His legs wobbled, and his arms jerked in every direction, as if he was slipping on ice and trying not to fall. Josie got him partially onto the seat of the pew, half falling and catching herself with one knee on the pew. Sister Theresa came from the other direction, helping Josie get him upright so she could disentangle herself. The Chief leaned forward and slapped the top of the pew in front of them. "Right here!" he said. "This is it! This is the pew!"

Josie looked past him to Sister Theresa. "Is this the same pew where Kelsey was killed?"

The nun shook her head. "No. Those pews were replaced. There was too much..." She glanced at the Chief, but his eyes were on the altar, his gaze following the light of the flickering candles. "Even if we had gotten them back, there was simply too much blood—I'm not sure we could have gotten the stains out. Both the pew behind her and the one that her arms were resting on were ruined."

"The police took them into evidence, right?" Josie asked. She knew her own team would have taken both pews in their entirety and kept them as evidence to be processed.

"Yes," said Sister Theresa. "They gave us a property receipt. I still have it somewhere, I'm sure—"

"That's not necessary," Josie told her. "I was just curious. They would have tried to get fingerprints from both pews. There should be a report. The Chief didn't have—" She broke off, not sure if Sister Theresa was privy to the Chief's personal file on his little sister. Instead, she turned to him and asked, "Did you ever see the fingerprint report? Ask your dad or his partner about it?"

"This is where it happened, Quinn," the Chief said as if he hadn't heard her.

Sister Theresa took the Chief's hand. Tears shone in her eyes. "This is the spot, Bobby, yes. I'm so sorry."

"Everyone is sorry," he mumbled. "But no one has paid."

"Bobby," said Sister Theresa. "We've talked about this before. Retribution isn't—"

Josie could tell by the flush of the Chief's cheeks that he didn't want to hear whatever it was that Sister Theresa was about to say. She tapped his shoulder, drawing his attention toward her. "How did you even get here?"

He stared at her for a beat. Then he said, "Uber. Hey, I've got whiskey, Quinn. You want a sip? I just have to find my bottle."

His upper body lurched forward, forehead slamming against the top of the pew in front of him before either Josie or Sister Theresa could catch him. A string of curse words erupted from his mouth as Josie eased him back. A pink mark was already forming across his forehead.

"All right," said Josie. "That's enough. Let's get out of here. I'm taking you back to the hotel. Thank you, Sister. I'm glad you called me. I'm very sorry about this."

Sister Theresa shook her head. "No need to apologize. Bobby has carried the burden of Kelsey's death all these years, but I'm not sure he ever truly dealt with it."

"I'm dealing with it just fine," the Chief said, his voice overly loud.

Josie felt a deep sadness as she looked into his glassy eyes. He'd dealt with Kelsey's death by simultaneously obsessing over her case and shutting out all possibility of love or companionship in his life. He was punishing himself, Josie realized. Year after year, he punished himself by never really living. Instead, he worked. Just like her. Work had always been the salve she used to manage her wounds. Alcohol had been the medicine she took to numb the pain from those wounds when work wasn't enough. She'd stopped drinking when she realized that all it did was cause her to make terrible choices and that when she sobered up, the pain she tried so hard to numb was still there. It was always there. There were things in life that could never be fixed, repaired, or even numbed. You simply learned to live with them—and with the pain. Josie had been lucky to have caring people in her life who refused to give up on her like her late grandmother, and her husband, Noah.

The Chief had no one. At least, no one he was willing to let in.

"Chief," Josie said softly. "Come on. I'll help you."

"You don't want a drink?" he asked, even as he let her slide beneath one of his arms and lift him to standing.

"I stopped drinking a few years ago," Josie said.

"What? Why?"

As they shuffled out of the church together, leaving Sister Theresa at the top of the stone steps, Josie said, "You'll know exactly why in the morning."

TWENTY-FOUR

THREE MONTHS EARLIER – CENTRAL PENNSYLVANIA

Prima tried to cover the girl with the blanket again, but she thrashed, kicking it away and landing a solid blow to Prima's stomach. She fell on her back and curled around the pain. Tears stung her eyes. It wasn't so much the pain as the entire situation. She was stuck in some weird place with some weird, naked girl who had obviously been tortured—she was chained up.

"Please," the girl whispered. "Just stay away from me. It's what's best for both of us."

Prima sucked in several breaths and sat up, wiping her tears with the hem of her T-shirt. "How do you know that?"

The girl put her back against the wall and hugged her knees to her chest, rocking slightly. "Are you stupid or something? Look at me!"

Prima's tears spilled over as she took a long look at the girl, noticing even more bruises along her legs and arms. Shiny skin stretched taut over her bones. Her hair was brittle, eyes sunken. "We can talk but you cannot help me, do you understand?"

Prima nodded although she didn't understand, not at all.

"You can't give me your covers or clothes or any of your food or water. You got that?"

Prima's lower lip trembled. "But you need—"

The girl lifted her chin, jutting it out in a look of defiance that startled Prima, given the emaciated, battered condition of her body. "I need you to listen to me and do what I say. That's what I need. I'm still alive. The girl who was here before you—"

Something squeezed Prima's chest, like a vise being tightened around her rib cage. "There was a girl here before me?"

"Yeah."

"Wh—what happened to her?"

"She did what they wanted for a long time and then one day, they took her and she never came back."

TWENTY-FIVE

Josie and the Chief sat in a corner booth inside a diner a few blocks from their hotel. Every time a member of the wait staff shouted something to the cook behind the dining counter or a busser tossed cups, plates, and utensils into a bin to take back to the kitchen for washing, the Chief flinched. A cup of coffee sat in front of him, untouched. His chin rested in one of his palms. He hadn't looked Josie in the eye yet. Not since he woke up and found her sleeping in one of the guest chairs in his room. It wasn't the best night of sleep, but Josie couldn't risk him leaving the hotel again, especially drunk. Once he woke, she'd stood up, told him to meet her in the lobby in a half hour and left.

"Why did you bring me here?" he muttered. "It's so loud."

Their waitress came over and slid two plates of steaming hot food in front of each of them. The Chief hadn't wanted anything, so Josie had ordered them both the same breakfast: two eggs, over easy, toast, hash browns, and bacon. The Chief's face paled. He pushed the plate away. "I told you I wasn't hungry."

"Just eat the toast," Josie said.

Normally, he'd respond to her—or anyone—telling him

WATCH HER DISAPPEAR   139

what to do with a whole lot of shouting. Josie could gauge how embarrassed he was about the night before by how little aggression he had left in him. She kind of missed the abrasive Chief she'd come to know.

"You need something in your stomach," Josie told him. "It's going to be a long day. Meredith called me while you were getting ready. She found Kelsey's file."

At this, he looked up from the table, finally meeting her eyes. "She did?"

"Yes," said Josie. "She said the case files appeared to have been swapped out in exactly the same way as before. Three cases, all mixed up in each other's boxes. Like you said, it seems purposeful. But regardless, she found Kelsey's file. We're heading over to the annex after this. You need to be... functional."

He picked up a piece of toast, cringing as he brought it to his lips. Josie waited until he had eaten both slices and washed them down with some coffee before she said, "There's something else we need to talk about."

"Quinn," he said. "Last night, I—"

She shook her head. "Not about last night. About the cases: Kelsey and Gemma Farmer. We found another connection. An important one."

She told him about the slashes on Kelsey's arm; how Harlan had talked the ME out of opining that Kelsey had self-harmed and how, instead, the ME had failed to mention the scars in the autopsy report at all.

"This damn place," the Chief said, his voice low and taut with anger. "The corruption is everywhere. We should hunt down that ME and talk with him."

"We can," said Josie. "Although even if he had included them, at the time they wouldn't have meant anything to anyone. They would have been considered an incidental finding. It's only in light of Gemma Farmer's murder and the fact that she's got five of the same types of slashes that Kelsey's scars become important. I talked with the team about it last night. Gretchen thinks the slashes mark the number of victims. If she's right, that means that Kelsey was his second victim and Gemma is the fifth."

The Chief took this in, staring into his coffee cup for several beats. "Three more victims. Quinn, I couldn't find them. I'm telling you. I looked."

"Then he changed his MO, or the others were never recovered. I don't know. We can discuss it further when we get back with the team. For now, we need to focus on reviewing Kelsey's file. Meredith said she'll make copies of everything so we can take it home. There was one other thing—I want to talk to the other detective on Kelsey's case, your dad's old partner. What did you say his name was?"

The Chief took another sip of coffee. "Travis Benning. He was a young guy back then. Only worked with my dad a few years."

"Do you know where he is now?" Josie asked.

"No. I only ever had maybe three conversations with the guy, but I don't think he stayed on here. I got the impression from him that he didn't like the way my dad handled things."

"You mean he wasn't corrupt."

"Right, and you saw with Meredith how the Brighton Springs Police Department handles officers who don't tolerate corruption."

"Do you think your dad knows what happened to him? Where he went?"

The Chief pushed the empty coffee cup away. "I doubt it."

Josie took out her phone and sent a text. "I'll ask Noah to track him down then. In the meantime, let's go see Meredith."

They drove to the Brighton Springs police cold case annex in silence. Meredith's desk was piled high with boxes, and she moved around them with a frenetic energy. Her eyes were wide, her cheeks pink. Either she had had way too much coffee, or she was excited about something. She pointed to a stack of letter boxes that were marked with Kelsey's name and case number. "Those boxes now contain all of the correct files and documents —those pertaining to Kelsey's disappearance and murder. Once you've had a look at everything, we can start making copies. I wanted you to look things over first so we can make sure you're getting copies of everything and that there's nothing I've missed."

"Fair enough," said Josie, opening one of the boxes and pulling out a stack of folders. "Thank you. You had a chance to look at the other cases this one was switched out with, right? Were there any similarities to this one?"

"I'm afraid not," said Meredith. "Listen, I'm sorry I don't have much room in here. I did clear a space in the back for you both. The copier's there, too. You'll have to use the floor, but—"

"That's fine," said the Chief. "We'll handle it. Quinn, grab a box."

"Before you do that," said Meredith, "there's something I wanted to show you."

She moved behind her desk and Josie and the Chief followed, squeezing into the small space together. Meredith sat in front of her computer, and Josie and the Chief watched over her shoulder as she clicked through several files. Josie could still smell the faint hint of whiskey under the Chief's aftershave. She wondered if Meredith could as well, but she seemed far too preoccupied with whatever she wanted to show them.

On the screen, she opened a PDF of what Josie recognized as a missing persons report on an official Brighton Springs police form. Josie searched for the date. April 5, 1999. Roughly two years after Kelsey Chitwood was found murdered in Saint Agnes's Church. "This girl," said Meredith, pointing to a line in the report. "Priscilla Cruz was fifteen when she went missing from a group home here in Brighton Springs. She left the home that day—everyone assumed she was going to school as usual, but she never arrived there and never returned to the group home. Also, she didn't take her backpack with her. The woman who ran the home said all her personal items were still in her room. The detective—guess who? Harlan Chitwood—questioned all the other residents and staff of the group home, her teachers, friends from school, and people living near the area. No one saw anything. No one thought she was acting strangely in the weeks before she disappeared. Everyone thought she ran away. She didn't get along with the house mother, apparently. They had even come to blows at one point. With no leads, the case stalled. Then Priscilla's body was found in 2003 behind her old high school. The medical examiner estimated her body had been there for approximately two to three years."

She clicked through more items in the file which included a grainy photo of Priscilla Cruz standing in front of a nondescript brick building as well as photos of her skeletal remains, blackened and unrecognizable in a bed of weeds, dirt, and rubble. "She was identified using dental records," Meredith continued. "She was too badly decomposed for the ME to determine cause and manner of death."

"What are you saying?" The Chief asked. "You think this girl... what's her name?"

"Priscilla Cruz."

"Priscilla Cruz. You think that she was killed by the guy who took and killed Kelsey?"

"I'm saying it's possible," said Meredith. "You said yourself yesterday that you hadn't found any other similar cases."

"This is great, Meredith," Josie said. "But other than the fact that she was fifteen and walked out of her home without any of her personal items only to disappear and be found dead later, I'm not sure we can prove that this case is connected to Kelsey Chitwood and Gemma Farmer."

"I thought the same thing," Meredith agreed. "But then, as I delved deeper into her file—not that there's much to it—I found one other thing that might connect her case to the other two. Look at this." She clicked a few more times and an aerial photograph appeared, showing a large, sprawling building, several parking lots, a sports stadium, and some undeveloped land. "This is the high school. This area here—" Meredith zoomed in on one of the undeveloped areas of land and pointed to what looked like a fence surrounding it. "This was supposed to be the site of a new football stadium. It had already been fenced off at the time that Priscilla Cruz disappeared. You can see there are some trees and such here, but for the most part it was cleared off and ready for building. Then the high school ran into some issues with a farmer whose land butts against this. He claimed that part of the land earmarked for the new stadium was actually his. Everything got tied up in court and so the erection of the new stadium was delayed a few years."

"So what?" Chitwood said irritably, sounding much more like his old self.

"So," Meredith said, looking back at both of them, her manic smile back. "They didn't break ground until 2003, and that's when they found her remains, but originally, they were supposed to break ground on August twenty-seventh, 1999—Priscilla's sixteenth birthday."

There was a long silence as Josie and the Chief digested this bit of information. "You're saying that if the construction of the new football stadium had gone on as planned, then her body would have been found on what would have been her sixteenth birthday."

"If she is the third victim, then yes, I believe the killer left her there on her sixteenth birthday. Construction of the site was scheduled to start that day. He probably thought that when construction crews arrived, they'd see her body. Except that the farmer got an injunction and no one went onto the land for three years."

"We can't actually know that," Josie said. "There is no way to tell for certain when her body was placed there. But it's very possible that she could be the third victim if the ME believed her remains were two to three years old."

"I know there's no way to prove that she was killed and left at the site on her sixteenth birthday, but if she was, it would fit with the other victims."

"What do you mean?" asked Josie.

Meredith swiveled in her chair to face them, hands flapping excitedly. "Kelsey was left at the church that was affiliated with her school. On the same campus as her school at that time. Had she never been taken or killed, she might have been at church. She would almost definitely have been on the campus. You said Gemma Farmer was found at a prom. Had she not been taken, she might have gone to the prom. Both girls were left where they might have been had they lived. Priscilla Cruz was sixteen. She would have been at that high school."

Josie had spent many hours wondering why the killer had bothered to elaborately stage both Kelsey Chitwood and Gemma Farmer's bodies. It required a lot of planning and time on scene, which was risky. The more time spent with the body, the greater the possibility he would be caught in the act. Not to mention he left both girls in public areas. Obviously, it had to do with his fantasy. Josie said, "That's an excellent observation. In a way, he returns them to what he sees as the life of a normal sixteen-year-old."

Meredith opened her mouth to say something but the Chief cut her off. "There are too many variables here. We can't prove definitively that this girl was killed by the guy who murdered Kelsey and Gemma Farmer, and no matter how he 'returns' them, we still have no idea who the hell he is!"

"But in twenty-five years, you haven't been able to find any other connected cases," Josie pointed out. "I don't believe for a second that Kelsey and Gemma are his only victims. Maybe we're not able to identify his other victims for reasons such as this: the bodies weren't found in time."

"Fine," said the Chief. "I don't know that it will do us any good, but can we get a copy of the Cruz file as well?"

"Of course," said Meredith. "I can look for other cases like this too, and if I come up with anything else, send it your way."

"That would be great," said Josie. "We'll get started on reviewing Kelsey's file. I wanted to see the fingerprint report from the church pews."

"Follow me," Meredith said, standing up from her desk. "I'll show you your 'work area.'"

Josie and the Chief grabbed boxes marked with Kelsey's name and followed Meredith deeper into the trailer. As promised, she had cleared a large space near the copy machine. While the Chief went back for the other boxes, Josie knelt on the floor and started looking for the fingerprint report. Soon after, the Chief joined her. "I asked my dad about the fingerprints," he said as he searched the boxes with her. "Right after Kelsey was found. He said there was nothing. Lots of prints. No leads. But it was a church pew. There were probably hundreds of prints on it."

"I'd still like to see the report for myself," Josie told him.

After a few more minutes of searching, the Chief found the report. He crawled over to where she sat and handed it to her. Pulling a pair of reading glasses from his collar, he looked over her shoulder as she perused it. "Well, you were right," she said. "Five hundred twenty-two latent prints pulled from the two pews in total. That's both full pews." She flipped a page in the report and studied the diagram of the two pews. "Of all of those, only two sets of prints were in AFIS. One was found on the seat of the pew behind Kelsey and the other was found on the top of the pew she was draped over."

"What?" the Chief said. "He never told me that. If I had known, I would have checked those people out myself."

"He probably did check them out and came up empty." Josie read off the findings in the report. "The print on the seat belonged to a thirty-seven-year-old sex offender named Donny Meadows, and the print on the front pew belonged to a nineteen-year-old girl named Winnie Hyde, who was convicted of retail theft the year before that, when she was eighteen."

"The sex offender," said the Chief. "We need to look him up."

"Of course," Josie said. "I'll text Noah and get him to track the guy down while we finish up here."

"Thanks," said the Chief. "Let's get this done. I don't want to be in this town a second longer than we have to be."

TWENTY-SIX

The next day Josie, the Chief, Noah, Gretchen and Mettner gathered in the conference room at Denton police headquarters. It had been over a week since Gemma Farmer's body was found at the alcove. The detectives sat around the table, all of them looking haggard, exhausted, and frustrated. Silently, Chief Chitwood stood in the corner of the room. Someone had hung up reports and photos along the walls. One side was devoted to Kelsey Chitwood, and the entire wall was nearly covered, while the other was dedicated to Gemma Farmer. On that side there was a lot more wall than anything else. Josie stood up and walked slowly around the room, taking in all the photos. She had looked at them many times already, but she couldn't shake the feeling that she was missing something. Or maybe she hoped she had missed something that would break the case wide open, even though she knew that wasn't how these things worked. She said, "What've we got on Gemma Farmer?"

Mettner used one foot on the floor to turn his chair back and forth. Looking at the notes app on his phone, he said, "We've got nothing. That's what we've got. Gretchen and I showed

Gemma's photo to just about every high school student and teacher in this city. No one recognized her."

"Or if they did, they wouldn't admit it," added Gretchen.

"No one from any of the restaurants recognized her either," said Mettner.

"We even managed to get footage from the night of the prom from all the restaurants within a forty-mile radius that served lobster that evening. Most of the footage is just the lobbies and parking lots, but still, you can see who comes in and out."

Josie stopped in front of the photos of Kelsey Chitwood in the church pew. She wondered if it bothered the Chief to have them on display. He hadn't said anything, but then again, he probably knew every photo by heart. He had worked this as a case for the past two decades.

"Gemma isn't in any of the videos?" Noah asked.

"Not one," said Mettner.

Josie left the crime scene photos and moved to a couple of the autopsy photos that someone had posted of Kelsey, copies of which she and the Chief had gotten from Meredith Dorton. Whoever had hung them had sensitively avoided including the more gruesome shots, given Kelsey's relationship to the Chief. The pictures were mostly of her face and the missing lock of hair. Josie was struck by the look of peace on her face. Gemma Farmer's expression had looked the same. She said, "What about the dress shops?"

Gretchen flipped a page in her notebook. "There's one shop that was still having issues accessing their footage. Technical difficulties. They promised to call the moment they can view the footage going back prior to the prom. The other shops don't keep footage of anything for longer than two weeks, but the managers went through all of their receipts going back to January the second to see if they sold the dress that Gemma

Farmer was wearing when she was found. So far we've got nothing."

Mettner said, "What about the Kelsey Chitwood file? That print you guys found in the reports from the sex offender—did we get anywhere with tracking him down?"

Noah said, "I found the guy, but he's in prison. Has been for the last five years. Reoffended."

"Then it can't be him," said Mettner.

Josie asked, "What about Harlan Chitwood's old partner? Travis Benning. Did you track him down, by any chance? I doubt he has much more to offer than Harlan did but as one of the original investigators, I'd still like to speak to him, especially since he wasn't as corrupt as Harlan."

Mettner looked over at the Chief. "You never talked with him? About Kelsey's case?"

"I did, a few times," said the Chief. "He was a good man, but he didn't have anything more to offer me than what was in the file, which you've now all seen. Still, if Quinn wants to talk to him, then she talks to him. She—all of you—are my fresh set of eyes on this."

Noah checked his notes. "Looks like he lived in Brighton Springs until about twenty years ago, and then he moved to Pittsburgh for about six years. Then he bounced around until he settled in Fairfield, down in Lenore County. He lives in an apartment there. He doesn't appear to be doing police work anymore. Also, I don't see any spouse or children associated with him. I gave him a call yesterday, and he said he'd be happy to come in and meet with us."

"Make it happen," Josie said.

Noah jotted something down.

"That still doesn't get us anywhere," said Mettner.

Gretchen sighed. "I have to agree with Mett." She spun in her chair, taking in the entire room. "We can't have all this evidence—two cases so closely connected—and not one lead. There's something we're not seeing."

"Let's go over it, then," Noah said. "Again. I made a list of similarities between the cases."

Mettner sighed, but watched as Noah stood up and walked to the back of the room where he'd brought in a whiteboard. He turned it around so that they could all see his handwriting in red marker. He went point by point, elaborating on the list he'd made.

"Both girls disappeared from their bedrooms, as far as we know. There was no indication of a struggle or any type of foul play. In fact, it looks like they both got up, got changed, and left on their own, leaving all their possessions behind. We also know that Josie and the Chief found another potential case in Brighton Springs from 1999, Priscilla Cruz, where the girl also disappeared from her bedroom as if she'd simply gotten up, gotten changed and left. But since we can't prove a connection, we're only going to consider Kelsey and Gemma's cases."

Josie walked toward the whiteboard, studying it as Noah continued.

"As we know, Kelsey disappeared when she was fifteen and was missing almost five months. Gemma was also fifteen and she was gone for four months. When they were found, neither girl appeared to be malnourished or had any indicators of torture or injury of any kind other than the fatal stab wound to their left leg. No obvious signs of sexual assault. Both Kelsey and Gemma were found on their sixteenth birthdays. Both had a lock of hair missing. Both had a femoral wound. Kelsey had two stab wounds, so I think the killer was not as sure of himself with her as he was with Gemma."

"If Gretchen is right about the slashes on the girls' fore-arms," said Josie, "that they indicate the number of each victim, with Gemma being the fifth, and Kelsey being the second, that makes sense. He might not have been as confident in severing the femoral artery the first or second time around."

"I agree," said Noah.

"But by the fifth victim, he's a pro," said Mettner. "Also, both victims were found in the evening. After dinner time."

"What about stomach contents?" asked Gretchen.

Noah returned to the table and searched for Kelsey Chitwood's autopsy report. Before he could find it, the Chief said, "She had eaten tacos."

They all turned to look at him. His voice wavered, infused with sadness. "They were her favorite. The killer gave her tacos and then killed her right before five o'clock Mass."

"They were her favorite?" said Mettner. "She had her favorite meal before her death?"

Now all eyes turned to him. Josie glanced at Chitwood's face, seeing a flicker behind his eyes. "Why do you ask?" he said, addressing Mettner.

Mettner looked around at each of them. "We are treating this as a serial case, right? 'Cause this guy is incredibly ritualistic. Most of the stuff he does isn't even necessary to committing the crime."

"You're talking about his signature," said Gretchen.

"Right," said Mettner. "Like the missing hair, killing them on their sixteenth birthdays, leaving them in a very obvious place, and this—their last meal. What if he feeds them their favorite meal before he kills them as part of his ritual?"

"It very likely is part of his signature," Gretchen said. No one argued. Gretchen was more intimately acquainted with the behaviors of serial killers than any person would ever wish to be. "Many serial killers have a fantasy they're trying to recreate and refine. It's less about the killing than the fantasy. He obviously keeps them for a certain amount of time—although that isn't entirely consistent—but it looks like when he decides he's finished with them, he dresses them for the occasion—church, the prom—"

"Or takes them to the place they might have been had they not been his captives on their sixteenth birthday," Josie said, echoing Meredith Dorton's theory.

Gretchen nodded. "Right. He gives them their favorite meal, which is laced with Benadryl so that they are sedated, and then he kills them."

Mettner said, "I'm wondering what Gemma Farmer's favorite meal was? Any chance it was lobster?"

There was a beat of silence. Then Gretchen said, "We can certainly find out."

Josie turned away from Kelsey's crime scene photos for a moment and said, "Let's go with this theory. We've got all these pieces. What about the kidnapping aspect?"

Noah said, "It doesn't look like either of them left under duress. From all appearances, they got out of bed, got changed, and left. Unless he lured them."

"How would he lure them?" Mettner said. "There's no evidence either of them was groomed in the weeks leading up to their disappearances. There's an older woman that Kelsey saw a few times at the bus stop, but that's it, and we have no idea who that lady was—could be completely unrelated to her case."

Noah said, "Gemma Farmer talked to that blonde girl at the mall a few times before she disappeared."

Mettner shook his head. "Can't tell if that's related or not either."

"They could have been taken at gunpoint," Gretchen suggested. "According to the records we have, there were no cameras at the dormitories where Kelsey lived, and she was gone before anyone woke up."

"It would have been difficult but not impossible to take her at gunpoint," said the Chief. "That would also explain why

Gemma Farmer didn't take her phone. What modern teenager would go anywhere without their phone?"

Josie said, "Unless he convinced her to leave it behind. Even teenagers know they can be tracked via their phones."

"With Gemma it would have been very easy to take her at gunpoint though," said Noah.

"There's no way we can say for sure," Mettner said. "All we know is that they go missing from their beds. Then on their sixteenth birthdays they are found in a public place, staged and stabbed. The killer takes a lock of their hair. They've been sedated with Benadryl—assuming Gemma Farmer's toxicology shows that—and fed their favorite meal before their deaths. The more I think about it, the last meal thing is really creepy. Why would he do that? What part of his sick fantasy is that fulfilling?"

Again, Josie thought about the almost merciful way that Gemma Farmer had been killed. Turning back to Kelsey's photos, she noticed the same almost respectful staging of the body. Kelsey hadn't been left naked or discarded like garbage. She had not been tossed aside somewhere. She'd been returned to a place of worship and comfort—literally to the house of God —and however awkwardly she was positioned, she had been left in an almost prayerful pose. The outlier was Priscilla Cruz, but they couldn't connect her to these killings anyway. "Maybe he thinks he is doing them some kind of favor? Freeing them from a cruel world?"

"There might be something to that," said Gretchen.

"Fine, but how does that get us closer to finding this guy?" asked Mettner.

Josie opened her mouth to speak but from the conference room table, her cell phone rang. She picked it up and swiped answer, listening to the person on the other end before hanging up. "We've got a lead," she said. "On Gemma Farmer's prom dress."

TWENTY-SEVEN

Anastasia's Boutique was located in South Denton inside an old stone house that had been converted into a store. It was one of the few structures in that part of South Denton that didn't look like a squat concrete bunker. Considered a business district, most of South Denton was just long stretches of strip malls, warehouses, factories and other businesses. Anastasia's Boutique looked out of place with its freshly black-topped parking lot lined with flower beds and shrubs. On the porch of the shop were several rocking chairs and potted flowers, adding a burst of color and giving the place an inviting, rustic look.

As Noah opened the door for Josie, he said, "This was the manager having technical difficulties accessing her footage?"

"Yes," said Josie. "That's what Gretchen said."

Inside, they spoke with a salesperson and waited until the manager finished serving a customer who was evidently purchasing a bridesmaid dress. She fixed a smile across her face as she approached them, and Josie realized that it probably wasn't good for business for two detectives to be lingering around. "Thank you for coming," she told them stiffly. "If you'll just come this way, I'll show you what I found."

They followed her through a door behind the glass display cases that surrounded the register and down a long hallway to what appeared to be an office. It was decorated in various shades of mauve with faux floral arrangements bursting from vases in every corner. A desk sat in the center of the room with a laptop open on it. Rolls of various types of fabric sat beside the laptop and stood leaning against the sides of the desk. The manager gestured to the chair and Josie sat down. Noah stood behind her so he could look over her shoulder.

"I don't know if this is relevant or not but as it turns out, we did sell a dress exactly like the one you showed us in those photos. It was sold one month ago to this girl."

She reached across Josie and clicked the mouse until a video appeared on the screen. The camera was positioned behind the register, taking in a wide pan of the entire store. In one corner of the store, a sales associate held up a bridal gown for the benefit of a woman with long dark hair. In the center of the sales floor, another sales associate showed various pairs of shoes to a woman already wrapped in a long, flowing blue dress. The door to the shop opened and a small, thin girl stepped inside. Her hair was flaxen blonde and tied in a ponytail. She wore an oversized brown jacket that looked more suited to a grown man than a teenage girl, together with loose-fitting jeans and a pair of brown boots. She looked like a girl wearing her dad's clothes. The sales associates stopped what they were doing and stared at her.

She wasn't deterred. Without a word, she headed directly to one of the dress racks nearby and began riffling through them. One of the sales associates broke away from her client and spoke with the girl. There was no audio, so Josie and Noah couldn't hear what was said, but the woman was clearly wary of the girl, her fake smile only barely kept in place. The girl shook her head, said something, and then the woman retreated although both sales associates kept a careful watch on the girl for the next ten minutes.

Finally, the girl chose a dress. Josie recognized it as the one Gemma Farmer had been wearing. She took it to the counter. Another discussion ensued and then the girl reached into her jacket pocket, pulled out a wad of cash, and tossed it onto the counter. Grabbing the dress from the clerk's hand, she turned and left.

"How much was the dress?" asked Josie.

"It was two hundred dollars," said the manager. "Plus tax. As you can see, she paid cash. She did not wait for change. My sales associates asked her if she wanted to try it on or if she would need alterations, but she refused."

Josie strongly doubted that was the content of the brief conversations the sales associates had had with the girl, but she didn't say anything.

Noah said, "Did you talk to these two sales associates once you found this?"

The manager nodded. "Only one of them remembered the girl. She said she was very strange and had 'dead eyes.'"

Josie suppressed a sigh. It was difficult to tell from the angle of the footage, but she wondered if the associate really thought the girl had "dead eyes" or if she'd made a snap judgment based on the girl's poor, unkempt appearance. "Did the girl say anything else? Anything at all?"

The manager shook her head. "No. She came in and said she needed a dress. My sales associate tried to get more out of her, such as what type of event it was for, what size, color, that sort of thing, and the girl refused to say. As you can see, she picked out a dress, threw the money onto the counter, and took off."

"Did anyone see whether she arrived or left in a car?" Noah asked.

"No, no one noticed."

"Do you have cameras in the parking lot?" asked Josie.

"I'm sorry, but we do not," said the manager.

"Is this the only camera angle you've got?" asked Noah.

"Yes, this is the only one. I'll be happy to send you along with your own copy if you'd like."

"Great," said Josie. She looked up at Noah. "Let's get back to the station and put everyone on this. We can pull some stills and see if anyone recognizes this girl—Gemma's parents, her friends or the students and staff at the city high schools. We'll start with Denton East."

TWENTY-EIGHT

Portia Beck knew a death rattle when she heard one, and her 2010 Chevy Caprice was choking out its last bit of life on a twisty mountain road just outside of Denton. The entire car shivered violently and then the steering wheel went stiff in her hands. Cursing, she tried her best to guide it to the side of the road but when it finally died altogether, the headlights even cutting out, its ass-end was still half in the road. She swore again and got out, scanning the road in either direction. Naturally, she had broken down on a turn in the road, which meant that the next car to come around the bend would probably rear-end her.

Her phone said it was almost eight thirty at night. It also said she had no service. Too high up on the mountain, she thought. There was a dead zone up here between Bellewood and Denton. Usually, it didn't matter. She tried to calculate how far she was from her trailer. It had to be four or five miles, at least, and she was exhausted from her shift at the grocery store. She hadn't even been able to take a lunch because things were so busy. Her feet throbbed. But, as with most things in her life, Portia had no choice. No options.

She gathered her vest and bag from the passenger's seat of

the car and started walking, trying not to cry. Her eyes burned with unshed tears, but she focused instead on the pain in her feet. If she thought about that pain, she wouldn't think about the other pain. The worst pain of all. Nine months ago, her car dying would have sent her into a tailspin. She would have rushed home and straight to her neighbor for a dose of OxyContin to get her through the night without thinking about how she was going to get the car off the side of the road; get to work the next day; and afford a new vehicle. Now it was a fleeting blip on her radar, barely worth thinking about.

She heard the hum of tires over asphalt a few seconds before headlights came around the corner, enveloping her in light. The car pulled around her and over to the shoulder of the road. The license plate sent her heart into overdrive. J-Rock.

The ache in her feet was suddenly gone as she hurried past the car, nearly breaking into a run to put distance between herself and the man who emerged from it.

"Oh, come on, bitch," he yelled at her.

Portia kept going, power-walking away from him as fast as she possibly could.

His car door slammed and then she heard the vehicle approaching again. She expected—hoped—it would career right past her and keep going but instead, it pulled up beside her, keeping pace. The passenger's side window rolled down.

"I saw your car," he shouted at her. "Are you really going to be like this?"

She ignored him.

"Get in," he told her.

When she didn't answer, he said, "I know you think I did something to Sabrina, but you're wrong."

She stopped and faced him. He slowed to a stop. He had lost weight since the last time she saw him. His hair was longer, hanging into his face, which was still greasy and pimpled with a pathetic excuse for a moustache trying to establish itself on his upper lip. The smell of pot wafted from inside the car.

"Where is she, Jonah?"

He shook his head. "I told you, just like I told the sheriff, I don't know. I don't know what happened to her, okay?"

She stepped forward and thrust a finger inside the window. "I heard about you, you know. You got some of the girls from Bellewood High involved in a sex-trafficking ring!"

He laughed. "Not true. You listen to too many rumors. I knew a couple of girls who got caught up in some shit like that, but I didn't do nothing. The sheriff checked me out."

"Not well enough," Portia hissed.

He rolled his eyes. "You want a ride or not?"

Portia weighed her options. Jonah Saylor had been under police suspicion since Sabrina disappeared—mostly due to Portia's own machinations. Would he try to do something to her? No one knew either of them were out here. This was how people disappeared without a trace. They'd find her car but nothing else. It would look like she'd gotten out and walked away and then vanished into thin air. Like Sabrina.

"Get in or I'm leaving," Jonah said. "For real."

She hesitated.

The tone of his voice changed then. Softened. "Look," he said. "You could get killed walking home from up here. I almost hit you when I came around the corner. What if Sabrina comes back? Don't you want to be there?"

Portia swiped at a rogue tear rolling down her face. Wordlessly, she got into the car. They didn't speak on the way into the city. All she could think about was what she would say to her daughter if she came back. The weeks before Sabrina left had been hell. They'd argued every minute they were in each other's presence. Gone was the sweet girl who had watched singing competition shows with Portia and helped her cook dinners. In her place was a sullen, angry young woman who told Portia, "I hate you," each and every time they spoke and insisted on staying over at her boyfriend's apartment forty miles away in Bellewood without so much as a phone call. Portia had thought it was simply because she'd forbidden her daughter to keep seeing Jonah and that she'd get over it. Then she was gone.

"Here," said Jonah as he pulled up in front of Portia's trailer. The tiny light outside her front door was on, as was the living room light. She left them on all the time now. In case Sabrina came back.

"You're welcome," he said as Portia got out.

She closed the door but then leaned back into the window. "It's been two hundred seventy-five days, thirteen hours, and twenty-three minutes since the last time I saw Sabrina. If you know where she is, just tell me."

He shook his head. "Get away from my car, you crazy bitch."

Portia barely had her head out of the window when he peeled way, throwing up gravel in his wake. She watched the dust he'd kicked up dissipate before walking into her trailer. She threw her stuff down on the kitchen table, dislodging some envelopes from the pile of unpaid bills. They cascaded to the floor. Ignoring them, she went to her fridge and found the half-finished beer she had left there that morning. After she downed it, she walked down the hall toward her bedroom, stopping short when she saw that Sabrina's bedroom door was closed.

In all the months that Portia's daughter had been missing, she had never closed the door.

Hope bloomed in her chest, a wild and irrational thing with beating wings and pointed talons that dug sharply into her heart. "Sabrina," she choked out as she threw open the bedroom door.

The tiny light next to Sabrina's bed twinkled, casting no more glow than a nightlight. It took a moment for Portia to make out a lumpy shape on the bed, beneath Sabrina's old pink comforter. Portia reached for the wall and flipped on the overhead light.

Rushing toward the bed, she tripped over the pile of dirty clothes that Sabrina had left on the floor before her disappearance and fell to her knees. "Sabrina!" she cried.

Her hands scrabbled over her daughter's face, but her skin was cold, her body stiff. "Sabrina!"

Portia shook her shoulders, but her daughter didn't move. She tossed the comforter away from Sabrina's body and that's when she saw the blood.

She was still screaming when the police arrived.

TWENTY-NINE

The Farmers had moved into a small, single-story home in one of Denton's working-class neighborhoods. Its small front yard was overgrown with weeds and tall grass. The porch was crowded with empty cardboard boxes marked "kitchen," and "basement." Patio chairs were stacked on top of one another. A trash bin lay on its side, empty. Diana Farmer answered the door weeping, a red sweater clutched in her hands. Wordlessly, she waved Josie and Noah inside.

"I'm sorry about the mess," she said.

The living and dining room were open concept, one bleeding into another. Both were filled with boxes, many of them marked *Gemma*. There was a single space on the otherwise buried couch. Neither Josie nor Noah sat there. The three of them stood just inside the front door, staring at one another.

"Mrs. Farmer," said Josie. "I'm so sorry to bother you. It's just that we have some questions that can't wait."

Diana nodded. Squeezing the red sweater between her thick hands, she said, "Why don't you come into the kitchen? It's about the only part of the house where there's room to move."

Dodging plastic bins and furniture piled high with more boxes, they followed her to the back of the house. The kitchen was tiled in white without a bin or box in sight. Diana walked over to the counter next to the fridge and punched some buttons on the coffeemaker. "I can offer you coffee if you're willing to wait twenty minutes. This damn thing. It's the only thing I asked for—a new coffeemaker—but Wes says we can't afford it. I'd sell half the stuff in here for a decent cup of coffee."

"We appreciate it, Mrs. Farmer," said Noah. "But that's not necessary. This is going to sound like a strange question right off, but what was Gemma's favorite meal?"

Diana gaped at him.

"Again, I know it's strange," Noah said apologetically. "But if you'd just humor us."

"Lobster," Diana blurted. "She loved lobster. We could never afford it but that was her favorite. She had it once on a trip to New York City. Special occasion. Asked for it constantly after that. I had to appease her with her second favorite thing."

"Cheesecake?" said Noah.

Diana's face paled. "How did you know that?"

Josie didn't have the heart to tell her the killer fed Gemma her favorite foods before he killed her. Managing a smile, she said, "Who doesn't love cheesecake? More importantly, there's something I need to show you."

Josie took out her phone and pulled up a photo of the blonde girl from the dress shop and turned it toward Diana. "About a month before Gemma was found, this girl purchased a dress identical to the one she was wearing, in cash, from Anastasia's Boutique. We were wondering if you recognize her."

Diana put the sweater down on the countertop and took Josie's phone. "You can scroll left," Josie told her. "There are four photos in total."

They waited while Diana studied the photos, swiping left and right and left again, her brow furrowed. Josie looked around the room, astounded by the juxtaposition of the uber-neat kitchen with the rest of the house. The only clutter was the profusion of papers and magnets on the fridge. A magnetic calendar from their real estate agent. A business card from a funeral home. A past-due bill for car insurance. A sheet listing family doctors in the area. Another business card listing a plumber. An information sheet from a place called the RedLo Group offering therapy services.

"This is the girl I saw at the mall," said Diana. "I told that other detective. What's her name?"

"Detective Loughlin?" said Noah. "Heather Loughlin?"

Diana nodded, handing Josie back the phone. "Yeah. You're saying this girl bought the prom dress that you found my Gemma in the night she died? Why would this girl buy Gemma a prom dress? Who is she?"

Josie said, "We were hoping you could tell us. Detective Loughlin mentioned that you never actually spoke to her. She said the girl 'took off' when she saw you approaching."

Diana reached behind her and tore a paper towel from the roll on the counter, dabbing at her cheeks. "That's right. I had never seen her before. I thought I knew all of Gemma's friends. But I'm not sure they were friends. I never saw her except when we went to the mall."

"Why were you there?" Noah asked. "Was it a specific store that Gemma wanted to go to?"

Diana's gaze dropped to her feet. "No. We didn't go there to shop." Looking back up, her eyes roamed everywhere but at Josie and Noah. "Look at this dump. Do you think we could afford to go shopping twice a month? We went there to get away from my husband."

Josie and Noah exchanged a furtive look. Josie said, "Was your husband abusive, Mrs. Farmer?"

"No, not in the way you think. He never hit us or anything. He never would. But he's... he's a lot to deal with. He can be mean, especially to me. Gemma didn't like it. She would defend me and then they'd fight—verbally. I tried to get them to go to their separate corners of the house but our place, even in Keller Hollow, was so tiny, it was impossible. It was freezing outside, and I just wanted to get Gemma out of there, so I thought we could be 'mall walkers.' You know what those are, right?"

"Yes," said Noah. "The mall is actually a great option for indoor walking. My mom used to do that."

Diana gave a wan smile. "I thought I was so smart, but the first time we went Gemma was embarrassed. She said she didn't want to be seen in the mall just walking, like we were too poor to buy anything. She refused to walk with me. I gave her five dollars and told her to wait for me in the food court while I 'walked,' but really I just cried in the bathroom for an hour and then went back to get her."

Josie couldn't stop the wave of sadness that crashed over her as she listened to Diana's recounting of events. "When you went to the food court, she was sitting with this girl?"

"Yes, they looked deep in conversation, which was weird because usually when the kids hang out together, they just sit around on their phones. The first time I saw Gemma with her, I thought 'great, she made a new friend,' but then the girl took off. I asked Gemma about her, and Gemma told me it was none of my business." More tears spilled from Diana's eyes.

Softly, Noah said, "Is there anything at all you can remember about her? Even if it seems insignificant, it might help us track her down."

Diana swiped at her tears with the paper towel and sniffed. "She didn't dress like other girls her age."

"How old would you say she was?" asked Josie.

"Probably Gemma's age. Maybe a bit older? It was hard to say. I didn't get the best look at her."

"What was unusual about the way she dressed?" asked Noah.

"She wore men's clothing. Baggy. Nothing like I've seen teenage girls wear these days."

"Gemma wouldn't tell you anything about her?" Josie said. "Her name? Anything at all?"

Diana sighed. She traded the paper towel for the red sweater, hugging it to her chest. "Detectives, I loved my daughter. More than the air I breathe. But she was very angry with me. If she had anything to say, she was not going to tell me."

It was completely dark by the time they left the Farmers' house. Noah drove toward home while Josie traded texts with Mettner and Gretchen. They'd spent the afternoon and early evening trying to find the mystery girl in the Denton East High yearbooks with no luck. Tomorrow they'd go back to the school with the surveillance photos to see if any students or faculty recognized her.

"You think she's involved?" asked Noah.

"She has to be," Josie said. "She bought the dress."

"Assuming it was the same dress that Gemma was actually wearing," Noah pointed out. "All we can really say for sure based on the video footage is that the blonde girl purchased the dress."

"The blonde was also seen with Gemma on three or four occasions at the mall near Keller Hollow as per Diana. It's the same dress."

"Okay," said Noah. "Let's say that the mystery teen is involved in whatever the hell is going on here. If this killer was doing this to girls twenty-five years ago, we know the blonde wasn't involved then. She wasn't even born yet. Where did she come from?"

"I don't know," said Josie. "But she's involved somehow."

"Do you think she's under duress? Maybe he's somehow keeping her as well?"

"It's possible," said Josie. "Maybe there's some kind of brainwashing going on. He convinces her to help him lure these girls, then he sends her out to get the dress for his big finale."

Before Noah could respond, Josie's phone rang. "It's Mett," she said, swiping answer.

"Boss," said Mettner without preamble. "Gretchen and I are over at Moss Gardens trailer park."

"Moss Gardens?" Josie echoed. She had grown up in that trailer park until her grandmother got custody of her.

"Yeah," Mettner replied. He rattled off the trailer number. "You guys are going to want to get over here right now. I've already called the ERT and Dr. Feist."

Josie was aware of Noah glancing over at her since he could hear Mettner's voice coming over the line.

"We've got another one," Mettner added. "Another murder. It looks very similar to the Gemma Farmer case."

THIRTY

Two hours later, Josie stood in a tiny bedroom inside a single-wide trailer in the Moss Gardens park dressed in a Tyvek suit watching Dr. Feist examine the body of Sabrina Beck. Her mother, Portia, was outside in an ambulance. Evidently, she had been so hysterical upon finding her daughter's body that the medics had had to administer Haldol to calm her down. Her shrieks had drawn the attention of the entire trailer park. A neighbor had called 911. Two uniformed officers responded and then quickly called for detectives. Since Mettner and Gretchen were available, they had driven to the scene immediately. Together with the uniformed officers and Noah, they now waited outside the trailer, watching Officer Hummel and his team pack up their equipment after processing the scene.

The ERT had removed the blanket found covering Sabrina and taken it into evidence together with several other items in the room, and now Dr. Feist knelt beside the twin bed and pointed to an inch-long slice in the pajama pants Sabrina wore. They were cotton, loose-fitting, and black with yellow stars on them that were now soaked red. The entire mattress beneath her was soaked through with blood. In the small confines of the room, the coppery smell was overpowering.

"Right here," said Dr. Feist. "Right through the fabric. A clean stab. Just like Farmer."

The stab wound might have been the same, but that was where the similarities ended. An expression of horror was etched onto Sabrina Beck's face. Her eyes were wide and glassy. Her lips stretched back from her teeth, as if she'd been about to unleash a scream.

Josie felt sick. "Check her forearm. Right side. There should be slashes. Scars."

Dr. Feist moved up from the girl's lower body and gently took her right arm. She pushed the long sleeve of the pajama shirt upward toward Sabrina's elbow. "Oh my," she said.

Even though she didn't want to, Josie took a step closer. She expected to see six pink or silvery slashes on Sabrina's forearm but instead, her gaze was drawn to the bruises and abrasions circling her wrist, some old and fading and others angry and red. One particularly red abrasion appeared to be in the shape of a chain link. "She was restrained," said Dr. Feist. "These are newer injuries superimposed over older ones."

She turned the forearm so that Josie could see it. There were no slashes. Yet, Josie was certain that Sabrina Beck's murder was linked to Gemma Farmer and Kelsey Chitwood.

"When I get her on the table, I'll see if her hair's been cut," said Dr. Feist. "It's hard to tell with her in this position. I heard her mother tell Detective Palmer that she went missing from Bellewood. One of the sheriff's deputies who worked the initial missing persons case should be here soon, and I think Detective Loughlin is involved as well. You should go talk to them. Apparently this girl has been missing for several months."

"And she reappeared in her bed tonight," Josie said. "Any chance today is her sixteenth birthday?"

"Find out."

Outside, the entire area in front of the Becks' trailer was awash in police lights. A crowd of onlookers stood alongside the nearest neighbor's trailer, watching as police personnel came in and out of the Beck home. Gretchen and Mettner worked their way through the crowd, likely questioning neighbors to find out if they'd seen someone bring Sabrina home. Josie spotted Noah talking to a sheriff's deputy and went over. As she drew closer, she recognized Deputy Judy Tiercar, a twenty-year veteran of the force that Josie and her team in Denton had found to be a reliable ally in cross-jurisdiction matters.

"It was August the fourteenth," Judy was explaining to Noah. "Her mom, Portia, hadn't heard from her in days so she drove out to Bellewood, to the boyfriend's apartment. Sabrina had been staying there. Several witnesses in his apartment complex confirm that. When Portia got there, the boyfriend was home but Sabrina wasn't there. The boyfriend said she had left that morning, but he thought she was just running out for a breakfast sandwich or something because all her stuff was still in his bedroom: backpack, phone, and a bunch of her clothes. We looked real hard at the boyfriend since Sabrina disappeared from his place. One of the neighbors saw her leave around six that morning but didn't see where she went or if she got into a car or anything. Sabrina's mom insisted the boyfriend had sold her to a human-trafficking ring. We found no evidence of that. We did ask for an assist from the state police, though. Detective Loughlin worked the case. I called her but she's a couple of hours away. The long and short of it is that we thought that Sabrina was a runaway. There was no evidence to support any other scenario and she often fought with her mother, got in trouble at school, had to get therapy because of her unruly behavior. There was no reason not to believe she was a runaway."

Josie greeted Judy. Noah asked, "How old is the boyfriend?"

"Just turned eighteen a few weeks ago. Believe me, we've

had eyes on him since Sabrina went missing. He's got a couple of drug charges, but we haven't caught him doing anything more sinister than smoking weed and speeding in this stupid, souped-up little car he tears around in. Actually, he's the one who brought Portia home tonight. Her car broke down between Bellewood and here. He picked her up on his way to see a friend who lives in East Denton."

"He's got an alibi for tonight then," said Josie.

"Sure looks that way."

"Dad's not in the picture?" asked Noah.

Judy shook her head. "Nope. Listen, we'll get you whatever we have in our missing persons file, but I can tell you it's not much. You should talk to Detective Loughlin."

Noah asked, "You didn't find anything on her phone? Social media?"

"Nothing that would help us find her or make us think something bad happened to her."

Josie said, "What about her friends? Did they say anything about her vanishing?"

"Nothing that raised any red flags, I can tell you that."

Noah met Josie's eyes. Then he looked back at Judy. "Do you remember whether or not her mother or her friends talked about her hanging out with someone new? A new friend, maybe?"

Again, Judy shook her head. "I would have to look at the file or talk with Detective Loughlin, but you could ask her mom. I'm sure she would remember."

They thanked Judy and walked to one of the ambulances. Its doors were closed and an EMT stood guard outside. They introduced themselves and he let them into the cab. Portia Beck lay on the gurney, her eyes drooping. She looked tiny and frail. Her shoulder-length blonde hair was mussed, sticking up in several places on one side of her head. Streaks of mascara had dried on her cheeks. Pale pink lipstick smudged beneath her lower lip. She gave them a slow blink. "You're that detective, aren't you? The one from TV. I bet if you'd had Sabrina's case since she went missing, she'd still be alive. Instead, 'cause she went missing in Bellewood, I got stuck with a bunch of people who didn't know what the hell they were doing. Now look. Look what someone did to my baby."

Josie sat on the small bench next to the gurney and Noah sat beside her. She leaned in toward Portia. "Miss Beck, I'm so sorry for your loss. You're right. You've seen me on television before. Denton is my jurisdiction. My name is Detective Josie Quinn. This is my colleague, Lieutenant Noah Fraley."

Portia nodded. "Those other cops should have called you right away. Maybe my Sabrina would still be here."

"I'm so sorry that she's not, Miss Beck," Josie repeated. "I just talked to Deputy Tiercar who advised me that State Police Detective Heather Loughlin was also involved in your daughter's case. I can assure you that both of them are excellent investigators."

Portia sniffed and shook her head, dismissing the notion that the Alcott County sheriff and state police had done everything they could to locate Sabrina. Josie forged on. "I know this is the worst possible time, but I'd like to ask you some questions."

Portia sat up and lunged toward Josie, grabbing her wrist. "You gonna listen to me? Really listen to me? Not just tell me my baby ran away? You can see she wasn't a runaway now, right? You believe me? You'll listen to what I have to say?"

Josie didn't back away. She held Portia's gaze. "I'm going to listen to every word."

Fresh tears streamed down Portia's face. Josie pulled a clump of tissues from her jacket pocket and handed them to her. Josie said, "Deputy Tiercar tells us your daughter went missing about nine months ago."

Portia nodded, dabbing at her tears with the tissues. "She was staying with that boyfriend of hers 'cause we were fighting.

Always fighting... but I knew she wouldn't just leave. She didn't call me for a few days though, and I got worried and went over there."

Noah asked, "Did she often stay over at her boyfriend's place and not call to check in?"

"Yes," said Portia. "She was a handful. Could never control her at all. I figured she would come back eventually, though. She usually did when she got tired of eating fast food or if he cheated on her. But she never went that long without at least a text message. I got a bad feeling so I went to his apartment and that's when I found out she was gone. I called the sheriff. They said they investigated and told me she ran away even though I told them it was Jonah who did something to her. They say he checked out. Then the state police investigated, and they said he checked out, too. I wouldn't have believed it myself except that he was the one who drove me home tonight."

"Did you notice anything unusual in Sabrina's behavior in the weeks before she went missing?" asked Josie.

"No, nothing I could think of. If I had, I would have told the sheriff or that state police detective."

"What about anyone new she might have been hanging out with?" asked Noah. "A new friend or something?"

"No," said Portia. "Nobody. If I knew somebody, I would have told the sheriff."

Josie took out her phone and pulled up the photo of the mystery blonde who had purchased Gemma Farmer's prom dress. She showed it to Portia. "Do you recognize this girl?"

Portia squinted at the photo and shook her head. "Well, I do recognize her, but I don't know her name. Who is she?"

"We're not sure," said Noah. "Where have you seen her before?"

"She dropped Sabrina off from work a few times," Portia said.

Josie and Noah exchanged a furtive look. Josie asked, "Where did Sabrina work?"

"She washed hair at a salon at that big mall out near the interstate. Oak Ridge Mall. She was only fifteen, so there were limits on how many hours she could work per week, but she got tips sometimes."

"What was the name of the salon?" asked Noah.

"Oh jeez, I don't remember. Avalon? Avalanche? Something like that. There aren't that many salons in that mall. There's probably some paystubs in her room. Is this important? 'Cause no one ever asked me about this girl before."

"We're not quite sure yet," Josie told her. "The girl dropped her off here? Outside of your home?"

"Yeah, right out front. She never stayed. Never came in. I asked Sabrina about her a few times, but she told me to mind my own business. She was so angry at me. Angry at everyone, really. At life. I got her some therapy through her school, but it never seemed to help. She didn't even like going to it. She stopped over the summer. I was going to make her start again when school came back but then she disappeared."

Steering her back to the mystery girl, Josie said, "You saw this girl from your window? Did you notice what kind of car she was driving?"

Portia's brows crinkled as she thought about it. "I'm not so good with cars, but it was black."

"Two doors? Four doors?" asked Noah.

"I'm not sure. Maybe four? I don't know."

"Small, large?" he continued. "Was it a sedan or an SUV?"

"It was a car," Portia said. "Kind of small, I guess? It was a black car. I only saw it a few times."

"If you saw a photo of it, would you recognize it?" asked Josie.

"I'm not sure."

Josie pushed her frustration down. It wasn't surprising that

Portia didn't remember details about the car. Most people didn't live their lives paying attention to seemingly insignificant things. Most things you saw in your daily life you had no need to recall later. "How many times did this girl drop Sabrina off?"

Portia shrugged and used the wad of tissues to dab at her eyes. "Three? Four? I'm really not sure."

Noah asked, "Did you see the license plate?"

"I'm sure I did but I don't remember it. You think that girl had something to do with what happened to my Sabrina?"

"We're definitely going to look into it," Josie told her. "How long before Sabrina disappeared had this girl been giving her rides home?"

"The summer. I only remember her bringing Sabrina home in the summertime, so that would have been starting in June."

"About two months then," Noah confirmed.

"One last question," Josie said. "When is Sabrina's birthday?"

Portia's face crumpled. "It's tomorrow. She would have been sixteen."

THIRTY-ONE

THREE MONTHS EARLIER – CENTRAL PENNSYLVANIA

"How did you get here?" asked Prima

The naked girl sighed and rested her chin on top of her bony knees. "I made a friend. At the mall. She was kind of weird but nice, too. Asked me for help one day in the food court. It was really strange, like she had never ordered food before."

Prima felt the color drain from her face. "I had the same friend. What did she tell you?"

A sigh came from behind the girl's mottled legs. "That I could get away. Go to a great place where I didn't have to listen to my nagging mom or my nasty teachers. No cheating boyfriends or backstabbing friends. It was like a retreat where I could do whatever I wanted for a while with total independence. It was only supposed to be for a couple of weeks. With her. Like a trip or something."

"She told me there were no rules," whispered Prima.

The girl scoffed. "Right. No rules. Pretty dumb to believe it, right? But at first..." She trailed off.

"At first what?" Prima coaxed.

The girl leaned her head down toward her shackled hands so she could scratch at her scalp. "I don't remember."

The exchange seemed to exhaust her. Prima watched her for a few more minutes, waiting for her to say more, but she didn't. On quivering legs, she stood and walked over to the door.

"It's locked," said the girl before Prima even had her hand on the knob. Still, she tried twisting it open. Nothing happened.

"What if we need to use the bathroom?"

"Bathroom runs are every four hours as long as you're in here. You'll get used to waiting."

"Get used to it?" Prima cried.

"If you have an accident, they'll clean it up."

Prima was so horrified, she couldn't get her vocal cords to work right away. She went back to the window and tried to lift it open but it wouldn't budge. The old frame had been nailed shut. Finally, her voice returned. "How long have you been here?"

The girl's frail shoulders lifted in a shrug. "Don't know."

Prima went back to the door and started pounding on it. She hammered against it with both fists until her skin was bruised and her body shook with fatigue.

"That won't work," said the girl.

Prima sank to the floor. "What are they going to do to me?"

"Depends."

Prima looked at her. "On what?"

"On whether you let them take you to the room or not."

"The room? What room?"

Ignoring her questions, the girl said, "First, you have to get your marks."

THIRTY-TWO

The next afternoon Josie and Noah stood in the exam room of the morgue. This time, the shrouded form before them was Sabrina Beck. The Chief had insisted on coming although he stood quietly brooding in the corner of the room. Before Dr. Feist could speak, the door to the hallway whooshed open and in walked Detective Heather Loughlin. Her gray suit was rumpled, and strands of hair escaped her ponytail. She looked as if she hadn't slept. A manila folder was tucked beneath one of her arms.

"I'm guessing Deputy Tiercar told you that Sabrina Beck was my missing persons case," she said without preamble.

Josie nodded. Heather's expression cracked, her professional façade slipping for just a moment. Sadness and distress flashed across her features. "I'm sorry," she said. "I didn't know."

"Know what?" Noah asked. "That there's a serial killer operating in our area right now who, by all accounts, was dormant for approximately twenty-five years before last week? You're kidding, right? How could you have known?"

Heather shook her head. "Portia Beck knew something was terribly wrong. I didn't listen to her—not well enough."

Josie said, "I find that hard to believe. Judy told us that Portia was focused on potential human trafficking, but that neither her department nor yours could turn anything up."

"That's true," said Heather. "I just can't help but think I could have—should have—looked harder." ˎ

"What do you think you would have found?" Noah said. "What else would you have looked at?"

Heather sighed and shook her head. "I don't know. I just feel like I should have seen this coming. But it looked so much like a runaway case. Just like Gemma Farmer. Maybe even more than Gemma Farmer's case because Sabrina routinely fought with her mother. But Portia told me this morning you two were looking at a friend, a blonde girl who had dropped Sabrina off from work a few times. I never even got that information out of Portia in the initial investigation and even if I had, I'm not sure I would have pursued it. I had spoken to all of her friends already. It just never occurred to me..."

"Sometimes we don't know what's important until we do," Josie said. "Did you speak with her coworkers?"

Heather nodded. "I did. It's all in the file. No one raised any red flags at all."

"What was the name of the salon where she was employed?" asked Noah.

"Avalanche Salon and Spa," Heather answered. "At the mall. No one noticed anything unusual about her behavior or anyone lurking around, although she only worked a few hours a week. They said she spent her breaks in the food court. Sometimes a friend would join her."

"A blonde friend dressed in men's clothes?" asked Josie.

"Coworkers said it was a teenage girl. Blonde. They didn't get close enough to give much more description than that. Again, I didn't think it bore more scrutiny or I would have pulled security footage before it was erased. If I had known this blonde girl was important—"

From the corner of the room, the Chief said, "It doesn't matter now, Loughlin. We have to start from where we are and right now, that's getting findings from the good doctor here."

From the other side of the exam table, Dr. Feist gave a grim smile.

"Right," said Heather. She held out the folder to Josie. "A copy of the Beck file."

"Thank you," said Josie. "We'll have a look at this when we finish here."

"Are you ready?" asked Dr. Feist.

They crowded around the exam table as Dr. Feist snapped on a pair of latex gloves and peeled the sheet away from Sabrina's face. Her brown hair was combed down the sides of her face with a part in the middle, but Josie could see where a lock had been shorn away. Dr. Feist pointed to it. "Here is the missing lock of hair, as expected."

She reached across the body and hooked a hand behind Sabrina's shoulder blade. Her other hand fit behind Sabrina's hip and she rolled the girl toward her, onto her side. "I found your slashes," she said, glancing up at Josie. "They're not on her arms."

Josie saw the thin silvery lines immediately at the base of Sabrina Beck's neck and extending down her back. There were six. Gently, Dr. Feist rolled her onto her back again.

"Why her back?" Noah asked.

Dr. Feist shrugged and straightened the sheet on her body. "Your guess is as good as mine."

Josie said, "Because she fought him. He had to restrain her. She's got ligature marks on her wrists."

"Right," said Dr. Feist. She adjusted the sheet to expose Sabrina's arms. "I showed this to Detective Quinn on scene, but here you can see she's got fresh ligature marks over older scars. They're patterned injuries—you can see that many of them match the shape of chain links. You can also see bruising along both arms. Same on her legs and torso. It's consistent with trauma that occurred within the last two weeks. She's also got a healed rib and jaw fracture. I got her medical records from her pediatrician. She did not have a history of fractures, so these had to have occurred after she disappeared. In addition, she's a bit malnourished. She weighed one hundred twenty pounds when her mother reported her missing. When I weighed her, she came out to ninety-eight pounds."

Josie winced. "He starved her?"

"Or she refused to eat," said Heather. "Her mom made no secret of how stubborn she was."

"It's possible," Josie said, "he might have hurt her because she didn't fulfill the fantasy he was trying to recreate."

"You mean she didn't go along with whatever he wanted?" Heather said.

"No, not necessarily," Josie said. "It's certainly a possibility that his other victims were more compliant. We don't know what kinds of threats or coercion he used or is using on these girls. It's possible the other victims were more frightened of him or they believed that if they just did whatever he asked, they would live and get to go home. Maybe Sabrina acted differently, and it set him off, made him more violent. Something was different about Sabrina—for the killer."

Noah said, "Just look at Kelsey and Gemma. Both were in perfect physical condition when they were returned. Other than their fatal stab wounds, they were healthy and well-nourished. They'd even had their favorite foods as last meals."

"Yeah," Josie said. "The killer displays a sick kind of loving care in the way he keeps them."

"He's collecting them," said Heather. "Like dolls."

A silent beat passed. Josie felt a heaviness in the air. She swallowed. "Maybe," she said.

"But at sixteen they're no longer of interest to him," Noah said. "Clearly."

Dr. Feist cleared her throat, reminding them that she was still there.

"Sorry," Josie told her. "We're getting off track. What else can you tell us?"

"There are no obvious signs of sexual assault. No indication of any recent sexual activity of any kind. It appears that she may have been sexually active at some point, but that's all I can tell you."

Heather said, "She had definitely been sexually active with her boyfriend, so that would account for her not being a virgin."

"Stomach contents?" asked Josie.

Dr. Feist shook her head. "Nothing except some fluid and what looked like dissolved Benadryl pills which, of course, I had to send to the lab for analysis."

"What about the stab wound?" asked Noah.

"Almost identical to the one found on Gemma Farmer's inner thigh. A single, efficient stab to sever the femoral artery with a knife. According to my measurements and examination, the blade is likely to be two to three inches in length and one half to five eighths of an inch in width. Single edge, not serrated. She likely bled out in less than five minutes. Cause of death is exsanguination."

"Same as Gemma and Kelsey," Josie mumbled.

"What about the pajamas she was wearing?" asked Heather.

Noah said, "We asked her mom about them when we were on scene. They were Sabrina's pajamas. Her mother thinks she had taken them with her to the boyfriend's place when she was staying there."

Josie added, "Gretchen and Mett tracked him down last night to interview him. He didn't remember what she was wearing before she went missing."

"Officer Hummel took them into evidence," said Dr. Feist. "You'll have to speak with him about whether or not he got anything of use from them. There is one last thing, but I'm not sure how relevant you'll find it."

"We'll take anything we can get," said Noah.

Dr. Feist walked over to the countertop along the back wall and flipped open her laptop. "We found dried blood on one of her temples."

Noah said, "That's not surprising. There was blood everywhere."

Dr. Feist shook her head as she clicked buttons on her computer. "The blood from her stab wound was located under her lower body. She had none on her upper body at all, which makes sense if we're operating under the theory that she was sedated before the killer stabbed her and that he placed her legs together and covered her with a blanket after he severed her femoral artery."

Josie said, "Meaning the blood would have collected beneath the blanket and that Sabrina would not have reached for her leg to try to stop the bleeding because she was already unconscious."

"Yes," said Dr. Feist. She beckoned them over and pulled up a photo of Sabrina Beck's face. Her hair had been pushed back to reveal a smudge of blood about the size of a quarter on her left temple.

Noah said, "She could have gotten blood on her temple from the ligatures. A couple of them look as though they were open."

"True," said Dr. Feist. "Except the blood I found on her temple wasn't human blood."

"What?" said Josie and Noah in unison.

On the laptop, Dr. Feist pulled up a series of graphs. She turned toward them. "This is a new technology they developed at SUNY Albany, so the test will need to be confirmed by the state police lab which is going to take weeks, but all the studies so far have found it to be extremely accurate. It's a rapid test to determine whether blood found at a scene is human or animal."

Heather said, "New technology? Defense attorneys love 'new' technology."

The Chief cleared his throat. Josie had nearly forgotten that he was there. "She's right. You better have an expert in this technology if you're going to use it."

Dr. Feist raised a brow at him. "I am aware of that, Chief. That's why the lab will confirm. But we're part of a trial using this since our area is still pretty rural. I'm working with Hummel. He said you guys get a lot of cases of people hitting things with their cars—especially at night on dark, rural roads—leaving blood, but not knowing what they hit."

"That we do," said Josie.

"What is the technology?" asked Noah.

"Like I said, it helps determine whether blood is human or animal. It can also accurately identify the blood of eleven specific animals. Basically—and I'm going to majorly simplify this for you guys, since I know you're not interested in the nitty-gritty of the science—we scrape flakes of the dried blood onto a crystal and then study the flakes using Fourier-transform infrared spectroscopy."

"I'm sorry," said Heather. "What?"

"An infrared light," said Josie.

"Yes," Dr. Feist agreed. "When the blood comes into contact with the crystal and is scanned with the infrared light, it emits a certain wavelength of light. Each type of blood gives off its own unique wavelength. Using a software program—" Here, she gestured to the graphs on her computer screen. "We can determine first, whether or not the blood is human and second, which animal it came from, as long as it's one of the eleven, within a pretty short amount of time, and we can do it right here in our own facilities instead of sending it out and waiting weeks or months for a result."

"What kind of blood was it?" asked Josie.

"Deer," said Dr. Feist.

"What?" said Heather. "How did deer blood get on her head?"

"It's your job to find out," said Dr. Feist.

THIRTY-THREE

Back at the stationhouse, Mettner and Gretchen sat at their desks, tapping away at their computers. It was late in the evening and Amber had left for the day. Josie, Noah and the Chief joined them, bearing gifts of coffee and pastries because the day was about to get longer than it already felt. Noah handed out coffees and set the plastic container of pastries in the center of their combined desks as Josie collapsed into her chair. The Chief paced round and round their desks, arms folded over his chest, his face an alarming shade of red.

"This can't be good," Gretchen said as she stood and leaned across the surface of her desk to snag a pecan tartlet.

Josie opened the file that Detective Heather Loughlin had made for them, scanning pages, while Noah gave Gretchen and Mettner a rundown of the Sabrina Beck autopsy, including the strange finding of deer blood on her corpse.

"Wherever she was being held, she was around deer blood," said Mettner. "The killer is a hunter, don't you think? The dimensions of the knife that these girls were stabbed with matches the dimensions of many caping knives."

Gretchen said, "What's a caping knife?"

"Part of a field dressing kit," Mettner answered. "Every deer hunter has one. They use the kit for when they have to field-dress—gut—a deer. There are usually a few different items, depending on the type and brand of field dressing kit and where they bought it, but the caping knife is pretty common among deer hunters."

"This killer would be a poacher, though," said Noah. "Deer hunting opens in the fall. The only thing open right now is Spring Gobbler."

Josie said, "We could still be looking at a hunter. A lot of people hunt out of season. If they're on their own property and no one reports them to the game commission, who's to know?"

Mettner said, "A remote property would make a lot of sense, especially if he is keeping these girls for months."

"The problem with that," sighed Gretchen, "is that everyone and their brother and their mother hunts in the area. And if he's doing it without a license, there's no way to track him."

The Chief said, "But you can pull hunting licenses, can't you? From all over the state?"

"We can try," said Mettner. "I can get a warrant for them—at least the ones in Alcott County. The issue is how we narrow that list, because it's going to be long."

"We know this guy was active twenty-five years ago," Josie said as she flipped more pages in the file in front of her. "Assuming that he was, at the youngest, eighteen at that time, he would have to be forty-three now at an absolute minimum. I think he skews older than that though, given the sophistication we saw in Kelsey's case and the fact that she was his second victim, if we're right about the slashes on the victims' arms."

"Right," agreed Noah. "He had her for almost five months. He would have to have had a place and the means to keep her—and any other victims."

"Which puts him probably in his mid-twenties to mid-thirties back then," said Gretchen. "So the age range of hunters we're looking for today would be mid-forties to mid-fifties."

"Take it to sixty," said Chitwood. "Just in case."

Gretchen took out her notebook and began jotting down notes. "I think we should look at hunters in the three counties that touch Alcott County."

Mettner said, "I agree, but just the hunters in Alcott County between forty-three and sixty... that's a lot of guys. We need to narrow that even more."

Noah said, "We can cross-reference with property records. Old addresses. Anyone on the list who has a remote rural property is someone we need to check out. Likewise, anyone who lived in or near Brighton Springs twenty-five years ago is someone else we flag."

"Speaking of Brighton Springs," Gretchen said, pointing to a large stack of papers on her desk, "Lamay and I finished going through all of the people associated with the Chief in any way from back then both in Brighton Springs and in Lochfield. We didn't find anyone who might have had bad blood with Chief Chitwood." She met the Chief's eyes. "At least, none that are still alive. There were a couple of candidates, but they died in prison years ago."

The Chief walked over and picked up the stack of papers. "I'll go through this if you don't mind. Make sure you didn't miss anyone."

"You've seen the list already," said Gretchen. "Is there anyone you had a beef with who isn't on it?"

"Just my father," Chitwood said with a sigh.

Filling the awkward silence, Mettner cleared his throat and said, "Besides looking for hunters and cross-referencing that with rural properties, I think we need to look again at the list we made of other missing persons cases in the county, specifically fifteen-year-old girls who appear to be runaways. I called each department and spoke with the lead investigators.

So far I haven't gotten anywhere, but maybe I missed something."

"I doubt that," said Gretchen. "It's more likely you just need to expand your search. I'd go outside the county. Maybe even look at the whole state, or at least include the surrounding counties."

Mettner already had his phone in hand, tapping away on his notes app. "I'll get on that, along with the warrant for the records of hunters in Alcott and nearby counties."

Gretchen said, "The other thing we should think about is trying to find connections between our two recent victims. If we can find a link between Gemma Farmer and Sabrina Beck, it might tell us how he is selecting them. If we figure that out, we may be able to find him."

Noah said, "The blonde girl is the connection."

"I agree," said Josie.

"Both victims were seen with her at the mall," Mettner said, looking up from his phone. "I think one of us needs to get over there and start showing her photo around the place. Maybe he's using her to select his victims. He sends her out to befriend these girls."

"She's the lure," said Josie. "If we find her, we find him."

Josie's desk phone rang. She snatched up the receiver, listened, and hung up. "Travis Benning—Harlan Chitwood's old partner—is here."

"Shit," Noah said. "I set up a meeting with him. With everything that happened last night, it slipped my mind."

"It's fine," Josie said. "It shouldn't take long. You and I can go speak with him. Gretchen, while Mett works on the warrant and the missing persons list, how about you head over to the mall?"

THIRTY-FOUR

They couldn't take Travis Benning to the conference room since it had been turned into a war room, so Josie and Noah walked with him to Komorrah's Koffee where they took a booth in the back of the café. They knew he was fifty-six from Noah's background search, but he didn't look it. Plump, with a thick head of brown hair and lively brown eyes, he had a kind and youthful way about him. When he spoke, his voice had a soothing quality, almost melodic. Once they were seated with coffees in front of them, Travis folded his hands on the table and smiled at Josie and Noah.

"I have to tell you that I haven't done any police work for over twenty years," he said. "I don't remember much from the cases I worked back then, but I'm happy to help in any way that I can."

"Thanks for agreeing to meet with us," Josie said. "We wanted to talk to you about the Kelsey Chitwood case."

A shadow passed over his features. His smile fell away, his face pinching with sadness. He wrapped his hands around his coffee cup and shook his head. "God, that was terrible. So terrible. I left the department before it was solved. If you're looking into it, I guess that means it was not solved."

"That's right," said Noah.

"Poor Bobby," Travis whispered. He looked away from them for a few seconds, taking in the rest of the café before returning his gaze to the cup of coffee in his hands. "I'm sorry. Bobby was her older brother. More like a father to her, to be honest. Bobby is the police chief here now, isn't he? I've seen him on the news."

"He is," Josie said. "We're aware of his relationship with Kelsey."

"Is Bobby the reason you're looking into it? Kelsey's case is a little out of your jurisdiction."

Josie smiled. "We had a case here recently that shows some similarities to Kelsey's case, so we're taking another look at it."

Travis's gaze dropped to the table. "Similarities," he said. "Like the missing lock of hair? The severing of the femoral artery? Benadryl toxicity? Artificial staging of the body?"

"You remember a lot," said Noah.

Travis met his eyes. "Hard to forget that one, especially since it was so personal. I have to ask—the new case you guys are working on. Does it have anything to do with the Gemma Farmer murder? I saw on the news that she had been identified as the 'Prom Queen' victim, or some such nonsense." Almost as an afterthought, he muttered under his breath, "I hate when the press does that. Gives cases those stupid names."

"Why do you ask?" said Noah.

"She's about the right age. Fifteen. That was also on the news, but the truth is that I met Gemma Farmer before."

"You did?" Josie asked. "Under what circumstances?"

"Like I told you, I haven't been on the force in twenty-some years. I'm a social worker now. After I left the Brighton Hills Police Department, I went back to college and got my master's degree. I've bounced all over the state working for various entities until I took this position as an intake counselor with an outfit called the RedLo Group. They're a non-profit that provides therapy or other interventions for at-risk youth, either for free or on a sliding scale. Gemma Farmer's mother brought her in about a year ago for counseling. I didn't remember her until her photo was released in the press."

Noah said, "You didn't think you should contact our department to let us know you remembered her?"

Travis spread his hands, palms up. "I met her once, maybe twice. I do intake and assign a counselor. The circumstances of her death weren't released in the press. It never occurred to me that she might be connected to a case I worked decades ago in a city three hours from here."

"We knew about the RedLo connection," Josie said, recalling the magnet on the Farmers' fridge. She thought about Heather Loughlin's file. There was no indication that RedLo had even come up. "How long did she get counseling there?"

"I couldn't tell you," said Travis. "We have a lot of kids come and go. Like I said, I only do intake. I see these kids once, maybe twice, and that's it. I'm pretty good with remembering names if I hear them."

Josie thought about how Portia Beck had said she'd gotten her daughter therapy, but it hadn't worked. "How about the name Sabrina Beck?"

Travis took a moment to think about it. "Sounds familiar, yes."

Noah took out his phone and pulled up a photo of Sabrina that Portia had provided the state police and sheriff right after she disappeared. In it, she sat on a couch, swimming in an oversized gray hoodie. Her hair hung loose around her face, mussed, and her smile was strained. Noah showed it to Travis. "Do you recognize her?"

Travis's face fell immediately. "Oh no," he said. "Oh no."

"She was a client at RedLo?" asked Josie.

He closed his eyes momentarily, breathing in deeply, trying to compose himself. When he opened them, he answered, "Yes. She was. I remember her because she was so resistant to being there at all. Don't tell me—is she dead? Was she—what happened to Kelsey, did it—"

He couldn't bring himself to say it.

Josie said, "The circumstances of her death were similar to those of both Gemma Farmer and Kelsey Chitwood."

Noah said, "This information has not been released to the press, so if you wouldn't mind keeping it to yourself."

"Of course," Travis said. "I won't mention it."

Josie said, "Do you remember the last time Sabrina was at RedLo for therapy?"

He shook his head. "I don't. Like I said, I'm just an intake counselor. I know I did intake for both Gemma and Sabrina—I do it for tons of kids—but I lose track of them once they are assigned a counselor. It's their therapist's job to monitor their progress. I only brought up Gemma Farmer because I thought you should know that there was a connection, given the fact that her murder bears similarities to Kelsey Chitwood's. If I didn't tell you, you'd suspect me more, right? You suspect me right now as it is—especially now that you know I'm connected to both Gemma and Sabrina. If I were still on the job, I'd suspect me."

"It does make you worthy of further scrutiny," Noah said.

Josie said, "Then you won't mind us asking where you were yesterday evening? Around eight p.m.?"

"Sure. I run a group for parents of kids with substance abuse problems on Friday evenings at the Episcopal church on Patterson Street in Bellewood. I usually get there around six thirty to set up. Meeting starts at seven, runs till nine."

Sabrina Beck had already been discovered by her mother by nine thirty p.m.

Noah asked, "Do you go right from work to that meeting?"

"I usually grab a bite to eat at Harry's between work and the meeting. I've got a receipt if you'd like it, although the wait staff there know me. They can verify that I was there."

If he ran the group on Fridays, then he would have been there the night of the Denton East prom, around the time that Gemma Farmer was murdered, Josie realized.

Noah said, "We're going to have to contact your coworkers, the wait staff at Harry's and the staff at the Episcopal church to confirm all this."

Travis gave them a weak smile. "Of course. It's fine. Speaking of full disclosure, have you spoken with Harlan yet?"

"I have," said Josie.

"That must have been fun. Did Harlan tell you about me?"

Josie raised a brow. "What do you mean?"

"You should know that I had to leave the police force because I screwed up a case. Majorly. Harlan went to bat for me, got the brass to keep me on for a few more years after that. I'm not even sure why because he knew I didn't like him. I think that he wanted to have something over me so that when he did something illegal I would either look the other way or help him. Anyway, I didn't last. I was pretty universally hated by my coworkers and the public after that. It got too hard so I left. I've been in social work ever since."

Josie tried to think of a screw-up so bad that even his own colleagues wouldn't stand behind him. Police departments tended to be tight-knit communities that rallied around their own.

Noah said, "What kind of screw-up are we talking about, Mr. Benning?"

Travis sighed and shifted in his seat. He gripped his coffee cup again, fingers tapping against the sides of it. "Have you ever heard of the Butcher of Brighton Springs?"

"No," Noah said.

"He was active in the early nineties. He took girls and

he... butchered them. It was—" he broke off. His eyes glazed over, as if he were looking into the past instead of at Josie and Noah. When he resumed, his voice was husky. "It was the worst thing I've ever seen. To this day. We had a task force. It wasn't just me and Harlan, although Harlan caught one of the first missing persons cases associated with him. By the time the fourth girl went missing, the whole department was working on it. I, uh, I made a mistake at a crime scene. Contaminated some pretty important evidence. I was going to get fired but like I said, Harlan intervened. The other guys did their best to build the case anyway but when it went to court, the guy—the Butcher—got off on a technicality."

"The technicality being the evidence contamination," Josie filled in.

"Yeah," whispered Travis. "A killer went free because of my mistake. I, uh, tried to kill myself a few times back then." He let go of his cup, pushed up his shirtsleeves and spread his hands across the table, palms up, exposing thick, gnarled scars that ran vertically down his wrists. "Harlan always brought me back," he continued. "He was a real bastard."

"That must have been hard on your family as well," Josie said as he pulled his arms back and covered the scars.

"It was. Damn near killed my mother. She just passed about ten years ago. My dad died while I was getting my master's degree. I'm glad I never had a wife or kids who had to be subjected to the scandal. It was very stressful."

"You never married?" Noah asked. "Not even after all that was behind you?"

"I was engaged to someone when the Butcher case fell apart. She left me. Since then? The women I've met tend to drop me pretty quickly when they find out I'm a disgraced police officer. I've accepted it, though. The single life isn't that bad. No one to answer to, no one to nag at you, boss you around. You don't have to compromise on anything..." He drifted off as his gaze flitted from Noah's left hand to Josie's and back, noting their wedding bands. "No offense to married people. I'm sure it has its perks."

"None taken," said Noah. "What happened to the Butcher?"

"I don't know," answered Travis. "The Brighton Springs PD kept eyes on him for a long time, until he moved on. Once he was out of their jurisdiction, there wasn't much they could do. To my knowledge, he never killed again—or if he did, he was smart enough not to get caught this time."

Discreetly, Josie took out her phone and googled the Butcher of Brighton Springs. Scanning the top few results, she saw that his name was Corben Thomas and that he'd been thirty-two when he was arrested, which would make him fifty-nine today—in the upper age range of the potential suspect pool that she and her team had come up with. She asked, "Do you think the Butcher could be the one committing these crimes?"

"I don't know," said Travis. "I don't know how he stopped killing unless he just got scared straight, or the public scrutiny was too intense, but he wasn't a one-stab kind of guy, if you know what I mean. He was savage. I still have nightmares about that case. You think you're cut out for police work until you see something like that. Even if I hadn't screwed up at the crime scene, the other guys were always making fun of me. Calling me names. Like, what kind of cop can't stand the sight of blood, right?"

"I guess you don't hunt, then," said Noah.

"The great Pennsylvania pastime? No. Could never stomach that, either. It hurt me in that department, too. All those guys were big-time hunters. I'm sure you two know how that is, living here."

"Was the Butcher a hunter?" asked Josie.

"Yeah, I'm pretty sure," said Travis. "I mean, not after he was released, but before that. Once he got out of jail, he didn't do much but stay in his house. Harlan and I looked at him for Kelsey's murder. Followed him around for a long time. Well, until his attorneys called our Chief and told him to make us stop. We could never link him to it."

Josie tried to remember if the name Corben Thomas had been in any of the documents from Kelsey's official file. It didn't sound familiar. Nor had the Chief mentioned it, and she was certain he would have looked closely at someone called "the Butcher of Brighton Springs" who'd been set free on a technicality. "There was nothing in the case file about him."

"There wouldn't be," Travis said. "Harlan didn't write up any reports. He didn't want the guy's name on paper unless we found something big, like a smoking gun."

"Why not?" asked Noah. "Was he afraid Thomas would sue the department for harassment?"

"Honestly?" Travis said. "I think Harlan intended to make him disappear except that, like I said, we couldn't connect him to Kelsey's case at all."

"How well did you know Chie—Bobby?" asked Josie.

"Not well. We only spoke a few times. He didn't come around much. As you probably know, him and Harlan hate each other, but I felt badly for Bobby, you know? He genuinely loved Kelsey. He was the one who raised her. Harlan never cared about her except when it got under Bobby's skin. Anyway, Bobby came to me for information about her case because he wasn't getting it from Harlan so I gave it to him."

Josie thought about what the Chief had said—how difficult it had been to get case materials out of the Brighton Springs Police Department file room at that time; how she shouldn't concern herself with how he'd gotten all the materials he had. "You gave him things from the file, didn't you?"

He gave a half-hearted shrug. "I suppose there's no point in lying about it now. I guess he didn't tell you in order to protect me, but I'm not even a police officer now so I'm not sure there's a point. Yes, I copied things from the case file little by little until I had a lot and then we would meet so I could deliver them to him."

Noah said, "Why would you do that? You'd already nearly been fired over the Butcher case. Why would you risk something like that?"

He hung his head. Another humorless chuckle escaped his lips. "Lieutenant, in case you haven't figured it out, my entire life since then has been about redeeming myself. I work with at-risk kids, trying to get them on track, keep them safe. I knew I wasn't going to continue being a police officer. It was only a matter of time. To be honest, I thought Bobby had a much better chance of solving Kelsey's case than Harlan. He deserved to know what was in that case file, and Harlan, always needing to control everything and manipulate everyone, was never going to share it. You don't know how bad things were between them. There was this one time at this bar..." He shook his head. "Never mind. I shouldn't say. It's not my business."

Josie knew it wasn't any of her business either, but she couldn't help herself. Curiosity got the best of her. "Tappy's Lounge? 1999?"

Surprise lit Travis's face. "How did you know?"

"The Chie—Bobby mentioned it, although he didn't tell me exactly what happened." She didn't mention that Harlan Chitwood now lived in a hovel over the top of Tappy's Lounge.

There were a few seconds of silence. Then Travis said, "Bobby almost killed Harlan. That's what happened. He came looking for him to discuss Kelsey's case. They got into an argument just like they always did except that it got physical. Bobby beat the piss out of Harlan. Literally. He was hospitalized for two weeks after that. The two departments got involved— Brighton Springs and Lochfield—but neither Harlan nor Bobby would talk about it. Harlan refused to press any charges and when asked about his injuries he just said he got drunk and fell.

I'm not sure why, but he would not throw Bobby under the bus. Everyone knew what really happened. Hell, it was in full view of about forty people, but it was clear that the incident was going to stay between those two so neither of them were ever charged with anything."

Noah said, "Mr. Benning, you know the Kelsey Chitwood case pretty well, it seems. You already talked about one thing that never made it into Kelsey's file. Is there anything else we don't know? Anything at all? Even if it seems inconsequential—"

Travis held up a hand to silence Noah and smiled. "I do remember how investigations work, Lieutenant. Off the top of my head, I can't think of anything else, but I'll take some time in the next couple of days, sit quietly, and try to recall everything I can about Kelsey's case. If I think of something, I'll be in touch. You obviously have my number. If you need anything from me, just call or text, and if you don't mind, say hi to Bobby for me, would you?"

"Just one last question," Josie said, bringing her phone screen to life. She punched in her passcode and pulled up the photos of the mysterious blonde girl in the dress shop. Sliding her phone across the table to him, she said, "Have you ever seen this girl before?"

He studied the photo, picking up the phone and pinching his thumb and index finger against the screen to zoom in. With a frown, he said, "I don't think so, but I see a lot of kids and at most, I only see each one of them twice before they're assigned to their regular counselors. Like I said, I'm better with names. What's her name?"

Josie took her phone back. "We're working on that. How many kids do you see per week?"

"Per week? It could be anywhere between five and fifteen. Sometimes more. There's a great need, and RedLo covers a huge swath of Central Pennsylvania."

Noah asked, "How do you decide which counselor to assign the kids to?"

"I take a complete history and get a grasp on their issues, and then I assign them a counselor based on the child's needs, location, and the counselor's specialty."

"Who was Gemma Farmer assigned to?" asked Josie.

"I couldn't tell you off the top of my head, but I can definitely check when I get back to work. I can look up Sabrina Beck's counselor as well, if you'd like."

"That would be helpful," Josie said.

Noah asked, "Is there anyone you work with at the RedLo Group that you think could be capable of these murders?"

There was a slight hesitation, so fleeting that Josie almost missed it. Just a quick twitch of his lips, as though he was going to blurt out a name and then stopped himself. He said, "I truly hope not, but you two know probably better than me that it's almost impossible to tell what people are capable of until you see it with your own eyes."

THIRTY-FIVE

They left Travis Benning at Komorrah's and walked slowly back to police headquarters. Josie's mind reeled. It seemed like every time they followed one lead, it led to ten others, and yet none of them brought them any closer to finding the killer. The string of bizarre associations grew exponentially with each new bit of information. It was a lot to contemplate. An hour earlier, the Brighton Springs Butcher hadn't even been a whisper of a thought. Now, they had to consider him. Harlan and Travis had never ruled him out; they'd simply stopped trying to connect him to Kelsey's murder. Given the fact that all three victims that they knew of—Kelsey Chitwood, Gemma Farmer, and Sabrina Beck—had died from a stab wound, and Travis and Harlan had worked on a case called the "Butcher of Brighton Springs"; as well as the fact that the Butcher's victims had been girls and Harlan had once suspected him enough to harass him, Josie had no choice but to try to track him down. The connection was tenuous, but after the mysterious blonde girl had slipped through the cracks in both the Gemma Farmer and Sabrina Beck investigations, Josie wasn't about to let any lead, no matter how dubious, sneak past her.

"What do you think of Travis Benning?" Noah asked.

Josie sighed. "I don't know. It's too much of a coincidence that he worked the Kelsey Chitwood case twenty-five years ago and that he also knew Gemma Farmer and Sabrina Beck. I mean, what are the odds? You said he lives in an apartment in Fairfield?"

"Yeah," Noah said. "From the background check I did, it looks like he's been there about eight years. I can check on his employment history. Take a closer look."

"We also need to look very closely at his property records," said Josie. "I don't see how he could successfully keep a teenage girl captive in an apartment for a long period of time, much less two of them at the same time, assuming he held them both at the same place. I'm sure it's possible but it likely wouldn't be easy. We need to see if he's got property elsewhere—a cabin or some type of rural getaway. Also, check out his family and see if there are any rural properties in his parents' names. We need to verify his alibi for both murders, as well."

As they came to the front doors of the police station, Noah pulled on one of the handles, gesturing for Josie to go ahead of him. "Will do. How do you want to handle the RedLo Group?"

Josie waved to their desk sergeant, Dan Lamay, as they passed through the lobby. "I'm going to call Diana Farmer and Portia Beck and see if they can tell us the names of their daughters' counselors. It might be faster than waiting for Benning to look it up."

They climbed the stairs to the great room. Mettner was still working at his desk. Noah brought him up to speed on the interview with Travis Benning. Josie checked her phone for any texts from Gretchen about her progress at the mall. Noah sat down at his desk and turned on his computer. "I'll work on tracking down the Butcher and do a deep dive on Travis Benning's employment and property records."

Plopping into her own chair, Josie made a quick phone call

to Diana, who confirmed that Gemma had been getting services from RedLo when they lived in Keller Hollow, but said that she couldn't remember the name of Gemma's therapist. All the paperwork from that period of time in their lives was still packed away in a box. Josie asked her to find it and call back. Next, she contacted Portia Beck who confirmed that Sabrina had been receiving services from RedLo via her school. She didn't remember the name of Sabrina's therapist either, as she had stopped going to RedLo about three months before she disappeared—which would have been a year ago—but she promised to try to find the paperwork. Josie could very likely get a warrant for RedLo's records given that both their victims had had the same intake counselor there, but she wanted to gather as much information as she could beforehand. If the killer was someone else who worked at the RedLo Group, then Josie didn't want to tip him off before she had some sense of his identity.

After she wrote up a report detailing her and Noah's interview with Travis Benning, Josie started preparing a warrant for RedLo's records pertaining to Gemma Farmer and Sabrina Beck. Once she got the name of their therapist or therapists, she could add that information to it, but at least it would be ready. While Noah kept searching for everything he could find on both the employment and property records of Travis Benning as well as the Butcher of Brighton Springs, Josie drove to Belle-wood and dropped in at Harry's restaurant as well as the Episcopal church where Travis Benning claimed to be every Friday evening.

All his alibis checked out. The restaurant even had surveillance of him for both evenings in question.

Josie arrived back at the stationhouse at the same time as Gretchen. Together, they tromped up to the great room. As they sat down at their desks, Gretchen blew out a breath. "I got nothing at the mall. A few regular employees at the food court and in other stores recognized our mystery blonde. They said they've seen her hanging around for a little over a year now. No one paid her any mind. As the manager of the pizza place said, 'Finding teenagers in a mall is about as shocking as finding fish in a pond.'"

Josie pinched the bridge of her nose between her thumb and forefinger, trying to stave off the headache that had begun behind her eyes. "Travis Benning's alibis for the nights Gemma Farmer and Sabrina Beck were murdered check out."

"Really?" Noah said.

Josie nodded. "I don't know why, but I kind of felt like he was lying to us. There's something not right about him."

"He's too helpful," said Noah.

Mettner piped up. "He's former law enforcement. That's probably why he seems too helpful."

Gretchen frowned. "Anyone want to tell me who the hell Travis Benning is and why we're looking into his alibi?"

"Sorry," said Josie. "Long day."

She explained that Travis Benning had been Harlan Chitwood's partner at the time of Kelsey Chitwood's abduction and then her death. She and Noah recapped their conversation with him at Komorrah's and all the information he'd given them, including the story about the Butcher of Brighton Springs case and the fact that he had a connection to both their victims.

Gretchen said, "Did you show him a photo of the mystery blonde? Did he recognize her?"

"Yes, and no," Noah answered. "Speaking of her, none of the people who saw her frequently at the mall ever spoke to her?"

Gretchen shook her head. "No one reported ever having spoken to her. A couple of Sabrina's coworkers at the Avalanche Salon and Spa remember seeing her with Sabrina in the food court and once in the mall after Sabrina went missing, but that was all."

Josie asked, "When's the last time anyone saw her there?"

Gretchen took out her notebook and flipped a few pages. "About three to four months ago. An employee from the taco place in the food court saw her. Alone. We went through all the footage that was still available—only going back one month—from inside the mall and the parking lots. We couldn't find her on video."

"But the mall has to be the killer's hunting ground," Mettner said. "Don't you think? The blonde is like bait in a trap. A lure. She befriends these girls, gets them to trust her, and then she brings them to him. We know she has a vehicle now, according to Sabrina Beck's mom."

"The mall is where he sets the trap," Josie said. "But I don't think that's where he selects them."

"If not the mall, then it's gotta be Benning," said Mettner. "If he's the intake counselor, that's how he meets them all. He selects a certain one and then he gets the blonde to do all the legwork."

"That's exactly what I thought," said Noah. "A lot of the pieces fit. Benning was living and working in Brighton Springs when Kelsey Chitwood went missing and also when she was found murdered. He worked both the missing persons and the murder case alongside Harlan Chitwood, which would have made it easy for him to manipulate evidence."

"Except the Chief conducted his own investigation," Josie said. "And he didn't find anything more, or different, than his dad and Travis did. We know that for sure now because we've seen the official file. There's nothing in there that the Chief hadn't seen before except the fingerprint report from the church pews which is essentially worthless. There were only two prints that came up as being in AFIS—one belonging to a nineteen-year-old girl and the other to a thirty-seven-year-old sex offender, and that sex offender has been in prison for the last five years so he can't be behind this."

Noah said, "Benning still could have easily removed things from evidence or from the case file."

"Yes," Josie said. "He could have found a way. But he's got alibis for the nights of the murders. Solid alibis."

Gretchen said, "Maybe the blonde does the killing."

No one said anything.

Finally, Noah said, "Okay, let's say he chooses them, sends this brainwashed girl out to lure them in, he keeps them for some amount of time and then he has her kill them. Where does he keep them while they're missing? His former addresses put him in the right geographic regions for all the murders at the right times, but he doesn't own any real estate at all. From what I can tell, he never did. He's always lived in rentals. I've checked each address with Google Street View and they're all in pretty congested areas. There were a couple of rentals that were houses but it's been twenty-five years since Kelsey was murdered. We wouldn't find any evidence in those now. For the last several years, he's rented an apartment in Fairfield which he's lived in since he moved to this area."

Gretchen said, "You can hold someone against their will in an apartment. I've seen it."

Noah said, "Sabrina was missing for nine months."

"And for nine months she was restrained," Gretchen responded.

Mettner said, "Noah's right, though. Gemma Farmer was gone for four months. They overlap. Keeping two teenage girls in an apartment at the same time without anyone getting suspicious could be pretty difficult."

Gretchen said, "What kind of apartment are we talking about, though? The one in Fairfield? Is it in a complex where a lot of people come and go and he's got neighbors on both sides of him and across the hall, or is it an old house that was converted into two or three apartments where he can come and go without being seen often and the number of other tenants who might hear any noise he makes is limited?"

"I looked it up," said Noah. "And did a Google Street View. It's a complex with thirty units. He lives on the second floor. Just like you said, he's got neighbors on both sides and across the hall and below him."

Josie said, "We should still pay him a surprise visit. Get a real look at the place."

"Definitely," Mettner agreed. "But I'm more interested in this Butcher. What did you find out about him?"

Noah grimaced. Leaning back in his chair, he put his hands behind his head, lacing his fingers together. "It's a horrible cautionary tale about the kind of devastating damage shoddy police work can do. He had his own house. Lived with his mother, who was, at the time of his crimes, bedridden with ALS. He was supposed to be caring for her but when the police finally found him, linked him to the missing girls, and went into the house, she'd been dead for weeks. He left her decomposing in her bed."

"Good lord," Gretchen said, letting out a low whistle.

"It gets worse," said Noah. "Between 1990 and 1994, he kidnapped four girls between the ages of eleven and fifteen and he quite literally butchered them, according to the reports I found. Only one survived. The early reports of his capture don't say anything about Benning or evidence being compromised, but in 1996 when he went to trial, the case was thrown out and Benning's name was released to the press. Looks like it was a pretty big shitstorm after that. The DA tried to pin Butcher's own mother's death on him, but the ME said in his autopsy report that she died of natural causes."

"That's a disgrace," Gretchen said. "I can't believe they let Benning stay on the force as long as they did if he screwed up a case that important that badly. Harlan Chitwood must have had a lot of power."

Mettner added, "And Brighton Springs must be even more corrupt than we initially thought."

Josie thought about Detective Meredith Dorton biding her time in the small annex trailer behind the main police building, banished there for blowing the whistle on just a tiny part of Harlan Chitwood's corrupt and damaging behavior over the years. "It is," she said. "Noah, Travis said that he and Harlan kept eyes on the Butcher until he 'moved on,' so he must have stayed in Brighton Springs for some period of time after his trial."

"The balls on that guy," Gretchen said. "Can you imagine? He must have gotten off on it."

"Probably," Noah said. "Looks like they razed his house once he was arrested. No one wanted to buy it, I guess."

"Understandable," said Mettner.

"But he still sold the land to a developer. He didn't get much for it at all, but it looks like he took that money and bought a cabin in the woods between here and Brighton Springs sometime in 1998."

"A cabin?" Gretchen said. "In the woods? Close to here? This is fitting some of the criteria we talked about before."

"Except there's no way this guy would be working for the RedLo Group," said Mettner. "Who's gonna let him work with kids?"

"Right," Noah said. "When he failed to pay his property taxes on the cabin from 1998 through 2001, his house was put up for a tax sale, at which time the county sheriff found the place vacant. A woman named Lorna Sims bought it at a tax sale for a song."

"Personal effects?" Josie asked.

"Gone," said Noah. "It made the local news: *'What Happened to the Brighton Springs Butcher?'* No one ever reported seeing him again. It became a pretty big focus of online true crime buffs. There's a Reddit thread devoted to him that goes on forever."

"He could still be alive," Mettner pointed out. "People have been known to change their names, take on false identities. He could have invented a whole new persona in the years between then and now. It could be him."

"Except for the RedLo Group connection," Josie pointed out. "I think that and finding the mystery blonde at the mall are our best leads right now."

The Chief's voice made them all jump. "For now, some of you need to go home and get some rest."

They all looked over to see him leaning against the wall outside of his office. How long had he been there listening, Josie wondered? She'd been so caught up in all of the new directions the investigation had taken that she'd forgotten to check in with him or check on him. He met her eyes and said, "I heard it all, Quinn. I agree that your focus should be on the mall and on this non-profit. But all of you have been chasing this thing like rabid dogs going after a steak—which I..." he coughed, as if he were choking on what he wanted to say, "...which I appreciate. Split up again. Two of you go home and rest and eat while the other two keep working. Rotate."

"We'll go home first," Noah volunteered. Josie opened her mouth to protest but clamped it shut the moment she saw the withering look on the Chief's face.

"Back at it in the morning, Quinn," he told her. "Maybe drop by Travis Benning's house before you come in tomorrow."

THIRTY-SIX

The surprise visit to Travis Benning's apartment wasn't as much of a surprise as Josie had hoped. It wasn't even possible to enter the building without being buzzed in. Once she pressed the button marked: *Benning, 2-H* and announced that she and Noah were outside, they had to wait a full five minutes for Travis to buzz them inside. Then it took another five minutes to get up the stairs and find his place.

"He's had ten minutes," Noah groused as they walked down a long, carpeted hallway on the second floor, searching for 2-H. "Plenty of time to hide evidence."

"Evidence of what?" she whispered. "He's got alibis for the nights of the murders."

"He could still be working with the mystery blonde, Josie. He could have abducted the girls and kept them."

The sounds of conversations, televisions, microwaves beeping, and phones ringing came from every direction of the hall. "I don't know," Josie said. "The walls are so thin here. If he had been keeping teenage girls against their will, all it would take would be one good scream, and the whole building would know something wasn't right."

The door to 2-H hung open slightly. From inside came the smell of coffee and eggs. Josie knocked on the door jamb and called out for Travis.

"Come on in," came a voice from inside.

Travis's apartment was even smaller than Josie imagined. The door opened into a living area that was only large enough for a single couch, a coffee table, and a television across from it. A thin metal transition strip separated the living room carpet from the kitchen tile. A small kitchen table took up most of the room. Travis was squeezed between one of the chairs and the stove, a spatula in his hand. He looked up and smiled at them. "I'd offer you some, but I'm kind of in a rush. Have to get to work. By the way, I found the name of the therapist."

"Mind if I use your bathroom?" asked Noah.

Josie knew he was only asking so he could get a better look at the rest of the apartment, not that there was much more to it.

"Sure," said Travis, using his spatula to point to a small hallway to the left of the living room. "Down the hall. There are only two doors. It's the room with the toilet in it."

Noah walked off. Josie asked, "The therapist? As in the same person for both Gemma Farmer and Sabrina Beck?"

"Exactly. It's the same guy. Kade McMichaels. He's out of the main office in Bellewood."

Josie committed the name to memory. "Do you know him well?"

"Not that well," Travis said. "He's kind of prickly. With the staff, anyway. Parents and patients never complain about him. I guess he saves all his manners for them."

"You don't like him?"

Travis shook his head and used the spatula to push scrambled eggs around a frying pan. "Not that much, but in our work it doesn't really matter whether I like him or not. I'm not the one getting therapy from him. Next you're going to ask if I think he looks good for the murders. I don't know. I mean, he's the right age, I guess. I think he's in his late forties, early fifties, but is he capable of kidnapping and killing girls? I don't know."

"We'll check him out," Josie promised as Noah came back into the kitchen. While Travis flipped his scrambled eggs onto a plate, Noah gave her a quick, almost imperceptible shake of his head. He hadn't seen anything out of the ordinary. Josie added, "If you wouldn't mind not talking to Mr. McMichaels about this issue, we'd appreciate it."

"Of course," he said. Directing his gaze toward Noah, he smiled pleasantly. "Find what you were looking for?"

Gamely, Noah smiled back. "Yeah. Thanks."

In the car, Josie said, "He knows what we were doing today. Dropping by unannounced, you looking around his place."

Noah put his seat belt on and turned the ignition. "Like he said, he knows how these things work."

"You didn't find anything?"

Noah shook his head and pulled out of the apartment complex parking lot. "Nothing concerning, but again, if he had some kind of incriminating piece of evidence lying around, he had a good ten minutes to hide it from plain sight. That said, that place is very small. One bedroom. I could hear his neighbors arguing through the walls when I poked my head into it. We're not getting anywhere with this guy. You think it's him?"

Josie shook her head. "I don't know. I don't see how it could be and yet, he's shown up in three cases, twenty-five years apart. You had a chance to look at his property and employment records, right? Anything there?"

"No red flags," Noah said. "Benning doesn't own any rural mountain getaways that would be perfect for keeping kidnapping victims. His employment history is unremarkable. He's been working at places just like RedLo between here and Lochfield since he got out of college."

"Maybe Mettner is right, and the mystery blonde girl is the missing piece in all this. In the meantime, we should definitely look up this therapist, Kade McMichaels."

She didn't wait for them to get back to the stationhouse, instead using the mobile data terminal to look him up while Noah drove. "Well?" Noah said after fifteen minutes. "Does he fit the criteria?"

Josie scrolled through her results. "He's fifty-two. Has two vehicles registered to him: a 2018 Nissan Rogue and a 2006 Chevrolet Malibu—oh wait, that's a salvage title."

"So he owns it but, according to the Commonwealth of Pennsylvania, it's not roadworthy because it won't pass inspection," Noah said. "That doesn't mean he's not driving it around illegally—or letting someone else drive it around illegally."

"Like our mystery blonde?" Josie said.

"Right. Plus, it's still a sedan. What color is it?"

Josie ran her finger across the computer screen until she found it. "Tan. Not black." With a sigh, she kept perusing every bit of information she could find on Kade McMichaels. "He lives between Bellewood and Denton."

"So probably rural," said Noah. "Those houses out there aren't close together."

"I'll Google Street View it in a minute. He's been here eleven years. Guess where he was before that?"

"Brighton Springs," said Noah.

"Close. Pittsburgh. Then Lochfield."

"He would have been in college at least some of that time, though, right? Where's his degree from?"

"University of Pittsburgh," Josie said. "He's got a master's in social work, just like Benning. Okay so it's not a perfect fit, but it's pretty close."

She used her phone to pull up Google Street View and inputted Kade's address. "This is interesting," she said. "It looks like he has maybe nine or ten acres of land so there's a buffer between him and his neighbors. There's a house directly across from his which looks like it has a pretty good view of the front of his place. It's not as rural as I imagined for this killer, but I think still feasible that he could have girls on his property without anyone knowing. I don't see any evidence that he's married or has any children."

"I guess no criminal record," Noah said. "Or they wouldn't let him work with kids."

Josie shook her head. "He's clean on paper." She read off the address. "Why don't we swing by?"

Fairfield, where Travis Benning lived, was about forty-five minutes from Kade McMichaels' house. Josie and Noah stopped there, pulling into the gravel driveway that was void of cars. The house was only one story. Its tan siding was clean. The flower beds around it were neatly kept. Although Josie didn't expect anyone to answer, she knocked loudly several times. They both listened to see if they heard anyone calling out from inside, but there was only silence. They walked the perimeter of the house, finding nothing out of place. Behind the house was a detached garage that looked new with its red brick and bright white doors. Noah was tall enough to look through the windows of the garage doors.

"From here, I see a lot of tools, a riding mower, and what looks like a car under a vinyl cover. Probably the salvaged Malibu. Still, this is a big structure. We'd need to get inside to see the rest."

"Maybe I can get a warrant for his house and garage, if we get the files from RedLo proving beyond a doubt that he's got connections to our two latest victims," Josie said. "I didn't get too far with the property records, but I'd like to do a more extensive search to make sure he doesn't own any additional properties, like a hunting cabin or something."

In her pocket, Josie's phone buzzed. She pulled it out to see the Chief's name flash across the screen. Swiping answer, she said, "Chief?"

"Quinn, we just got a call from a mall employee who thinks she saw the mystery blonde in the food court this morning. I need you and Fraley to meet me over there ASAP."

THIRTY-SEVEN

By the time Josie and Noah pulled into the Oak Ridge Mall parking lot, the Chief was calling her again. As she and Noah got out of the car and hurried inside the nearest mall entrance, Josie answered.

"Quinn," he shouted. "Where the hell are you?"

"We're here now," she said. "Coming in through the entrance near the arcade. Did you find her?"

"No, but I'm in the security office now. We've got her on video in the food court this morning. She might still be here. I've already got mall security covering all exits, as well as searching the parking lot for a small black sedan. I need you two inside looking for this girl. I've also called in some uniformed units from our department and asked for an assist from the sheriff's department, but they're still a few minutes out."

"What's she wearing?" Josie asked.

"Blue jeans, brown boots, boxy brown jacket. Everything oversized."

Josie hung up and dropped her phone into her pocket. She waved at the mall security guard as she and Noah rushed through the doors. A wide hall with storefronts on each side led

into the central area of the mall. Josie briefed Noah while they
walked. As they emerged onto the concourse, Josie realized they
were on the second floor. "One of us is going to have to go
downstairs."

"Where's the food court?" asked Noah.

"Not sure, come over here." She jogged over to a mall direc-
tory, scanning it as quickly as she could "Downstairs, all the
way at the end."

"That seems to be where she has been seen the most times,"
Noah said. "One of us should start there. Or start on this end
and work our way there."

"I'll go," said Josie. "You search up here. Once the
uniformed officers show up, the police presence is going to be a
lot more noticeable which could spook her, so let's cover as
much ground as quickly as we can."

"You got it," said Noah. He reached down between them
and gave her hand a brief squeeze before she sprinted away,
down the first set of stairs she found, onto the first floor. The
inner ceiling of the mall was glass, allowing great shafts of
sunlight to slice through the cavernous space. As she dashed
through the first-floor concourse, she had to shade her eyes from
time to time so she could see ahead. She panned each store and
center kiosk as she went, eyes trained to pick out blonde hair.
Luckily, since it was mid-morning on a weekday, there weren't
many shoppers or even mall walkers crowding the building. A
salesman at a kiosk that offered some sort of miracle anti-aging
cream tried to flag her down for a demonstration. Instead, Josie
showed him the photo of the girl and asked if he'd seen her.
Puzzled, the man said no. Josie ran off before he could get
through his second spiel about why she needed his wonder
lotion.

The myriad smells of the food court reached Josie's nose
before she found it. It was circular in shape, food counters
jammed side by side surrounding a large area of tables, chairs,

and trash cans. Here it was far more crowded, almost every table filled. Lines amassed outside of each establishment. It was louder as well. Josie didn't even hear her phone ring. She was only aware of the vibration of it in her pocket. She tore her gaze away from the crowded food court only long enough to see Noah's name on the screen. "Did you find her?" Josie asked right after swiping answer.

"Not sure. I think it's her. If it is, she's headed your way. I'm upstairs but I can see her from here."

Josie looked behind her. "Where? What store is she near?"

"She's passing the Spur Mobile store right now. I see a bunch of kiosks ahead."

"I know where that is," Josie said. "Heading that way."

Quickly, she texted the Chief: *Center kiosk area. First floor.* Then she sprinted back the way she had come. The kiosk salespeople were aggressive. Surely one of them would try to stop the girl, to try to sell her copious amounts of their products. Maybe not the miracle face cream man, Josie thought, since the mystery blonde was so young. Maybe the sunglasses or jewelry kiosk minders. Sweat pooled at the base of Josie's spine but she didn't stop to take off her jacket. It was the only thing covering up the gun at her waist, and she wasn't sure how the girl would react to that. She didn't want to scare her off.

The miracle lotion salesman signaled to Josie as she approached the area. A quick glance above revealed that Noah was searching frantically. He caught her eye and lifted both hands as if to say he had lost her. "Miss, please," said the salesman.

Josie opened her mouth to rebuff him but he clamped his mouth shut, widened his eyes, and gave a stiff nod toward his right. Then he mouthed, "The girl."

Looking over, Josie spotted the girl, caught between the sunglasses and the cell phone case salespeople. She was waving both women away—or attempting to. Josie strode over.

"If I could just show you this case," said one of them. "It's got all kinds of features. What kind of phone do you have, honey?"

"We've got sunglasses for any style. You can try on any pair. It looks like you've got a more... masculine style. I think I've got something you'd really like," said the other.

"No, no," mumbled the girl, speeding up.

Josie noted the heavy boots on her feet that looked too large for her—like the kind men on construction sites wore. Baggy jeans bunched at the tops of the boots and disappeared beneath a brown button-down corduroy shirt whose collar dwarfed the girl's slender neck. It was just as the Chief said—everything she wore looked too big for her. Her blonde locks were tied up in a messy ponytail. She carried nothing with her and from what Josie could see, wore no jewelry, which made her a prime target for the salesperson at the next kiosk which boasted several glass cases of costume jewelry.

"Miss? Miss?" called the man. "I've got a necklace that would go perfectly with that shirt."

Josie stepped between the man and the girl, plastering a big fake smile across her face. "There you are!" she said to the girl. "I've been looking all over for you."

The girl's eyes bulged. For a split second, Josie thought she might bolt. Quickly, Josie turned to the man and said, "I'm sorry, but we can't talk right now. My sister has an appointment, and we can't be late."

Josie beckoned for the girl to follow her and she did, until they were out of earshot of the jewelry salesman and away from the kiosks. Then the girl stopped in her tracks. Josie halted as well, turning back to face her.

"What do you want?" said the girl.

"I want to talk to you," said Josie. From her periphery she saw Noah moving along the concourse above them, keeping watch. His phone was pressed to his ear.

"About what?" said the girl. "I don't know you. You don't know me."

Josie took a step closer, taking in the girl's features. Her eyes were dark brown, hair a flaxen blonde, thin and wispy. A smattering of freckles covered her nose and cheeks. Josie thought about how one of the sales associates from the dress boutique had said she had "dead eyes," but now, face to face with her, they looked wary, suspicious, not dead.

"I don't know you, that's true," said Josie. "But I think you knew—or at least met—two girls who used to come to this mall."

The girl dropped her chin down to her chest and speed-walked around Josie, but Josie caught up to her easily, walking alongside her. From the corner of her eye, she saw two uniformed sheriff's deputies approaching from one of the halls that led out to the mall exits. "Gemma Farmer and Sabrina Beck," Josie said. "You knew them. You bought Gemma a dress and you gave Sabrina rides home from work. I need to talk to you about them."

The girl stopped in front of a bookstore and narrowed her eyes at Josie. "Who are you?"

"What do you think?" Josie asked.

"I'm not going to talk to you," she replied. "I don't have to talk to you. I know that."

"That is true," Josie agreed. Behind the girl, more uniformed officers approached, wearing Denton PD uniforms. "But it really is in your best interest that you do talk to me. Why don't you tell me your name? Mine is Josie. Josie Quinn."

The girl studied Josie for a beat. "You look familiar. You that cop who's on TV all the time?"

"I'm a detective, yes, and I have been on television many times. Do you watch a lot of television?"

The girl nodded. "I like to watch television. I saw Gemma's picture on television."

"Yes," said Josie. "We had to put her photo on television

because we needed help solving her case. I think you could help a lot with that. What if the two of us went into the food court and sat down and talked? Just the two of us?"

"I can't."

"Why not?" asked Josie.

The girl slid her hands inside the overly long sleeves of her shirt. "I can't talk to anyone I'm not supposed to talk to."

"Who told you that?"

The girl gave a half-shrug with her right shoulder. "I can't say."

"Can you tell me your name at least?" asked Josie.

"Only if I can leave," said the girl. "I know you can't keep me here. You can't make me stay here."

"Where will you go?" asked Josie.

"Can't say that either."

"Who told you these things?" Josie said, trying to keep her voice calm and casual and not belie the frustration she felt.

The girl shook her head, eyes cast downward, her face lined with disappointment. "I can't say that. Why aren't you getting the picture? Now, I have to go."

"Your name," Josie said. "That's all I'm asking right now."

"They call me Daisy," the girl said reluctantly.

Josie smiled. "Daisy. How old are you?"

Confusion blanketed her face. She said, "I have to go now."

But as she turned away from Josie, she was met with a wall of uniformed police officers both from the sheriff's office and Denton police. She didn't turn back around but Josie heard her words. "You can't keep me here."

Josie said, "No one is going to hurt you, Daisy. We just need to talk. If you need us to call a parent or guardian to come be with you, we can do that before anything else happens."

"I've already said too much," whispered Daisy.

In the blink of an eye, she spun on her heel and charged at Josie, both her hands connecting with Josie's sternum, knocking her off balance. Josie stumbled backward, arms flailing in an attempt to stay upright. A Denton officer lunged forward, catching her before she fell as the other officers surged past her in pursuit of Daisy. Their boots thundered across the linoleum as they pushed past a handful of shoppers who had stopped to watch the spectacle play out. Josie sprinted after the other officers, her mind working through the layout of the mall, trying to determine where Daisy might be headed. She might be able to get lost in the crowds of the food court but eventually they'd catch up to her.

Shoppers and mall walkers froze in place and watched the stampede of police officers chase a frail teenage girl. Several of the uniformed officers yelled for her to stop and freeze, but she kept running, zigzagging around unsuspecting patrons and mall planters filled with greenery. She passed a large fountain and one of her hands shot out, tossing something into the water. Josie heard shouting among the other officers. Someone stopped to retrieve what Daisy had discarded. Josie kept going.

Daisy hung a left at the food court, weaving through packed tables. As Josie caught up to the rest of the officers, she watched Daisy bump into several diners and accidentally knock people's meals to the ground. She kept running even when angry bystanders jumped from their seats and hollered after her. Snaking through the tables in no discernible pattern, with people leaping from their seats as she passed by, she caused a commotion throughout the entire food court. Josie lost sight of her among the crowded tables.

The other officers appeared to have lost her as well. On either side of Josie, they stopped or slowed, eyes searching the crowd, their gaits hesitant. Some muttered into radios clipped to their shoulders. There was no exit from the food court, Josie thought, but there was a hall, off limits to patrons, that ran along the back of each establishment. Josie panned the signs above each food counter. In the center of them was a small red neon sign that read: *Restrooms* and beneath that: *Employees Only.*

"This way," she called to the officers nearest her and took off in a dead run. Just as she reached the hallway beneath the two signs, she saw a flash of brown fabric and blonde hair disappear into the women's room at the end of the hall. As Josie reached the door, a young mother and her toddler walked out, hand in hand. The toddler paused in the doorway to point to some unidentified stain on the tile.

"Excuse me," Josie said.

Annoyance creased the woman's forehead until she looked past Josie to the approaching wave of police officers. Scooping her child into her arms, she stepped aside. The bathroom had five regular stalls and one accessible stall. It smelled like urine, feces, and some sickly-sweet industrial cleaner that only made the combination of smells worse. Josie's sneakers stuck to the tile as she walked, making a sucking noise each time she took a step. Water was splashed across the countertop that held a row of sinks. Ribbons of toilet paper littered the floor. Two of the seven stall doors had handwritten signs taped to them reading: *Out of Order.* Three others were closed.

"Daisy," Josie called. "No one is going to hurt you. We just want to talk."

Josie squatted down to see if any feet were visible below the stall doors but there were none. Behind her, she heard the whoosh of the door. In the large mirror that ran the length of the bathroom wall, she saw two uniformed Denton officers slip inside, their weapons drawn. Josie pressed her index finger to her lips and then held it out to them, indicating for them to be quiet and give her a moment.

"Daisy," she tried again. "I know this is scary, but you've really got nowhere else to go. Because you pushed me and ran from us, I'm afraid we'll have to take you back to the station, but I promise that no one will hurt you."

One by one, Josie checked the closed stalls, pushing each door inward. The last closed stall was larger and wider, made for people who used wheelchairs. The door opened outward. "Daisy?" Josie said. "I know you're in there. I'm going to open the door so we can talk."

Keeping her body angled away from the center of the stall opening, Josie slowly pulled the door open. In the two seconds it took for Josie to register Daisy perched with both feet on the toilet seat like some kind of gargoyle, the girl jumped toward the stall opening. She turned away from Josie when she crossed the threshold but pulled up short when she saw the uniformed Denton officers blocking her exit. Josie let the stall door swing closed.

"Daisy," she said. "Please come with us. We just want to talk to you."

Spinning, Daisy lunged at Josie. A high-pitched screech tore from her throat as her body slammed into Josie's, sending Josie flying backward. Josie's shoulder smashed into the hot air hand dryer affixed to the wall. She wrapped her arms around Daisy, struggling to keep her flailing fists from striking, but the girl was strong and wild, almost feral in her desperation to hurt Josie. Their fused bodies lurched to the side. Josie's lower back smashed into the edge of the countertop. Then her head bumped something small and hard. Water sprayed down the back of her neck.

Daisy made another sound that was more animal than human as Josie fought to keep them both upright. The entire thing happened in only seconds, but it felt like an eternity before the other officers pried Daisy away from her.

Breathing hard, Josie watched two of them carry her off, arms cuffed behind her. Craning her neck, Daisy peered over her shoulder. Josie expected to see rage in her eyes, but there was only fear.

THIRTY-EIGHT

TWO MONTHS EARLIER – CENTRAL PENNSYLVANIA

Prima woke to weak morning light seeping around the blinds. Her mouth stretched open as if to scream, but nothing came out. That's how it was now. Her sleep was fitful. She always startled awake, on the edge of a primal howl that was trapped inside her. She lived in a waking nightmare with a strange, naked girl at the foot of her bed who accurately predicted everything. Like the marks. Prima sat up and gingerly touched her right forearm where she had been slashed seven times in her sleep. They were still red and crusted over but healing more each day. Prima wondered if they would scar. The naked girl had them too, on the back of her neck, but she had only received six.

"What are these for?" Prima had asked her during one of the long, interminable days when nothing happened except that they were provided food and bathroom breaks.

"I don't know," said the girl, sounding more weary than usual.

Now, Prima looked over at her, sleeping soundly, a heap of bones and skin. Once, Prima had covered her with a blanket in her sleep. For that, the girl had received a beating and Prima had been denied a day's worth of meals.

The sound of the doorknob rattling startled Prima, but it also sent an irrational hope soaring through her heart. When she wasn't pitying herself and her roommate, she fantasized about being rescued. But this time, it was the man again. They'd met before but she didn't dare bring that up. She was already terrified by the fact that he didn't wear a mask. Prima had seen enough crime dramas on television to know that once the kidnapper showed you his face, you were as good as dead.

He closed the door behind him and made a show of tiptoeing over to the bed, like they were conspirators of some kind, trying not to wake the other girl. He stood over Prima, smiling.

She felt sick.

"We need to talk about something," he said.

"I don't want to talk," she mumbled, looking anywhere but at his face.

"But this is very important," he said. "It's time for you to go to the room."

"I don't want to," blurted Prima, at once regretting it.

His expression morphed, sadness replacing his smile. He looked meaningfully at the sleeping girl on the floor. "I can't make you," he said. "But think about it. Think about what will happen to you if you don't."

THIRTY-NINE

At the stationhouse, Josie felt the collective excitement like a vibration in the air. The item that Daisy had tossed into the fountain turned out to be a cell phone. It had been retrieved from the fountain and placed in a bowl of rice on Josie's desk in the great room. While Josie prepared a warrant to get the phone powered on and a separate warrant to search it, Noah and the Chief stood behind her chair, observing the phone, as if it might start spitting out information at any moment. Josie knew they were all desperately hoping that the rice would work so they could peruse the phone's contents as soon as possible, rather than spending a week or more trying to determine the phone's carrier and then serving that carrier with a warrant for records. Once they had their warrants signed, as long as the phone powered on, they'd very likely be able to get into it using a Gray-Key, which was a machine that would allow them to bypass the need for any password that Daisy might have set.

Whatever was on that phone could break the case wide open.

Gretchen and Mettner came in early to be briefed on all the developments, and then the Chief sent them right back out to assist in finding the small black sedan that Portia Beck had seen Daisy driving. A single car key had been found in one of Daisy's jacket pockets when she was taken into custody. The assumption was that she had driven to the mall, but there were well over one hundred cars in the parking lot. It didn't take Gretchen and Mettner very long to locate the sedan in question, but they'd needed a warrant to search it, which had taken more time.

Josie got the warrants to power up and search the phone signed and then she had Hummel retrieve it so that he or another member of the ERT would be able to periodically check to see if it would power up. Then she went down the hall and sat at a table in a room next to one of their interrogation rooms. When Gretchen finally called with news about the car, Josie nearly dropped her own cell phone in her scramble to answer.

Gretchen said, "There's no identification in this car. In fact, there's almost nothing in it at all. We found a knife and a shit-ton of empty Cinnabon containers, some loose change, and a hair tie."

With her free hand, Josie patted her hair. It had dried hours ago, but she still couldn't shake the feeling of damp that seemed to cling to it. She hadn't fallen on the floor of the mall restroom, but she still felt as though she couldn't get the stink of it off her. Trying to push the phantom smells out of her mind, she turned to the large CCTV monitor. In the adjoining room, Daisy sat calmly at a scarred table. She didn't speak, even when Noah entered and offered to get her something to eat. But once he had left the room, she took several sips from the water bottle he had left for her.

"A knife? Like a caping knife?" Josie said. "Single edge, not serrated, measuring two to three inches in length and one half to five eighths in width?"

"A caping knife like the kind you'd find in a deer hunter's

field dressing kit?" asked Gretchen. "Boss, I don't think this kid is a hunter."

"We're in Central Pennsylvania, Gretchen. "Lots of kids hunt. Even girls."

"No, this isn't a caping knife. This is a two- to three-inch blade with a dull tip and a sharp gut hook. Mett says it's used to gut deer."

"Yeah," Josie said. "I know the kind you mean. If someone had used that on Gemma Farmer or Sabrina Beck, there would have been extensive tissue damage from when the killer pulled the knife out."

Gretchen sighed. "We're bagging it anyway. Hummel will see what he can get from it. Prints, DNA, anything that can tell us where it's been."

"What about the license plate?" Josie asked.

"Stolen from a car in Fairfield three years ago. Guy left his car in his driveway one night and the next morning the plate was gone. He reported it missing right away and was issued a new plate."

"VIN?" asked Josie.

The Vehicle Identification Number would tell them everything they needed to know about the vehicle, including its previous owners.

Gretchen sighed. "We've only got a partial VIN. Someone scratched off a good portion of it—in all the places it could be found. We're trying to find a match, but it might take a while. In the meantime, Hummel's having it impounded and he'll process it for evidence."

The door to the room opened and the Chief walked in. For a moment, he stood and watched Daisy on the CCTV screen.

"What kind of car is it?" Josie asked.

"A Chevy Malibu," Gretchen said. "But I can't tell you more than that. Not without the VIN."

Josie felt a jolt. Kade McMichaels owned a salvaged

Malibu, only it was tan. Was it a coincidence that the vehicle Daisy had been driving was also a Malibu? It wouldn't take much to get someone to paint the vehicle black—or even to do it himself. "How's the paint job?" asked Josie.

"Not great."

"We might have Kade McMichaels' vehicle there."

"The RedLo therapist?" Gretchen asked.

"The very same. I looked him up. He's got a salvaged Chevy Malibu registered to him, 2006. Tan."

"Send me the VIN, will you?" Gretchen said. "Mett and I will see if we can match it up. You talk to McMichaels yet?"

"I plan to as soon as I'm finished here."

They agreed to keep each other posted and Josie hung up. Daisy hadn't moved.

While Josie pulled up Kade McMichaels' information again and texted the VIN of his Malibu to Gretchen, the Chief paced behind her. "What do you think of this kid, Quinn? You talked to her at the mall."

Noah came into the room, closing the door behind him and leaning against it. He watched the Chief walk back and forth across the small space with the steady rhythm of a metronome.

"She's definitely odd," Josie replied. "Something is…"

"Off," Noah filled in. "She hasn't spoken since we took her into custody. She had nothing on her person except for a single car key and thirty dollars in cash. That was it. No identification."

Josie said, "We've got a couple of issues here. One is that we don't know who she is and she won't tell us—so far. We digitally printed her when we brought her in, since technically she's in custody for assaulting an officer, but she's not in the system. Two, is that we don't actually know her age. She appears to be a minor, but we can't tell for sure, and she wouldn't tell me when I spoke with her at the mall."

"We need to call Children and Youth Services then," said Noah.

"Agreed," said the Chief. "We also need to check statewide missing persons reports to see if she matches up with any of them."

"Children and Youth Services could help with that," Noah said.

"Call them," said the Chief.

Noah left. The Chief continued to pace. Josie said, "If she is a minor, and I believe that she is, we cannot talk to her without her parent or guardian present. Not while she's in our custody for an alleged crime, and not if she's considered a suspect in the Farmer and Beck murders, which means she's going to sit in there until Children and Youth send someone over or we figure out who she is and get in touch with her parents or guardian, and if we can't..."

The Chief stopped walking and pointed to the camera. "Look at her, Quinn. Do you really think she even understands what's happening to her?"

Daisy sat unmoving, back straight, both palms face down on the table in front of her, looking directly ahead. Now, Josie saw the "dead eyes." It wasn't that there was nothing behind them; it was more like she had gone to a place inside her own mind that was so real to her that she had left her present reality altogether. But Josie thought about the conversation they'd had in the mall. *You can't make me talk to you. You can't keep me here.*

"I think she understands some things. Things that were maybe told to her, but I'm not sure she understands the entirety of the situation."

"If Children and Youth Services come and we can't figure out who she is or where her parents or guardians are, they'll take her into protective custody."

"Well, she needs a psychological evaluation for certain," said Josie.

The Chief walked over to the table and leaned down so he was face to face with Josie. His breath smelled of coffee. "Go in there, Quinn. Try one more time."

"Chief, I can't talk to her—"

"I'll record it. Just explain to her what's happening and see if she'll tell us her full name, where she came from, anything. Once she goes into state custody, there's going to be a whole ton of red tape between her and us. She's our only lead, Quinn."

"She's not our only lead," Josie pointed out. "There's still Kade McMichaels, the therapist from the RedLo Group who treated both Gemma Farmer and Sabrina Beck before they went missing. He lives in a semi-rural area, and he lived near Brighton Springs at the time that Kelsey went missing. He's in the right age range. Noah and I stopped at his house today— that's where we were when you called. There is even a chance that the sedan Daisy was driving is registered to him. Gretchen and Mett are looking into it now. When we're done here, I'm going to finish writing up my warrant for the RedLo Group and his files and then I'm going to pay him a visit."

"Quinn," the Chief said. "I'm asking you, one more time, to go in there and just try to get a last name from her. Anything we can use to identify her. Don't ask her anything else. Nothing about the cases or where she's been or how she's getting around or any of that stuff. If she's got parents out there looking for her, and we can get them in here before Children and Youth take her into custody, we might have a chance at getting her to talk."

Josie saw the desperation in his face. With a sigh, she put one hand on his shoulder and gently pushed him back. Standing up, she said, "Record every second. I'm not kidding."

"I know," he said.

Daisy's face remained impassive as Josie entered. The only indication that she noticed Josie at all were two blinks. Rather than sit across the table from her, Josie walked around the table and sat beside her. Daisy used her feet to inch her chair away from Josie, putting two feet of space between them.

"Daisy," Josie said. "Do you understand what's happening right now?"

She focused in on Josie's face. "You arrested me because I pushed you, and now I have to stay here."

"Yes," Josie said. "That's right. A lot of what happens to you from this point on depends on your age. Can you tell me how old you are?"

Daisy said nothing.

"We know that you drive, so you must have a driver's license, which makes you at least sixteen. Is that right? Or are you older than that?"

Still, Daisy did not respond.

Josie waited a long minute before trying again. "Okay. I'm just going to explain to you what happens now. Because we believe that you are a minor, we have called Children and Youth Services. Do you know what that is?"

"Yes."

"They're going to take you into protective custody until we have more information about you, like your full name, date of birth, address, the names of your parents. They'll keep you in their custody until things get sorted out, legally. If we find out that you are not a minor—that you are eighteen or over—then you can make your own decisions as to how to proceed in terms of hiring an attorney or taking on a public defender to help you navigate the legal process."

Another long moment passed. Josie glanced at the camera, knowing the Chief was watching her get precisely nowhere with this girl. Josie was about to give up when Daisy said, "There is no license."

"Okay," Josie said. "You've been driving without a license?"

Daisy nodded.

With everything in her, Josie wanted to follow this line of

questioning, especially since Daisy had finally volunteered something, but she had to be careful. She couldn't break the law by interrogating the girl if she was a minor with no parent or guardian present. She said, "What about your age? Can you tell me how old you are? It's really important, Daisy."

Josie saw the faintest flicker of uncertainty flash in the girl's eyes. She bit her lower lip and then said in a small, childlike voice, "I don't know how old I am."

"Okay," Josie replied, again wanting to ask follow-up questions she knew she could not ask in this situation.

"Can you tell me your last name?"

No response.

"How about your address?"

She shook her head. Josie could see the faraway look returning to her eyes. She was shutting down again.

"Is there anyone we can call for you, Daisy? Anyone you would like to call yourself? You are allowed to make a call."

"I can't. I don't know the numbers."

"That's okay," Josie assured her. "I could help you. Are there numbers in your phone? We have it. We're waiting for it to dry. I can get numbers from your phone if you want."

When Daisy didn't speak, Josie continued, "Or you could tell me the name of a person you'd like to call. I can look them up if I have a name."

Silence fell between them again. Josie waited, counting off the seconds as the clock on the wall ticked them down. Daisy stared directly at her, but Josie knew she wasn't seeing anything in the room. She stood to leave. Her hand was on the doorknob when Daisy said the last thing she would utter for the rest of that day.

"I don't know his name."

FORTY

Kade McMichaels was tall and sturdy and, with his crisp suit, shaved head, and intense brown eyes, he looked like he belonged behind the coaching bench of a sports team rather than a desk at the RedLo Group. The non-profit took up the first floor of a four-story, historic red-brick building in the center of Bellewood, the Alcott County seat. McMichaels' office was deep inside the building, through a maze of halls painted a bland yellow. As they followed him there, Josie saw Travis Benning at a desk inside a room marked "Intake Counselor." He met her eyes but didn't acknowledge her or Noah.

McMichaels closed his office door and gestured for Josie and Noah to sit. Two wingback chairs and a small couch surrounded a narrow coffee table. Josie and Noah took the couch and McMichaels positioned himself across from them in one of the chairs. He rested his right ankle on top of his left knee, leaned back and regarded them with a wary smile. "Denton PD, huh? I'm surprised to see you guys. Usually when one of our kids gets in trouble, it's the state police or the sheriff we hear from. What can I do for you?"

Josie slid the warrant across the table. "You'll see from the warrant that we're requesting a number of records. We'd also like to talk to you about Gemma Farmer and Sabrina Beck."

He put his right foot on the floor and leaned forward to take the warrant, but he didn't look at it. "I'm sorry, who?"

Noah said, "Gemma Farmer and Sabrina Beck. They were clients. You were their therapist."

"Those names don't sound familiar," Kade replied, "but I have an extremely large caseload. We all do. I might have seen them, but I don't remember off the top of my head."

Josie said, "The last time you saw Gemma would have been sometime last year, well over four months ago, at least, and with Sabrina, that time period is longer—roughly a year."

He held the warrant between his thumb and forefinger. His other hand rubbed at his bald head. "Like I said, I don't remember. In this business, five or six months, a year, that's an eternity. I can barely handle my current caseload, let alone worry about kids who never came back. I'd help you if I could."

With that, he slid the warrant back toward Josie and Noah. Smiling insincerely, he said, "I'm really sorry."

Noah let out a long breath. With deliberate movements, he placed an index finger on top of the warrant and slowly pushed it back toward McMichaels. Mirroring the man's fake smile, Noah said, "You've got records. Check them."

McMichaels remained still, a phony smile plastered on his face. "If those two girls were patients of mine, then yes, I have records. But Detectives, you both know there are privacy laws in place that prevent me from disclosing anything personal or private about my clients."

Josie said, "Gemma Farmer and Sabrina Beck are dead."

She noted the reaction from McMichaels—a stiffening of his posture, two rapid eyeblinks, and a hard swallow.

Josie went on, "We're investigating their murders. Our investigation supersedes the privacy laws in this case. That's a warrant, signed by a judge. You're required by law to honor it."

Again, he picked up the warrant and made a show of reading it, slowly. Josie was aware of sounds from outside of McMichaels' office, elsewhere on the floor: muffled voices; a radio playing indistinct music; phones ringing, and the hum of what sounded like a printer or copy machine. Finally, McMichaels said, "I can get these ready for you. If you come back—"

Noah cut him off. "We'll wait."

McMichaels sighed. "It might be a while."

"We have a while," Josie assured him. "But before you get started, let me ask you, where were you the afternoon and evening of May sixth?"

He raised a brow. "I don't remember. Why—"

Noah interjected, "How about May twentieth?"

His answer came more slowly this time. "I don't—I don't remember. I'd have to check my calendar, but other than being here at work, I'm usually home."

"Do you live alone?" asked Noah.

Two more quick eyeblinks. "Uh, yeah. Why are you asking me this?"

Josie said, "The better question is why haven't you asked us about our homicide investigation? We came here with a warrant for records pertaining to two of your former clients and you haven't even asked us what happened. Why is that?"

He gave a slow smile and shook his head. "Oh, I see. You think because I'm not crying and quaking in my boots that I had something to do with those girls' deaths?"

"Murders," Noah corrected. "Both girls were held against their will for several months before they were brutally killed."

"Okay, okay," said McMichaels. "Look, I know I'm coming off as insensitive, but I've been doing this a long time. I see a lot of kids come through here. Most of them are beyond help. We're a non-profit. We offer free and sliding scale services. This isn't a place you come because you need help. This is a place you end up at because you have no money to pay for a therapist who isn't overwhelmed with patients. A lot of our kids? They end up here as part of a court-ordered sentence for some crime they've committed. A fair percentage of our kids die by suicide in spite of our efforts. Then there are kids who come for therapy because their parent or guardian or some well-meaning school administrator insists on it. They do the bare minimum, leave and end up in trouble. The kind of trouble that gets them killed. You think you're the first detectives to show up here because a couple of our kids got killed? Last week the sheriff's office was in here for a boy who got shot by his drug dealer. The kids who want help? The kids who listen to me? I'm here for them. I remember them. They're important to me. I can turn their lives around. But the rest of them? Again, I don't want to sound cruel —I'm being realistic—but with a lot of these kids, all my efforts are wasted. It's not that I don't care that these two girls you've mentioned..."

He drifted off, looking from Josie to Noah and back until Josie finally filled in the names, her face hot with anger at his callousness. "Gemma Farmer and Sabrina Beck."

"Right," he went on. "It's not that I don't care that they were murdered, as you say. I'm very sorry to hear it, and my heart goes out to their families, but Detectives, I just don't see how this concerns me."

Josie risked a furtive glance at Noah, and she could tell by the muscle twitching in his jaw that he was just as angry as her. He said, "Mr. McMichaels, both girls were killed in the same way. In fact, the similarities in their cases suggest we might be dealing with a serial killer. The only connection we can find between the two girls is you."

McMichaels' eyes blinked rapidly again. Josie counted the blinks. Four. His chuckle came again but this time with a note of nervousness. "Me? That's absurd. Because I was their therapist? I told you, I've got an extremely large caseload. I've seen hundreds of kids in the last two years. It may seem meaningful to you that they were both clients of mine, but I can assure you that it's just a coincidence. RedLo serves a very wide area. It shouldn't be surprising that they were both former clients."

Noah said, "You own a 2006 Chevrolet Malibu, correct?"

Five blinks. "I don't understand," he said. "Why are you asking me about my car all of a sudden? I thought you were here about my former clients."

Josie answered his question with one of her own. "When is the last time you drove your Malibu?"

McMichaels cleared his throat. "Not for years. I have a salvage title on it."

Noah said, "So it just sits... in your garage?"

"Yeah. It sits in my garage. So what? What does my old car have to do with anything?"

"A 2006 Chevy Malibu," Josie said. "That's not a classic car."

"So?" McMichaels' voice rose in pitch slightly.

Noah picked up on Josie's line of questioning. "Why bother with a salvage title? Why keep the car?"

"Because it was never totaled. I drove to Pittsburgh one weekend to see a Pirates game. It got stolen. My insurance company paid out for a new vehicle. About a year later, the police found it and returned it to me but by that time the insurance company had already written it off as a total loss. I had to take a salvage title even though there was nothing wrong with it. It runs fine. I meant to get it retitled but I just haven't gotten around to it. Happy? Or is that not nefarious enough for you two?"

"Have you painted it since you got it back?" asked Josie.

Three blinks. "No. I told you. It sits in my garage."

Noah asked, "How long ago was that Pirates game?"

"I don't know. Four years? You don't already know? You seem to know everything else about me. Look, are you going to accuse me of something, or can we finish up with... whatever this is?"

Ignoring his questions, Josie took out her phone, pulled up Daisy's mug shot, and showed it to McMichaels. "Have you ever seen this girl before?"

He took a second to compose himself, pulling in a deep breath and straightening his posture. Still, there were those tell-tale rapid blinks.

"Mr. McMichaels?" Josie coaxed.

The warrant crinkled between his fingers. "No," he said. "Should I?"

Josie put the phone away. "Does the name Kelsey Chitwood ring a bell?"

She expected him to end the meeting or complain about their questions once more but instead, he leaned back in his chair again and shook his head. "No. Should it?"

"How about the Butcher of Brighton Springs?" asked Noah.

He laughed, although behind it, Josie could hear an undertone of anxiety. "The what? Did you say Butcher?"

Josie said, "Mr. McMichaels, do you hunt?"

His gaze snapped toward Josie, and she could see by the way his expression faltered, like a mask slipping off-kilter on his face, that their rapid-fire questions and the sudden change in subject had thrown him off. Again, he tried to contain his agitation, taking three deep breaths before answering, "Doesn't everyone around here?"

"What do you hunt?" asked Noah.

"Is this relevant?" he responded, this time with a note of weariness. "I don't understand what's going on here."

"Lieutenant Fraley asked what you hunt," Josie said, being purposely obtuse. "I think he means do you hunt small game? Deer? Turkey? Bear? That sort of thing."

"Uh, deer mostly. Sometimes small game."

"Archery?" Noah asked. "Or rifle? Or both?"

"Rifle," answered McMichaels.

"Me too," Noah said, even though Josie couldn't recall him hunting the entire time she'd known him. "Where do you hunt? Here in Alcott County?"

"Sure," he said. "Yeah. Usually."

"When you lived in Pittsburgh, did you hunt there?" Josie asked.

He opened his mouth to answer and then clamped it shut. There were two more beats of silence. He stood up and waved the warrant in the air. "I'll get these records for you. If you don't mind waiting out in the reception area."

FORTY-ONE

"Can you believe that guy is a therapist for troubled teenagers?" Noah said as they drove back to Denton, Kade McMichaels' files on a flash drive tucked inside a pocket of Josie's jeans.

"According to him, it doesn't seem like the kids who get services through RedLo have much choice in the matter," she replied. "They're stuck with him. I guess if you're one of the kids he thinks he can help, he treats you well, but otherwise I wouldn't want to be his client."

"Which is terrible," Noah said. "That guy is a jerk. Benning was right. He was downright hostile and definitely hiding something."

"I agree," Josie said. "The question is what? A string of abductions and murders stretching back twenty-five years, or something else entirely?"

"He got pretty flustered when we asked him about the car," Noah pointed out. "Speaking of which, if Daisy was driving it around, then how was it in McMichaels' garage when we were at his house this morning?"

"You didn't actually see it," Josie pointed out. "It had a cover on it. We just assumed that's what was under it."

Noah shook his head. "We need to get onto his property—inside the house and the garage."

"If Gretchen and Mett can link the sedan Daisy was driving to McMichaels, and if we can get her phone powered up and find out she's been in contact with him, or we can get another shot at questioning Daisy and she gives us something on him, then we can get a warrant," Josie said.

Back at the stationhouse, the Chief paced the great room in a steady rhythm. Round and round the four detectives' desks he went. Only Mettner was seated there, a pen between his teeth, his brow wrinkled as he focused on his computer screen. "Phone won't power up yet," he said before either of them could ask.

"You get anywhere with that VIN?" said Noah, as he and Josie took their own seats.

The Chief didn't acknowledge them, continuing his circuit, but he answered for Mettner. "No, he hasn't."

Mettner waited until the Chief circled behind him before rolling his eyes. "I'm doing the best I can. How about you guys? You get anywhere with McMichaels?"

Noah recounted the conversation while Josie plugged the USB drive into her computer and pulled up the files that McMichaels had provided. The Chief stopped walking, grabbed Gretchen's chair and wheeled it over to Josie's desk. He sat down and used his legs to propel himself closer to Josie, their armrests bumping against one another.

"Personal space," Josie said to him.

Noah and Mettner froze in place, both of them staring at Josie and the Chief, as if waiting for the Chief to explode at her. A few weeks ago, Josie would have expected the same. He didn't like to be told what to do. He didn't like to be told anything, really. But since then she'd been in his garage, heard his life story, been stuck in a car for hours with him, and dragged his whiskey-soaked ass off the floor of a church. The invisible barrier that normally kept her from stepping on his toes was gone.

He said, "What about personal space?"

Josie elbowed him. "Stay out of mine, that's what."

"We don't have time for that nonsense, Quinn," he said, almost at his normal shout, but he scooted his chair away from her a few inches, giving her room to maneuver her computer mouse and keyboard.

She was aware of Noah and Mettner staring at them as she pulled up the files on the USB drive. The Chief didn't notice. He was too intent on the screen, pointing a finger toward the file marked *Farmer, Gemma*. "Open that one first," he said. "Print all this stuff out. I want to read it myself."

Josie began opening documents and sending them to the ancient inkjet printer in the center of the room.

Noah asked, "Where's Gretchen?"

"Impound lot," said Mettner. "She's at the evidence processing unit there with Hummel. She wanted to be there when he went over the car."

Josie said, "What about Daisy? Did Children and Youth Services come yet?"

"They're in holding with her now," said the Chief. "I made it clear that we needed to talk with her, but those people won't be rushed."

Noah stretched his arms over his head with a groan. "It feels like we're close to finding something that will break this wide open."

The Chief stood up and walked over to the printer to retrieve some of the records pertaining to Gemma Farmer. "Then we keep working," he said. "Until we find it."

Hours passed. They worked in relative silence, only stopping to eat takeout that Mettner ordered for them. Josie and the

Chief read over the Gemma Farmer and Sabrina Beck records. Each file painted the picture of a girl who was unhappy, somewhat rebellious, having academic difficulties and strained relationships at home, in spite of their parents' efforts. Neither the Farmer nor the Beck household was without problems, but all of the reports and documents Josie read showed parents who were trying to get their daughters the assistance they needed. There was nothing in either file that helped their investigation. Kade McMichaels' notes were sparse and matter-of-fact.

Josie was printing out McMichaels' client list when Gretchen returned with news that Hummel had pulled what prints he could from the interior and exterior of the car and put them through AFIS. Both Gemma Farmer and Sabrina Beck's prints had been found on the interior and exterior of the car, but that wasn't surprising. They already knew that Sabrina had been in the car. That Gemma also had was new information, but it didn't bring them closer to solving the case.

They needed more.

The Chief put them on a rotation again, sending Josie and Noah home for the night while Gretchen and Mettner kept working. The last thing Josie felt like doing was resting, but she knew there wasn't anything they could do in the middle of the night.

She and Noah were fast asleep with Trout snuggled at their feet when Josie's cell phone rang. It was five a.m. Mettner's face flashed across the screen, lighting up the darkened room. Her voice was groggy when she answered. "What's going on?"

He sounded like he'd spent the night mainlining coffee. "We've got big developments," he said.

"Daisy's phone powered up? You got into it?" Josie croaked, the fog in her head clearing as hope sailed into her heart.

"Oh, no," Mettner said, the excitement in his tone fading a bit.

"What is it?" Josie asked.

"I matched the VIN. The car that Daisy was driving was Kade McMichaels' Chevy Malibu. Boss, did you hear me? The mystery girl was driving McMichaels' car!"

FORTY-TWO

It was after eight in the morning by the time Josie and her team reached Kade McMichaels' house. They arrived in a convoy—Josie and Noah; Gretchen and Mettner; the Chief; two uniformed Denton PD officers; and Hummel and his colleague Jenny Chan from the ERT in one vehicle with two of their other team members in another. It had taken some time to prepare the warrant and have it signed by a judge as well as to rouse the ERT and inform the Alcott County sheriff that they'd be serving a warrant in their jurisdiction. Josie didn't know what time Kade McMichaels arrived for work, but he wasn't home when they knocked at his door and announced their intentions. Josie waited a few minutes and then tried again. Still there was no response and no sounds from inside the house. She looked over her shoulder, past the crowd of her colleagues bunched at McMichaels' front stoop, at the Chief.

"He's at work. We could call him—or even go get him," she said.

"No," said the Chief. "We don't need his permission to force entry. Do it."

Josie sent Gretchen and Mettner around to the rear of the

house in the event that someone was inside and tried to escape that way when Josie's team came through the front door. Josie, Noah, and the Chief stepped aside and two of the uniformed officers came forward with a battering ram. Moments later, they entered Kade McMichaels' house. They worked in silence, moving with assurance, looking through every drawer, under every piece of furniture, in every closet. McMichaels' house was the unremarkable abode of a single man. Sparsely furnished, nothing overly personal, not too messy but not sparkling clean either. Mail sat unopened on his kitchen table. The trash bin needed changing. An empty beer bottle sat alone on the coffee table in his living room. Beneath his television was a video gaming system with a mass of tangled wires bursting from each side of it. Facial hair shavings peppered his bathroom sink like discarded confetti. A towel lay in a heap on the tile floor. In his bedroom, the bedclothes were rumpled. Several work shirts were draped haphazardly over the top of a chair in the corner of the room. Another empty beer bottle stood on his nightstand.

He had one spare bedroom which appeared to be used mainly for storage. A few boxes were stacked along one wall containing clothes, old textbooks, and various extension and charger cords. There were two dust-covered printers on the floor in front of the boxes, their cords coiled around them like thick black snakes. Josie noted a vacuum, a bicycle missing its front wheel, and a gun safe. Beyond all of the mess was a futon mattress on the floor. Josie catalogued the items scattered across it, her heartbeat tapping like a drumbeat in her chest. A crumpled UPitt blanket, a pillow, men's clothes—a white T-shirt, a pair of jeans, a brown corduroy button-up shirt. Next to those was a pair of what looked like women's underwear, white cotton, with a tiny white bow on the front of them.

Although she was wearing gloves, Josie resisted the urge to touch them. "Hummel!" she yelled. "Spare room!"

Stepping closer, she leaned over the pillow, searching the white pillowcase until she found the telltale blonde hair.

"Hummel!" Josie hollered again.

From behind her came Noah's voice. "He's out in the garage. You've got to get out there. It's important."

Josie motioned toward the futon mattress. "More important than this?"

She turned and looked at Noah's face. Rarely had she seen him so pale. "Okay," she said. "I'll go to the garage. Get Chan or someone else from the ERT and have them take this stuff into evidence. I need photos of everything first. The clothes and bedding will need to be processed for DNA. There are some strands of hair, blonde, that may belong to Daisy."

Noah nodded.

She left him in the spare room and made her way out of the house and around to the rear, where the garage stood. There was a little wobble in her knees when she saw that almost everyone who had come with them was gathered around one of the bay doors. They parted to let her through. Inside, the smell of gasoline, sawdust, and cut grass mixed together, making an unpleasant odor. The bay was empty except for some oil stains in the center of the concrete. To her left was the other bay where the vinyl car cover had been pulled back to reveal a four-wheeler, a tractor, and a snowblower all bunched together. She looked back at the oil stain. That was where he had kept the Malibu all along. That's why the space was empty. She had seen the tire ruts along the side of the house, likely from him parking his new vehicle there daily. It was much closer to the house than the garage.

Over the machines, Josie saw the backs of several people's heads: Hummel, Mettner, and the Chief. They were looking down at something. Josie's heartbeat got louder in her ears with each step she took toward them. Inside the vinyl gloves she wore, her palms were sweaty. As she rounded the four-wheeler, she saw that McMichaels had built a two-tiered wooden shelving unit into the wall. Tools and hunting supplies took up the top tier. Mettner pointed a gloved finger at a set of knives with bright orange handles.

"This is a field dressing kit," he told the Chief. "You've got your skinning knife, a boning knife, a bone saw, and a caping knife... the only thing missing is the gut hook knife which we found in the car Daisy was driving. It's safe to assume that that knife came from this set."

Hummel said, "We'll bag these and process them, see if there's a way to match the set to the gut hook knife from the car. Looks like the same brand, but we'll also check for prints and see if we can pull any DNA or blood from the caping knife."

Gretchen knelt on the concrete floor, her gloved hands feeling along the back of the second tier of shelving. On the floor in front of her was a red metal toolbox. Its lid lay on the floor beside it.

Two more steps brought Josie inches from the box. She stared down at its contents, feeling a tightness in her chest. "Oh God," she said.

She looked away long enough to meet the Chief's eyes. She was certain she saw a glimmer of tears. His Adam's apple bobbed in his throat as he swallowed. He didn't speak and Josie realized that it was because he couldn't, without losing his composure. For a fleeting moment she tried to imagine what it must feel like to have answers after almost three decades. But they were still a long way off from having all the answers, or the most important thing—justice. As if reading her mind, the Chief nodded.

Josie stared back down at the contents of the box. There was no removable tray as was common with toolboxes of its size. Instead, a thick bed of dark blue velvet had been placed inside it. Spaced evenly apart were tiny white cards, maybe only one inch by one inch. Each of them bore a number written in thick black ink. *1, 2, 3, 4, 5, 6, 7.* Pinned beneath almost every number was a clear plastic bag containing a single lock of hair, tied with a white ribbon. Most of the locks were a shade of brown except numbers 1 and 2, which were blonde. The hair pinned beneath the number 1 was so light it looked almost white. The only numbers that were missing hair were 4, and 7.

Gretchen looked up at her. "Time to get ourselves an arrest warrant, boss."

FORTY-THREE

The mid-morning sun warmed Josie's back as she stood next to her vehicle in a CVS parking lot a few blocks down from the RedLo Group. Sweat gathered at the nape of her neck. It wasn't even ten a.m. and the temperature had already reached sixty-five degrees. In the foliage that lined the lot, birds hopped and flew from tree to tree, chirping and calling to one another. It was the kind of lush spring Pennsylvania day that made the whole world seem alive with possibility. That a few blocks away, in a building where teenagers came and went freely, a serial killer went about his day with no one the wiser, seemed incongruous.

Shoppers drifting out of the store looked up from their cell phones, staring instead at the growing police presence. Joggers slowed as they ran past on the sidewalk, taking in the sight. Deputy Judy Tiercar waved all of them off. "Keep moving," she called. "This is just a training exercise."

Josie had called the sheriff's office to let them know they were making an arrest since Bellewood was their jurisdiction. Deputy Tiercar and two of her colleagues had joined Josie, Noah, Gretchen, Mettner, the Chief and two uniformed

Denton officers at the CVS. Deputy Tiercar looked at Chief Chitwood. "What do you want to do here, Chief?"

"We go in now and get him. I don't want him out in the world for another minute, especially if he's got easy access to teenage girls all day."

"All right, let's go," said Gretchen.

They started disbursing, donning their tactical vests, and getting into their cars for the short ride to the RedLo Group. Josie was halfway into her seat when she realized the Chief hadn't moved. Getting back out, she strode over to where he stood, eyeing the convoy. A warm breeze blew wisps of his white hair straight into the air. "Chief?" she said.

"I can't be there, Quinn," he said.

"What do you mean?" she said. "You should be there. Not doing the arrest, but seeing it. Witnessing it."

He shook his head, gaze still lingering over her head. "Remember Travis Benning? The Butcher went free because of him."

"Because he contaminated evidence," Josie said. "This isn't the same thing."

"I can't be there. I want to, but I can't. I don't want there to be any question, not ever, about my personal stake in this."

Josie pointed out: "You've overseen this investigation. Your hands are all over this, Chief. You—"

When he met her eyes finally, Josie was startled by the emotions that flashed across his face. Real emotions. Not the ever-present annoyance and pseudo-anger they had all grown used to. This was real anger, true hatred. A need for vengeance. Josie recognized it. She had been pushed to that brink before, had gone plummeting over the edge into a darkness so profound it had taken her a long time to fight her way back to the light.

The Chief said, "I don't want to be like my father."

He didn't trust himself, Josie realized. Face to face with the man who had kidnapped, held, and killed his baby sister, at the moment of arrest, the Chief didn't trust himself.

Josie said, "You're not like him. You were never like him, and you'll never be like him. I'll call you when it's done, and you can meet us back at headquarters."

She started walking away, but he called after her. "Quinn?"

Turning back to him, she waited.

"You'll do it, right? You'll put the cuffs on?"

She nodded.

In the car, Noah said, "What was that about?"

Josie pulled out of the parking lot. Gretchen and Mettner followed in one vehicle and behind them was a marked Denton PD unit and Deputy Judy Tiercar in a sheriff's vehicle. "He'll meet us back at the stationhouse," Josie said.

It took fewer than sixty seconds to traverse the three blocks to the RedLo Group, but it was enough time to send Josie's heart rate into overdrive. She sent Gretchen and Mettner around the back of the building in case McMichaels decided to run. Deputy Tiercar and the two uniformed Denton officers remained outside. Josie and Noah marched past a very confused receptionist and four waiting clients, giving a terse explanation as they went, headed directly to McMichaels' office. The door was open, McMichaels behind his desk, his pen scrawling across a piece of paper. He looked up as they entered, his slack-jawed expression morphing into some combination of surprise and fear.

"Kade McMichaels," Josie said. "You're under arrest."

"Sir, please stand up," Noah directed as the two of them rounded the desk, one of them on each side. "And put your hands behind your back."

McMichaels stood up, wobbling a bit, the backs of his legs sending his office chair bouncing off the wall behind him. Fisting the pen, he said, "No, no. This is a misunderstanding."

Josie and Noah flanked him. Josie said, "Sir, please put the pen down and put your hands behind your back."

"It's not what you think," McMichaels spluttered, looking back and forth between them, panic making his voice reedy and high. "I was trying to help. I—nothing happened. Not before, and not this time."

"Drop the pen, sir," Noah said firmly.

The pen fell from McMichaels' hand. Josie and Noah moved in, instructing him again to put his hands behind his back. Noah recited his Miranda rights. As Josie clasped the handcuffs onto his wrists, she felt him tremble.

"Let's go," she said, grasping his upper arm firmly and guiding him from behind the desk.

"It's a misunderstanding," he cried. "I never touched them. I swear to you—I never touched any of them."

FORTY-FOUR

By the time they reached the police headquarters, Kade McMichaels had clamped his mouth shut and had no intention of talking to anyone except the lawyer he requested. Josie was mildly disappointed but not at all surprised. He hadn't been forthcoming with them the first time they interviewed him. Now, in custody for the murders of Gemma Farmer and Sabrina Beck, she doubted he was going to offer them anything incriminating. The officers in the holding area took over for Josie and Noah, getting him processed and allowing him to contact an attorney.

Josie and Noah trudged up the stairs to the great room, pulling off their tactical vests and plopping into their chairs. Gretchen and Mettner, who had worked over twenty-four hours with no real sleep, had both gone home for some much-needed and much-deserved rest. Josie had called the Chief from the car but only gotten his voicemail. "It's over," she had said. Now his office door was closed, inscrutable. She tried to recall if she had seen his car in the parking lot out back, but her mind was still turning over Kade McMichaels' words: *It's not what you think. I was trying to help. I—nothing happened. Not before, and not this time. I never touched them. I never touched any of them.*

"Did you hear what I said?" asked Noah.

Josie turned away from the Chief's door and blinked, staring across their desks at him. "What?"

"Hummel texted me. He said to call him right away. I'm going to put him on speaker phone."

Noah put his cell phone on his desk and dialed Hummel. He answered after four rings. "I have some findings for you that you're going to want to know about."

"I've got Josie here. You're on speaker."

Josie jumped right in. "Did you get Daisy's phone to power up? Did the GrayKey work?"

"Oh," said Hummel. "No. Chan tried this morning but it wouldn't power up. We'll try again though. No, I'm calling because you know we searched the rest of McMichaels' property, right? He's got ten acres of land. We didn't find any kind of other structures, man-made or natural, in which he could have kept a human or more than one human."

Noah said, "Maybe he was holding them in the house or the garage."

"Could be. We took prints and any DNA we could find from both buildings. I haven't gotten any hits on the prints besides McMichaels and the Daisy kid from inside either of them. So unless he wiped down everything Gemma Farmer and Sabrina Beck touched, he wasn't keeping them in his house or his barn. However, we did find a firepit in the woods near the back of his property within walking distance of a back road that runs behind there. We collected the ash, whatever was there, including several bottles of tequila and peach schnapps and a few cans of beer. I was able to pull a couple of prints from some of the bottles."

"Did you get any hits?" asked Josie.

"Kade McMichaels. Daisy. Gemma Farmer. Sabrina Beck.

Some unidentified prints. That was from one of the peach schnapps bottles. Also several pieces of broken glass from other bottles that were scattered around the area. I'll email over the report, and you'll see which prints were on which items, but Kade's and Daisy's prints were on most everything. We have a piece of glass with Kade's and Gemma Farmer's prints as well as another piece with Kade's and Sabrina Beck's. With weather conditions and not knowing how long those bottles were out there, that was the best I could do. Also, that caping knife you found in his garage with his field dressing stuff? His prints are on the handle, although I guess that's not that surprising. I'm sending it to the lab to see if they can pull any DNA from it."

"Hummel, that's incredible," said Josie.

"Don't get too excited," Hummel replied. "I don't think the knife will yield anything but from what Dr. Feist told me, I'm pretty sure we can match the size and shape of its blade to the wounds of our two victims."

"What about the creepy toolbox of hair?" asked Noah.

"That's where it gets weird," said Hummel.

Josie had a sinking feeling in her stomach. "Weird in what way?"

"Well, McMichaels' prints are on the outside but none on the inside."

Noah said, "Any partials? I'm wondering how much he would have needed to touch the inside of the box if he was taking stuff in and out of it—or if he was just putting hair inside."

"Nothing," Hummel replied.

Josie said, "What about the plastic bags? The cards with the numbers on them?"

"No prints from McMichaels, but on one of the cards—only one: the one marked number four which had no hair attached— there were two prints from the same person."

"Who?" asked Noah.

"I'll email you the report," said Hummel. "But it's some woman I don't think is related to the case at all. Her name is Winnie Hyde. She has a conviction for retail theft in Brighton Springs from 1996."

Josie didn't hear the rest of their conversation. Her mind was working back through the serpentine details of the case to where she had heard the name Winnie Hyde before. Nudging her computer screen to life, she started clicking through case files, looking for it.

Noah said, "You're not listening to me."

"I'm sorry," said Josie. "It's just that Winnie Hyde—I've heard her name before. I'm trying to figure out where."

"The Kelsey Chitwood case?" asked Noah. "Hummel mentioned Brighton Springs."

"Right," said Josie, closing out the Gemma Farmer file. "Let's go down to the conference room so I can search."

Noah followed her downstairs and helped her search, talking as they went. "Hummel impounded McMichaels' 2018 Rogue and is going to start processing it today, but I'm going to write up a warrant for its GPS data. If he's been coming and going to some secondary location, we need to know about it immediately. I'm worried because a lot of what we have is circumstantial."

Josie nodded as she riffled through one of the many stacks of boxes marked with Kelsey's name. "True, but the DA has gotten convictions on circumstantial evidence plenty of times."

"This is too important," Noah said, leafing through a stack of reports. "I think we need to push harder, maybe see if we can get Daisy to tell us something. Right now, we have nothing that ties McMichaels directly to Gemma Farmer's or Sabrina Beck's bodies."

"But the box of hair," Josie said with a slight shudder. "His prints all over everything."

"All over everything at his house. Nothing connecting him

to the murder scenes or the body. Not directly. You heard Hummel—the lab probably won't get DNA from the knife. Even if we can say his prints are on it, his attorney will argue it's his knife, so of course they are. If we match its size to the wounds, his attorney will say there are thousands, if not more, of that size knife manufactured every year. I just think we need more."

"Then we'll get more," Josie told him. "We can call Children and Youth Services to see if they'll allow us to talk with Daisy. She's implicated in this murder, too, you know. For all we know, she could be the actual murderer, just like we discussed before. Maybe the DA will offer some kind of deal if she cooperates and tells us everything."

As Josie thumbed through another stack of pages, she saw the fingerprint report from the church pews flash past. Like a lightning strike, she remembered that was where she'd seen the name Winnie Hyde. She plucked it from the stack.

Noah said, "That's a good place to start. I'll call Children and Youth Services and see what I can arrange."

Josie waved the report in the air. "Go ahead. I'm right behind you. I found the name. Winnie Hyde left a fingerprint on one of the pews Kelsey Chitwood was resting on when she was found dead. I'm going to look her up and call the cold case detective in Brighton Springs to see if she can dig up any more information."

Noah already had his cell phone in his hand. Frowning, he said, "You think this woman is important? Like she's involved?"

"I have no idea," Josie said. "But her fingerprints showed up twice now across these cases. We shouldn't ignore it."

"You're right."

Josie followed him upstairs. Once seated at his desk, Noah punched a number into his cell phone. Moments later, he was speaking quietly to a representative from Children and Youth Services. Josie fished her own cell phone from a stack of reports on her desk and dialed Detective Meredith Dorton, explaining the situation. Meredith promised to find Winnie Hyde's file, if it still existed—including a mug shot—and send it over. Hanging up, Josie nudged her computer mouse, bringing the screen to life.

A search of the TLO database for Winnie Hyde yielded almost nothing. A birthdate. There was no driver's license or state ID. A single address for an apartment in Brighton Springs from when she was eighteen years old. The retail theft conviction was listed, but how had she been arrested and convicted with no state ID, Josie wondered? In Pennsylvania you had to be sixteen to get a driver's license, but you could get a state-issued photo ID as young as ten years old. However, there was no requirement that you get one. People got them because they were necessary to do just about everything in adulthood: get a job, rent an apartment, buy a house, open a bank account. Basically, if you wanted to exist and move in the world, you needed a photo ID. So why hadn't Winnie Hyde ever had one? Was she was deceased? Josie found no evidence of a death certificate. Had she gone missing at some point?

Josie logged into their system to see if Hummel had uploaded any of the photos from the search warrant they'd executed on McMichaels' house that morning. He had. Scrolling through, she found a photo of the toolbox and enlarged it on her screen. They didn't know the identity of Girl One. According to their theory—that McMichaels numbered his victims and then marked them with cuts—the hair of Girl Two belonged to Kelsey Chitwood. If Detective Meredith Dorton of Brighton Springs' cold case annex was correct, then McMichaels' third victim had been Priscilla Cruz, whose badly decomposed remains had been found in an abandoned lot behind a high school. They knew that Gemma Farmer was Girl Five and Sabrina Beck was Girl Six. The state police lab would have hair samples from those two girls and would be able to match the samples from the creepy box to those two victims at least, although without root cells, they wouldn't be able to match DNA.

But what about Girls Four and Seven, Josie wondered? Why was there no hair? Had he intended to keep a lock of Winnie Hyde's hair? Josie did some quick math. According to Winnie Hyde's birthdate, she would have turned sixteen in 1994. If Kelsey Chitwood turned sixteen in 1997 and she was Girl Two, then Winnie Hyde couldn't be Girl Four.

How was she involved? Had McMichaels used Winnie to lure Kelsey and Priscilla and whoever Girls One and Four were? Josie thought about the woman at the bus stop that Kelsey had spoken to before she disappeared, but that woman had had white hair. It couldn't be Winnie. An eighteen-year-old wouldn't have white hair.

Josie put thoughts of Winnie Hyde out of her head for a minute and concentrated on the photo of the toolbox again. The missing locks of hair. Had things not gone as McMichaels planned? Or, Josie wondered, feeling a chill envelop her entire body, were Girls Four and Seven still out there being held somewhere? Priscilla Cruz had been found in 2003. The next known death was that of Gemma Farmer. Sabrina Beck had been found only two weeks later. They'd been held at the same time for at least part of their captivity. If he had been holding multiple girls at once, where had he done it? Besides the futon in McMichaels' spare room with the blonde hair and pair of women's underwear, there wasn't any evidence that Gemma Farmer or even Sabrina Beck had ever been there. It didn't mean that they hadn't. Maybe he was really good at cleaning up evidence. It would explain why he had never been caught.

Or maybe he had another place that he was keeping girls.

Had he taken Girl Four at some time in the last couple of years and still had her? Was that why there was no hair in the box? What about Girl Seven? Was there no trophy because she was also still being held, or was it because he had chosen her but not abducted her yet?

Noah's voice startled her from her thoughts. "We can't talk with Daisy."

"What?" Josie said.

"Children and Youth haven't been able to identify her. She doesn't match any missing persons. They don't know her age, and she's not telling them anything. They want to consult with legal counsel and a psychologist before they let anyone speak to her. They've also taken a DNA sample."

"Shit," said Josie. "This is not good. Noah, I think there might be more girls out there, and they might still be alive."

FORTY-FIVE

Josie took Noah through her thought process—how there were no souvenirs for Girls Four and Seven and what that could mean. Noah snatched the phone receiver up again. "I'm going to call Children and Youth Services back," he said. "Maybe if we tell them that one or potentially two other girls' lives hang in the balance here, they'll be more inclined to let us talk to Daisy. If McMichaels was keeping them in a place we haven't found yet, then they could be on limited time. We don't know what kind of conditions they're living in or what kinds of supplies he left them. We have to get to them before they die of dehydration or starvation."

Josie raided Mettner's desk, looking for the list of missing fifteen-year-old girls he had been working on before things with the case exploded. While Noah argued with the representative for Children and Youth Services, Josie compared the names on Mettner's list with Kade McMichaels' client list.

By the time Noah hung up, Josie's heart was thundering so hard she felt like it might burst right out of her chest. "I found one," she told him. "This girl's name appears on Mettner's list of missing fifteen-year-old girls and on Kade McMichaels' client list."

"Who?" Noah said, standing up and coming around to her desk.

"Erica Mullins. I don't think that Mett flagged this one because the way she went missing was a little different than the others. Three months ago, she was in Quakertown staying with her grandmother for the weekend while her parents were out of town, and on Sunday when her grandmother went to wake her to get ready to go home, she was gone. All personal items left behind. But her parents live in Bowersville."

Bowersville was just outside of Denton and it was so tiny, it barely qualified as a town.

"When is her sixteenth birthday?" Noah asked.

Josie pointed to her date of birth. "It's in two days."

"It's possible that he didn't have a chance to kill her—or if Daisy is the actual killer, then she didn't have a chance to kill Erica. She could still be alive."

"But where is she?" Josie said. "The only people who could tell us are Daisy and McMichaels. What did Children and Youth say about us meeting with her?"

"At the earliest? Sometime tomorrow. They'll do their best to set something up."

"Then we need to go after McMichaels," said Josie.

"He's already got a lawyer," said Noah.

"Then we just need to find out who it is and talk some reason into them. If Erica Mullins is one of his victims and she's still alive somewhere, we need to find her as soon as possible unless he wants another murder charge."

"Let's talk to her parents then. Call them, see if they'll meet with us. We can find out if Erica had been hanging out or seen with a new 'friend' before she went missing. Maybe a blonde teenage girl who dressed in men's clothes."

FORTY-SIX

Erica Mullins' parents readily agreed to speak with Josie and Noah. Bowersville was west of Denton, just a smattering of houses nestled in a valley between mountains. It had a strip mall and a couple of churches but no post office, no police department and no funeral homes. Its crowning jewel was a new mini-golf course that did a surprising amount of business given Bowersville's remote location. The Mullins house was easy to find, sitting alone on a cul-de-sac between the strip mall and the Baptist church. It was a white, two-story craftsman with a large porch that held two wooden rocking chairs, a number of potted plants, and a profusion of ceramic frogs.

Faith Mullins threw open the front door before Josie or Noah had a chance to knock. She was tiny and thin, dressed in gray sweatpants, a Denton University T-shirt and a black cardigan. Her dark hair was thrown up on top of her head in a messy bun. Her heart-shaped face was pale, with large circles under her eyes.

Josie made introductions and Faith ushered them inside. The living room was decorated in distressed white wood and eggshell-colored furniture that sat low to the ground. Sprawled across the couch was a man in jeans and a polo shirt that hung loose from his pants. The logo embroidered on his left breast was for an auto parts shop in Denton. He jumped up when they entered and shook their hands. "Oscar Mullins."

Faith and Oscar sat on the couch, gesturing for Josie and Noah to take the loveseat, which they did. "Do you have news?" Faith asked.

Discomfort took root in Josie's stomach. She hated this part of the job—looking into the hopeful, desperate face of a family member and having to deliver news that would either make it harder for them to hold out hope or destroy that hope entirely. "We're here because we recently arrested Kade McMichaels for the homicide of two girls close to Erica's age."

Faith and Oscar looked at one another. "McMichaels," Oscar said. "Isn't that the therapist?"

"I don't understand," said Faith.

Josie said, "Those two girls were clients of Kade McMichaels. Former clients at the time they went missing. They were also both fifteen years old. Their disappearances were similar to Erica's—it appeared as though they had simply left all their things behind and run away. But we know now that was not the case."

Faith said, "Wait, you think her therapist kidnapped her? Is that what you're saying?"

"Former therapist," Oscar pointed out.

"Erica disappeared from my mother's house in Quakertown," Faith said. "That's a couple of hours from here. How could he—how would he... You think he traveled there and took her?"

Noah said, "At this point, we can't say for certain. We're still investigating."

Faith covered her mouth with a fist and made a strangled cry. "Is she—is she dead? Is my baby dead?"

Oscar blinked several times and took his wife's free hand.

His knuckles went white but if he was hurting her, Faith didn't notice.

An ache spread through Josie's chest.

Noah said, "We don't know. That's the truth. We're not even sure that Erica was taken by Kade McMichaels. We only know that she was on his client list and that she's been missing for three months."

"Then why are you here?" asked Faith. "You're scaring us."

"I'm so sorry, Mrs. Mullins," said Josie. "That's not our intention. What we're trying to do is figure out if your daughter could have been taken by him. If there is a chance that he took her, even though she was in Quakertown, and she hasn't been found yet, she may still be alive, but we need to work as quickly as possible to figure out where he is keeping her."

"Can't you just ask him?" Oscar said. "You said you arrested him. Ask him! Our daughter's life might be at stake here."

Noah said, "We have every intention of asking him. But we have to go through his lawyer. There are legal issues here that are making things more difficult."

"But we are going to do everything we can to get Erica back to you—if McMichaels took her," Josie added.

"How will you know if it was him?" asked Faith. "How could you possibly know?"

"That's why we're here," Noah said. "We need to ask you a series of questions about her disappearance that might help us figure out if McMichaels was involved or not. Some of them might seem strange, but there are elements of the investigation that we can't disclose at this time."

"Fine," Oscar said, his voice betraying a hint of impatience. "Ask whatever you need to ask. Just get on with it."

Josie said, "Can you take us through the few days before she went to stay with your mom?"

Faith and Oscar looked at one another as if trying to decide who would tell the story of their daughter's last week at home.

Finally, Faith said, "It was a normal week. She went to school—"

"Failed a biology test," Oscar put in.

Faith gave them a weak smile which immediately faltered. "Yeah, that was ugly. We—we punished her."

Oscar rolled his eyes. "Then she put on a big show, crying and being melodramatic about it, like her life was over because we took away her phone for a few hours."

Faith bristled. "You think everything she does is melodramatic. She's fifteen! Everything is huge when you're fifteen!"

Oscar's face flushed with anger. A vein throbbed in his temple. "She cries over everything. Every little thing, Faith! She needs to grow up."

"No, you need to be more empathetic toward her. No wonder she's got anxiety! It's because of you! If it wasn't for you, she wouldn't have needed to go to that stupid therapist in the first place. Now look!"

He shot up from the couch, a snarl on his face. "This is my fault? It's my fault that some freak kidnapped her? Anxiety? That's a crock of shit that you and the school kept trying to push on her until she believed it. That had nothing to do with me. I didn't even want her to go!"

Noah stood up and moved closer to Oscar, putting a hand on his upper back. "Mr. Mullins," he said. "I have to ask you to calm down. It's important that we get as much information as we can so that we can help Erica. How about if we step outside for a few minutes? Get some air."

Oscar glared at his wife before silently letting Noah guide him out onto the porch.

Alone with Josie, Faith squeezed her eyes closed but tears snuck from beneath her eyelids and rolled down her cheeks anyway. Josie looked around until she found a box of tissues on one of the end tables. Beside it was a candid photo of Erica with a golf club in her hand and one of the mini-golf holes in the background. The dimple in her right cheek was disarming. She looked younger than fifteen, with a sweetness about her that many teens lacked. Josie plucked a tissue from the box and sat beside Faith on the couch.

"Here," she said, handing her the tissue.

Faith opened her eyes and took it, swiping at the snot leaking from her nose. "I'm so sorry," she croaked. "So sorry. I didn't mean for that to happen. You can't imagine what this is like. I want to scream my head off and pull out my hair. He thought she ran away. He always thinks the worst of her, but Erica is a good kid. She wouldn't do that. Someone took her. I know it. Whether it was McMichaels or some other monster..."

"Why would your husband think the worst of her?" asked Josie.

"She just... she's had a hard time since she got to high school. Her grades got worse. I found out she was being bullied at school. She's been depressed and anxious. Even the teachers noticed. But my husband doesn't think that mental health is a real thing. He thinks she should just 'get over it' and 'study harder.' It's led to a lot of fights, and I think it's made things harder on her. He thinks she's just saying she's anxious as an excuse to get out of studying. I tried to explain to him that there were a lot of factors at work, but he just says that all teenagers are lazy and trying to get one over on adults, and any kid who seems like they're not is just acting. All teenagers are overdramatic, according to him. Anyway, he was convinced she ran away and that she would come back when she realized how hard it is to be out on her own—especially down by where my mom lives. She doesn't know anyone there. But now..."

Josie said, "Did the police there send someone here to interview all her friends?"

"Yes. But her friends weren't helpful. No one knows anything."

"Was there anyone that Erica was talking to or hanging out with you hadn't met before? Anyone new?"

Faith shrugged. "Not really. I mean, a couple of times when I picked the kids up from mini-golfing—that's all there is to do here in this godforsaken town—I saw her talking with this blonde girl about her age, but when I asked her about it, she said the girl didn't live around here."

Josie's heartbeat went into overdrive. She took out her phone and pulled up Daisy's mug shot. "Is this her?"

Faith studied the photo. "Yes," she said. "That's her. How did you—what's going on? Did McMichaels take her, too?"

Josie said, "We're not sure how she fits in exactly, but she was seen talking to the other victims before they disappeared as well."

"Who is she? Is she... is she dead, too?"

"She's in the custody of Children and Youth Services," Josie said. "We don't know who she is because she won't tell anyone, but we have physical evidence linking her to Kade McMichaels. Did Erica say where she was from?"

"No. She only said the girl didn't live around here. But wait, I don't understand. She knows something and she won't tell?"

"We didn't know to ask her about Erica until now," Josie said. "Lieutenant Fraley has been pressing Children and Youth for a meeting with her so we can try to get some information from her. We're hoping to speak with her tomorrow."

Faith dug her fingers into Josie's forearm. "When you see her, you tell her that Erica's mother wants her back. I need my baby back."

FORTY-SEVEN

The next morning, the team gathered in the great room. The Chief lurked on the periphery, pacing. Josie had already contacted Hummel to see if he had had any luck with Daisy's phone. Her heart soared when he said he'd gotten it to power up finally but then sank when he told her he was having issues with the GrayKey bypassing Daisy's password. He promised to keep working at it.

Noah held up a photo for Gretchen and Mettner to see. "This is Erica Mullins. She was also a client of Kade McMichaels. She is fifteen, same as the others, and turns sixteen tomorrow. She has been missing for three months." He recapped everything they knew about Erica's case. "We believe she came into contact with Daisy prior to her disappearance."

"We have to find her," Josie said. "As soon as possible. We're waiting on the GPS data from McMichaels' 2018 Rogue to see if it helps us find wherever he's been keeping these girls—it's clearly not at his house or their prints and DNA would be all over it. No one's that good at cleaning up."

"We might not have time to wait for the GPS data," Gretchen said.

"We agree," said Noah.

"That only leaves us with two options," Mettner said. "Getting the information from either Daisy or McMichaels himself. For all we know, Daisy did the killing. We can't actually prove which one of them is the murderer at this point. The evidence is too circumstantial. We need more."

Noah smiled. "That's exactly how I got us a meeting with Daisy—by telling her Children and Youth caseworker we were considering murder charges. They got her an attorney who is bringing her over here today." He swiveled in his chair and looked at the wall clock. "They should be here in the next half hour or so."

Josie said, "I've left a message with Kade McMichaels' attorney, but I don't expect much to come from it."

Gretchen sighed. "Yeah, I can't imagine any attorney wanting him to talk with the police at this point. Unless you can get the DA to offer some kind of leniency in exchange for telling us where to find Erica."

The Chief said, "No leniency. Quinn will get what she needs from Daisy."

Josie looked at him. Daisy had been as unreadable and reticent as any subject Josie had ever questioned—and she had once tried getting information from a girl who didn't speak at all. She wasn't sure she was getting anything at all from Daisy, but she knew she had to try.

Erica Mullins' life might depend on it.

An hour later, Daisy was back in the interrogation room. This time she wore a pair of jeans and a plain yellow T-shirt that looked more her size, and she was accompanied by two women in their forties. One introduced herself as Daisy's Children and Youth caseworker and the other as Daisy's attorney. A bottle of water sat before the girl, unopened. Her hands were folded in her lap, and she stared straight ahead. Josie again opted for the seat beside Daisy. This time, she didn't move away as quickly or as far as she had last time, seeming a little more willing to give up some of her personal space to Josie, who hoped this was a sign of trust.

Once Josie was seated, Daisy turned to her and said, "If I tell you things, I can go?"

Josie met the eyes of the attorney and then the caseworker. The attorney said, "I've attempted to explain the situation to Miss—to Daisy—but I'm not sure she comprehends what's going on." The caseworker nodded in agreement.

Turning back to Daisy, Josie smiled. "I wish it was that easy, Daisy, but it really depends on what we find out today. First, I need to talk to you about your rights, okay?"

Daisy didn't respond. Slowly, Josie took her through her Miranda rights. When she asked if Daisy understood them, she said yes.

"Okay," Josie said. "Now that that's finished, let's talk about some other things. Right now you're being held for your assault on me—when we were in the mall. You tried to run away, and you pushed me. Then you attacked me in the bathroom."

Daisy said nothing. Her unblinking stare was unnerving to Josie and for the first time since she had met the girl, she found something vaguely familiar about her wide-eyed expression, but couldn't place it.

"While I'd be willing to drop those charges, you may be facing some far more serious charges."

"Like what?"

"Like murder."

"Murder of who?"

"Gemma Farmer and Sabrina Beck."

Daisy shook her head vehemently, a flush creeping across her pale features. "No, no. I didn't hurt them. They were my friends."

"Gemma and Sabrina were your friends?"

"Yes, we talked about things. Like, girl talk. They were nice to me."

"Do you know what happened to them?"

Daisy's gaze dropped to her lap. "I know they're dead because I stopped seeing them."

"Seeing them where?" Josie asked.

Daisy's voice grew small and weak. "At the place I was supposed to take them."

"What place was that, Daisy?"

She hesitated before answering, "The firepit out in the woods. We had a fire and ate chips and we had... we drank alcohol and stuff like that. I was supposed to give them alcohol and the pink pills. So they would fall asleep."

"You were supposed to do that?"

"Yes."

"Who told you to do that, Daisy?"

"I don't know his name. He's in charge of everything, that's what I know, but I don't know his name."

Josie took out her phone and pulled up Kade McMichaels' mug shot. "Is this him?"

Daisy looked at the photo for a long time but didn't answer. The screen went black.

Josie said, "We know you were driving his car—did you paint it black?"

She shook her head no.

"We also know you were staying at his house for some period of time. You were driving his vehicle, staying in his house, but you don't know his name."

Daisy remained silent and still, eyes on the blank phone screen.

Josie waited a long minute, but Daisy didn't offer anything else. "Daisy, who asked you to buy a prom dress for Gemma Farmer?"

Nothing.

Josie punched her passcode into her phone to bring up McMichaels' photo again. "Was it this man?"

No answer.

Josie pulled up photos of Sabrina and Gemma and swiped back and forth between the two for Daisy to see. "Did you kill these girls?"

"No," came her small voice.

"Did you help Gemma get dressed up for the prom?"

"No."

"Did you drive her to Denton East High School?"

"No."

"Did you stab her?"

"No."

"What about Sabrina Beck? Did you take her home?"

"From work. I gave her rides home from work."

"But on the night of May twentieth, did you drive her to her mother's trailer and stab her in her bed?"

"No, no. I would never do that. I told you, I wouldn't hurt them. They were my friends."

Josie swiped back to McMichaels' photo. "Did he stab them?"

"I don't know."

Next, Josie pulled up a photo of Erica Mullins. "Did you take her to 'the place,' the firepit?"

"Erica. Yes. She wanted to go so I took her."

"What happened then?"

"She drank a lot. A whole lot. And she took the pills. She didn't wake up."

Josie met the eyes of the attorney before looking back at Daisy. "Did she die? At the firepit?"

"I don't think so. I don't know. I left her there like I was supposed to."

"Who told you to leave her there?"

No answer.

Josie pointed to Erica's smiling face. "Where is she, Daisy? Where is she now?"

"I don't know."

"Daisy, this is very important. Was Erica your friend, too?"

"Yes."

"Erica might be in danger. Very serious danger. She might die, Daisy, if we don't find her. If you are her friend—if you are a good friend—you'll help us find her before that happens. Can you do that for me?"

For the very first time, tears glistened in Daisy's eyes. "I want to," she choked out. "I do. But I can't."

"Why?" Josie asked. "Why can't you tell me where to find Erica?"

"Because I promised and I have to keep my promises."

"Even if that means that your friend might die?" Josie asked gently. "Who made you promise such a thing?"

A tear spilled down Daisy's cheek. "I don't want to talk anymore."

Josie tapped a finger against her phone screen to keep Erica's photo there. "Daisy, I know this is hard. I think that you've had a very difficult life. I suspect that the adults you've been with your entire life have made you believe things that are simply not true. Saving a friend—like Erica—is worth breaking any promise in the world. Don't you think?"

More silence. Each time Josie's phone screen darkened, she tapped it again, keeping Erica's face front and center.

"How about the password to your phone? Can you tell us that?"

Without meeting Josie's eyes, Daisy mumbled five numbers. Josie knew that the team was watching from the other room and that someone was already on the phone to Hummel with it. "Thank you," Josie said. "That wasn't so hard, was it? Can you tell me where we can find Erica?"

Josie continued to keep Erica's face aglow on her phone screen. Finally, Daisy asked, "What happens to me if I can't leave here?"

Josie pointed toward the caseworker. "That's up to Children and Youth Services. You'll have to stay with them for some time. If you're found guilty of any criminal charges, you'll have to go to jail. I'm sorry. If you help us find Erica, there's a chance that we could keep you out of jail. If you help us find her, I will do everything I can to make that happen."

Daisy's gaze swept from the caseworker to the photo of Erica, then to Josie, and then to the two-way mirror on the other side of the room. "I want to go," she said.

"I'm afraid it's not that easy," Josie said softly. "But help us find Erica and I'll see what I can do."

More silence.

Josie said, "Are you afraid of someone, Daisy?"

No answer. Josie swiped back to McMichaels' photo. "Are you afraid of him?"

Still no answer.

"Because he's in jail now, Daisy. He can't hurt you or anyone else anymore."

Nothing.

"Is there someone else you're afraid of?"

Daisy's face began to close off, the life draining from her eyes, her skin smoothing out.

Changing tacks, Josie asked, "What's your last name, Daisy?"

"I don't know."

"Where are your parents?"

"I don't have parents."

Josie looked over Daisy's shoulder to see the caseworker's eyes wide, a pen poised over a notebook in her hand.

"Who gave you the phone?"

No answer.

"Okay," Josie said, smiling again. "How about this: can you tell me where you were before you stayed here?" She swiped to a photo of Kade McMichaels' house. "We know you were staying here because we found your fingerprints and some of your things inside this house."

"Another place," Daisy said, as if that explained everything.

"What place was that?" Josie asked.

No answer.

"Can you take us to it?"

She shook her head.

"Are there other people there?"

No response.

"How old are you, Daisy?"

A shrug. "I don't know."

Josie went back to the photo of Kade McMichaels. "Did this man ever touch you or try to touch you in any way?"

Again, she shook her head. "I think... I think maybe he wanted to but he never did."

FORTY-EIGHT

The Chief, Noah, Gretchen, and Mettner were all crammed into the adjacent CCTV room, crowded around the television screen. When Josie entered, they all turned to her. On the screen, the attorney and caseworker were packing up and urging Daisy out of the room. Josie felt wrung out and exhausted, like she'd just emerged from a murky swamp in which she'd been swimming for her life all morning. Not her life. Erica Mullins' life. She felt as close to crying at work as she ever had.

"I'm sorry, Chief," she said.

He swallowed. "You'll find another way, Quinn. I know you will."

Josie looked at Noah hopefully. "Anything from Hummel on the phone?"

"Not yet," he said. "But I gave him the password."

The quiet in the room was filled with the soft rustle of clothes as each one of them shifted uncomfortably. The trill of a cell phone ringing sent them all checking their pockets. "It's me," said Noah, holding up his phone. He swiped answer. They couldn't hear the other side of the conversation but after issuing a number of words of agreement, Noah finally said, "We'll be ready."

He hung up. "Looks like we might get another chance at this. That was Kade McMichaels' attorney. McMichaels wants to talk to us. His attorney will be here soon. I'll have someone bring him up from holding."

Mettner said, "He wants to talk?"

Gretchen added, "And his attorney is okay with it?"

Noah shrugged. "I'm just telling you what she said."

The Chief looked at Josie. "You ready to go another round, Quinn?"

"If it's all the same to you, Chief," she said, "I think someone else should take a stab at this one. Maybe Gretchen. She's the most experienced."

He looked at Gretchen. "Palmer, you up for it?"

"Of course," said Gretchen.

"You'll go in together, then," said the Chief. "Palmer can lead."

Twenty minutes later, Josie and Gretchen were seated across the table from Kade McMichaels and his attorney in the same room where Josie had just questioned Daisy. His attorney was younger than him, perhaps in her thirties, dressed in a power suit, her hair long, dark, and straightened to within an inch of its life. Her features were severe, and judging by the austerity of her perfunctory smile, Josie imagined she was a fierce litigator. She started the meeting by saying, "Detectives, in the spirit of cooperation, and because we believe you have arrested the wrong man and your efforts would be better spent looking for the real killer, my client would like to go on record about a number of things."

"May we ask follow-up questions?" Gretchen said.

"Ask whatever you want," the attorney said coolly. "I'll let my client know which questions are appropriate for him to answer."

"If he's innocent, then wouldn't it be appropriate for him to answer all of our questions?" asked Gretchen.

The attorney ignored her and gave McMichaels a meaningful nod. He put his hands on top of the table and looked at Gretchen. "About a year ago I met a young woman at the public library. She told me that her name was Daisy. She appeared to be homeless. I... became friends with her. I let her stay at my home indefinitely, and I gave her use of my vehicle."

It was rehearsed, the attorney's words coming out of his mouth.

Gretchen said, "Did Daisy tell you her age?"

He shook his head.

"How old did you believe she was?" asked Gretchen.

"I don't—"

"That's not relevant," said his attorney. "Mr. McMichaels tried to help a young woman who was obviously struggling. She needed shelter, food, and transportation, and he provided it."

Josie said, "What happened to helping kids who couldn't help themselves being a waste of your time?"

All eyes swiveled toward her, but she kept her gaze locked on McMichaels. His eyes blinked at warp speed. Six blinks.

"She needed help. She asked for my help."

Gretchen said, "You gave her a vehicle that wasn't even legal to drive. She doesn't have a license. You thought that was a responsible decision?"

"I didn't think—I mean, she promised to be careful. She said she was looking for a job at the mall and she would only drive there and back."

"Did you give her a phone?" asked Josie.

"What? No. She had a phone when I met her. She said it was prepaid, she bought it at a grocery store."

"Who painted your car?" asked Gretchen.

"She did. I don't know why. One day she brought it back to me and it was black. I was upset, of course, but what could I say? It was more important that she was getting her life on track."

"You're a social worker," Josie said. "You meet a homeless girl and instead of directing her to the appropriate services, you just take her in? Feed her. Then you give her a vehicle that has no business being on the road. She's been wearing your clothes, hasn't she?"

He hung his head.

Josie continued, "When I showed you her photo in your office, you denied knowing her."

"I was afraid of what you would think—"

"Did you have a sexual relationship with her?" asked Gretchen.

He recoiled, lips peeling back from his teeth. "God, no."

"Then why would you be afraid of what we think?" asked Josie.

He dropped his chin to his chest and sighed. "Come on, Detectives. I'm fifty-six years old. Daisy never told me how old she was but she's young. You can tell. How would that look?"

Gretchen said, "You're saying any time a man in his fifties gives shelter to a younger person, we should automatically assume there is something inappropriate going on? What aren't you telling us?"

"Kade," his attorney said, a note of warning in her voice.

He sighed again. "Not every man. I have a... history."

"What kind of history?" Gretchen asked.

"When I was first out of graduate school, I lived in Lochfield—out near Pittsburgh—and I worked at a facility there doing basically the same thing I do here, which is to act as a therapist to teenagers dealing with depression, anxiety, social issues, family problems, drug and alcohol abuse. You name it. I left that practice because several of the girls—clients—misunderstood my behavior."

By the time he finished, his face was the color of beets.

Josie said, "What does that mean? They *misunderstood your behavior*? In what way?"

"It doesn't matter," the attorney cut in. "Although there was an in-house investigation, the accusations were found to be not credible. My client resigned in the interest of putting the entire thing behind him. No charges were ever brought. The police never became involved."

Josie said, "I think it is relevant, given the fact that two of his clients were murdered in the last two weeks and another one of his clients is missing."

"Detective Quinn is right," said Gretchen. "It's relevant because we found his prints with the prints of the two murdered girls on bottles of booze near the firepit on his property. Not to mention the toolbox we found in his garage—which also had his prints on it—containing samples of hair that we're in the process of matching to Gemma Farmer and Sabrina Beck."

McMichaels glanced at his attorney, but she didn't have a chance to direct his answer. He turned back to them and began spluttering, "My prints are on that box because it's my toolbox, but I swear to you, the only thing I ever put in it were tools! I don't know where the hair came from. Maybe Daisy put it there. Maybe she's behind all of this. I didn't kill those girls. I haven't seen either of them since the last time they came to my office for therapy... and who else is missing? You never said anything about another client being missing. But it doesn't matter because I'm telling you that I didn't do anything wrong. That old firepit at the back of my property? I haven't been out there in years. I don't use it. If kids were out there drinking, I didn't know about it. It's Daisy. She took the booze from my house. That's how it got out there. It has to be her. She's setting me up. She's weird. Something is off about her."

"If something was off about her, why did you bring her into your home? Give her use of a vehicle?" Josie asked.

He lowered his face into his hands. "I don't know, okay? I don't know. I liked her. I... sometimes I just like them, but I never, I would never—"

"Kade, stop," said the attorney, clamping a hand down on his shoulder.

"What did Daisy tell you about her background?" asked Gretchen, and Josie knew she was changing the subject before the attorney ended the meeting entirely.

He took in a couple of breaths and put his hands back on the table. "She said a long time ago she had a mom, but then her mom made her leave—pretty recently. She said she was trying to find her way."

"Did you ask about her mother? Her name? Where she lives? Contact information?" asked Gretchen.

"Of course I did. She wouldn't tell me. She wouldn't tell me anything—her age, birthday, not even her last name. She said she didn't know that stuff, but I think she was lying. Some kind of trauma response, probably. I thought that if I could gain her trust, she would open up to me, and we could get it sorted out."

"She was with you a year?" asked Josie. "You're a trained therapist and you couldn't get anything out of her in a year?"

He looked down at his hands. "No, I couldn't, and she was with me on and off, not the entire year. She disappeared for long periods of time. I just figured one day the police would call and say they'd found my car abandoned somewhere and that I would never see her again, but she kept coming back. Now I know she was setting me up. You have to believe me. I didn't do the things you're accusing me of—I didn't."

"The evidence suggests otherwise," Gretchen said.

He slapped both hands against the table. "The evidence is

wrong! Daisy did this, and she planted the evidence to make it look like I did these things."

"Why?" asked Josie.

He froze. "What?"

Josie leaned forward. "Why? If what you're saying is true, why would Daisy frame you for two murders? After you took her in, fed her, clothed her, gave her transportation for a year, why would she plant evidence in your home that implicates you in multiple murders?"

His mouth hung open. Both Gretchen and Josie let the moment stretch out, waiting for him to fill the silence. Finally, his attorney said, "It doesn't matter why. It's not Mr. McMichaels' responsibility to do your jobs for you. He can only tell you what he knows. He didn't kill those girls and he has never seen the hair that was planted in his toolbox. He has never consumed alcohol with minors at the firepit on the back of his property. He may be guilty of poor judgment, but he is not guilty of the homicides of Gemma Farmer and Sabrina Beck."

Without missing a beat, Gretchen took out her phone, tapped and swiped until she found a photo of Erica Mullins and slid it across the table. "Okay, then let's talk about the abduction of this girl. Also a client of yours."

He stared at the photo. "I didn't abduct anyone."

"Do you remember her?" asked Gretchen.

"I-I remember her face, yes. What's her name?"

"Erica Mullins," Josie said. "She was abducted three months ago but she was only your client for a few months last year."

"I don't remember—I didn't kidnap her. I know you've got a problem here—girls going missing and turning up dead—but I swear on my mother's grave, I didn't hurt anyone. I wouldn't. I swear to you, I wouldn't."

Gretchen tapped an index finger over Erica's face. "Tell us

where she is and we'll work something out on the murder charges. Maybe we'll keep you off death row. I can talk to the DA's office. If you help us find Erica before she dies, I'm sure the DA will be inclined to make some kind of a deal."

Kade opened his mouth to speak but his attorney went first. "My client has already told you everything he knows. This meeting is over."

Josie stood and leaned across the table, her face inches from his. "You want to help? You want to stop wasting time? Help this girl. Save her. Tell us where she is before it's too late."

The attorney rose. "I said, this meeting is over."

Josie ignored her. "Right now, you're facing two murder charges. First-degree murder. That's two life sentences if you're lucky enough to get life. But there were seven slots in that box we found in your garage. There may come a time when the other jurisdictions where the other girls were killed—those departments will want to charge you for those murders. That's four more murder charges in jurisdictions who might not be so interested in keeping you off death row. But we can talk to them. Let them know that you cooperated, that you told us where to find Erica Mullins, that you saved her life."

Again, he opened his mouth to say something, but his attorney stopped him with a hand on his shoulder. Her face was red with fury. "This meeting is over, and you should not ever expect another opportunity like this to talk with my client. I will defend him vigorously against any charges he faces. I suggest you turn your efforts to finding the real killer in these cases. Whether you want to hear it or not, he's still out there. When that girl, Erica Mullins, turns up dead while my client is in police custody, don't be surprised. Truly, I wish you the best of luck explaining to Ms. Mullins' parents how their daughter died because your team had tunnel vision."

FORTY-NINE

"She's right."

Josie stood in the great room, facing her team at their desks, and the Chief who stood beside Gretchen.

Noah, who had been tapping away at his computer, looked up and said, "What are you talking about?"

"McMichaels' lawyer. She's right. We've got tunnel vision. I'm not so sure anymore that he killed those girls or that he kidnapped Erica Mullins. I don't think he has any idea where to find that girl."

Mettner said, "But the evidence. We followed the evidence. It led to him."

Gretchen sighed. "The boss is right. Yeah, there's evidence and yes, it is linked to him, but there are too many problems with it."

"So it's circumstantial," Mettner said. "Lots of cases move forward with circumstantial evidence."

Gretchen said, "But we can't connect McMichaels to the girls other than that he was their therapist."

"And through Daisy," Mettner argued. "Daisy was staying at his house! He gave her the car. She went out and picked the girls up, took them to the firepit at the back of his property, and fed them alcohol and Benadryl!"

"It appears that way," Josie said. "But if that's how things really happened, we can't prove anything that took place after that."

"That's why he used the girl," said Mettner. "For exactly this reason. It muddies everything. If anything, it makes Daisy look like the killer."

"She could be," Noah agreed, eyes still on his computer screen. Josie wondered what he was looking for. "But then how does she select the victims? It can't be a coincidence that they were all clients of McMichaels."

"Daisy being behind all this doesn't account for the murders that happened twenty-five years ago," Gretchen pointed out.

"Maybe that's this guy's thing," said Noah. "He creates a killer. He finds a young woman and convinces her to kill for him."

"I don't think Daisy is a killer," said Josie, sitting down at her desk.

The Chief spoke finally. "Then who is it, Quinn? If not Daisy and not McMichaels?"

Josie explained, "There is only one other person with enough connections to the earlier cases and the present-day cases: Travis Benning. He was your dad's old partner. He had access to Kelsey and to Priscilla Cruz, assuming she is the third victim, and he had enough access to the police files and investigation to cover up whatever needed covering up. He was also the intake counselor for at least two of the three girls in our cases. McMichaels thinks that Daisy set him up, but she can't possibly be behind Kelsey's murder. She wasn't even born. However, she has been perfectly positioned all along to set McMichaels up—maybe at someone else's direction. Like Benning."

"We checked him out," said Mettner. "We found no

evidence that he was involved at all. He's got credible alibis for the nights of the murders. He lives in a second-floor apartment in a thirty-unit complex with paper-thin walls—which you and Fraley visited. You guys said there was nothing there. No one. He doesn't own any other properties. No one has implicated him. We haven't found any evidence that he's involved in this. You're the one who always says we have to follow the evidence, boss. There's no evidence against Benning."

Noah clapped his hands together suddenly, drawing everyone's attention. "Got it!" he exclaimed. "Check this out. Kade said that he had to resign from a facility in Lochfield because of accusations against him years ago, remember? Well, guess who else was working there at that same time?"

"Travis Benning," said Josie.

Noah nodded.

Mettner said, "So what? They worked together in Lochfield. That doesn't mean anything."

"Benning was law enforcement," Noah said. "What if he killed Kelsey twenty-five years ago and maybe even Priscilla Cruz—if she really is victim three—and then he stops. Maybe he got spooked, afraid of being found out, so he takes a break. Then he's working with Kade McMichaels at the time and place when McMichaels is accused of inappropriate behavior by teenage girls. Benning sees an opportunity: he can set McMichaels up for the killings. Maybe it's no coincidence that Benning ended up here, working at the same place that McMichaels is now working. He's perfectly positioned to manipulate everything and he knows enough about police work to keep himself off our radar. He uses Daisy to do all his legwork so that again, nothing can ever be traced back to him. You saw her—there's no way she's ratting him out."

Gretchen said, "That makes perfect sense. The problem is that we can't prove any of it."

Noah opened his mouth to speak again but the stairwell

door whooshed open and Hummel strode through with a sheaf of papers in his hands.

"Boss," he said, addressing Josie. "I got what you needed from Daisy's phone."

Josie stood up as he approached. He handed her the pages. "That's the report, but here's what you need to know. The call history only goes back six months—for anything more than that, you'll have to get the records directly from the carrier—but I don't think that's going to help. There are no texts. She wasn't logged into any social media apps. The only thing on this phone is a call history. There's only one number that she's called and received calls from for the last six months. It's a cell phone number. You guys were pretty busy so I did some digging—as much as I could without a warrant. The number that Daisy has been calling and receiving calls from is from another prepaid cell phone. However, it's a model that requires an email to even set it up."

Gretchen said, "You can set up an email address without giving any real biographical information, especially if it's a free one."

"True," said Hummel. "But in this case, the email address associated with the phone that was in contact with Daisy is registered with Spur Mobile as belonging to a Laura Claxon, who is, in fact, a real person."

In the back pocket of her jeans, Josie felt her cell phone buzz. Ignoring it, she flipped through the report to find the parts about Laura Claxon. She had no criminal record. She was in her seventies and she lived at an address in Brighton Springs that was very familiar. In fact, it was the same address that Josie had found for Winnie Hyde the day before but with a different apartment number.

Josie's phone buzzed again. She handed the reports off to Gretchen and took it out so she could check her notifications.

There was a text message from Meredith Dorton of the Brighton Springs cold case annex. *Check your email.*

"Who the hell is Laura Claxon?" asked Mettner.

"I'm not sure," said Josie. She sat down at her desk, opened her browser, navigated to her email inbox and found the email from Meredith Dorton. Its subject line read: *Winnie Hyde.* Josie clicked on it. Meredith had written: *I found a lot more than I bargained for in our database. I scanned everything I could find into a single PDF. This one's a doozy! Hope this helps. —M*

"She's somehow related to Winnie Hyde, though," Josie added. She clicked on the PDF.

"Winnie Hyde?" asked Gretchen.

Josie blinked and reread the information in the PDF.

"Quinn?" the Chief said, speaking for the first time in several minutes.

She turned to him. "Put one unit on Benning for now. Just one. We can spare that." The Chief raised a brow. Josie didn't have to look at her colleagues to know they were staring at her like she was nuts. Erica Mullins didn't have much time.

She said, "Gretchen's right. If Benning is the mastermind behind all this then he's put all the pieces into place so that we can't tie anything to him, and he knows it."

"Which means he's not going to confess to anything," Noah said. "No matter how hard we pressure him."

Josie looked around at the faces of her team, everyone looking defeated and frustrated. "But we talked about how important the fantasy part of these killings is, which means that even with us coming down on McMichaels and Daisy, he might still risk killing Erica Mullins. She turns sixteen tomorrow. He won't be able to carry out the parts of the fantasy involving leaving her in a public or semi-public place, but he can still kill her."

"He might go to her," Mettner said. "We can follow him."

"Right," Josie said. She hit print to send the PDF to their

inkjet printer. "You guys go after Benning. The Chief and I are going back to Brighton Springs."

Everyone in the room went completely still. Mettner said, "You just told us to follow Benning."

"I did," Josie said. She walked over and snatched up the pages from the printer. Holding them up, she said, "But there's a lot more to this entire thing than we can see. I'm not sure Benning is our only lead here. I don't want to put all of our eggs into one basket. It could cost Erica Mullins her life. The Chief and I need to go back to where all of this started. If we're wrong about Benning, it could be our only opportunity to find Erica alive."

FIFTY

She went into the room. She wanted to resist. The thought of "the room" was chilling, mostly because she had no idea what would happen to her there. The naked girl—whose name she'd finally found out was Sabrina—kept talking about how the other girl had gone to the room many times and then one day, failed to return.

"Didn't she tell you what happened in the room?" Erica asked Sabrina. "How do you know it's so awful?"

"I know because she wouldn't talk about it."

Now Erica knew that she wouldn't talk about it because she wasn't allowed. There were rules. So many rules. All of them revolved around the room. For example, you had to take a shower and dress in nice clothing—even though it didn't fit exactly right—if you were going to the room. Your hair had to be combed, your teeth brushed. You had to maintain a positive attitude in the room. *A positive attitude of gratitude*, the man sometimes quipped. You had to do all the things you were told to do in the room, and if you did, you could stay there for a very long time.

By the time she made it to the room, it wasn't exactly hard

to put on an "attitude of gratitude." Erica had no idea how many days or weeks or maybe even months she'd been shut away in the smelly bedroom with Sabrina, not even able to go to the bathroom alone. Or shower. Or wear anything except the pajamas she'd been given which hadn't been laundered since her arrival. The odor was ungodly.

She hated herself for it but there was a small part of her that was excited to go to the room. The shower felt glorious. The clothes were clean and unwrinkled and smelled fresh like the outside. Her hair felt clean and almost silky again. The first time she stood before the door to the room—a heavy, exterior door that looked out of place inside a cabin—she felt so nervous that she couldn't draw enough air to breathe. Her skin prickled and the air around her seemed to shimmer. She worried she might pass out.

Then the room was nothing like she expected.

FIFTY-ONE

For the fourth time in an hour Sharifa Hagstrom used the handle of her broom to bang against her ceiling. This time, she yelled, "Can you be quiet, please? Some of us are trying to work!" Afterward, she paused and listened, but still she could hear the blare of the television in the apartment above hers and the steady drip, drip, drip of some kind of leak. She was worried that sooner or later, whatever was dripping up there was going to come right through her ceiling. The last thing she needed was a plumbing issue. The landlord hadn't even properly fixed her kitchen sink from the last problem she'd had, but she hadn't had time to fight with him over it. She didn't have time for anything right now except her dissertation.

Drip, drip, drip.

Sharifa banged the ceiling again. The sound of muffled cheering came from overhead. Whoever it was must be watching a game of some kind. "Great," she muttered, returning to her desk.

Drip, drip, drip.

She told herself she'd shut it all out, all the noise, and focus only on her work. She had typed three sentences when the sound of applause from the upstairs television invaded her apartment once more. She actually heard an announcer holler: "It's outta here."

Pushing away from her desk, she stood. "That's it!" she said, even though she was alone. "I've had it."

She took the steps to the next floor, wondering why none of the neighbors on this floor were complaining about the noise, which grew louder the closer she got to the offending apartment. They were probably all at work, she thought. In the entire building, it was only her and the assclown who lived above her who were home in the middle of the day. Or so it seemed.

"That's a grand slam for Rhys Hoskins! The Phillies go up six to two in the seventh inning!" bellowed the announcer as she reached the midway point of the hall.

The door to the apartment above Sharifa's was ajar, the noise of the television so loud she could no longer hear the dripping.

"Hello?" she called, knocking against the doorframe. "Excuse me? I'm the tenant just below you. Hello? I was wondering if you could turn your TV down."

There was no response. She knocked again, this time on the door. "Excuse me? It's really loud. I'm trying to work. Also, I think you've got a broken pipe or something. There's dripping—"

The door swung open, giving Sharifa a full view of what lay inside. Within seconds, her shrieks overtook the sound of the television.

FIFTY-TWO

Josie was pretty sure she could make it to Brighton Springs in under two hours if she used her detachable beacon light. It flashed red as she sped down the highway, doing nearly twice the speed limit. In the passenger's seat, the Chief braced one hand against her dash. "Quinn," he said. "Slow the hell down. We're not going to find Erica Mullins in Brighton Springs."

"No," said Josie. "But we might find out where she is, and if I'm right, we have less than twenty-four hours to get to her before she's murdered, and I'm not confident that Benning is the only one involved in these killings."

"I'm sure you're right," said the Chief. "But I'm not sure how you expect to find answers in Brighton Springs."

"Me either," Josie admitted. "But the alternative is sitting at our stationhouse watching the last day of Erica Mullins' life drain away, minute by minute. This is a Hail Mary, but it's all we've got."

A sigh. Then, "Fair enough. I was just hoping not to have to see my dad ever again."

"Sorry about that," Josie replied. "We'll visit him after we see the Claxons."

The Morgan Arms Apartments was a stately old six-story brick building shaped like a U with a large courtyard nestled inside the three sections of the building. A lot like the Denton East High alcove, Josie thought, except this space was more like a garden with its center fountain, stone benches, lively garden beds, and stone paths that wended throughout. With the Chief in tow, Josie followed one of the paths to the entrance to the "C" wing. Inside the entryway, she punched the up button for one of the elevators.

The Chief had reviewed the documents Detective Meredith Dorton had sent over on the ride. He said, "This is Winnie Hyde's last known address, isn't it?"

"Right," said Josie. "But Dennis and Laura Claxon, who lived across the hall from Winnie Hyde, are still here. They've lived here for forty-three years."

A ding sounded overhead, and the elevator doors lurched open. They stepped inside. Josie pushed the button for the third floor. "According to the reports that Meredith sent over, Winnie Hyde was raised by a single mother. Winnie and her mother had no other family. No support system—except for Dennis and Laura Claxon. They were like grandparents to Winnie."

The elevator rumbled as it came to a stop. Its doors creaked open and Josie and the Chief stepped into a wide hallway with a threadbare dark red carpet running its length. Josie checked the numbers on the nearest doors and then turned left. The Chief had to jog to keep up with her brisk walk. "You think this Laura Claxon, who's been in contact with that kid, Daisy, is going to just tell you everything, Quinn?" he asked.

"I don't know."

She found Unit 117 and rang the bell. The Chief huffed behind her. "What if they're not home?"

The door swung open. Before them stood a tall, white-haired man with a kind smile. "Can I help you?"

"Dennis Claxon?" asked Josie, holding out her credentials.

"I'm Detective Josie Quinn and this is Chief Robert Chitwood. We're from Denton, Pennsylvania."

Reluctantly, the Chief held out his credentials as well. As Dennis studied them, a thin woman with sandy hair walked up beside Dennis. Adjusting her glasses on her face, she too studied their IDs. "I'm Mrs. Claxon," she said. "What's going on?"

Dennis said, "I don't know where Denton is, do you?"

The woman said, "Nowhere near here."

"What is this about?" asked Dennis.

Josie said, "Mrs. Claxon, we're here about your cell phone." She rattled off the number. Laura's puzzled expression deepened. "I don't own a cell phone," she said. "My husband has one but it's a different number from the one you just said."

"I can show it to you," said Dennis, but his wife put a hand on his forearm before he could turn to go fetch it.

The Chief said, "You didn't purchase a prepaid cell phone in the last six months to a year?"

"No," said Laura. "We've got a landline and like I said, Dennis has a cell phone if we need it, which we hardly ever do."

Josie recited the email address Hummel had found associated with the phone. "Is that your email address?"

Slowly, Laura shook her head. "No, we've had the same email address for the last twenty years! We share one."

Dennis said, "I think this is identity theft."

Laura said, "Yes, I think you're right." She looked Josie and the Chief up and down, eyes sharp and appraising. "But you two wouldn't come all this way from Denton to talk to me about identity theft."

Josie studied them. They seemed genuinely bewildered. Having read over the entirety of the PDF that Meredith Dorton sent over, as well as the background check that Hummel had done on Laura, Josie's instinct from the beginning had been that someone else was using Laura's name. She said, "You're right.

Can we talk to you about Winnie Hyde? We understand you two used to be close to her and her mother. I realize it's been decades, but we really need to ask you some questions about Winnie."

There was a noticeable stiffening of their posture. Dennis said, "It's been decades but that's hard stuff to forget."

Laura's mouth turned downward. Sadness pooled in her eyes. "Come in," she said.

She led them right into the kitchen. Its dark wood cabinets made it look dated but the cheery yellow accents in the form of wall art, hand towels, and curtains brightened the room. Laura instructed them to sit at the yellow Formica table in the center of the room. "How do you know Winnie?" asked Dennis as he and Laura took seats across from them.

"We don't know Winnie," said Josie. "What we know is that she was the sole survivor of the Butcher of Brighton Springs."

Laura shuddered at the mention of the Butcher.

Josie continued, "We know that Winnie was rescued from the Butcher in 1994, when she was sixteen years old. In 1997, a girl named Kelsey Chitwood went missing from Brighton Springs. Four months later, her body was found in Saint Agnes's Church. Prints from one of the church pews on which she was found belonged to Winnie Hyde."

Dennis and Laura looked at one another, confusion deepening the lines on both of their faces. Finally, Laura said, "By 1997, Winnie was gone again."

The Chief asked, "Did Winnie go to church? Was she Catholic?"

"No," said Dennis. "She wasn't."

Josie asked, "What do you mean, Winnie was gone again, Mrs. Claxon?"

Laura said, "Winnie left here soon after she turned eighteen."

"We think she left," Dennis clarified, giving his wife a meaningful look.

"Right," Laura said softly. "Winnie's mother had a heart attack shortly after Winnie turned eighteen. That was in 1996. It was right after—after the Butcher went free. Winnie stayed in the apartment—" Laura lifted an arm and gestured in the direction of the front door. "They lived across the hall from us. Anyway, Winnie stayed there for a time. How long do you think she was there after her mother passed, Dennis?"

He shrugged. "I don't remember now. A couple of months? We checked on her now and then, but she wanted nothing to do with us. With anyone."

Laura added, "Anyway, one day we noticed she wasn't coming in and out of the apartment anymore. We had the landlord check, but she wasn't there."

"Were her things left behind?" asked the Chief.

"It was hard to tell," said Laura. "It's possible she took clothes with her and some personal effects, but we weren't privy to her daily life the way we were before... her ordeal. The Butcher had her for a long time. Did you know that? How long was it, Dennis? A year and a half?"

Dennis said, "It was two years. She was fourteen when he took her. He snatched her right off the street on her way home from school. She walked the same route every day. Never a problem. Then one day, she didn't make it home. Her mother was frantic. The police searched and searched. All the neighbors in the building looked for her. People from her school."

"It was terrible," said Laura. "But not as terrible as when she was rescued."

The Chief spoke again. "What do you mean?"

Dennis leaned forward, elbows pressing into the tabletop. His blue eyes darkened. "For two years, the Butcher tortured her, made her watch all the things he did to those other little girls. It changed her. Warped her, somehow."

"She wasn't the same when they brought her home," said Laura. "It was heartbreaking. At first, we thought it was just the pain. She had a lot of injuries. Physically, she did heal, though."

Dennis's eyes were glassy with tears. "And the scars. So many scars from where he cut her."

Laura nodded solemnly and patted her husband's shoulder. "It was very bad. Hard to see. Hard to imagine that a grown man could do such savage things to a girl."

"Multiple girls," Dennis reminded her.

She nodded. "Winnie's mother, God rest her soul, said sometimes she thought it would have been better for Winnie if he'd just killed her. It was so hard to watch Winnie struggle. What kind of life can you have after that? Did you know that her hair turned white?"

Josie felt the Chief's eyes on her and knew he was thinking of the white-haired woman seen talking to Kelsey at the bus stop in the weeks before she went missing. They'd always assumed that the woman was elderly. Josie kept her focus on Laura Claxon. "She was arrested for retail theft when she was eighteen. In her mug shot, which we just received a copy of today, she's got white hair."

"It was the Butcher," said Dennis. "When he took her, her hair was brown. By the time she was rescued, it had turned completely white. It never did change back to brown, although sometimes with the sun it looked almost blonde. He ruined her. That bastard ruined her, and he didn't even go to prison."

"How did she—" the Chief began, voice raspy. He cleared his throat and tried again. "How did she act after she came home?"

Laura and Dennis exchanged a glance. Dennis reached up to wipe a tear from his eye and then Laura took his hand, squeezing. She said, "Winnie was sad, terrified... different."

"The Winnie who came home was not the Winnie who left here the morning she was taken," Dennis said. "You know, we damn near raised her, helping her mother with everything. We never minded. We loved that girl. Loved her like our own. We have a son but he moved to the West Coast and he chose not to have kids. Winnie was like our grandchild."

Laura smiled. "We loved to spoil her. Her and her mom. Those years before Winnie was taken were wonderful. We had such good times, the four of us. Winnie was sweet and thoughtful. She liked books and playing dress-up and dolls. When she got older, she liked to put on make-up and do her hair. I'd let her do my hair and make-up as well. She just loved it."

"She ran track," said Dennis. "And she was good. We went to all her meets. Her mom did, too, when she wasn't working. She was a nurse. Lots of long shifts."

"And after?" the Chief prompted.

"She stared at the walls," said Laura. "Wouldn't talk."

"Except to her mother," said Dennis. "But she was cruel toward her. Mean. Winnie had never been like that before. So nasty. Throwing things at her mother, calling her a bitch, telling her she was going to—" He broke off.

Laura said, "It's okay, hon."

He swallowed. "Telling her she was going to carve her up while she slept. Honestly, I think Winnie's mom was afraid of her toward the end."

Laura nodded. "She ended up living in her bedroom with the door locked while Winnie had the run of the apartment. I don't think Winnie would ever have hurt her—or anyone, for that matter—I just think that she couldn't process what happened to her, what she saw. Who could? She had a therapist after she came home but apparently, she wouldn't speak to her either."

"The therapist was a woman?" asked the Chief.

Laura and Dennis nodded.

Josie tried to steer the conversation back to what had

happened to Winnie. "What did you do when you realized Winnie wasn't in her apartment any longer?"

Laura sighed. "We called the police. The Butcher had just been released only a month or two earlier. We worried that maybe he had come back to finish what he started. We were worried about her."

"Understandably," said Josie. "What did the police say?"

Dennis scoffed. "They were completely useless. They said that she was eighteen and she could take off if she wanted to—"

"And because we weren't next of kin," Laura cut in, "we had no business filing a missing persons report."

Next to Josie, the Chief tensed. "I know it's been a long time," he said. "But do you remember who you spoke with? Was it a uniformed officer? A detective?"

"It was that detective who was always solving the big cases in Brighton Springs," said Dennis. "If you lived here back then, you would know him. There was this big socialite murder case he cracked."

"Harlan Chitwood?" asked Josie.

Dennis frowned. "I'm not sure. I think that's right."

"It was him," said the Chief.

"He was on the Butcher case," Josie said. "Part of the task force. He wasn't concerned that the Butcher might have come after Winnie?"

Laura shook her head. "He said the department had been watching the Butcher and he hadn't taken any girls."

"What do you think happened to her?" asked Josie.

Laura said, "I don't know. If she left, like that detective thought, I can't imagine where she went. Sometimes I even wondered if she had killed herself. Everyone tried so hard to help her, but she was beyond reach."

Josie asked, "After she was rescued from the Butcher, did you notice whether she had any new people in her life?"

Laura shook her head but Dennis said, "There was that

man. We thought he was some kind of therapist at first. Remember, Laura? He used to come every week? Winnie couldn't go anywhere after it first happened. Because of her injuries. Too much pain. But this guy kept coming to see her every week, sometimes more. We had no idea who he really was until after the Butcher was freed."

Laura looked at her husband for a long moment, her lips pursed as she tried to access the memory. Finally, she said, "I can't believe I forgot that. Yes, it was terrible. Just terrible."

Josie asked, "Who was he?"

Dennis said, "The police officer who screwed up the whole entire case. I don't remember his name anymore, just his face. All those weeks he came to see Winnie, knowing what he had done."

The Chief said, "What was he doing with her?"

Laura said, "We have no idea. We never did. Winnie's mother said sometimes he talked to her and sometimes he just sat with her. Sometimes they walked together. I couldn't figure out why her mom would trust her with a man after what happened with the Butcher, but apparently, he was the only person Winnie seemed at peace with."

Dennis's face hardened, anger boiling beneath his words. "After the Butcher went free, I caught that officer in the hallway and I told him to leave them alone. I told him never to come back, that if I ever saw him in this building again, he'd be sorry."

"We never did see him again," added Laura.

Josie did some calculations. That would have been 1996, a full year or more before Kelsey Chitwood went missing. What had Benning been doing? Grooming Winnie? He'd visited her weekly since she was rescued, all the while knowing that he had likely killed the case against the Butcher. Out of guilt? Something else? Guilt made the most sense, except that within a couple of months of the Butcher going free and Winnie's mother dying, Winnie disappeared—right after her well-meaning neighbor threatened Benning.

But Benning lived alone near Denton. He'd bumped around all over the state. Did he take Winnie with him? Had they somehow been together all these years? She had to still be alive. Benning wouldn't have bought a prepaid phone and opened an email account using Laura Claxon's name. But Winnie might. She'd obviously had an emotional attachment to the couple. But where was she? Where would Benning have kept her all this time? Neither one of them owned any property and yet, if Benning was behind the murders, he would need a place to keep the girls. He would need help. But he'd made it clear he had no one in his life. Certainly no one loyal enough to him to help him keep the Butcher's only surviving victim off the grid for twenty-five years.

Or did he?

The Chief said, "I just want to make sure we're talking about the same guy, if you don't mind."

He looked at Josie and she took out her phone, pulling up a photo of Kade McMichaels first, to ensure there was no confusion or foggy memories. "He's a lot older in this photo," she explained, turning the screen toward them. "Is this the man you saw with Winnie?"

Their response was immediate. Dennis shook his head and Laura said, "Oh no, that's not him."

Josie took her phone back and swiped to a photo of Travis Benning she'd pulled from the RedLo Group website. "How about this guy?"

"Oh yes, that looks like him," said Dennis. "Older, of course, but I'll never forget his face. The gall of him, coming around here for almost two years like he was a friend when all along he knew what he had done. Made me sick."

"You know," Laura said. "You could probably find the old newspapers and get his photo, or old footage from the local news stations. They had his face splashed all over the place right after the Butcher went free. The families of the other victims sued the police department. Do you know they never even fired him? They put him on leave. I'm pretty sure he was allowed back to work after a year, like they could sneak him back onto the force and no one would notice. When it came out that he was back at work—I remember it was in 1996 because it was right around the time they caught the Unabomber—a bunch of people went to the police headquarters and protested."

Dennis said, "Yeah, we went, too, and tried to get him fired once and for all, but without the pressure of the press, the police chief didn't care. The press wasn't even interested in the story. They were too focused on the Unabomber story instead of anything local. By that time, the Butcher case was old news. No one cared anymore. It was like they were always protecting him. Looking the other way no matter what."

Laura nodded along. "I suspect that guy had someone inside the police department pulling strings for him, too."

"I think you're right about that," the Chief muttered.

Josie knew exactly who had been pulling the strings.

FIFTY-THREE

Tappy's Lounge was just as dim, dank, and smelly as it was the first time Josie stepped through its doors. This time, Harlan Chitwood was the only patron, sitting alone in front of a glass of amber-colored liquid. Again, the bartender ignored their arrival until the Chief walked over to Harlan and knocked him off his barstool with a punch to the mouth.

"Chief!" Josie yelled.

"Hey!" boomed the bartender, coming around the bar with a baseball bat in his hands.

Flat on his back, Harlan looked up at them, a grin spreading across his face. Blood dripped from where the skin of his cheek had split. Josie put herself between the two Chitwoods and the bartender, holding up a hand.

"You son of a bitch," spat the Chief, hands fisted at his side, chest heaving. "What did you do?"

The bartender stepped closer, but Josie put her hand on the bat and lowered it.

Harlan laughed and touched two fingers to his cheek. They came away wet and red. He stared at them. Then he sat up, wiping the blood on his pants. "You wanna do this again, Bobby? It's been decades. When are you gonna move on?"

"I'll move on when you tell me what you did, you bastard," said the Chief. "And if you don't, I'll kill—"

"Stop," Josie said firmly. "Stop it now." She looked down at Harlan. "Get up."

Harlan shook his head. "This is how you treat a man in his nineties? This is elder abuse, you know. I got—"

"Get. Up," Josie told him. "I'm not asking."

Slowly, he climbed to his feet, chuckling the entire time. "You got yourself a firecracker, there, Bobby. Young, firm, feisty. That's how I always liked 'em."

The Chief flew at Harlan again but this time, Josie tucked her body between the two men, digging her heels into the sticky, scuffed floor and using her weight to keep the Chief from going after his father again. The bartender stepped in and helped Harlan over to a stool, out of the Chief's range. "That's enough," Josie told him. "Finding Erica Mullins is our priority. Remember that. She still has a chance."

He clenched and unclenched his jaw, but she felt some of the tension in his body slacken. "Sit," Josie instructed.

She sat on the barstool between father and son. The bartender returned behind the counter, stowing his bat and setting three shot glasses on the bar, one for each of them. As he poured whiskey into them, Josie covered hers with her hand. She hadn't wanted a drink this badly in a very long time, but she wasn't about to break her promise to herself on someone as morally bankrupt as Harlan Chitwood.

The bartender handed Harlan a towel and he held it to his cheek. Using his other hand, he downed the shot of whiskey. "Ahhh," he sighed with pleasure and smacked the glass back onto the bar. The bartender refilled it.

Josie said, "You were on the task force assigned to the Butcher case. Winnie Hyde was one of his victims."

Harlan rolled his eyes. "You really do like rehashing old shit, don't you, sweetheart?"

"When it's connected to bodies found in my jurisdiction in the present, yeah, I sure do, champ. You knew Winnie Hyde."

"Everyone working that damn case knew her," he said.

"When her prints showed up on one of the pews where your daughter was found murdered, you didn't think that was odd?" Josie asked.

His eyes darkened. He lowered the towel, now smeared generously with blood.

Josie went on. "You and your colleagues rescued Winnie Hyde from the Butcher in 1994. In 1996, she was arrested and charged with retail theft. You were the arresting officer. After that, her mother died, she disappeared, and her neighbors tried to report her missing. You went to their apartment and told them there was nothing you could do. In 1997, your daughter disappeared and then four months later, Kelsey was discovered in the church and Winnie Hyde's prints were on one of the pews. Why didn't you look into it?"

He knocked back another shot. "Look into what? Why some crazy, messed-up kid's prints were at the crime scene? Who cares?"

"The lead investigator on the case should care," the Chief said. "You should have cared. You knew Winnie Hyde. She wasn't just some random kid. You would have known from working the Butcher case that her hair turned white. Kelsey was seen talking to a woman with white hair at the bus stop several times before she disappeared. It never occurred to you that there might be a connection?"

Harlan waved a dismissive hand. "Come on, Bobby. You know not everything is important in these cases. Kelsey was talking to someone with white hair. You know how many people in this city have white hair? You two are making a lot out of nothing. Kelsey's dead and she ain't coming back. Move on."

He pointed to his glass and the bartender poured again. Josie pushed the glass just out of Harlan's reach. She leaned in close enough to smell his foul breath and the coppery scent of the blood congealing on his cheek. "The great Harlan Chitwood doesn't miss things. Does he?"

Harlan didn't answer, instead trying again to grab his glass. Josie kept it just out of reach. "You know, Harlan, your hands are on everything in this town. Your son couldn't get custody of Kelsey because you had a judge in your pocket. All your old cases are carefully protected so that no one finds out how badly you botched them."

"Hey—" Harlan protested.

"Shut up," said the Chief.

Josie continued, "Your partner, Travis Benning, did something so egregious on the Butcher case that it allowed a serial killer to go free. A serial killer of young girls. Yet, not only was he not fired, he was brought back to work, in his old role as a detective. The families of the Butcher victims protested and still, he was allowed to keep his job. Because of you."

"Those families got paid, that's all that mattered," Harlan said.

"How'd you do it, Dad?" asked the Chief. "Why? Why did you do it?"

Harlan leaned in across Josie and pointed a gnarled finger at the Chief. "You still don't get it, do you? You don't get what police work is all about. It's about keeping yourself on top. If you got the law on your side, you don't need nothing else. It's power, son. That's what you never understood. You don't even need money when you've got all that power. The way to do it is to collect secrets. The things people don't want other people to know. You make everyone owe you and you'll always be on top. That judge who wouldn't give you custody of Kelsey? He had a rape case coming down the pike. I made it disappear. He owed me. The chief of police in 1994? He was stepping out on his wife with a prostitute. I had tapes! He owed me."

"You did Travis Benning a favor," Josie said, using her free hand to push him out of her space. "You must have had to cash in on a lot of those I.O.Us. What did you owe him?"

She took her hand away from his shot. He grabbed for it hungrily and drank it, some of the whiskey dribbling down his chin. When he didn't answer, the Chief said, "Quinn asked you a question. What did you owe Travis Benning?"

Harlan kept his eyes on his empty shot glass. He waved at the bartender, but the man shook his head and put the bottle of whiskey on a shelf. Pushing the shot glass away, he took in a deep breath and let it out on a sigh that held decades' worth of tension. His shoulders folded in on themselves. For just a moment, he looked every one of his ninety-plus years. Dabbing the towel against his cheek again, he said, "Everything. I owed him everything. Benning was in bed with the Chief and DA, on some special mission to take me down, apparently. Like some kind of internal affairs bullshit. He was recruited while he was on patrol. They brought him up, promoted him to detective, and then saddled me with him. He was supposed to get as much dirt on me as he could and report back to them. Document everything."

Josie said, "They wanted whatever you had on them."

Harlan nodded. "That, too. But mostly they were after me."

"How did you turn Benning?" asked the Chief.

Harlan chuckled. His fingers fidgeted with the bloody towel. "That kid was never cut out to be in the business. Sure, he was fine for traffic stops but anything heavier than that and he was getting sick all over himself. It was easy. Saved his life once, early on, and he came clean. Told me everything. Said he couldn't be a part of anything I did, but he wouldn't report me. When the Chief and DA asked for evidence of my 'misconduct,' he'd come up empty."

Josie asked, "What happened with the Butcher case?"

"What? You mean with Benning? He was engaged to some chick. Her daughter was one of the missing girls. The Chief pulled Benning off the task force. He was too emotional, acting erratic. I think he was under a lot of pressure from his lady to find the kid. But he was still around, you know? When we got the lead on the Butcher, he asked me to tell him when and where the raid was going to be. I didn't think it would matter. I just figured he wanted to know 'cause his girlfriend's kid was probably there. But he showed up before all of us. Snuck into the house. Touched things in almost every room. I'm telling you, he cracked up. I've never seen anything like it. We rolled in, trying to clear the house, and he'd already been through the entire thing. We found him in the killing room, covered head to toe in blood. It was everywhere, like someone used a damn spray nozzle to paint the room. There he was, in the middle of the room, with his girlfriend's kid in his arms, crying like a little baby. That older girl, Winnie, she was sitting up on top of a dresser like a damn gargoyle, watching the whole thing. Never said a word."

A chill drilled down Josie's spine but she suppressed the shudder. Inside her jacket pocket, her cell phone buzzed. Ignoring it, she said, "Winnie wouldn't testify against the Butcher? Even with the tainted evidence, wouldn't her testimony be enough?"

Harlan shrugged. "Maybe. Everyone thought so, although there were some issues with her credibility. She wasn't restrained when we got there. She could have gotten out, but she didn't. Maybe he broke her and that's why. After all the damage he inflicted on her, maybe she had Stockholm syndrome or something. She wouldn't talk. At first, she wouldn't talk at all. For months. Never said a word. Her mother said she wouldn't force her to testify. Without her on the witness list, the defense filed a whopper of a motion to suppress evidence. They won."

Anger heated Josie's face. "None of you told her that you needed that testimony? That the case hinged on it because Benning had tainted every aspect of the crime scene?"

"Wasn't my job, honey. Besides, Benning tried to get her to talk, to testify."

"That's how it started," said the Chief.

Josie glanced over at him, saw the pain in his eyes.

"How what started?" Harlan said.

The Chief's cell phone rang. Josie recognized the ring tone —like an old-fashioned rotary phone. He took it out of his pocket and silenced it without even looking at the screen. His eyes were fixed on Harlan.

Josie said, "You didn't ignore it when Winnie's prints were found at Kelsey's murder scene. You did look into it because you knew where Winnie was—or you knew someone who did. Travis Benning had been visiting Winnie Hyde every week since she was rescued from the Butcher's killing room. Her mother died after she turned eighteen and then she disappeared. It was like she fell off the planet. She was with Benning, wasn't she?"

Harlan held up his hands. "I had plenty of relations with young women. I wasn't about to get in the middle of that. She was safe. That's what he cared about."

Josie felt the buzz of her cell phone once more, but she kept her attention on Harlan.

The Chief said, "You asked him about Winnie's prints. What did he say?"

Harlan hung his head. "You two aren't going to leave me alone till you know everything, are you?"

Josie thought about explaining to him that a girl's life might be in danger, but a man like Harlan Chitwood wouldn't care about that. For some people, becoming a police officer was a calling; it was the call to serve the public, protect people, and deliver justice whenever possible. For others, it was only about power—the power the badge gave you and the protections it provided. Many times, they were protections that were not warranted. The only thing Harlan Chitwood had ever cared about was power and himself.

Josie signaled the bartender. He poured a shot into her glass, and she pushed it to Harlan. "You tell us what you know —the truth—and you'll never see us again."

Harlan downed the shot and wiped his mouth with the back of his hand. "I knew something was going on with Benning and Winnie Hyde, but I didn't know what. I confronted him about the prints. He said he'd talk to her. I wanted to bring her in. He said he had to find her."

"She wasn't living with him?" Josie asked.

Harlan traced the rim of the shot glass with one finger. "He said she wasn't. She'd come by now and then and stay but then disappear for long periods of time. He said he didn't know where she went. I told him he needed to find her and bring her in. He didn't want to. She was already traumatized enough, he didn't want her interrogated. He talked to her. She told him she'd been going to Saint Agnes's a lot to pray, trying to find religion or something, and one night she saw the Butcher coming out of the church. She got scared, waited till he was gone and went inside. She found Kelsey. That's why her prints were there. She didn't call the police because she was afraid."

"But she didn't tell Benning either?" asked Josie, feeling her cell phone ring again. "You bought this story?"

Harlan pushed his glass away and it fell over, rolling back and forth on the bar. "It was the Butcher. Of all the girls in the whole city to take, he takes my kid? Stabs her to death and leaves her in a public place? It was a message. I was the lead on the task force. I put the cuffs on the guy. He was taunting me. He even changed his MO so we couldn't connect it to him."

"Let me guess," said the Chief. "Winnie wouldn't testify that time either."

"I needed more than her testimony," said Harlan. "Benning and I followed that creep around for damn near a year trying to find enough evidence to arrest him."

"Then he moved away," said Josie. "Disappeared."

Harlan laughed. "'Cause Benning and I made him disappear. That's what I finally got on Benning. He helped me kill the Butcher. He had that cabin way out in the middle of nowhere. We paid him a visit one night. No one to see anything. No one for miles. We took our time, buried him in the woods, although if you two ever try to put me away for it, I'll deny I ever told you. My friend over there—" he pointed to the bartender. "He didn't hear a word."

"Hear what?" said the bartender before turning back to the television on the wall.

"Why didn't you tell me any of this?" said the Chief.

"You kidding me, Bobby? You been looking to nail me for something since the day you put on the uniform. Anyway, that's not the best part. The best part is that a few years later, that cabin went up for tax sale."

Josie thought back to what she had seen in the file. It hadn't been Harlan Chitwood who purchased the Butcher's cabin. "You couldn't let it go to just anyone," Josie said. "The Butcher's body was out there. What did you do?"

"I had a girl I was messing around with at the time. Young thing. Big-time addict. Trying to turn her life around. She was an informant on this series of murders between two rival gangs —all of it over drugs. After the case wrapped, I still wanted to see her, and she wanted to get out of Brighton Springs. So I helped her out. Gave her some money. She bought the cabin for a song. In exchange, she didn't tell anyone about our arrangement. Any of it. I saw her for a while after that but then I got tired of driving out to that cabin."

"Lorna Sims?" asked Josie, remembering the name Noah had found when he looked up the cabin.

"Right," said Harlan. He smiled at her. "You're good, kid. Lorna lived in the cabin. There was also an old barn on the property. Benning set his girl up out there—Winnie. He said she couldn't be around people, that she needed a quiet, out-of-the-way place. I asked him, did it bother her that she was living on the Butcher's property, and he said no, she actually took pleasure in it. Anyway, Benning worked and went up there when he could, same as me with Lorna. It worked out. Even after I was tired of Lorna, he was still there to make sure no one ever nosed around the place."

"Is Lorna still there?" asked Josie.

"Nah, she left probably ten, eleven years ago. Benning's girl moved up into the cabin."

"Who pays the property taxes on the cabin?" asked Josie. "It's still in Lorna Sims' name."

"Benning and his girl," replied Harlan. "She set up some kind of business in the barn doing some kind of thing for the locals. I don't know what. Don't care. It's not on the books or anything, but apparently she makes enough cash to pay the property taxes each year."

The Chief's phone rang again, and he silenced it.

Josie said, "Where is that cabin?"

FIFTY-FOUR

Clutching the crude map that Harlan had drawn them on the back of a napkin, Josie got into her SUV and fired up the engine. She punched the cabin's address into the GPS. As Harlan had predicted, the GPS couldn't locate it. He had told her to instead use the address of an auto repair shop in the nearest town. "It's on the corner of the road that leads up to the cabin," he had told them. "Make a left, drive a few miles. When you see the barn, you'll know you're there."

She entered that address instead and it popped up. But the GPS would fail once they got within forty or fifty miles of the place, Harlan had warned. The middle of nowhere was an understatement, thought Josie, as she tapped against the screen, pulling up an aerial satellite view. Miles and miles of green forest appeared. She pinched her thumb and index finger, trying to zoom out, but the green seemed to go on forever. The road wasn't even on a map, Harlan had said, which is why he'd drawn one. The only landmark he could give them was the two-story red barn sitting on the side of a dirt road.

Re-centering the GPS map, she checked the time. One and a half hours away. She could make it in half that time. More than enough time to reach Erica Mullins before she turned sixteen.

The Chief climbed in next to her. "My phone's been ringing off the hook," he said, taking it out and scrolling through his missed calls. "Gretchen, Mett, Noah."

"Mine, too," Josie said as it vibrated in her pocket once more. She slapped the beacon light onto the roof of the car and tore out of Tappy's parking lot.

"Quinn, don't you want to find out what they've got before we head deep into the woods looking for this place?"

"Call Noah back," Josie instructed, jerking the car around two vehicles in front of her. "If I'm right, Erica Mullins will be at the barn or the cabin at least until sometime tomorrow afternoon, but I don't want to lose any time in case things go sideways."

The Chief dialed Noah and put him on speakerphone. "Fraley," he said when Noah answered. "What the hell's going on?"

Noah said, "It's Travis Benning. He's dead."

There was a long silence. Josie took her eyes from the road for a second to look at the Chief. He was preternaturally still, the phone held out in front of his face, his gaze locked on it as if it was some completely foreign object.

Josie returned her focus to the road ahead. "What happened?"

"We put Mett on him. He went down to his apartment building, saw that Benning's car was still there, so he parked out front and waited. Pretty soon, a whole mess of Lenore County sheriff's deputies show up. Downstairs neighbor said she couldn't concentrate because Benning had his television on too loud and there was some kind of dripping noise. She went up to ask him to keep it down and his door was open. He killed himself, Josie. Sliced his wrists open and bled out. The dripping she heard? It was his blood. He was sitting at the kitchen table."

"My God," Josie said. As she sped through the streets of Brighton Springs headed toward the interstate, the vehicles in front of her pulled to the side to make way.

"That's not all. He left a note."

Dread coiled in Josie's stomach like a venomous snake ready to attack. "What did it say, Noah?"

The Chief still hadn't moved.

"Noah!" Josie shouted.

"It was addressed to you, Josie. It says, '*I'm sorry. Check your email.*'"

For a moment, Josie was speechless.

Finally, the Chief spoke. "That's what his note said? *Dear Detective Quinn: I'm sorry. Check your email?*"

"I can send you a photo if you'd like," said Noah. "It was on the table next to your business card. That's where he got the email address from."

Josie knew that Noah could have easily guessed her login credentials for her work email. He knew most of her passwords and pins. "Did you check it?" she asked.

Noah hesitated.

Voice rising, the Chief said, "Fraley? Did you check it?"

With a sigh, Noah answered, "Yeah. I guessed your password, Josie. We couldn't get hold of you and we were concerned that there might be something about Erica Mullins on there. I didn't think either of you would mind. Exigent circumstances and all."

"What did he send me?" asked Josie. Her heartbeat thrummed, a vibration through her entire body.

"Video files," Noah said. "Lots of them. We were only able to view a few so far but they appear to be of Gemma Farmer."

Josie willed herself not to vomit. "What happens in the videos, Noah?"

"That's the weird thing," he said. "We were all bracing for the worst—the absolute worst—but so far it's just her in this room. It's like a bedroom but for a little girl. It's painted pink and decorated with princess tiaras and flowers. She comes in wearing pajamas and she changes into clothes from one of the dressers. Again, more like clothes that a young girl would wear, not a teenager. Then she stands there. There's no sound but it's like she's hearing someone give her directions because she goes from activity to activity: laying on the bed, brushing her hair at the vanity, reading a storybook—again, not age-appropriate— watching what appears to be a cartoon show on a TV, even coloring in a coloring book."

The Chief said, "What? That's it? Is there anyone with her?"

"Benning is in the second and third video that we watched," said Noah. "He brings her a dress and makes her put it on. He has her twirl around for him and then he makes her dance with him. In the next video, he dresses her in some new outfit and makes her sit at his feet while he reads her a book. It's not what we expected, but I'm telling you, it's creepy."

"Nothing more than that?" The Chief asked.

"We're only on the third video but so far, no."

"It's the fantasy," Josie said. "It's his fantasy. When we found Gemma Farmer, other than her stab wound, she was in excellent health. No signs of abuse or torture."

"Because she went along with it," said the Chief. "Sabrina Beck didn't, and he was violent with her."

Noah said, "Gretchen and Mett are working with Lenore County on the scene while I get through as many of these as I can. I'm looking to see if Erica was ever in the room or if I can figure out where this room is—it obviously wasn't at his place."

"It has to be the cabin," Josie said. "It's the only thing that makes sense. Benning and Winnie have been using that property for twenty-one years, according to Harlan, without ever having their names attached to it. Noah, I need you to stop what you're doing and get me a search warrant for that cabin. There's a barn on the property as well, so we'll need a warrant for that, too. Notify the sheriff in the county where the cabin is located and email them copies."

"You got it," Noah said.

Josie swerved around car after car, the red beacon slicing through the night around them. The highway flew beneath them, its broken white lines zipping past like shooting stars.

The Chief said, "Benning and Winnie have been at this the whole time."

"Yes," said Josie. She thought of the white-blonde hair in the toolbox pinned beneath the number 1. "I think Winnie was Girl One. She's been with him all along. She lured Kelsey. They couldn't have been keeping her at the cabin back then since the Butcher didn't even own it yet, but they found a place to keep her until they were ready to dispose of her. Same with Priscilla Cruz, assuming she was Girl Three."

"Benning made a mess of the Butcher case. Lost everything over that case. He tried to kill himself. More than once. Shit. He just succeeded. Why would he take girls just to murder them? Why would the Butcher's surviving victim help him?"

"I don't know," Josie admitted. "But early on you asked me what I saw. This is what I see. Benning loses his fiancée's daughter during the Butcher case. Because of him, the killer goes free. His fiancée leaves him. His career is in shambles. Out of guilt, he starts visiting Winnie Hyde."

"Who was just as messed up and broken as he was," the Chief murmured.

"They have the shared trauma of the Butcher's killing room," Josie pointed out. "I don't know how it started or whose idea it was to take girls, keep them, and then kill them. I don't even know why, other than that it was obviously some fantasy recreation for Benning."

"Like, the girls get kidnapped but instead of being tortured, they're given what he sees as a young girl's ideal experience."

"His pink, lacy room with its castles, unicorns, and flowers replaces the Butcher's killing room."

"But once he's taken them, he can't exactly release them. They'll tell," said the Chief. He hesitated and then, in a choked voice, asked, "Why Kelsey, though? Why my Kelsey? He knew me, knew my dad. She was innocent, just like the girls the Butcher killed. Why would he do this to her?"

"Chief, you know we're not dealing with a sane or rational person in this scenario, right? Something was badly broken in Benning. That said, think about what all the victims had in common."

"They were all fifteen? Full of promise with their whole lives ahead of them?"

"Yes," Josie said. "But also, they all came from home situations that were chaotic. Kelsey's home life wasn't exactly stable once your dad decided he was sending her to boarding school. Gemma Farmer's parents fought all the time. Sabrina Beck's mother did her best, but Sabrina kept getting into trouble. Erica Mullins' parents also seemed like they had a strained relationship with her and each other. All three of our recent victims were getting counseling for stress, anxiety, and other issues."

"He thought he was rescuing them?" said the Chief. "That's absurd."

"Benning's warped. To his way of thinking, it probably all seemed very reasonable. If he thought like a normal, rational, reasonable person, he wouldn't have done any of this."

"He worked with kids, though," the Chief said. "He worked in the damn mental health field!"

Josie nodded. "There's a very good possibility he tried to stop as well. After Priscilla Cruz, no victims were found until Gemma Farmer. We don't know if Girl Four came right before Gemma and we just haven't found her yet, or if she came right after Priscilla Cruz in the early 2000s but either way, there's a definite gap in his crimes. Without knowing Girl Four's identity and when she was taken, it's hard to narrow it down, but the gap between Priscilla Cruz and Gemma Farmer is over fifteen years."

"What made him stop? He wasn't in prison."

"I don't know," Josie said. "There's only one person left on earth who might know and that's Winnie Hyde."

"Who had a definite part in these crimes. She was the one calling Daisy on the burner phone under Laura Claxon's name. Has to be. You think we're just going to walk up to her weird little serial killer fetish cabin and ask her to answer all our questions?"

"No," said Josie. "Not alone. You need to find out which county sheriff covers the area where the cabin is located. Call it in, let them know what's going on. Then call the state police, too. It's dark. This place is remote. Erica Mullins' life is on the line and if everything we've talked about so far is right, then Winnie Hyde is dangerous. She also knows the terrain intimately which puts us at a disadvantage. We need backup, and we need it fast because we're about to enter a dead zone."

FIFTY-FIVE

At the auto parts store that Harlan had told them about, Josie and the Chief were met by two Wendig County sheriff's deputies and a single state trooper. The trooper had printed out a topographical map which showed an overhead view of where they now stood; the turn-off to the dirt road a mile away, and then, about two miles along that, the red barn Harlan had told them about. From the map, it looked like the barn had a small dirt parking lot along one side of it. Behind it was a trail that wasn't quite wide enough for a vehicle, but it led uphill to where the cabin sat in a clearing. They'd have to park at the barn, search there first, and then walk up to the cabin. Josie studied the map, but she didn't see any other way to approach the cabin, unless one or more of them tried to get through the woods.

Josie punched a finger against the map. "How well do you know these woods, Deputy?"

The man smiled and shook his head. "Not well enough to find your cabin in the dark, if that's what you're getting at. How about this? My colleague and I here will search the barn while the rest of you walk up toward the cabin. Then we'll follow and surround the place. We'll be right outside in case you need any help."

"It'll have to do," Josie answered.

Noah had emailed Josie a copy of both search warrants, and one of the Wendig County deputies had been kind enough to print them out for her and bring them. Josie tucked them into her back pocket and strapped on a tactical vest. She would have preferred a lot more manpower, but technically she and the Chief were only there to check the barn and cabin to see if Erica Mullins was present and if possible, question Winnie Hyde. The Chief hadn't brought a vest, but Josie had one of Noah's in her trunk. He strapped it on, they checked their weapons and flashlights and got back into their vehicles.

As they parked next to the red barn and cut their headlights, Josie looked at the Chief. He hadn't spoken in over an hour.

She flicked on her flashlight. "You ready for this?"

The light caught his eyes for a second. He gave her a glare harder than any she'd ever received from him before. "Quinn, I've been ready for this for twenty-five years. Let's go."

Flashlights bobbing, they made their way around to the back of the barn. The beam of Josie's flashlight bobbed over the small sign next to the barn's side entrance. It read: *Hyde's Game and Deer Processing.*

As the two sheriff's deputies gained entry into the darkened barn through a rear door, Josie, the Chief and the state trooper kept moving. They turned their flashlights off when they reached the path to the cabin. With no major source of ambient light nearby, the silver light of the moon was enough for them to make out the terrain, once their eyes adjusted. Around it, thousands of stars burst across the black sky in a brilliant tableau. They trudged up the rock-strewn path in silence, the only sounds the chirp of crickets, the hoot of an owl, and their own labored breath. Finally, the golden glow of the cabin's windows came into view. The cabin itself was just an inky silhouette against an even darker background but still, it was larger than Josie had anticipated. She and the Chief stepped onto the small porch, which was empty save for a single rocking chair, while the state trooper waited outside, out of sight.

Josie unsnapped her holster. Her heart thumped so hard it felt like an elephant was stomping on her chest. She raised her hand and knocked firmly on the door. "Hello?" she called loudly. "This is the police. My name is Detective Josie Quinn with the Denton Police Department. I've got a search warrant for these premises."

No response.

The Chief reached forward and twisted the doorknob. It turned easily in his hand. Both of them took out their pistols, holding them at the ready. Josie crossed the threshold first and went right, with the Chief only a second behind her, panning left. Again, Josie shouted out her name, department, and their intention to serve a search warrant. While part of her mind was hyperaware and poised to neutralize any threat, another, muted part quickly took in the details of the room: hardwood floor with a braided oval area rug. Rustic furniture—a sofa, chair, and coffee table—all dark, distressed wood. Gauzy curtains on the windows. Cedar paneling on the walls. A laptop partially visible beneath an afghan on the couch. Recording equipment and USB drives scattered across the coffee table.

"Clear!" the Chief said.

Josie chanced a glance in his direction where the living room opened into a small kitchen. A wooden table that looked like it had been made from the trees outside. Four chairs. Chipped green laminate countertop. The usual array of appliances. A photo on the fridge that Josie didn't have time to study. Next, they were making their way down a dark, narrow hall. Bathroom—small but functional—clear. A bedroom with a queen-sized bed, covers rumpled, nightstand and a single dresser. Another photo on the dresser that Josie had no time to examine. A closet filled with clothes and shoes—women's and men's—all in drab colors. Clear. A second bedroom, this one with nothing but a stained mattress on the floor and a set of steel chains hanging low along the wall. Clear.

Then came the last door at the end of the hall. An exterior door for an interior room. Josie knew before they even opened it that behind it was the room from the videos Noah had described. Pastel pink, everything frilly and lacy, stuffed animals on the bed, white furniture, a vanity with dozens of hair accessories neatly lined up across its surface. A closet bursting with colorful dresses. Windows that had been boarded up and painted over—pink. A drop ceiling with fluorescent lights. Two cameras affixed to the wall high above them, dead eyes watching the room below.

"Clear!" said the Chief.

They lowered their weapons. Disappointment fell heavy across Josie's shoulders. "I thought for sure Erica would still be here. Maybe I missed something. Maybe they're not here until the last day. When the girls are killed, they're left in a different place. A place they might have been on their sixteenth birthday. Kelsey was at church. Gemma was at a prom. Sabrina was in her bed. A last meal is prepared somewhere, only a couple of hours before they're taken to their resting place. I was sure it was here, in this cabin."

The Chief stared at her. Holstering his weapon, he said, "Quinn, look at this place. The lights were on in half the rooms, including this one. We just missed someone. Maybe they saw us coming or heard us or something and snuck out the ba—"

Before he could finish, one of the panels from the drop ceiling gave way, falling, pieces of it breaking off when it hit the Chief's shoulder. He flinched. Confusion flitted across his face. Then a figure fell from the ceiling, crashing down onto the Chief. The next few seconds hurtled past in a fury of shouts and a blur of frenzied motion. The Chief toppled to the floor, the figure atop him. It was only when Josie saw shock-white hair that she realized that it was Winnie Hyde. They rolled, both of them flailing, trying to hit or subdue one another. Josie's pistol was useless in her hands. She couldn't take a shot at Winnie without risking the Chief's life. Shouting at the top of her lungs, hoping the trooper outside would hear her, Josie holstered her weapon and jumped into the fray, leaping on Winnie's back and trying to pry her off the Chief. She was all hard bones and sinew beneath a threadbare pair of jeans and a man's tank top that brushed against Josie's cheek. The Chief bucked beneath her and threw up his forearms, trying to block her attacks. Josie started to slide her right arm beneath Winnie's chin for a choke-hold that would render her unconscious but not permanently harm her when the back of Winnie's head came flying at Josie's face.

She took the impact right between the eyes. Stars streaked across her vision. Dazed, her body went momentarily slack. Winnie took the opportunity to shrug Josie off. She fell back against the dresser, catching one of the drawer knobs in the back of her head. A gasp erupted from her diaphragm. Her tactical vest kept her midsection from taking any major abuse, but it made it more difficult to maneuver in close quarters against an opponent who was both lightning-fast and savage in her attack.

Josie was only vaguely aware of the Chief's voice. He was just feet from her, but it sounded like he was shouting from several rooms away. "Quinn! Get out! Find the girl!"

Winnie landed a solid blow to the Chief's jaw. The crack it made sent an instant spiral of nausea from Josie's stomach to her throat. He stopped shouting. Blood poured from his mouth. "No!" Josie shouted. She started to stand up, and that was when she saw the flash of a blade.

Josie lunged for Winnie's arm, but she was met with a boot to the sternum. The blow sent her careening back into the dresser so hard, she heard wood splinter. The breath left her body. With horrifying clarity, she watched Winnie Hyde rise up onto her knees, now between the Chief's legs. Josie wasn't even sure he was aware of her any longer. His head was turned to the side, palms trying to catch the flow of blood from his lips. Winnie brought the knife high overhead before plunging it down into the Chief's inner thigh.

Trying desperately to take air into her lungs, Josie tried to scream, to rage, to beg for his life. Nothing came out but a limp wheeze. Winnie left the blade in his leg, stood up, and looked down at Josie. She didn't look that much older than the mug shot Josie had seen of her when she was eighteen. Except that Josie had only seen her from the neck up in the mug shot. Here, Josie could see her bare arms and they were covered in thick, ropy, silver scars. The Butcher's work. Josie knew she was forty-five now, but she didn't look it. Didn't move like it, either. The Butcher had scarred and aged her, but he hadn't ever cut her face. Time had been kind to her visage as well. Her olive skin was smooth and unblemished. Some wrinkles gathered in the corners of her eyes and across her forehead. Long, straight nose with a smattering of freckles across it. Full, wide lips. Dark eyes that gleamed with malevolence.

The Chief writhed and coughed.

Winnie smiled at Josie. Then she ran.

FIFTY-SIX

Josie counted off the seconds until her breath returned to her body, watching helplessly as the Chief squirmed in front of her. One, two, three, four... at five, it came rushing back. She tried to crawl toward him and nearly fell straight over onto her head. A wave of dizziness washed over her. Keeping her eyes on the knife handle sticking out of the Chief's thigh, Josie clambered across the floor.

"Don't move," she told him.

She leaned over him and touched his shoulder.

"Chief!" she said. "Don't move."

"Qu—Qu—" he burbled.

Josie leaned in closer, until their faces were inches from one another. "Look at me," she said, all the sensation in her body coming back, the colors and condition of the room around them growing sharper with each passing second. "Chief."

His eyes searched blindly, not seeing her. "Bobby," Josie said, squeezing his shoulder firmly. "Look at me."

He found her.

Josie's heart pitched into her throat. In the last few weeks she had seen the man behind the bluster and exacting rules.

She'd watched him cycle through anger, hurt, vulnerability, profound sadness. But not this. This was terror.

"Bobby," she said. "It's okay. I'm here. It's okay."

"Qui—"

The state trooper raced into the room, pulling up short when he saw them. His right hand held his left forearm. Blood seeped through his fingers. "Oh God," he said. "What the hell happened? This crazy... woman came bursting out of the front door. I tried to catch her but she stabbed me. I lost her in the woods. The others are still at the barn, I think—"

"Go get them and start looking for her," Josie said. "And one of you call for backup. I don't care what you have to do. Get help. We need an ambulance. Maybe even life flight. Go."

He looked at her for a moment, as if unsure, until she shouted, "Go!"

Alone with the Chief again, Josie gently ran her fingers across his forehead. She dared not touch his cheek. Winnie Hyde had definitely broken his jaw.

"Qui—" he tried again, but it was hopeless.

"Don't talk," Josie said. "Just listen. Your jaw is broken. You're going to need surgery for that. But more importantly, there's a knife in your leg. There's a good chance it's lodged in your femoral artery. I don't know for sure but I'm not taking any chances. If you move or try to take it out, you could bleed out, so what I need from you right now is for you to be perfectly still. Blink if you understand."

He gave a slow blink. One of his hands fumbled for hers, catching it and squeezing it tightly. A single tear formed in the corner of his right eye and slid across his nose. "Stop it," Josie said firmly. "You're not going to die. I lost a Chief before you. Did you know that?"

He blinked.

"He was a good man and he died saving my life. He saved a lot of lives. I'm not going through that again."

Tears stung the backs of her eyes as she spoke but she pushed them away. She took the emotion welling inside and closed it up into a tiny box in her mind. Later. Later, she would feel all the things this room and these moments evoked. Right now, she had a job to do.

She fumbled inside her pocket and found the rosary bracelet. The beads were warm against her skin. The sound of them clinking against one another brought an immediate rush of comfort. She pressed the bracelet into the Chief's palm. His eyes widened. Managing a smile, Josie said, "You were right about me knowing when it was time to give them back. You hold onto these. Keep all your focus on them. Not anything else. That will help you stay still until help comes. You got that?"

Blink.

"And Chief? Do me a favor. Pray."

FIFTY-SEVEN

Outside, the night was pitch-black. The beams of three flashlights bobbed among the trees all around the cabin. Josie found her flashlight and turned it on again, taking the path that led back to the barn. As she drew closer, she saw that the rear door hung open but the lights inside the barn were off. The deputies would have turned them on while they searched it. They wouldn't have bothered to turn them off when the state trooper came to ask them to help search the woods. Winnie Hyde had had a chance to flee when Josie and the Chief knocked on the cabin door, yet she had stayed and hidden. Josie hadn't seen any vehicles near the cabin or even down near the barn, although it was certainly large enough to house a vehicle or two. The state police trooper and the sheriff's deputies had given chase through the woods. If Winnie had had an escape route, she would have taken it. She'd flown under the radar for decades. A woman who had ceased to exist at the age of eighteen. A ghost. Clearly, she had learned to fight; had honed her rage so carefully and artfully that she'd made herself into a weapon.

But she had not planned for this. Josie was sure of it.

According to Harlan, the barn had been Winnie's long before Lorna Sims had vacated the cabin. The barn was Winnie's sanctuary. The place she knew best. Winnie had been invisible for so long, she was probably counting on being invisible now. At least long enough for her to figure out the best way to escape and where she would go.

Josie unholstered her pistol and snapped the safety off. She held it at the ready, her flashlight positioned beneath it. Moving into the barn, she panned the cavernous space with the beam of light.

"Winnie Hyde," Josie called. "This is Detective Josie Quinn with the Denton PD. I'm here to place you under arrest for the attempted murder of Robert Chitwood. Come out where I can see you, hands above your head."

She moved as quickly as she could, keeping her back to a wall of shelving packed with items she couldn't decipher and steadily worked her way toward the front of the building. More calls for Winnie went unanswered. Outside, more vehicles arrived, their headlights and the emergency strobe beacons lending a great deal more light to Josie's torch. Most of the barn was devoted to game and deer processing. The chrome of the various meat-processing machines gleamed in the light coming through the windows. A set of long metal tables ran almost the entire length of the center of the barn. Josie stayed between the shelving and the tables, every sense heightened, listening for any sound, eyes tuned to any movement. But the only noise was men shouting from outside. On the other side of the tables were stalls formerly used for livestock. Along the walls of one stall hung every knife imaginable that a hunter or butcher might need. Josie sucked in a breath, thinking of Winnie Hyde in the same space as all those blades.

She had literally become a Butcher. She had reclaimed

what happened to her all those years ago. But instead of healing, Winnie had become more and more poisoned.

Josie edged past a stall which held filing cabinets. The next, more equipment Josie couldn't fathom. After that, she reached a stall with beams suspended over it. Metal hooks had been drilled into them. From one set of hooks hung the carcass of a deer.

In the next stall was a car with front-end damage. Josie rounded the tables, carefully approaching the vehicle. As she got closer, a flash of light from one of their torches illuminated a clump of brown fur in the grill of the car. That explained the deer blood on Sabrina Beck's temple. Not poachers; Winnie had hit a deer with the car, likely the very same night she was transporting the girl. Then she'd brought the carcass back here and processed it. It wasn't uncommon in Central Pennsylvania. There were many times Josie had hit deer on a rural road, driven far enough away to get cell service so she could call the game commission only to return and find that someone had come along and taken the deer. Many families in Central Pennsylvania had trouble making ends meet. A single deer could provide many meals for a struggling family.

Josie crept up to the driver's side and shone her light inside. The seats were empty. She moved to the backseats, also empty. A knocking sound drew her to the rear of the car. Josie kept her eyes, pistol and flashlight up as she moved toward the trunk of the vehicle. The knocking got louder. Josie lowered her flashlight and used it to tap lightly against the trunk. The knocking ceased. Then came a muffled voice. "Help."

A rush of air escaped Josie's body. "Erica?" she said. "Erica Mullins?"

A high-pitched squeal sounded from inside the trunk. Relief pulsed through Josie as she went to the driver's side door, threw it open and tried to find the trunk release. Before she could locate it, another noise came. From somewhere else in the barn. A female voice.

Josie stepped out to the front of the stall and took up a guard position near the hood of the car. "Winnie Hyde?" she called, pistol and flashlight back at the ready.

"You can't take her," came a disembodied voice.

Josie stayed frozen in place, waiting for the voice to come again, hoping she'd be able to pin down Winnie's location from the sound of it. When she didn't speak, Josie said, "Winnie, I'm taking Erica home. It's over. Just come out."

"You can't take her. I've already prepared her."

Josie turned to her right—in the direction of the stall with the hanging deer carcass. Her flashlight beam bobbed but didn't catch any bit of Winnie. She needed her to talk more. "You're the one who prepares them? You're the one who kills them?"

"I prepare them but I don't kill them. It's not killing. I send them somewhere else. Somewhere that's better than here."

Josie took a step closer to the next stall, the stink of the carcass invading her senses. "How do you know the place they're going is better than here?"

Winnie's laughter seemed to come from nowhere and everywhere at once. "Wouldn't anywhere be better than here?"

In the deepest depths of her grief over losing her grandmother, Josie would have agreed, but now she thought about her husband, their dog, their families—both the ones related by blood and the ones they had chosen. She thought of Sister Theresa and her rosary bracelet, of the compassion she'd shown the Chief over the years. She thought of the Chief taking in his little sister, sacrificing his own relationships for her. She thought about Meredith Dorton stuck in the Brighton Springs cold case annex, eyes bright with enthusiasm over doing the right thing, no matter what it cost her. Joy, comfort, care, acts of love—they weren't givens in this life, not by a mile but if you found them, if you created them, it was worth the work.

"If you think anywhere else is better than this place," Josie said, "then you haven't been doing it right."

A loud exhale, again coming from no direction and every direction all at once. Then, "I saw when the Butcher sent those little girls to another place. I saw the peace that came over them when he finally sent them away. There's nothing like it. I do that for these girls. Travis gives them a taste of what a perfect life could be like here and when he is finished, when he has what he needs, I send them away."

Josie took another step, now at the threshold of the next stall. The hanging deer loomed. She said, "Whose idea was it? Yours or Travis's?"

"He needed it. He needed to heal, to stop blaming himself, so I helped him. He is the only person who ever saw me after I was taken from the Butcher's house. He saw what I really was, what the Butcher had made me, and he loved me anyway. He is my soul mate. But he kept trying to leave me behind."

Josie moved into the stall, certain now that the voice was coming from somewhere to her left but her flashlight beam revealed only a table with a field dressing kit on top. "He tried to kill himself, you mean," said Josie. "You thought recreating his trauma from the Butcher case would help him."

"It did help him. He was so much better after we did it. When he started to become depressed again, we would find another. I did the hard things so that he could live in peace, like the peace he's given me by loving me all these years."

A stack of boxes sat in the corner. Josie inched closer to them, closer to Winnie's voice. "You were Girl One? The first girl?"

"Oh, our marks? Yes, I was the first one. I did my best to help him, but I wasn't enough. That's why we needed more. But we were judicious. We only did it when it was absolutely necessary, when Travis was in danger of losing himself."

Josie peeked behind the stack of boxes. Nothing. "Who was Girl Four?"

"She was the most special of all," Winnie said, and for the first time, Josie thought she heard some kind of real emotion for someone besides Travis Benning. "She was a found thing. An unexpected gift. We kept her the longest and she made it so that Travis didn't need help for many, many years."

"What's her name?" asked Josie.

More laughter.

Josie turned her body toward the carcass. "Winnie, I really need to get Erica back to her family as soon as possible. Don't make this any harder than it has to be. Come out where I can see you. Hands above your head."

Seconds ticked past. Josie thought back to what Harlan had said about finding Winnie in the Butcher's home. Sitting on top of a dresser, watching. Just like she had hidden herself inside the drop ceiling—watching.

"Winnie," she said. "I've got bad news about Travis. I took a team to his apartment to arrest him this morning. Things got out of hand. He fought us and so I shot him. Travis is dead, Winnie."

The moment the lie was out of her mouth, Josie aimed her pistol and flashlight upward, at the beam the deer hung from. A scream ripped through the air. There was a flash of white hair, the gleam of a blade and then Winnie flew at Josie from above, knife extended toward her.

Josie fired two shots. Winnie collapsed to the floor in a heap.

Josie moved in, kicking the knife away from Winnie. Then she returned to the car, fingers fumbling under the steering wheel to find the release lever for the trunk. Finally, she found and pulled it. Then she ran to the back of the car, shining her flashlight on the teenage girl curled inside the trunk. She wore pajamas. Her brown hair was greasy with sweat. She closed her eyes tightly when Josie shone the light on her face. A pink and white crust clung to her lips. Next to her, on the floor of the trunk, was dried vomit, mostly white foam and small chunks of pink pills.

"Who are you?" Erica croaked. "Can you help me?"

"My name is Detective Josie Quinn. I'm here to take you back to your family."

FIFTY-EIGHT

DENTON, PENNSYLVANIA – ONE MONTH LATER

Josie set a glass of iced tea on the tray table next to the Chief's recliner. She peeled a straw and stuck it into the glass. Then she tried to bring it to his lips, but he waved her off, irritated. Through gritted teeth—his jaw had been wired shut to heal—he groused, "I can get my own drinks, Quinn. When are you going to go home?"

"I just got here," she said.

He started to get up and then hissed in pain. Settling back into his chair, he glared at her. Luckily for him, Winnie Hyde had not severed or even nicked his femoral artery, but she had left him with a significant wound which was still tender. The Chief was under strict orders from his doctors to stay out of work another month. The team had been taking turns stopping by his house to make sure he had everything he needed and that he didn't overdo it. Well, Josie came every day. The others took turns during the times she wasn't there.

There was a knock at the door. The Chief sighed. "You might as well just get it."

Josie knew it would be Noah before she opened the door. He had come with some very important information. "Hey

Chief," he said, entering the living room, a folder beneath his arm.

"Fraley. Listen, I don't need two of you here. Who the hell is working?"

"Gretchen," said Josie. "I asked Noah to come over because we just got a couple of things in that you need to hear."

The Chief waved a hand in the air. "Winnie Hyde died?"

Noah shook his head. "I'm afraid not."

It was hard to believe but somehow, Winnie Hyde had survived both her leap from the beams above the barn stall and the two shots that Josie had put into her center mass. She'd already been charged with a number of crimes, but the team was still combing through evidence found at the cabin to make sure they had enough to convict her on every charge brought. In Brighton Springs, Meredith Dorton was working on bringing charges against Winnie for Kelsey's murder. McMichaels had been released.

"It's about Daisy," Josie said as Noah handed her the envelope. "While you were in the hospital, someone at Children and Youth Services noticed that she had slashes on her right forearm. They worried she had been cutting. She wouldn't talk to them about it."

"But she would talk to Josie," Noah said. "We saw the slashes. They're the same as the rest of the victims, except Daisy's got four."

The Chief looked at Josie, then Noah, then back at Josie. "I don't understand. She's Girl Four? But she's still alive."

"Winnie told me she was special," Josie said. "Right before I shot her. 'A found thing,' Winnie called her. I pieced it together between what we knew, what Winnie told me through her attorney, and what Daisy was able to tell us once she knew that Travis was dead, and Winnie was in prison. Remember how Harlan told us that his informant, Lorna Sims, lived in the Butcher's cabin? Well, Daisy lived there with her. Then when

Daisy was about seven, Lorna got back into drugs and over-dosed. Winnie was living at the barn. She was the one who discovered Lorna's body and found Daisy all alone. She and Benning took Daisy and raised her at the cabin. She's on several of Benning's videos. We think that was actually her room. Remember when we went into the cabin, there was a photo on the fridge and another framed picture in the master bedroom? They were of Daisy when she was much younger. We think that having Daisy there for so long helped keep Benning and Hyde from killing, at least for a while. Then Daisy turned sixteen and that became a problem for them. Well, for Benning. I think Winnie cared for Daisy, so rather than kill her like the others, she put her to work."

Noah said, "We were able to track some of their movements from the burner phones. Last year, Winnie brought Daisy here. They stayed at the Patio Motel for a month. The manager confirmed it. Long enough for Daisy to 'meet' Kade McMichaels and manipulate him into taking her in. Then she and Winnie only needed to communicate by phone. Winnie told her where and when to meet Benning in person so that he could show her a photo of the next victim and tell her where to find them. Daisy would befriend them and bring the girls to the firepit at the back of McMichaels' property, get them drunk with alcohol she took from McMichaels' house. Sometimes she drugged them with the Benadryl as well. Then she called Winnie, who would come get them."

"All Daisy knew is that she was supposed to make friends, bring them to the firepit, get them drunk and wait for Winnie to come get them."

"That's really messed up," said the Chief.

"Benning wasn't around for most of Daisy's life. She never even understood who he was to her. She barely remembers Lorna. Winnie is the closest thing to a mother she's ever had," said Josie.

Noah said, "That's why Daisy's social skills are... wanting."

"Jesus," said the Chief. "That's terrible. She got any other family?"

Josie and Noah exchanged a glance. Then Josie handed him the envelope. "Yeah," she said. "You."

"She's your sister," Noah said.

"Remember, Harlan said he was having a relationship with that informant? He must have gotten her pregnant."

The Chief did his best to laugh through his wired jaw. "Come on, Quinn. My dad would have been in his early seventies then."

"Right," said Josie. "A man can still produce a child at that age. It's not common, but it is possible. I had the state lab run her DNA just in case. She's definitely Harlan's daughter. The reports are in there for you."

He stared at the folder but didn't open it. It trembled in his hand.

Josie said, "Do what you will with that information, but we felt you had a right to know."

The Chief didn't look at them. The envelope shook so badly in his hands that he had to put it in his lap. They waited for any response from him but he simply stared at the envelope. After a few minutes, he said softly, "Quinn. Fraley. I'd like to be alone."

"Of course," said Josie. "You know how to reach us."

A LETTER FROM LISA

Thank you so much for choosing to read *Watch Her Disappear*. If you enjoyed the book and want to keep up to date with all my latest releases, just sign up at the following link. Your email address will never be shared, and you can unsubscribe at any time.

www.bookouture.com/lisa-regan

As always, I consider it a privilege to continue to bring you Josie Quinn books. It is my absolute pleasure to write these stories for you. *Watch Her Disappear* spans many different locations. Most of them, like Lochfield, Brighton Springs, and Wendig County, are fictional. Longtime readers will already be aware that Bellewood, Bowersville, Fairfield, and the two other counties referenced, Alcott and Lenore, are also fictional. I have done my best to make the police procedural elements as authentic as possible. A few things were modified for the sake of pacing and entertainment. As always, any errors or inaccuracies in the book are my own.

I feel so blessed to have such faithful and wonderful readers. I love hearing from you. You can get in touch with me through my website or any of the social media outlets below, including my website and Goodreads page. Also, I'd really appreciate it if you'd leave a review and perhaps recommend *Watch Her Disappear* to other readers. Reviews and word-of-mouth recommendations go a long way in helping readers discover my books for the first time. Thank you so much for your loyalty and enthusiasm for this series. Thank you for continuing to come back to Denton book after book, even though it has an extremely high crime rate. I am so grateful for you and to you! I hope you'll return for the next adventure!

Thanks,

Lisa Regan

www.lisaregan.com

 facebook.com/LisaReganCrimeAuthor
twitter.com/LisaIRegan

ACKNOWLEDGMENTS

Fabulous readers: thank you for coming back to join Josie and the team on their latest adventure. You are truly the best readers in the world, and I am so thankful for you and grateful that you keep reading these stories!

Thank you, as always, to my husband, Fred, and my daughter, Morgan, for your patience and for helping me stay focused and on task. Thank you to my first readers: Dana Mason, Katie Mettner, Nancy S. Thompson, and Torese Hummel. Thank you to Matty Dalrymple and Jane Kelly. Thank you to my incredible friend and amazing assistant, Maureen Downey, for reminding me that I can, in fact, do this. Thank you to my grandmothers: Helen Conlen and Marilyn House; my parents: Donna House, Joyce Regan, the late Billy Regan, Rusty House, and Julie House; my brothers and sisters-in-law: Sean and Cassie House, Kevin and Christine Brock and Andy Brock; as well as my lovely sisters: Ava McKittrick and Melissia McKittrick. Thank you as well to all of the usual suspects for spreading the word—Debbie Tralies, Jean and Dennis Regan, Tracy Dauphin, Claire Pacell, Jeanne Cassidy, Susan Sole, the Regans, the Conlens, the Houses, the McDowells, the Kays, the Funks, the Bowmans, and the Bottingers! As always, thank you to all the lovely bloggers and reviewers who continue to read Josie's adventures as well as the ones who met Josie somewhere in the middle of the series and have been so generous with their support!

Thank you, as always, to Sgt. Jason Jay for answering all of my endless questions especially when the last one (I promise!) is never the last one. Thank you to Lee Lofland for answering my law enforcement-related questions and getting me in touch with experts whenever needed. Thank you to Lisa Provost for the most excellent crash course on latent fingerprints. Thank you to Stephanie Kelley, my fabulous law enforcement consultant, who so generously and painstakingly read this book and helped with all the nitty-gritty procedural stuff. Thank you to Amanda Schmeltzer for Chief Chitwood's favorite caffeinated drink, and to Sandy Klodzinski for the mall name!

Thank you to Jenny Geras, Noelle Holten, Kim Nash, and the entire team at Bookouture including my lovely copy editor, Jennie, who is absolutely brilliant, as well as my proofreader, Jenny Page. Last but never least, thank you to the best editor in the entire world, Jessie Botterill. I can never thank you enough for holding my hand through each and every step in the book-writing process. Thank you so much for finagling the schedule again and again to accommodate me. You're so patient and encouraging. I don't know what I did to deserve someone as wonderful as you are, but every single day I wake up incredibly grateful that I know you. There is no one else I would want to do this with!